Praise for

Kiki Strike: The Empress's Tomb

A Book Sense Children's Pick
A New York Public Library Book for the Teen Age

"These characters are sassy, spirited and smart, and their adventures will appeal to young readers cut from the same mold." —*Kirkus Reviews*

"The latest tale about these friends is just as thrilling and as much fun as the first. A well-paced plot keeps the momentum while unexpected surprises help round out many of the characters introduced in the first adventure." —*SLJ*

"This book is every bit as delightful as the first in the series. The characters are very colorful, and you feel as if they are your friends." —*VOYA*, teen reviewer

"Kiki Strike is *GL*'s hero!" —*Girls' Life*

"Strong memorable characters, well-written, fast paced, exciting, touching, hilarious . . . And, of course, indispensable information like how to appear mysterious, how to know if your house is haunted, how to take advantage of the power of scent, and much, much more. You absolutely must read this book. Trust me." —TeensReadToo.com, Gold Award

Praise for

Kiki Strike: Inside the Shadow City

A Teenreads.com Best Book of the Year

"If Harry Potter lived in New York City, he'd have a mad crush on 14-year-old Kiki Strike . . . the next literary idol of the tween-to-infinity set." —*Vanity Fair*

★ "A fascinating, convoluted mystery/adventure, which features early adolescent girls with talents and abilities far beyond their years." —*Booklist*, starred review

"Non-stop thrills starting from page one challenge the reader to put it down while the mysteries deepen, leaving the curious begging for answers." —Teenreads.com

KIKI STRIKE

THE
EMPRESS'S
TOMB

Also by Kirsten Miller

**KIKI STRIKE
Inside the Shadow City**

THE EMPRESS'S TOMB

Kirsten Miller

BLOOMSBURY

NEW YORK BERLIN LONDON

Copyright © 2007 by Kirsten Miller
First published by Bloomsbury U.S.A. Children's Books in 2007
Paperback edition published in 2008

Published by Bloomsbury U.S.A. Children's Books
175 Fifth Avenue, New York, New York 10010

The Library of Congress has catalogued the hardcover edition as follows:
Miller, Kirsten
Kiki Strike: the Empress's Tomb / by Kirsten Miller. — 1st U.S. ed.
p.   cm.
Summary: Fourteen-year-olds Ananka Fishbein, Kiki Strike, and the other Irregulars encounter a
Chinese mummy, a ghost, trained squirrels, and old enemies as they try to stop an art forgery ring
and safeguard the secret streets hidden beneath New York City.
ISBN-13: 978-1-59990-047-6 • ISBN-10: 1-59990-047-5 (hardcover)
[1. Underground areas—Fiction. 2. Crime—Fiction. 3. Identity—Fiction.
4. New York (N.Y.)—Fiction.] I. Title.
PZ7.M6223Kit 2007   [Fic]—dc22   2007012000

_____

ISBN-13: 978-1-59990-297-5 • ISBN-10: 1-59990-297-4 (paperback)

Typeset by Westchester Book Composition
Printed in the U.S.A. by Worldcolor Fairfield
4 6 8 10 9 7 5 3

All papers used by Bloomsbury U.S.A. are natural, recyclable products
made from wood grown in well-managed forests. The manufacturing processes
conform to the environmental regulations of the country of origin.

The advice given in this book, including first aid information, is meant as a
literary device and an amusing sidebar. The author and publisher are not responsible for any
accidents or injuries that may occur by following it. Refer instead to the American Red Cross.

For SD, whose secrets are my inspiration

The Traitor Empress

The whispers began the day she arrived on horseback at the gates of the Emperor's palace. They knew her long journey had begun beyond the great wall being built to the west. A princess of the Xiongnu, the barbarian tribes who waged endless war with China, she had come to marry the Emperor's son. When they saw her, most members of the court agreed. Peace had been bought at too high a price.

No one dared question the princess's beauty, so they sneered at her round cheeks blasted pink by the winds of her native land. They couldn't deny her nobility, but they scorned a woman who could shoot an arrow farther and straighter than any man. Even the palace servants found something to mock in the fact that her loyal attendant, a lowborn barbarian horsewoman, could always be seen at her side.

The Emperor's son thought nothing of the gossip. He adored his wild bride-to-be and lavished her with silk, jade, and gold. She was draped in heavy robes that made it impossible to ride and paraded before the court like an exotic creature from the Emperor's zoo. Over time, she began to look the part of a Chinese empress. But the women tasked with teaching her the feminine virtues of humility, subservience, and obedience knew that the girl could never be tamed. It would be easier to teach a tiger to tiptoe.

At night the Princess dreamed only of home—of the deserts, grasslands, and mountains that lay outside the empire she was one day to rule. Finally, in desperation, she traded her robes for the frock of a peasant and fled the palace walls. She and her servant were free for three glorious days before they were captured by soldiers as they crossed the Yellow River.

The old Emperor was a wise man, and he had long known that the girl could never be Empress. Servants were dispatched to deliver a meal spiced with poison, so her body would remain unmarked and her murder kept secret from his son. But the Princess refused to die. Instead, she drifted into a sleep so deep that her heartbeat was little more than a faint tapping.

The Emperor's son was told that the Princess had expired from fever. A royal funeral was planned, even as court gossip branded the girl the *Traitor Empress*. It was whispered she'd been unmasked as a spy and buried alive as punishment for treachery. The Princess's faithful servant was powerless to prove the girl's innocence. All she could do was bribe a guard to smuggle two items into the Princess's tomb. One was a small statue of herself on horseback, so she could serve her mistress in the afterworld. The other was the truth.

She knew that in time all secrets are discovered.

CHAPTER ONE

You've Been Warned

Before we begin, take a quick peek out your window. It makes no difference if you look down on a crowded street in Calcutta or a strip mall in Texarkana. Wherever you might be, all the people you see share one thing in common. They've all got a secret they'd like to keep hidden. The dapper gentleman with the briefcase robs parking meters in his spare time. The kid on the bike enjoys eating ants. And the little old lady on the park bench was once known as the Terror of Cleveland. I'm kidding, of course. I don't know their secrets any more than you do. That's the point. You never know.

There are many lessons in life that can be unpleasant to learn. Don't dry a hamster in the microwave. Flip-flops aren't appropriate cocktail party attire. And mayonnaise shouldn't come with a crust. But for a girl detective, there's one lesson that's hardest to learn. No matter how hard you try, you can never know everything about the people you care for the most. Even if you've shared countless adventures and faced death side by side, there may still be secrets between you.

When this story began, I had five best friends. I knew all about their unusual hobbies, life-threatening allergies, arrest records, and shampoo preferences. What I didn't know was that two of my friends still had secrets they were hiding—and that one of those secrets was powerful enough to destroy us all.

· · ·

It all started at eight o'clock on a Saturday morning. I was sitting at my kitchen table, reading a book and enjoying a well-balanced breakfast of butterscotch pudding, when I looked up to find my mother standing in the doorway, clutching a newspaper. I don't recall feeling particularly guilty that day, but I let loose a shriek at the sight of her. Her short black curls had broken free from their hairpins and surrounded her face like a cloud of toxic smoke. There were bags under her eyes and mismatched sneakers on her feet.

"What are you reading?" she inquired in an oddly formal voice.

"*Phantoms, Fiends, and Things That Go Bump in the Night*," I informed her. "I found it under the bed in the guest room. What are you doing up?" In my fourteen years, I'd never seen my mother standing upright before noon on a weekend.

"There was a story on the news last night. I thought you might find it interesting, so I got up early to buy the newspaper." On her way to the table, she stepped over a pile of books that had spilled across the kitchen floor. A week earlier, what most people assumed was a minor earthquake (I knew better) had toppled the tall towers of books that had lined the walls of our apartment. But the task of putting my parents' large and bizarre library back in order was too tedious to consider, and most of the books were still lying where they fell. My mother lowered herself into a chair across from me, keeping her eyes trained on my face.

"What was the story?" I asked, trying to remember if I'd done anything that might have made the papers. On Wednesday I'd helped nab a flasher in Grand Central Station, but that didn't seem terribly newsworthy. And as far as I knew, the source of that earthquake was never determined. I was trying to keep a low profile.

"See for yourself." My mother slapped the newspaper down in front of me. The front page of the *New York Post* featured a picture of a young orangutan wearing a pair of purple boxer shorts and brandishing a set of salad tongs. I started to laugh until I read the headline: *Is This the Work of Kiki Strike?* the paper asked. The smile slid off my face as I glanced up at my mother.

"Go ahead. Read it," she insisted. "The story's on page three."

As my mother watched, I skimmed the article. Apparently, at eight o'clock the previous evening, a woman by the name of Marilyn Finchbeck had woken to find a three-foot iguana crawling into bed beside her. Her next-door neighbor, hearing Marilyn's terrified screams, was dialing 911 when he stepped into the nursery to discover his one-year-old son playing peek-a-boo with a family of hairy-eared lemurs. Not long after, a man on the third floor of the same building leaped from his bedroom window when confronted by the orangutan pictured on the newspaper's cover. At the time, none of the residents of 983 Broadway had noticed that the animals that had invaded their apartments were all wearing handwritten notes tied around their necks.

When police had responded to calls from Marilyn Finchbeck's building, they quickly discovered the source of the mayhem. Someone had picked the locks to a pet store on the ground floor and liberated the animals inside. Rotweiller puppies were found gorging themselves on bags of premium dog food. Half a dozen cockatoos and one foul-mouthed parrot screeched from the rafters. But rather than search for the animals' mysterious benefactor, the police instead arrested the pet store's owner. In the back of his shop, behind a hidden door, they had found a series of secret cages. Most were empty. Only two drugged koalas remained inside, both too woozy to join the party. The zookeepers who were called in to capture the lemurs and orangutan (along with a young snow leopard that had chased a deliveryman for thirteen blocks) knew a crime when they saw one. The animals that had been locked away in the secret cages were all members of endangered species. They had no business being in New York. Around each of their necks was a note that read *I want to go home*.

The *New York Post* believed Kiki Strike was responsible. A man in the neighborhood was reported to have witnessed a pasty-looking elf in dark clothing casing the pet store the week before. (Not the most flattering description of Kiki, but not entirely inaccurate, either.)

"So. Where were you last night, Ananka?" my mother asked.

"*Here*," I insisted, relieved to be able to tell her the truth. "I don't know anything about this."

"You know Kiki Strike. She was here on Thursday watching kung fu movies in our living room."

"Yeah, but the girl I know is fourteen years old and couldn't care less about the animal kingdom. The *Post* is just trying to sell papers, Mom. Everybody wants to believe there's a teenage vigilante running amok in New York."

My mother snorted like an angry bull preparing to charge. "Let me get this straight. You *still* expect me to believe that your friend had nothing to do with foiling that kidnapping plot a couple of months ago?"

"Do we have to go over this again? You saw the news," I told her, sidestepping the truth. "The Kiki Strike story in June was a hoax. That girl who claimed Kiki rescued her from kidnappers was lying. She made up the story because she wanted to be on TV. Who knows where she got Kiki's name? She could have picked it out of the phone book."

My mother leaned back in her chair and glared at me through narrowed eyes. She had something else on her mind, and I knew it couldn't be good. I saw a mouse take a cautious step out of the cabinet under the kitchen sink. He took one look at my mother and scurried back to safety.

"Principal Wickham called yesterday afternoon," my mother finally announced. "Your history teacher says you haven't been paying attention in class. He claims you slept through a lecture on the founding of New York. Apparently you didn't even bother to clean up your drool when you left." At last I had identified the species of bee in her bonnet. My extracurricular activities weren't the issue. I could dress up like Wonder Woman and fight the forces of evil as long as I got good grades.

"I don't *drool*. Mr. Dedly doesn't like me because I know more about New York history than he does." It may sound conceited, but I wasn't exaggerating. I'd spent two years picking through my parents' massive library and gobbling up every book I could find on the subject. I knew how many unfortunate workmen were entombed in the Brooklyn Bridge, which burial grounds had once supplied the city's medical students with fresh corpses to dissect, and the location of the secret underground railroad built for the Vanderbilt family's personal use. I could have taught the class myself—and with much more flair than Mr. Dedly, I might add.

"That may be true, Ananka. But Mr. Dedly isn't the only teacher who's caught you taking cat naps."

"Who else complained?" I snapped, not entirely surprised to find that the snooty Atalanta School for Girls was filled with spies and traitors.

"It doesn't matter," said my mother. "What matters is that classes started three weeks ago and you're already in trouble. I don't want more report cards like last year's. Any more C's or D's and I'll send you to boarding school. I'm not joking, Ananka. I'll find one so far away from civilization that you'll have nothing to do *but* your homework."

"You're bluffing." I laughed nervously. My mother had never threatened me before, and I wasn't sure if I should take her seriously. But I couldn't imagine a fate more horrible than being banished from Manhattan.

"I don't think you want to find out what I'm capable of. I suggest you start spending more time studying and less time hanging around with your friends. Some of those girls don't seem to care about school, and a couple of them are downright shifty. Oona Wong never even knocks when she comes to visit. She just picks the lock on the front door and lets herself in."

I felt myself wince. I'd asked Oona to stop picking the locks, but it was a habit she was finding hard to break.

"My friends are geniuses" was my pathetic response.

"I don't doubt it for a moment. They may even help you win a scholarship to the community college of your choice." My mother rose from the table. "You and Kiki Strike are up to something," she said. "I don't know what it is, but if it keeps affecting your schoolwork, I'll make it my business to find out."

As she shuffled out of the room, I glanced down at the open paper in front of me. If Kiki was responsible, she should have been more discreet.

· · ·

Of course my mother was right. My friends and I *were* up to something. But even if the possibilities had been presented in the form of a multiple-choice question (*Ananka and her shifty friends have been . . .* A: *spending time with radical animal-rights groups*; B: *sniffing Sharpies and neglecting their homework*; C: *falling under the influence of a tiny Svengali who will ensure they end up working at Better Burger*; D: *saving the city of New York*), my mother could never have guessed the truth. Like many people her age, she suffered from a bizarre form of amnesia that prevented her from remembering what it was like to be young. Despite her suspicions, she couldn't bring herself to believe that a group of fourteen-year-old girls were capable of anything more than petty mischief.

Since I'm in the mood for sharing, I'll let you in on the truth. At the age of twelve, I had joined the Irregulars, a band of disgraced Girl Scouts led by the infamous Kiki Strike. Together, the six of us shared a remarkable secret. We had discovered a vast maze of forgotten passages beneath downtown New York that had been constructed by the city's criminal community more than two hundred years earlier. Hidden entrances to the Shadow City could be found in the basements of banks, boutiques, and fancy homes throughout Manhattan, and anyone with access to the rat-infested tunnels could enter and rob the buildings at will. Of course the Irregulars weren't interested in lining our pockets with ill-gotten goods. We just wanted to keep the tunnels to ourselves. But we knew our underground playground came with a price. Instead of letting the authorities ruin our fun, we took responsibility for keeping a new generation of criminals out of the Shadow City.

I'd like to say we succeeded. But like the bloated bodies of giant squid that wash ashore on the coast of New Zealand, even the best-hidden secrets surface sooner or later. Six months earlier, an incomplete map of the Shadow City had fallen into the very worst hands, and Kiki Strike's murderous relatives—the evil Queen of Pokrovia and her morally challenged daughter—had used it to plot her destruction. After the Irregulars foiled their attempt on Kiki's life, Livia and Sidonia Galatzina fled to Russia. But it was only a matter of time before they returned—and as far as we knew, they still had a copy of our map.

While we waited for the Galatzinas to make their next move, the Irregulars stayed busy. Over the summer, we explored new tunnels and expanded our map of the Shadow City, collecting the treasures (gold coins, silver watches, surprisingly valuable antique bedpans) we found along the way. Whenever we came across an entrance in danger of discovery, we either blocked it or set booby traps. It was exhausting work, and much of it was done at night while most girls our age were snuggled up in their beds. We had hoped to complete our map before school started in September. But by the time Principal Wickham decided to rat me out, there was still one tunnel left to explore. Nothing my mother might have threatened could have kept me from finishing the job.

It's not that I didn't take her warning to heart. As my friend Verushka would say, when a quiet dog begins to bark, it's best to pay attention. I even tried tackling the geometry homework I'd long been neglecting. But math has always made my mind wander, and it didn't help that every room in our apartment was littered with books on more interesting topics. (Lost South American civilizations, forensic analysis of prehistoric dung, and the MI5 plot against Princess Diana, to name just a few.) While brewing a pot of strong coffee, I spotted a book titled *Female Poisoners of the Seventeenth Century* leaning against a box of Sweet'N Low. Unable to resist, I convinced myself

I needed a short break from numbers and let my eyes sink into the story of the greedy Marquise de Brinvilliers, who poisoned half her family before being burned at the stake. When I looked up again it was almost nine o'clock in the evening. As I threw on a pair of black pants and a black T-shirt, I cursed my lack of discipline. Books have always been my weakness.

I locked the door to my bedroom and scrambled down the fire escape outside my window. I'll admit that there wasn't much call for Cat Woman–style stealth. My mother and father weren't even home. I had put on such a convincing show of studying all day that they had decided to toast their success at a nearby restaurant. A simple *Studying: Do Not Disturb* sign would keep them out of my room when they returned. But since I was meeting Kiki Strike for an evening of adventure (perhaps my last for a while), going out the front door just didn't seem fitting.

· · ·

The weather had been unseasonably hot for weeks, and the air was thick with the rancid smell of a million garbage cans. Lightning crackled in the clouds above, warning of a storm that was slinking toward the city. As I headed for the Marble Cemetery, a hidden graveyard with an entrance to the Shadow City, I counted the rats that ducked into the sewers at the sound of my footsteps. I'd made it past forty when I turned into a short unlit thoroughfare named Jersey Street. The hair on the back of my neck began to levitate, and my fingers gripped the small can of pepper spray I had hidden in my pocket. I tried to prepare myself for an encounter with a gang of quick-fisted hooligans or one of Manhattan's fabled mug-gers. Instead, I found myself face-to-face with an enor-mous rodent.

. . .

Painted on the side of a building, the squirrel stood over six feet tall, and he didn't look pleased to see me. Two black, beady eyes stared out from beneath bushy brows, and a sinister sneer revealed a set of buckteeth. One of the squirrel's meaty hands held a sign written in block letters. It read YOUR MONEY WILL SET ALL THE ANIMALS FREE. I peered over my shoulder, hoping a flesh-and-blood squirrel wasn't there to make good on the threat. The alley was empty. I reached out and brushed my fin-gers against the paint on the wall. It was still wet. Who-ever had painted the squirrel had only recently finished the job.

On any given night in New York, there are hundreds of artists slipping through the shadows, leaving their marks on the walls of the city. Some are adrenaline junkies hooked on the rush; others have something to say and want the whole world to hear it. There was little doubt that the squirrel artist was on a mission—I suspected it might even be the same person whose pet store adventure had made the front cover of the *New York Post*. But one thing was certain: It wasn't Kiki Strike. She could speak a dozen languages and kick butts twice her size, but she couldn't draw a convincing stick figure. There was a new vigilante in town.

Having cleared Kiki of the animal-liberation caper, I was itching to tell her about the squirrel I'd seen. I made it to the Marble Cemetery with three minutes to spare and paced in front of the gates, consulting my watch every few seconds like a famished fat man checking a batch of brownies in the oven. Nine o'clock passed without word from Kiki. At nine fifteen, a pet supply truck drove past with a punk squirrel emblazoned on its side. The squirrel held a sign that announced LET THEM GO FREE OR SUFFER THE CONSQUENCES. I wondered what the consequences might be as the sky rumbled like the bowels of a constipated giant. At nine thirty I stood huddled under the awning of the neighborhood undertaker. It was pouring rain, and I was starting to worry. Kiki Strike prided herself on her punctuality. If she was late, there had to be trouble. I dialed her cell phone, but there was no answer. At nine forty, I hailed a cab and gave the driver directions to Kiki's house.

· · ·

For anyone who might think I was overreacting, I've included a brief list of the people who wanted Kiki Strike dead. The list has grown considerably over the years, but given the fact that, at the time of this story, Kiki wasn't old enough to drive (though she often did), I think you'll find it rather impressive.

1. **Livia Galatzina, (Exiled) Queen of Pokrovia.** A power-hungry monarch with a penchant for tacky home furnishings, Livia Galatzina had poisoned her older sister's entire family in order to ascend the throne of the tiny European kingdom of Pokrovia. Kiki Strike,

Livia's unfortunate niece, was saved by
Verushka Kozlova, a member of the Royal
Guard. After the people of Pokrovia gave Livia
the boot, she moved to New York. Kiki and
Verushka soon followed, intent on revenge.

2. **Sidonia Galatzina, Princess of Pokrovia.**
Livia's daughter and my former classmate at the
Atalanta School for Girls, the Princess had
once been labeled New York's *It Girl.* She, too,
had tried her hand at killing Kiki Strike. To lure
Kiki into her clutches, the Princess had kidnapped two girls whose parents had access to a
dangerous map. When the Irregulars managed
to rescue the girls, Sidonia and her mother fled
to Russia, where they were last spotted playing
croquet at the home of a notorious gangster.

3. **Sergei Molotov.** A corrupt former member
of Pokrovia's Royal Guard and Livia's right-hand
man, Molotov pinned the murder of Kiki's
parents on Verushka Kozlova, forcing Kiki and
Verushka into hiding. Later, the dapper
assassin shot Verushka in the thigh while
trying to capture Kiki Strike. He, too, escaped
punishment.

4. **The Entire Fu-Tsang Gang.** While exploring
the Shadow City, the Irregulars discovered
that the Fu-Tsang, a gang of Chinese
smugglers, were using rooms in the Shadow

City to hide its booty. We alerted the police, and in retaliation for the raid that followed, the Fu-Tsang joined forces with the Princess to kill Kiki Strike. Most of the gang had been jailed, although a few members remained at large.

5. **Lester Liu.** The mysterious leader of the Fu-Tsang, Lester Liu was rumored to be running his business from Shanghai.

6. **Hot Dog Vendor on the Corner of Fourteenth Street and Sixth Avenue.** Let's put it this way: Since Kiki reported his activities to the Health Department, I've never eaten another hot dog. Having skipped bail, the vendor was still wanted on multiple charges of animal cruelty.

When a queen, a smuggler, and a hot dog vendor are all determined to kill or capture you, it's best not to stay in one place very long. In July, Kiki and Verushka had moved to new living quarters on Eighteenth Street. Originally a carriage house, the long, narrow brick building had a single floor. Since Sergei Molotov had shot her two years earlier, Verushka had slowly lost the use of one leg, so stairs were out of the question. Over the summer, Luz Lopez, the Irregulars' brilliant mechanic, had spent three weeks crafting a one-of-a-kind wheelchair for Verushka's sixtieth birthday. When finished, it featured a seat that could rise three feet in the air, a robotic arm, and a small cannon for launching tear gas canisters. Late at night, when the city's traffic died down, Verushka could be seen racing the chair down Seventh Avenue. A policeman had once clocked her going fifty-three miles an hour. Verushka often bragged that he'd been far too impressed to give her a ticket.

At Eighteenth Street, I stepped out of my taxi and into a river of rainwater that coursed along the curb. Squinting past the streetlights at their building, I couldn't tell if Kiki and Verushka were home. A voracious ivy vine had swallowed the two small windows that faced the street, and its hungry tendrils were now attacking neighboring buildings. I walked up to the tall, arched wooden doors, reached deep into the ivy, and pressed a hidden doorbell. When no one answered, I waited for a nosy pedestrian to turn the corner and started to climb the wall.

If you're anything like me, you've seen a hundred movies in which people scale buildings using a wide variety of clinging plants. Trust me when I tell you that it's far more difficult than it looks and shouldn't be attempted unless you're saving lives or running from the law. Before reaching the edge of Kiki's roof, I slid back to the ground half a dozen times, skinning my knuckles in the process. Finally, I pulled myself over the top and peered down at the massive skylight set in the building's roof. The lights were on, but Kiki and Verushka were missing. The entire dwelling was as still and as silent as a dead child's dollhouse. I could see no evidence of a struggle—from what I could tell, everything was in its

proper place. In fact, there was only one sign that something was wrong. In the middle of the room sat
Verushka's empty wheelchair.

As much as I would have liked to investigate, I couldn't
break into Kiki's house. The Irregulars had spent weeks
booby-trapping the building for Kiki's protection. Break
the skylight and a cloud of laughing gas would send you
chuckling over the side of the building. Jimmy a lock and
you'd find yourself trapped in a net of skin-searing lasers.
I squatted on the roof and considered my options. There
was really only one, and I didn't like it: I'd have to wait.

As I prepared myself for a trip down the ivy, I checked
the street for passersby. At the end of the block, I spied a
thin, dark figure standing by a brick wall, sheltered by the
building's eave. Given his posture and lack of umbrella,
I assumed he was answering nature's call. My cell phone
vibrated, and I fished it out of my pocket, hoping to hear
Kiki on the other end of the line. Instead I saw the text
message icon. Distorted by raindrops, a sentence flashed
on the phone's screen. "*Meeting Tomorrow. 7:00 a.m. Fat
Frankie's. Oona.*" Disappointed, I started to inch my way
down the side of the building. Only when I landed safely
on the sidewalk did I realize I might have been spotted. I
hurried toward the figure I'd seen by the wall. The person
was gone, but he'd left his mark—a fierce six-foot squirrel
with a sign that read YOU'VE BEEN WARNED.

HOW TO APPEAR MYSTERIOUS

Despite what some books will tell you, you don't need magical powers or
friends in the faerie kingdom to enjoy a thrilling adventure from time to

time. What you *do* need is a little common sense—and some practical advice. That's what I'm here to offer. I may not be the world's greatest adventurer, but what I've learned, I've learned from the best. (And I tend to take *very* good notes.)

Let's start with something simple. How would you like to intrigue other people, inspire novels, and possibly become a legend in your own time? You don't need a criminal past, a dangerous secret, or even a trench coat to appear mysterious.

Silence Screams
If you're the sort of person who's willing to tell her entire life story to someone she meets on the subway, you may find it hard to cultivate an air of mystery. (Don't worry—you'll probably enjoy a fabulous future as a talk-show host.) Nothing will make you seem less mysterious than a bad case of verbal diarrhea. That doesn't mean you should be sullen or unfriendly. Simply keep your mouth shut and let people do what they enjoy most—talk about *themselves*.

Invent a Secret
Choose a subject to avoid in conversation. It could be your job (or a parent's profession), what happened on your summer vacation, or why there's always a bodyguard following you. Whenever the topic comes up, just smile and change the subject.

Look the Part
Bold colors and exposed flesh don't say *mysterious*. Instead, think black, streamlined, and sophisticated. Also, have at least one curious item that you're never seen without. It doesn't need to be a set of nunchakus—an old locket, a strange Indian armlet, or a well-worn copy of *International Affairs* could work just as well.

Flaunt Your Scar
Few things are more intriguing than a scar. If you already have one, consider yourself lucky. If you don't, you should be able to find a reasonable alternative at a costume store. Once again, it's best not to discuss it. No story you invent will be as fascinating as the ones people will concoct for themselves.

Choose an Area of Expertise

Take a lock-picking course. Learn how to hot-wire a car. Work toward a black belt in karate. Get to know the stock market. But never brag about your expertise. Instead, wait for the right opportunity to showcase your skills and watch all the jaws drop.

Learn How to Vanish

Disappearing is easier than it seems. Always have lunch with your friends in the same spot? Pick one day to eat your tuna fish in a new location. Don't explain your absence. Refuse to answer your phone or respond to e-mails for twenty-four hours. Tell people you were *busy*. When out with a group, wait until no one's watching and ditch them. When asked, say you *had something to do*.

Start a Secret Society

Once you've managed to create an aura of mystery, it may be time to pass your knowledge on to a few friends. Find a cause you can all rally around—whether it's saving baby squirrels or world domination—and start your own secret society. Consider creating your own logo, but remember—in order to be a *secret* society, it must always remain a SECRET.

CHAPTER TWO

Who's Been Sleeping in My Bed?

I think it's safe to say that most fourteen-year-old girls with criminal histories would have steered clear of Fat Frankie's diner. Every morning, dozens of police officers crammed the small coffee shop to scarf down breakfast before their morning shifts. But over the summer, Fat Frankie's had become Oona Wong's favorite hangout. However illicit her business might be, she preferred to conduct it in public. She knew she had nothing to fear. Few of her fellow customers could have imagined that the elegant girl with the doll's face had once been one of the most notorious forgers in Chinatown. Oona claimed she enjoyed living on the edge—but I've always suspected she had a fondness for policemen.

As I pushed my way through the crowded coffee shop, I wondered what Oona's latest scheme might be. One year earlier she had opened the Golden Lotus, an upscale nail salon where wealthy women flocked to freshen their pedicures and swap gossip with their friends. Arrogant and ignorant, they assumed the young Chinese women who worked in the salon could speak no English. But as they silently clipped cuticles and trimmed toenails, Oona's employees carefully recorded their clients' conversations. Oona had made a small fortune trading on socialites' secrets and stock tips, but that never stopped her from searching for new ways to pump up her bank account.

What Oona *did* with her money was a mystery the rest of us had never been able to solve. Painfully blunt, she never hesitated to point out that your lip gloss didn't suit your complexion or a giant pimple was about to emerge on your forehead. But as a matter of principle, she refused to discuss her own personal life. Though we'd known her for years, we had no idea where Oona lived or who cooked her waffles every morning. My single attempt to satisfy my curiosity had ended in a showdown on a Chinatown street when Oona caught me following her home, disguised as an unusually youthful bag lady. In the end, I promised to leave her alone. I knew one day the truth would be revealed, and having a sneak preview wasn't worth losing a friend.

· · ·

I found the Irregulars clustered around a table at the far end of Fat Frankie's, a few feet from the bathroom. Dressed in a gray mechanic's jumpsuit, Luz Lopez sat with her work boots propped up on the back of a chair. Her head was bent in concentration, and her lips formed silent curses as her fingers fiddled with her latest invention. DeeDee Morlock, the Irregulars' chemistry expert, was chatting with a bald Hare Krishna who could only be Betty Bent, our master of disguise. While the other girls paid little attention to their surroundings, Oona sat with her back to the wall, her fierce black eyes skipping from person to person. I had the sense she'd been counting the seconds until the meeting could begin. When she spotted me making my way to the table, she cocked her head and crossed her arms, silently demanding an explanation for my tardiness. Oona Wong did not like to be kept waiting.

"Thrilled you could finally make it, Fishbein. Were you abducted by aliens on the way here? Or did you stop off to bore another tourist with that lecture you give on the secret history of Washington Square Park?" Oona loved a confrontation, and on most mornings I might have indulged her. Instead I kept quiet as I pushed Luz's boots off the chair and sat down across from DeeDee.

"Where's Strike?" Oona demanded.

"I don't think Kiki's coming," I said.

Betty bit her lip and Luz's fingers froze as we all prepared for what would come next.

"What are you talking about?" Oona's pretty face wrinkled with rage. "She's *got* to be here. When one of us calls a meeting, everybody has to show up. That's the *rule*."

"Lower your voice. It's too early for shouting." Of all of us, DeeDee had the least patience for Oona's outbursts. "Let Ananka finish for once, would you?"

Oona's mouth clamped shut with enough force to bite a fork in half.

"Kiki's missing," I told them. "She was supposed to

meet me last night to finish the map. She never showed up at the Marble Cemetery."

"She was probably breaking into another pet store," said Luz, returning to her tinkering. "Any of you check the papers this morning? I'll bet somebody saw an albino leprechaun releasing more monkeys into the streets last night."

"Kiki didn't set those animals loose. She'd never be that irresponsible. It's a miracle none of them got squashed by a bus." Sweet natured and gullible, Betty never believed Kiki capable of anything objectionable. The rest of us knew better.

"Sometimes I wonder if we know the same person," I told her. "But this time you're right. Kiki didn't have anything to do with the pet store. Have you guys seen the giant squirrels?"

"I saw one on the way here," said DeeDee.

"What about them?" Luz shrugged.

"I'm pretty sure the same person who's been painting the squirrels set the pet store animals free. I think I saw him last night. He left a squirrel not far from Kiki's house."

"So you went to Kiki's house?" asked DeeDee. "What did Verushka say? Does she know where Kiki is?"

"Verushka's missing, too. And she didn't take her wheelchair."

For a moment, the Irregulars sat in silence as the information thumped around in our brains like a bowling ball in a washing machine. Oona sighed and rolled her eyes.

"There goes *my* meeting," she muttered.

"I'm sorry your latest get-rich-quick scheme has been temporarily put on hold." The volume of DeeDee's voice rose with each word. "Don't you think this is a *little* more important?"

"It's too early for shouting," Oona mocked her. "Kiki disappears all the time. That's what she *does*. I don't know why everyone's so worried. None of you would even notice if *I* didn't show up for a meeting."

"Your family isn't trying to kill you," Betty tried to explain.

"What would you know, baldy?" Oona said. "Maybe they are."

"So where is the homicidal royal family of Pokrovia these days?" Luz asked, dragging the conversation back on track. "Still hiding out in Russia?"

"We don't know," I admitted. "Livia and Sidonia vanished two months ago. Verushka's sources claimed they'd left St. Petersburg, but the other day I got wind of a rumor that made me wonder if the Princess and her mother might still be there."

"Could they have made it back to New York by now?" Betty wondered. "Have you heard anything at the salon, Oona?"

For a moment, it seemed as if Oona's lips wouldn't budge. Her anger had vanished, and she'd started to sulk. "I haven't been spending much time there lately," she finally said. "But Livia and Sidonia are top-priority topics. Someone would have called me if there had been any news."

"Should we check Kiki's house?" asked DeeDee. "If you give us a couple of hours, Luz and I can disable the booby traps."

"And destroy all that work?" moaned Luz. "Come on, guys. Oona's got a point. This isn't the first time Kiki's disappeared. It isn't even the *fourth* time. Shouldn't we wait a day or two before we start ripping everything apart?"

"Maybe Luz is right," said Betty. "Our weekly meeting is tomorrow. If Kiki doesn't show up for that one, we can break into her house and search for clues."

"Okay," I said, standing up from the table. "If you all want to wait, we'll wait. I just hope we're doing the right thing."

"Where are you going?" Betty asked.

"I have research to do. If Livia and Sidonia are back in New York, there might be an item in the gossip columns."

"But Oona called the meeting, and we haven't even let her talk," Betty protested. Oona said nothing. She just concentrated on the table in front of her as if she were willing it to fly through the window.

"Sorry, Oona," I said. "What did you want to discuss?"

"Never mind," Oona mumbled.

"Pleeeeeease," Betty begged, trying to lure Oona out of her funk.

"I'll wait. It's not that important," said Oona, and I suddenly suspected it was.

· · ·

That night, the weather worsened. Even with the windows open, my bedroom was hot enough to roast a goat. I lay on my bed in my nightgown, using the *Daily News* as a fan. Since returning home from the meeting, I'd combed through every New York newspaper. There was no mention of Livia or Sidonia Galatzina. The giant squirrels were the day's big story.

As if to prove to the city that they couldn't be ignored, the squirrels had invaded the Central Park Zoo in the early hours of the morning and freed hundreds of animals from their cages. At 6:00 a.m., a jogger reported a pack of penguins feasting on fish in the Harlem Meer. An anaconda was seen sunning itself on the steps of a Fifth Avenue mansion, a poodle-shaped bulge in its belly. Jewel-colored tree frogs clung to pine branches like Christmas tree ornaments. Among the only animals left behind at the zoo were several enormous squirrels. The one that made the front cover of the *New York Times* had been painted on a plastic iceberg in the polar bear's habitat. It was a thuggish-looking beast with a sign that said bluntly WHAT ARE YOU LOOKING AT?

According to the papers, security tapes at the zoo had captured a shadowy figure skipping past several sleeping guards, pausing from time to time to moon the cameras. Since the vigilante's face had been cunningly disguised, and his butt lacked distinguishing features, the police were without solid leads. They had begun staking out pet stores and interrogating art students, but the culprit remained at large. Everyone in New York was anxious to see what he'd do next.

A gust of wind blew through the room, rustling the newspapers I'd tossed to the floor. I turned my sweat-speckled forehead to catch the breeze and caught sight of an unnaturally pale face framed by wild, white hair peering at me from the fire escape. When I shrieked in terror, the face grinned and disappeared. Seconds later, my bedroom door swung open and my bespectacled father poked his head inside.

"Still alive?" he asked, checking the room.

"Barely." I was feeling a little faint from the shock.

"Boogeyman?" he asked.

"Spider."

Having earned a degree in entomology, my father's sympathies lay with the insects of the world, and he never missed an opportunity to bad-mouth an arachnid. "Repulsive little creatures," he said, shivering with disgust. "Did you know they dissolve their prey's innards and then suck them out like a Slurpee? They're the eight-legged serial killers of the arthropod phylum. But just remember: You're bigger than they are."

"Thanks for the advice," I said.

"That's my job," he replied as he shut the door with a smile.

Once I heard his footsteps fade, I ducked through the window and onto the fire escape. Kiki Strike was leaning against the wall, waiting for me, her chic black clothes blending into the night. She wasn't exactly the picture of a princess—at times it was hard to believe she was human. Though the poison she'd consumed as an infant hadn't killed her, it had drained her skin and hair of color. And because the attempt on her life had left her allergic to most forms of food, she was unlikely to grow more than five feet tall. At fourteen, she was like a creature from a sci-fi movie, shockingly beautiful and strange.

"Sorry I'm late," she whispered. Even in the dark, I could tell there was something wrong. Her ice-blue eyes were bloodshot, her cheeks had sunk to new depths, and she hadn't brushed her hair in days.

"Twenty-four hours. I think you've set a new record for tardiness. Where have you been? I was sure you'd been kidnapped. I've spent all day trying to locate Livia."

"Verushka was sick. I had to take her to the hospital."

"Verushka's in the hospital? What's wrong with her? Is she going to be okay? Can I see her?" The questions shot from my mouth like badly aimed bullets, and my vision blurred as tears flooded my eyes. Not only was Verushka the kind of guardian I always wished I had—funny, understanding, and handy with a bazooka—I knew it was she who'd convinced Kiki to invite me to join the Irregulars. Without her intervention, I might have died of boredom long before I reached high school.

"Verushka's back at home. She's doing fine. There was something wrong with her leg—the one that Sergei Molotov shot. It started turning blue a few days ago. But the problem's under control now. In fact, she'd be mad if she knew I told you. She wouldn't want to you to worry about her. She's a tough old lady. I once watched her stitch up her own head wound with a sewing needle and some fishing wire. She'll probably outlive us all."

"I wouldn't be surprised," I said. "But how are *you* feeling? You look like you've been dipped in Wite-Out. Are you sure you didn't catch something at the hospital?"

"Nothing a little danger can't cure. What do you say we finish the map tonight?"

"I can't. Some of us have to go to school in the morning. My teachers have been complaining that I keep passing out during class."

"Want me to take care of them?" asked Kiki with an arched eyebrow that I was afraid to interpret.

"I think I can handle them on my own," I assured her. "But I really do need to get some rest. My mother threatened to have me deported to the middle of nowhere if my grades don't improve."

"Come with me tonight, and I promise you'll get a nap tomorrow afternoon."

"Oh yeah? How are you going to do that?"

"It's a surprise. It won't get you into any trouble."

"But I don't want to go to the Marble Cemetery tonight," I moaned. "It's too much work."

"See," Kiki countered with a cocky grin. "I thought of that, too. If you get dressed fast, we can use the entrance in Iris's basement. Her parents are at a cocktail party."

"And her nanny?"

"The nanny locked herself in the bathroom an hour ago. She polished off a bottle of cooking sherry, and now she's singing show tunes to herself."

"I don't know, Kiki."

Kiki's smile faded as she chipped a piece of paint off the rail of the fire escape. Beneath all the bravado, something was still troubling her.

"You win," I huffed. "Stay here while I slip into something a little more practical. But you better think of a foolproof plan to get me out of school tomorrow." Back in my room, I reached out the window and handed her the front page of the *New York Times*. "Here's a little something to read while you wait."

"Yeah, I've seen the squirrels," Kiki said. "As long as they're on the loose, they should keep *me* out of the papers. Thanks to the zoo footage, nobody's looked twice at me all day. That butt on the surveillance tapes was undeniably male."

I poked my head out the window. "Worried your fifteen minutes of fame are finally up?"

"Relieved," Kiki corrected. "Another fifteen could get me killed."

. . .

In June, the Irregulars had rewarded eleven-year-old Iris McLeod with an honorary membership. Not only had she saved Kiki's life, she had also discovered a foul-smelling perfume that kept the man-eating rats of the Shadow City at bay. Without Iris's help, we could never have continued our explorations once our Reverse Pied Pipers stopped working. The kazoolike devises had been designed to produce a noise that rodent ears couldn't bear. For a while, the Reverse Pied Pipers had worked wonders, leaving only a few deaf rats to roam the tunnels. But over time, that handful of beasts had multiplied into a million-rat army. The large, fierce, hearing-impaired rodents were again on the hunt for trespassers, and anyone without the protection of Iris's perfume quickly took his place beside the hundreds of rat-picked skeletons that littered the passages and chambers of the Shadow City.

I squeezed my eyes shut and held on to Kiki's black leather jacket as she steered her Vespa motor scooter onto Bethune Street without bothering to slow for the curve. When we skidded to a halt in front of Iris's brownstone, the first thing I saw was the Irregulars' logo stamped on the sidewalk. An *i* in the shape of a girl in motion, it marked all known entrances to the underground tunnels. Beneath an old trunk in Iris's basement lay an ingeniously disguised trapdoor. A long, rusty ladder led to a hidden room seventy feet below street level that had once belonged to a bootlegger named Angus McSwegan. According to *Glimpses of Gotham*, a nineteenth-century guide to the *dark side* of New York, each bottle of Angus's whiskey was spiked with a dash of formaldehyde, which gave it a nasty kick. It had been the beverage of choice in the Shadow City, which lay just outside Angus's door.

I saw Iris watching at the window as Kiki and I climbed the steps of her stoop. Before we had a chance to ring the bell, the door flew open, revealing a tiny blond girl in an oversized white coat.

"Greetings, Irregulars," said Iris. Like Kiki, Iris was unusually small for her age. Unlike Kiki, she possessed a set of cherubic cheeks that were often pinched by strangers who mistook her for an eight-year-old.

We brushed through the door and into a front hall lined with the hideous masks and shrunken heads that Iris's parents collected on anthropological expeditions.

"What's with the lab coat?" Kiki asked Iris. "Don't tell me you've been experimenting on the nanny again. There are laws against that sort of thing, you know."

Iris giggled. "I forgot I had it on. I was getting ready for tomorrow."

"What's tomorrow?" I asked. "Are you in a play?"

"I've been practicing for the meeting tomorrow, remember?" Iris looked offended when I shook my head.

"DeeDee and I are presenting our big discovery. The one we've been working on all summer? Remember now?"

I didn't, but I figured it was best to play along. "Oh right, *that* presentation. Yeah, we're all really excited."

"You *should* be. My discovery's going to make the rat-repelling perfume look like toilet water."

"Speaking of rat-repellent," said Kiki, "we'll need a new bottle for tonight. I ran out last time, and I had two hundred rats chasing me like I was made out of marzipan. By the way, want to come?" It was her way of apologizing for forgetting Iris's presentation.

"I'd love to," Iris said. "But my parents will be home any minute. Plus, I want to make sure everything's perfect for tomorrow. If you need perfume, there's an extra bottle in the trunk downstairs. Just make sure you're superquiet on the way out. My mom thought there was a burglar the last time you guys were here."

"Sorry about that," said Kiki. "Oona slipped on her way up the stairs."

Iris's nose twitched at the sound of Oona's name. "That was *Oona* making all the noise? Little Miss Criminal Mastermind?"

"Can't you two get along?" Kiki sighed. "All this arguing is beginning to bore me."

"I get along with *her* just fine," Iris complained. "It's not *my* fault she doesn't like me. On Monday she said that if I didn't get any taller you guys were going to sell me to the circus."

"She did?" Kiki sounded both appalled and amused.

"Just because she teases you doesn't mean she doesn't

like you," I tried to assure Iris. "Oona teases all of us. She doesn't know any better. It's like she's socially retarded."

"Retarded or not, she'd better watch out," Iris fumed, "or one day somebody's going to teach her some manners."

We heard a door open upstairs, and a tone-deaf rendition of "Hey, Big Spender" rang through the house.

"Time to go," whispered Kiki, pulling me toward the basement. "See you tomorrow, Iris. And whenever you feel the urge to put Oona in her place, be my guest."

"Thanks," said Iris with a mischievous giggle. "Maybe I will."

· · ·

The temperature dropped with every step we took down the ladder that led from Iris's basement to the lost city beneath Manhattan. At the bottom, I shivered as I shined my flashlight around a chamber decorated with crates of rotgut whiskey and the rat-picked skeleton of Angus McSwegan, whose jaw hung open in a toothy smile. I unfolded my map. The last unexplored tunnel was on the east side of the Shadow City, more than a mile away.

"We'd better get going," I said with a yawn. "We've got a long walk ahead of us."

"Good!" For the moment, Kiki's worries were forgotten. "I'm in the mood for a stroll."

Beyond the chamber lay a broad, stone-lined tunnel. One side was blocked by a mound of rubble, the result of an unfortunate explosion two years earlier that had sent DeeDee Morlock to the hospital and Kiki into hiding. The other side of the tunnel stretched ahead of us. A monstrous gray rat bolted from a hole in the wall and vanished into the darkness. As we passed the doorways that led to the Shadow City's abandoned saloons, gambling parlors, and thieves' dens, we could hear the patter of a million tiny feet all around us. Thanks to Iris's rodent-repelling perfume, the rats kept their distance, but we both knew they were waiting for an opportunity to attack.

We had just turned a corner in a familiar part of the tunnels, fifty feet below the crypts of Saint Patrick's Old Cathedral, when Kiki grabbed my arm and pressed a finger to her lips. A wooden door stood open, blocking the path in front of us. At first I felt the same unnerving sensation you might experience if you returned from school one day to find your books rearranged or your bedspread upside down. But when I saw what was painted on the door's wooden boards, I almost sprinted for an exit. While the Irregulars loved nothing better than a new chamber to explore, we were always careful to avoid doors that were locked from the outside and labeled with a single red cross. We knew all too well what we would find. Whoever had opened the door, it wasn't one of us.

On the silent count of three, Kiki and I leaped in front of the doorway and lit the chamber with our flashlights. The floor of the room was stacked with skeletons, some still dressed in moldy dresses and moth-eaten suits. These were the citizens of the Second City—the criminals and con men who had met their Maker when the plague of 1869 swept through Manhattan's hidden tunnels. The few survivors had locked the sick and dying in rooms labeled with a red cross. Their cruelty had prevented the disease from spreading to the world above and ensured that the Shadow City would lay forgotten for over a hundred years.

"I don't see anybody," I told Kiki as my flashlight circled the room. "Do you think the door could have opened on its own?"

Kiki examined the lock. "I doubt it," she said.

Just beyond my flashlight's beam, something moved and I was overcome by a familiar terror. As many times as I'd visited the Shadow City, I had never been able to shake the feeling that some of the dead were still roaming the tunnels.

"Maybe it was one of them," I said, training my flashlight on a skeleton wearing a straw boater. "Maybe it was a ghost." A large bulge appeared beneath the dead man's shirt and crept slowly across his chest. A rat emerged at the collar and bolted past us as if it had been called to dinner.

"You're such an optimist, Ananka," Kiki joked. "Let's *hope* it was a ghost. But keep your eyes open. There may be somebody down here. Haven't you noticed anything strange in the past few minutes?"

I was about to shake my head when I finally figured it out. "It's quiet," I said. "I don't hear the rats anymore."

"Exactly," said Kiki. "That was the first rat I've seen in a while. Kind of makes you wonder where they've gone, doesn't it?"

· · ·

The last uncharted tunnel of the Shadow City snaked beneath Manhattan's Lower East Side. Its crumbling brick

walls were less impressive than the high, arched passages found elsewhere in the city, and at times, it felt as
if we were strolling down the hallway of an abandoned
penitentiary. I took measurements and scribbled notes
as Kiki investigated the rooms we passed. Most were
empty, though we discovered one storeroom stocked
with enough barrels of pickled oysters to have fed a
small town for a year (though I suspect most townsfolk
would have preferred to starve). To our disappointment,
none of the chambers appeared to have an exit to the
surface. When the tunnel came to a dead end at a plain
wooden door, I silently worried that our final exploration
had been a dud.

In the cavelike room beyond, we found ten rickety
cots lined up in a row and a large wardrobe set against
the far wall. Nine of the beds were made—the sheets
and woolen blankets crisply folded and tucked beneath
the mattresses. The tenth bed, however, was rumpled,
and its sheets lay in a lump in the center of the mattress.

"Who's been sleeping in *my* bed?" I joked, but Kiki
had her ear pressed against the wall beside the wardrobe
and wasn't paying attention. I picked up an old book that
lay on a bedside table. The title page read *A Canadian
Woman's Guide to Housekeeping*. I thumbed through the
book, pausing to skim chapters that offered handy instructions for making your own burlap panties and cooking a nutritious moose stew.

"Hey," Kiki called. "Do you hear that?"

"Hear what? Are the rats back?"

"No. Sounds like water," she said. "Help me move this wardrobe."

Together, we pushed the heavy piece of furniture away from the wall. Behind it was a narrow tunnel just high enough to crawl through. It led up to the surface at a steep angle. The roar of rushing water filled the void.

"Just as I suspected," said Kiki.

"Looks dangerous," I said, pointing to a pair of boards on the roof of the tunnel that were bulging with the weight of the earth above. "I don't think we should check it out until Luz can have a look. It might be ready to collapse."

"That's all right. I'm pretty sure I know where *this* tunnel goes. It's an escape route to the river. But you're not getting out of climbing up *that* one." She lifted her eyes to the ceiling. There, above our heads, was a circular opening carved into the earth—an exit from the Shadow City.

We found a ladder in one of the storerooms and dragged it back to the final chamber. Inside the hole, a series of metal rungs led to a trapdoor high above. Although most exits from the tunnels looked the same, you never knew where you might emerge. You could find yourself interrupting a mafia dinner party, gazing in wonder at the jewels stored in a secret vault, or staring into the eyes of a smuggler's pit bull. When Kiki's head hit the trapdoor, she listened carefully before pushing it open and hoisting herself into the darkness.

"You're not going to believe this," she whispered.

I pulled myself out of the hole and followed her

spotlight as it circled an enormous room. The walls were painted with murals of ancient buildings and palm-speckled landscapes. Neat rows of wooden pews lined the floor. At the front of the room stood a two-story ark made of wood and gold, which was decorated with a pair of weeping lions.

"It's beautiful," Kiki whispered.

"I think I know where we are."

"Looks like a temple."

"It's the Bialystoker Synagogue," I informed her, wishing Mr. Dedly were there to get a taste of my expertise. "A hundred and fifty years ago, it was known as the Willet Street Church. I've heard rumors that it once was a stop on the Underground Railroad, but nobody's been able to prove it. Until now."

"So that's what the beds are all about?"

"Yep, before the Civil War, somebody must have been hiding escaped slaves in the Shadow City and smuggling them out to boats in the river at night."

"How about that," marveled Kiki. "Our last unexplored tunnel, and we finally discover that somebody put the Shadow City to good use. My faith in humankind has been restored."

"Do you have any idea how important this is? This trapdoor, that room, the ten little beds—they're all a part of American history. There's nothing like them anywhere."

"That's why it's a shame no one will ever know about them but us." Though it was too dark to see, I could hear the warning in Kiki's voice.

As we climbed down to the room below, my heart was still pounding with excitement, and a thousand thoughts bounced around in my brain. What if the discoverer of King Tut's tomb had sealed it up and let the desert reclaim it? What if the explorer who found the Lost City of Machu Picchu had left it hidden in the clouds?

"Kiki, sit down for a second. We've got to talk about this," I said.

Eyebrow arched, Kiki settled on the side of the rumpled bed. Suddenly, her brow creased. She patted the sheet beside her.

"Save the lecture for later. There's something in the bed," she said, carefully unknotting the sheet. A small clay figure fell onto the mattress. It was a woman wearing ancient Chinese armor and riding a fat black horse. There was no doubt it was far older than anything else we'd found inside the Shadow City.

"Were stops on the Underground Railroad usually decorated with ancient Chinese art?" asked Kiki.

"Probably not," I admitted.

"There goes your ghost theory. Somebody's been down here. So I guess that leaves one question." Kiki gave me a wicked grin.

"What?" I asked.

"Who wants to look under the bed?"

HOW TO DETECT THE PRESENCE OF AN INTRUDER

Concerned that your private space might be invaded but don't have the money for armed guards or laser beams? No need to fret—there are dozens of options available to you. The following cheap and effective security devices will not only signal an unauthorized entry, many will also scare the pants off an intruder (which can be quite amusing if you're watching the scene through binoculars).

Door and Window Contacts

These small, inexpensive magnetic devices are designed to issue an ear-splitting alarm whenever a door or window is opened. They can be found at any hardware store and are also handy for drawers, jewelry boxes, coffins—or anything you can think of that opens and shuts. (Be forewarned: A determined intruder may go online for tips that will help her disable these gadgets.)

Motion Detectors

Believe it or not, for little more than the price of two movie tickets, you can purchase your own motion alert system. Place the sensor in just the right spot and wait for someone to sneak into your room while you're immersed in your favorite kung fu film. The sensor will send a signal to your portable receiver, which will alert you with a piercing alarm or flashing lights. (Motion detectors can also work well for ghost hunting.)

Voice-Activated Tape Recorder

The previous two items are great for protecting your belongings when you're not far away—but what if you suspect someone's snooping around when you're not at home? Unless you're rich or have a talent for installing electronic security systems, I recommend a simple voice-activated tape recorder, which will start recording at the sound of movement. You won't catch your snoop red-handed, but at least you'll have some hard evidence that a break-in has occurred.

Trip Wires

If you're running low on cash—or you need an alarm in short order—a trip wire may be your best bet. Take some fishing line and stretch it across an entryway or well-trafficked area. (Make sure it's about a foot above the floor.) Anchor one end of the line to a piece of furniture and attach the other end to a small plastic cup. Fill the cup with some water and place it on top of a newspaper. If the newspaper's wet—or missing—when you get home, you'll know someone's been in your room. (Warning: This trick may work only once.)

Do-It-Yourself Alarms

If you're good with your hands and you want an alarm that will make lots of noise, a quick online search will lead you to instructions for making a wide variety of alarms with supplies that might already be in your garage.

CHAPTER THREE

Eau Irresistible

At eight o'clock the next morning, I shuffled into the Atalanta School for Girls, a private academy on the Upper East Side of Manhattan, and found the hallowed halls buzzing with a thousand whispered conversations.

"She's almost entirely plastic, you know."

"Forget jail. If the police ever call my house, I'll end up sleeping in a box on First Avenue."

"Guess who had dinner with you-know-who's boyfriend on Saturday?"

"The President was at our house this weekend, and he said . . ."

Though many of my wealthy schoolmates couldn't tell time without a digital clock, they all excelled at one subject—gossip. At least once every year, usually in the aftermath of a vicious rumor that had sent a student into hiding, one of our teachers would take it upon herself to warn us that gossip is mean, petty, and a waste of our time. While I'm inclined to agree with the first part, the second couldn't be further from the truth. Gossip is merely information that's been cleverly packaged, and it can be a powerful tool if you know how to use it. Revolutions have started with a single whisper. A little idle chatter can bankrupt a movie star. And any good detective will tell you that one careless comment can uncover a crime.

When dealing with gossip, the trick is keeping your mouth shut. Swapping stories is like skinny-dipping in the Hudson River. It seems like great fun until you wake up in the morning with a nasty rash in all the wrong places. I've found that it's best to watch (and listen) from a distance and resist the urge to jump in.

Since school had resumed, I'd taken to lingering in the hallways, pretending to go about my business while I snapped up the snippets of information that flew through the air. For weeks, the hottest topic had been Kiki's cousin, Sidonia Galatzina, whom everyone at Atalanta knew as the Princess. Rich, royal, and thoroughly evil, the Princess had ruled our school for years before she finally succumbed to scandal. In June, four of her closest friends had been arrested on kidnapping charges, and the Princess had disappeared before the police could ask any questions. Some, like the authorities, believed the Princess had been a victim herself. I was one of the few who knew that the pretty girl with the jet-black hair and golden eyes had masterminded the entire affair.

It seemed that everyone at Atalanta had a theory about the Princess's whereabouts. In September, I'd eavesdropped on two juniors who had managed to convince each other that Sidonia was living in an Alpine castle, secretly betrothed to Prince Uder of Lichtenstein. (Kiki had a good laugh at that one.) Later, I heard that Dylan Handworthy had spotted the Princess in a Japanese ad for toilet bowl cleaner. (Though the model was only a look-alike, color copies of the ad were quickly posted in every bathroom stall in the school.) But the most promising theory was never made public. Alex Upton insisted she'd run into the Princess while touring the Hermitage's Rubens Room in St. Petersburg, Russia. I wasn't particularly interested when Alex bragged that Sidonia had introduced her companion as Oleg Volkov, a Russian gangster believed to be one of the ten richest men in the world. What caught my attention was the date. If Alex was telling the truth, the Princess and her mother were still in St. Petersburg as late as August—a full month after the Irregulars had lost track of them.

I had been shadowing Alex for over a week, hoping for more information. But that morning, I was too exhausted for detective work. It was only by chance that I happened to pass by as she chatted with a friend outside the biology lab.

"Squirrels don't *attack* people," her friend insisted. I stopped and pretended to shuffle through my notebook, dying to inform them that one quick Internet search would prove that squirrels are indeed prone to violence against humans.

"I'm just *telling* you what I heard," said Alex. "I don't care if you *believe* it."

A third girl joined the group. "Believe what?"

"One of the scholarship students says she got attacked by squirrels yesterday."

"Squirrels?" repeated the newcomer in disbelief.

"That's what *I* said," the second girl sneered, feeling more confident now that backup had arrived.

"No, it's just that my brother's friend had a squirrel steal his iPod yesterday," said the third girl.

"See?" Alex looked triumphant.

"Yeah, he'd just come from some exhibit at the museum and he was walking home through Central Park when a squirrel dropped out of a tree and landed on his head. Then it grabbed his iPod and took off for the bushes."

"How could a squirrel pick up an iPod?" asked the skeptic.

"He said it wasn't an ordinary squirrel. It was huge—like two feet long. He tried to tell a policeman, but the guy just laughed and told him to say no to drugs. Hey, what's that smell?"

"What smell?"

"You're telling me you can't smell that? It's like a Porta Potti at a chili cook-off."

It took one quick whiff to confirm that there was, indeed, a hint of sewage in the air. As the odor grew stronger, it began to drift through the school. Hundreds of noses were pinched in disgust, and the halls rang with a chorus of *"Ewww!"*

"Attention!" Principal Wickham barked from the loudspeaker. "We've just gotten word from the Sanitation Department that there has been a sewer backup in the building and we must evacuate. Grades eight and below, please gather in the courtyard. Grades nine and above, you are dismissed until tomorrow morning."

A hundred nasal voices let out a cheer. Kiki Strike had made good on her promise.

. . .

As I started home for a much-needed nap, a small, pale girl in a black wig and dark sunglasses joined me on the corner of Sixty-eighth and Lexington. Having briefly been a student at the Atalanta School, Kiki couldn't risk being recognized. We walked in silence to the downtown subway and waited on the far end of the platform.

"Great job!" I commended her once no one was listening. "How did you back up the sewers?"

"I didn't. I just placed a call to Principal Wickham," she boasted. "Oh—and then I tossed some of these beauties through the bathroom windows." She opened her hand just enough to reveal a plum-sized stink bomb. "DeeDee has a whole box of these in her laboratory. Guess what her secret ingredient is?"

"Manure?" I hazarded.

"Fresh from the sidewalks of the Upper West Side. She's got a deal with a dog walker in her neighborhood."

"That's vile," I told her. "I hope you wash your hands when you get home."

"See how far I'll go to keep you out of trouble?" said Kiki.

"I'm grateful, believe me. I just hope I can make it home. It'll be a miracle if I don't fall asleep on the subway and end up in Brooklyn. By the way, I heard something interesting before you cleared the school out."

"Where do they say Sidonia is now—herding goats in Uzbekistan?" Kiki laughed.

"No, it wasn't about Sidonia. It was about the squir-rels. They started mugging people over the weekend."

"So I've heard. I was thinking of doing a little squirrel spotting while I'm uptown. But kleptomaniac rodents aren't my biggest concern right now."

"You're right. We need to find out who's been in the tunnels first."

For the briefest of moments, Kiki looked confused. "Of course," she said, nodding vigorously. "The intruder's top priority."

A train rolled into the station with a deafening screech. I stepped aboard, but Kiki stayed behind on the platform. I think she could sense the question I was dying to ask.

I leaned out the doors. "Are you coming?"

"On second thought I could use a walk in the park," said Kiki. "See you at the meeting."

· · ·

"Hurry up! You're late!" DeeDee practically shouted as she threw open the door to her town house near Colum-bia University. "Everyone else is upstairs in the lab, and Oona's driving us nuts."

"Sorry. I overslept." I followed DeeDee as she bounded up five flights of stairs to the attic. The seat of her chinos looked as though she'd sat in a puddle of grease, and a purple blob that jiggled like Jell-O clung to her dread-locks. "Kiki used one of your stink bombs to shut down the Atalanta School so I could take a nap."

"I'm glad somebody got some use out of them. My par-ents threatened to move if I didn't stop production. The whole house stank like a fertilizer factory. I can't tell you how relieved they were when I started working with Iris."

"So what *is* this big discovery Iris keeps talking about?" I asked.

"My lips are sealed, Nancy Drew. Iris would kill me if I ruined her surprise," DeeDee replied. "We've been working on it all summer."

"I hope you didn't let her use any dangerous chemicals," I said, knowing that Iris's many gifts did not include gracefulness. "I'd rather not die today."

"Why does everyone treat Iris like a little kid?" DeeDee sniffed. "I was making my first explosives when I was eleven."

"Yeah, and look where that got you." I pointed to the scar that ran across her forehead, the unfortunate result of a bad batch of explosives.

"Don't you think it makes me look interesting?" DeeDee took everything seriously except her appearance. "At *my* school, everyone wants to know the girl with the scar."

.   .   .

At the top of the stairs lay DeeDee's bedroom and laboratory. She'd tried her best to tidy up for the meeting, but the closet bulged with dirty clothes, and an impressive collection of Chinese take-out containers peeked out from beneath the bed. I couldn't bear to think what had been swept under the rug. A softball-sized lump was emitting an odor that could be described only as rank. But DeeDee didn't seem to mind. As far as she was concerned, housework was for people with too much time on their hands and too little on their minds. Only her laboratory, which took up half the large room, was kept perfectly spotless. Glass beakers, flasks, and test tubes sparkled like crystal, and a rainbow of chemicals—some of them glowing—were arranged neatly on shelves.

In front of the lab, six folding chairs had been positioned in a semicircle, and all but two were filled. Luz was impatiently yanking on her ponytail while Betty Bent reapplied a set of false eyelashes that had come unglued. I was hoping I'd have a chance to ask Kiki what was bothering her, but Oona was already sitting at her side.

"How long is this going to take?" I overheard Oona ask. "I've got something *important* to talk about."

"It's going to take as long as Iris needs it to take," Kiki said curtly. "Ananka and I have news, too, but we're willing to wait our turn. Iris has been looking forward to this for months."

Oona rolled her eyes and gazed at the ceiling. I took the chair as far away from her as possible. DeeDee rapped at the bathroom door, and Iris's little blond head peeked out into the lab.

"Are they all here?" she whispered to DeeDee. "Can we start now?"

"We can hear you, Iris," Oona called. DeeDee shot her a nasty look.

"Yes, everyone's here," she told Iris. The bathroom door closed again while DeeDee took a seat.

Exactly ten seconds later (she must have been counting), Iris made her entrance. She was wearing an enormous white lab coat that reached down to her ankles and a set of orange-tinted safety goggles. Her hair had been pulled into an official-looking bun.

Oona cracked up. "Why didn't anybody tell me it was Halloween?" she cackled.

"What's wrong with you?" DeeDee snarled.

"SHHHH!" Kiki insisted.

Iris did her best to ignore the commotion. "Good evening, fellow Irregulars."

"Hey, Iris," said Betty. In honor of Iris's big day, she was dressed in a vintage Chanel suit and wearing her favorite red wig.

"Thanks for coming today. I hope you all find my presentation both entertaining and educational." Iris opened a cabinet and retrieved a silver serving tray. On top of it sat two crystal bottles filled with amber liquid.

Luz turned to DeeDee. "What's that, more perfume?"

"Iris will be answering your questions tonight," DeeDee responded.

"So you've been making perfume?" Luz asked Iris with a yawn. She had little interest in anything girly.

"You *could* say that." Iris forced back a grin.

"Can I smell it?" asked Betty, eager to play along.

"Sorry, Betty. I was hoping Oona would be the first to try my new creation. I call it *Fille Fiable*."

"Forget it, Iris. I'm already wearing perfume," said Oona. "I had it custom made by a professional nose, and it cost four hundred dollars an ounce. I'm not interested in smelling like a chemistry lab."

"I understand completely." When Iris appeared to take the insult with good humor, I began to get worried. "What if I put a little on my own wrist and let you take a whiff?"

"Iris . . . ," said DeeDee in a warning tone. I saw one of Kiki's eyebrows rise.

"It's okay, DeeDee," Iris insisted. "Oona doesn't have to *wear* it to appreciate it."

"I'm sure I'll survive," said Oona, rolling her eyes and rising from her chair.

Iris chose one of the crystal bottles from the tray. Pulling back the sleeve of her lab coat, she dabbed a little liquid on her forearm and waved it in the air before offering her arm to Oona. Oona bent down and inhaled deeply. Her nose instantly wrinkled in disgust.

"I think you need a better name for it," she said. "How about Eau de BO? It's almost as foul as your rat-repelling perfume."

Iris nodded thoughtfully. "I thought you might say that. It's just not special enough for a girl with your taste. I mean, look at you. Those must be real diamond earrings you're wearing, right?"

"Two carats each," Oona bragged. Everyone has a weakness, but Oona had more than her fair share. At the top of a list that included alligator handbags and cashmere socks, was diamonds.

"They're *nice*," said Iris, making it perfectly clear that she meant the opposite. "But they make you look a little cheap. I think they'd look better on Ananka, don't you?"

The rest of us held our breath, waiting for the carnage to begin. I slid forward on my seat, preparing to leap to Iris's rescue. That's when Oona surprised us all.

"You know, you're right," she agreed. "I always thought they were kind of tacky. Want them, Ananka?" She took the diamonds out of her ears and tossed them into my lap.

"And that dress," said Iris. "It's not very flattering. I read in *Vogue* last week that it's much more fashionable to wear just a slip during the day."

"Really?" said Oona. "I must have missed that issue. Do you think I should take the dress off? I have a slip on underneath. But won't it be a little chilly?"

"Cold, shmold," Iris declared. "A girl should be willing to suffer for fashion."

"I couldn't agree more!" announced Oona, stripping out of her dress. She posed in front of us in a hot-pink slip. "How's this? Fabulous, right?"

Luz fell out of her chair, laughing.

"Are you on drugs, Lopez?" Oona snipped. "*Whatever.* I wouldn't expect a girl who dresses like Mr. Goodwrench to understand."

"Um, Iris," I said, choking down a guffaw. "How far are you going to take this?" Iris ignored me.

"You look great, Oona. After the meeting, we should go over to your house and get rid of all the ugly stuff in your closet. By the way, I've always wondered where you live. Nobody's ever been to your house, right? Why don't you tell us about it?"

"That's enough," Kiki barked before Oona had a chance to speak. She picked up Oona's dress and handed it to her. "Go to the bathroom and put your clothes back on," she instructed.

"But that dress is hideous!" Oona moaned.

"Trust me," Kiki insisted.

Once Oona shut the bathroom door, Kiki slid a proud arm around Iris.

"Impressive," she said. "Cruel, but impressive."

"Thanks!" chirped Iris. "Oona was begging for it."

"True, but I hope you didn't take it too far. You don't want Oona as an enemy. Did you know about this, DeeDee?"

DeeDee smiled. "No, but I agree with Iris. Oona's been asking for it."

"I'm with DeeDee. Nobody's made me laugh that hard in months," said Luz. "So the perfume can make people do what you want?"

"I wish. Fille Fiable just makes people trust you. If you give them a nose full, they're more willing to tell you their secrets—or believe whatever *you* tell them," Iris explained.

"How long does it take to wear off?" I asked.

"Only a couple of minutes," DeeDee assured me. "Oona should be coming to her senses soon."

I looked at Iris. "In that case, I would recommend running for your life."

The bathroom door banged against the wall, making DeeDee's glass beakers tinkle. For a moment, I thought I might have to break up a brawl, but Oona simply walked up to me and snatched her diamonds.

"Funny trick," she muttered to no one in particular before she stormed out of the attic and down the stairs.

As the rest of us stood speechless, Betty and DeeDee sprinted after Oona.

"Uh-oh," said Luz, digging her hands deep into the pockets of her jumpsuit. "Looks like Oona just overdosed on her own medicine."

"I didn't mean to hurt her feelings," cried Iris. "I was

just trying to pay her back for all the times she's made fun of me."

"You must have hit a weak spot," I said. "She'll forgive you."

"You think so?" Iris asked hopefully.

"Sure." My lie wasn't convincing, and Iris started to sniffle just as Betty and DeeDee returned, out of breath.

"She won't come back," DeeDee announced. "Let's get on with the show. I've had enough of Oona today anyway. Actually, I can barely remember when I *wasn't* sick of Oona. If you ask me, the girl's more trouble than she's worth." DeeDee clapped a hand over her mouth. "Whoa—did I just say that? That perfume really loosens your tongue."

"Oona's just upset," said Betty. "Something's not right. She's been acting strange all week. Don't you think we should postpone the meeting?"

"We can't," said Kiki. "Let's let Iris finish her presentation. Then the rest of us have important business to discuss. I'll speak to Oona tonight. She'll come around. We're going to need her help. Iris? Are you ready?"

A slightly teary-eyed Iris returned to her presentation.

"Um. Where was I? Okay. After the perfume my parents brought back from Borneo worked so well on the rats, I started thinking about other things I could make. Then I read in the newspaper about these scientists in Switzerland who had come up with a spray that makes people seem trustworthy. When I told DeeDee about it, she offered to help me improve their formula."

"The Swiss had been using oxytocin, a hormone

secreted by the pituitary gland, which functions as a neurotransmitter . . . ," DeeDee began.

"Could you try speaking English?" I asked.

"Sure." DeeDee grinned. "For those of you who prefer to sleep through biology class, oxytocin is a chemical in our bodies that helps us bond with other people. It's part of what helps us fall in love. But in small doses, it makes you trust the people around you. For instance, oxytocin is one of the reasons that girls like to gossip and swap secrets. It's good stuff. We didn't need to change the Swiss formula; we just made it a little more powerful. That's how we came up with Fille Fiable.

"We tested our first batch at a movie theater down the street. There were only R-rated movies playing, and I thought we might be able to convince the people at the ticket counter that Iris was seventeen. It wasn't the best idea I've ever had. The woman selling tickets was behind two inches of glass and she couldn't smell the perfume. But the people standing in line behind us were so outraged when we couldn't get in that they demanded to see the manager."

"They were *soooo* nice." Iris was starting to enjoy the presentation again.

"They got banned from the theater," said DeeDee. "Iris and I had to book it before the perfume wore off and they figured out they were fighting to let an eleven-year-old watch a dirty movie."

Iris jumped in. "But then I came up with another way to test the perfume. My dad once told me that there are hundreds of dinosaurs in the basement of the Museum of Natural History that nobody ever gets to see. So

DeeDee and I talked one of the security guards into taking us on a tour."

"It's a little more complicated than that," DeeDee explained. "You've got to be careful with the formula. You can't just make up something that's one hundred percent unbelievable. We couldn't tell the guard that we were visiting paleontology professors or anything, so we came up with something a little more realistic. We told him that Iris's father was doing research in the dinosaur archives and that we needed to let him know that Iris's mom was about to have a baby."

"We said his cell phone was turned off," Iris added.

"It worked perfectly. The guard took us through the whole basement. Iris was right. I couldn't believe what they have stored down there. We saw bones that I swear didn't come from any Earth creature I've ever read about. Of course, we had to keep reapplying our Fille Fiable every time the guard turned his back. When we were about to run out, Iris pretended to get a text message that said her dad was already on his way to the hospital."

"Smart." Kiki nodded with approval.

"So what's the stuff in the other bottle?" I asked.

Iris held up the crystal vial. Its amber contents shimmered in the light. "This is *Eau Irresistible*. Our second masterpiece."

"We realized that with a few tweaks, our potion might have other uses," said DeeDee. "We haven't tested it yet, but if our calculations are correct, it should live up to its name."

"It's a love potion? Go ahead and spray a little here," Betty offered, holding out her arm.

DeeDee shook her head. "I don't think that's a good idea. Like I said, we haven't tested it yet."

"You've got to start somewhere," said Luz. "Betty looks like a pretty good guinea pig to me."

"Okay, Betty, but don't come complaining to me if you start sprouting hair in weird places," DeeDee warned.

"Why would I complain about that? Do you know how much a convincing fake mustache costs these days? I'm ready when you are, Iris."

Iris removed the bottle's atomizer and passed it to Betty. "I don't think you should have a full spritz. DeeDee was kidding about the hair, but it might cause a rash."

Betty dabbed a little Eau Irresistible on her wrist and inhaled. "Wow. Smells like feet. Let's see if it works." She turned to Luz and batted her false eyelashes. "Do you find me irresistible?" she asked in a sultry voice.

Luz leaned toward Betty, as if drawn in by the scent of the perfume.

"You know, Betty, I've never met anyone so completely . . ." Luz paused as if searching for the right word. "Resistible."

The rest of us laughed and Betty shrugged.

"It was worth a try, right? All in the name of science."

"Maybe it works only on the opposite sex," said DeeDee. "Or maybe you didn't put enough on. We'll have to do some tests before we know for sure."

Iris stepped toward Betty to retrieve the bottle of Eau Irresistible when her foot caught the edge of DeeDee's rug. Seeing Iris lurch toward her, Betty leaned back too far and her chair toppled over. Kiki snatched the bottle of perfume, but not before most of the contents had spilled. Betty looked up in shock, her red wig drenched with perfume, as the smell of feet filled the room. Iris watched, petrified, as DeeDee grabbed the hair off of Betty's head and flung it into a corner. Then she dragged Betty to the bathroom and threw her into the shower fully clothed.

"Rinse off as much of it as you can while you still have your clothes on," we heard her instruct. "Then go ahead and take a shower. There are towels in the cabinet. I'll bring you something to wear."

"I'm so sorry!" cried Iris as DeeDee closed the door of the bathroom and returned to the lab.

"Accidents happen," DeeDee mumbled as she ransacked her closet for clean clothes.

Iris ran to the bathroom door. "I'm sorry, Betty!" she called through the crack.

"What about the rest of us?" Luz moaned. "It smells like a giant sweat sock in here."

"I'll open the windows," I said, pinching my nose.

"You know, DeeDee, I don't think applying more of the stuff is going to make it work any better," Kiki informed our host. "Nobody in this room seems very appealing right now."

"Yeah," DeeDee admitted. "I think it's back to the drawing board with Eau Irresistible."

. . .

Ten minutes later, Betty emerged from the bathroom and took a seat next to a miserable Iris. She was wearing a chemistry club T-shirt and a pair of DeeDee's jeans, which were three inches too short and covered with green blotches. Despite her unflattering outfit, it was a little unnerving to see Betty out of disguise. Beneath all the makeup and rubber noses, she was remarkably pretty.

"I thought your presentation was fascinating," she said, more concerned about Iris than herself. "Don't worry about me."

"You still stink a little," sniffled Iris. "It might last a couple of days."

"I don't mind. I've got a new garbage collector's uniform I've been dying to try out," said Betty. "You can learn all sorts of interesting stuff by going through people's trash. The smell should make the disguise more convincing."

"That's true," said Iris, perking up a little. She handed Betty a plastic bag. "Luz was going to throw your wig out the window, but I know it's your favorite, so I saved it. But you might want to wash it before you wear it again."

"Or burn it," said Luz. "Are we done here? I told my mom I'd be home by eight."

"Not yet," Kiki said. "Take a seat. There are a couple more things on the agenda."

"Is this about the squirrel attacks?" Betty wondered.

"You've heard about them?" I asked.

"Sure. A girl at school had her wallet stolen. Everybody was talking about it."

"Yeah, some kid was mugged in Morningside Park yesterday," Luz added. "And a giant squirrel popped up on the window of my friend's cousin's dog grooming shop the other night. Those rodents are getting to be a real menace."

"We'll look into the squirrel issue later," said Kiki.

"We've got bigger problems right now. Ananka, you want to tell them?"

"Someone's been inside the Shadow City. Kiki and I were down there last night. First we found one of the doors with a red cross standing open, and then we discovered this." When I held up the Chinese statue, I saw three girls grimace. They knew it meant trouble, and only Iris seemed prepared for the next adventure to begin.

"Could it be the Fu-Tsang?" Betty asked. Thanks to Sidonia Galatzina, the gang of Chinese smugglers had made it into the Shadow City once before. "Don't they smuggle stuff like that?"

"I doubt it's the Fu-Tsang," said Kiki. "Most of them are in jail. The rest are probably too scared of the rats to go back to the tunnels. Three of them *did* get eaten last time."

"Then who do you think it could be?" asked Luz.

"We don't know," I admitted. "We don't even know how they got inside."

"But we have to find out," Kiki said. "Anyone have any ideas?"

"I have some motion detectors I just made," said Luz. "I was going to use them to keep my sisters from snooping through my workshop, but I guess that can wait. I'll have to make a few more, but it shouldn't take very long."

"When could they be ready?" asked Kiki.

"If I stay up late, I could have everything done by tomorrow. But there's one thing I'm gonna need."

"What?"

"If we want to put the motion detectors in all the right places," said Luz, "I'm going to need the map of the Shadow City."

I shuddered when she said it. All summer, I had taken sole responsibility for protecting the map. After all, there were only two copies left in the world. The first unfinished map was on a disk stolen by Sidonia Galatzina. The second was a single sheet of paper that I usually kept tucked away between the pages of *Glimpses of Gotham*. There were no other copies, no more computer files. After everything that had happened, the Irregulars couldn't risk letting the final version fall into the wrong hands. I've never claimed to possess psychic powers, but the moment the map was no longer in my possession, I knew we were all in trouble.

THINGS YOU CAN LEARN BY GOING THROUGH THE TRASH

Several years ago, a mysterious British man began supplying London's journalists with embarrassing stories about the private lives of famous people—and no one could figure out where he'd gotten the information. Many suggested he was hacking into celebrities' computers or staking out their homes with fancy cameras and listening devices. The truth was far . . . dirtier. All of the scoops came from one low-tech source—the trash.

In the United States, your trash is public property. As soon as you set it out on the curb, anyone is welcome to have a look. It's a treasure trove of information for detectives, journalists, parents, and criminals who have no qualms about picking through your banana peels and used tissues to find what they're after. Just one bag of garbage may reveal the following:

Everything a Crook Needs to Go on a Shopping Spree
Be careful when throwing out any documents that list bank account or credit card numbers unless you're willing to foot the bill for a stranger's Las Vegas vacation or her calls to the psychic hotline.

Your Telephone Numbers (and Who's Been Calling Them)

One cell phone bill will give a snoop a full list of the calls you've made or received for an entire month. So be careful who you talk to—or shred your bill before it hits the Dumpster.

A List of Your Friends, Loved Ones, and Mortal Enemies

Been swapping notes with your friend's crush? Did your grandmother foolishly ignore the advice of the witness protection program and send you a birthday card? Have you been doodling unflattering pictures of your loathsome math teacher? Dump them properly, or be prepared to pay the price.

Your Academic Achievements (or Lack Thereof)

If you're a star student, this may not be your biggest concern. But if your test scores reveal you've been spending way too much time exploring noneducational sites on the Internet, you might want to dispose of the evidence in a discreet manner.

A Menu of Your Favorite Foods

Any outspoken vegetarian who enjoys a secret hamburger from time to time—or health nut who harbors a forbidden love of Twinkies—should keep in mind that one look through her garbage can reveal all of her weaknesses.

Your Bad Habits

You know what they are. Would you care to share them with others?

All the Places You've Been

Countless items in your trash—receipts, shopping bags, airline tickets, surgical dressings—can help someone piece together your activities. Toss them only if you've been on your best behavior.

CHAPTER FOUR

Attack of the Squirrels

For the first time in weeks, I was tucked into bed at a reasonable hour, but no matter how many pigeons I counted (I wasn't that familiar with sheep), I couldn't fall asleep. Oona was angry, Kiki was worried, squirrels were attacking innocent park-goers, and someone was inside the Shadow City. But worst of all, the map was in Luz's hands—and out of my control.

The next morning, I practically sleepwalked to school. By the start of first period, I had already left my geometry book on the subway, injured my pelvis by walking into a parking meter, and forgotten to turn off my cell phone. Just as I began to drift off in the middle of Mr. Dedly's lecture on Dutch wall construction, it began playing the theme from *Jaws*. Cell phones were forbidden at the Atalanta School, and I would have rather been caught with a dead body in my locker than a ringing phone in my hand. I winced as every head in the classroom turned toward the purse that was hanging from my chair.

"Out, Ananka," Mr. Dedly bellowed. "Deliver your musical handbag to the principal's office immediately."

A girl named Petra Dubois had the nerve to snicker as I stood up.

"Wonder if Principal Wickham would like to know who wrote your last essay?" I whispered as I passed by her desk, winking when she gasped. Gossip may be petty, but it certainly has its advantages.

"OUT!" Mr. Dedly shouted.

Once I was in the hallway, I quickly ducked into a bathroom and answered the phone.

"This better be somebody's one and only call from jail," I growled.

"It's worse," said the voice on the other side. "Did I get you in trouble?"

"Let's just say I may be looking at a very bleak future. What do you want, Betty?"

"I just heard from Kiki. Luz got mugged on the way to school this morning." There was a brief pause. "By the squirrels."

The idea that Luz Lopez had been the victim of a robbery, particularly one perpetrated by wildlife, was staggering. Her surly disposition usually succeeded in keeping most people and animals at a distance.

"Where?" I asked. "Is she hurt?"

"She's a little scratched up, but she'll survive. She said she was cutting across Morningside Park when three huge squirrels jumped her. A jogger pulled them off, but by that time her backpack was gone."

"The squirrels have moved uptown? How much money did they get?" I asked.

"There wasn't any money, Ananka." Betty was trying to break the news gently.

"No," I moaned.

"Yeah. They got the motion detectors. And the map."

My worst fears had come true. "What's Kiki say?"

"She wants us all to meet at her house after school. We're going to Morningside Park to get the map back."

"Are you kidding?" I asked. "There's no way the squirrels will still be there."

"Kiki said you'd say that. She told me to give you a message."

"What is it?"

"She wants to know if you have a better idea."

"I'll try to think one up on my way to reform school," I huffed and hung up.

· · ·

The walk to Principal Wickham's office was known as *the plank* (as in "Jordan was forced to walk the plank yesterday, and nobody's seen her since"). Her door sat at the end of a gloomy hall in a part of the school that most people avoided. It was a well-known fact that, back in the days when the building was a home for wayward children, the office had belonged to a doctor who enjoyed practicing his surgical techniques on hapless delinquents. While I'd always felt a certain fondness for Principal Wickham, there were plenty of Atalanta girls who swore she could be equally cruel.

I knocked at the door before opening it a crack. Principal Wickham was paging through a stack of files, and she looked tiny and old behind her enormous oak desk.

Judging by the stories floating around, one might have expected to find the heads of naughty students mounted like hunting trophies on the walls. Instead, dozens of dusty photographs clung to the dingy plaster. In one, a well-known painter posed beside her masterpiece at an exhibition of modern art. Another photo had been snapped at the recent inauguration of New York's first female senator. The rest of the pictures spanned at least four decades, but they all shared two things in common. They each focused on famous women—directors, writers, CEOs, and surgeons. And in each one, hidden somewhere in the background—her face blurry or half concealed by a champagne glass—was Principal Wickham. Even in the black-and-white photos taken in the days when women never left the house without their hats, gloves, and stockings, she looked a hundred years old.

"I had a hunch I'd be seeing you soon, Miss Fishbein," the principal murmured without looking up. "Come in. Make yourself comfortable."

I plopped down in one of the hard leather chairs. While I waited for her to finish her paperwork I stared at a defective smoke bomb that sat on her desk. The fuse was singed, but it hadn't burned.

"So," the principal finally said, laying down her pen and removing her bifocals. When her eyes met mine, I realized that even without her thick glasses she could see things that others couldn't. "What do you make of that?"

"What is it?" I asked in my most innocent voice.

"That is the cause of the disturbance yesterday. I believe you would call it a stink bomb. A particularly effective one, I might add. Whoever made it deserves a suspension from Atalanta and a scholarship to Harvard. I'd ask if you knew anything about it, but I've seen your chemistry grades, Miss Fishbein, and I doubt if you're up to the task."

"Do you have any leads?"

"Not one," said the principal. "Perhaps I should ask your friend Kiki Strike to take the case." She delivered the blow so smoothly that I barely realized I'd been hit.

"Kiki Strike?"

"Please don't play dumb, Ananka. Your grades are atrocious, but I know you're intelligent. Kiki Strike was a student here a couple of years ago. I checked the files after your mother mentioned her name. She seems to think your friend is the same girl who keeps making the papers."

"That was all just a hoax, Principal Wickham."

"So they say. But I don't believe everything I hear on television. Now, Miss Fishbein, let's be honest. What you do when you're not at school is none of my business. But staying awake between the hours of eight and four is a requirement here at Atalanta. If you don't think you can manage that, I believe your mother may have a few other options for you."

"Yes, Principal Wickham. But I *have* been staying awake."

"Have you? So to what do I owe this visit?"

"My cell phone rang in Mr. Dedly's class. It was an emergency."

"Oh dear," said the principal, shaking her head in exasperation. "I think you're well on the way to making an enemy of Mr. Dedly, Ananka. What, may I ask, was the emergency?"

"A friend of mine who goes to school uptown just got mugged." I expected her to scoff, but instead she nodded solemnly.

"Yes, one of our students was recently mugged as well. By squirrels, strangely enough. I must say, I've never been a fan of squirrels. Greedy little creatures. All fur and teeth. But the paintings around town are impressive. The person behind them has great talent, but that's another matter, isn't it? Is your cell phone off now, or do I need to confiscate it?"

"No, ma'am. It's off."

"Then I suggest you don't miss another of Mr. Dedly's fascinating lectures. But, Ananka, if I see you again, I won't be so lenient. Do you understand?"

"Yes, Principal Wickham," I said, wondering how I'd gotten off the hook so easily. I scampered out of her office before she had a chance to change her mind.

. . .

My brush with trouble was long forgotten by the time the last bell rang. I left all my school books in my locker and jumped on a bus to Kiki's house. When I arrived, the massive wooden door opened just wide enough for me to slip inside. The large, uncluttered room was furnished with one sofa, one coffee table stacked high with books, and a large archery target, which stood at the end of the room. The brick walls showcased an astounding array of martial arts weapons. Butterfly swords, battle-axes, and chain whips gleamed in the sunshine that streamed through the skylight in the ceiling. Beyond the living area was a glass conservatory that looked out on an overgrown garden. Rare orchids, their blooms the shape of caterpillars, spiders, and crabs, sprouted from dozens of clay pots.

A cloud slid across the sun, and the room grew dim as an arrow whistled through the air and lodged itself in the target's bloodred center.

"Luz didn't go to school today," Kiki explained. "Verushka's been teaching her how to use the crossbow."

"I'm glad Verushka's feeling better," I noted, watching her deliver a second arrow into the heart of the target and wondering why she was wearing a pair of blue gloves indoors.

"She feels better than she looks," said Kiki.

"What do you mean?"

"You'll see." Kiki led me across the room. "Try not to make a fuss."

"Hi, Ananka." Three Harry Potter Band-Aids covered the squirrel scratches on Luz's nose and cheeks. They seemed out place with her olive-green, army-inspired ensemble. "Sorry about the map."

"We'll get it back," I assured her, though I held little hope of seeing my map again. "I'm just surprised that anyone would mug a girl dressed like Fidel Castro's niece."

Luz's eyes narrowed and her Band-Aids crinkled. "I'm going to do you a favor and forget you said that. For your information, I got the idea for this outfit from a picture of Verushka back in the day."

"And I am flattered by the tribute." Verushka wheeled around and offered me the crossbow. "You would like to try, Ananka?" Kiki watched with a grin as I struggled not to show my shock. The tiny gray-haired woman looked like she'd spent a week trapped in a dairy freezer. Her skin was a pale blue that darkened to navy at her lips and fingertips. "It is not smart to stare at a woman with a crossbow," Verushka said with an oddly girlish giggle.

"I don't understand," I mumbled. "I thought your leg was the problem."

"Yes, but you see my leg is still attached to the rest of my body," Verushka pointed out.

"Will the blue go away?" I asked, relieved that I hadn't insulted her.

"The doctors say it is temporary," said Verushka. "But I am afraid my days as a sex symbol are over."

"Maybe, but you'd make a great Smurf." Luz had a habit of taking things a little too far, and I decided to change the subject.

"What's with all the books, Verushka?" I picked up a few of the books on the coffee table. *Conversational Urdu? The Art of War? Homemade Poisons and Antidotes? Royal Babylon?* It looks like you tried to read an entire bookstore today."

"When you are as old as I am," said the little blue woman in the wheelchair, "you will not want to waste any time."

"Verushka's trying to catch up on our lessons," Kiki explained with a sigh. "It's not easy being homeschooled."

"This is your schoolwork? I'd trade Atalanta for this any day. Why study something useless like geometry when I could be learning how to speak Urdu instead?"

"Without geometry, there would be no tunnels. Without tunnels, no Shadow City. No Shadow City, no Irregulars," Verushka announced. "You owe more to math than you think."

The doorbell rang, and Kiki ran to answer it. Standing at the door was Oona Wong wearing a white manicurist's smock and a scowl on her face. DeeDee and Betty were close behind her. Oona marched inside, ignoring them both.

"Oona doesn't look thrilled to be here. Any idea how Kiki convinced her to come?" I asked Luz.

"Who knows?" Luz whispered as Oona approached. "Maybe she promised Iris's head on a platter."

"Talking about me?" snipped Oona.

"Get a life," Luz responded.

"We're just glad you came," I said, elbowing Luz.

"Yeah, I bet you are. Who else would provide the entertainment?" Oona dropped onto the sofa, crossed her arms, and stared into space. Verushka wheeled her chair over to the girl and whispered in her ear. Oona nodded solemnly, and the old woman rolled out of the living room.

"Let's get to work," said Kiki. "We need to be at the park before sunset. Luz, want to tell everybody what happened this morning?"

"Sure." Luz unrolled a map of the park and held it up for us to see. "At seven thirty this morning, I entered Morningside Park through the north gate. My destination was the southeast gate, approximately thirteen blocks away. I was almost to the waterfall when I felt something land on my head. At first I thought I'd been beamed by a pigeon, but when I saw the thing's tail, I knew it was one of those giant squirrels. I dropped the bag I was carrying and tried to pull it out of my hair. Shortly after that, two more rodents attacked me. A jogger stopped to help me, but it wasn't till I heard a whistle that the squirrels disappeared. That's when I saw the bag was gone."

"Luz Lopez, squirrel victim," sneered Oona. "What will you do for an encore? Get mauled by mice?"

"Shut up, Oona!" Luz raged.

"Oona, you promised," said Kiki. "Can we all play nice long enough to get the map back? After that you and Luz can duke it out, for all I care."

I raised my hand.

"Yes, Ananka, I *know* you don't think the squirrels will still be there. But we've got to give it a shot. Otherwise, we're going to be staking out parks for the next few months. Luz and I spent the afternoon coming up with a plan. The six of us are going to set up an ambush. DeeDee, how would you like to be bait?"

. . .

I stood on the edge of a rocky precipice, feeling dangerously dizzy. Two inches from my toes, the earth plunged a hundred feet, until it came to a halt in Harlem. A narrow path wound down the side of the cliff to Morningside Park, where the trees swayed in rhythm as if the land were moving beneath them. Through my binoculars, I could see two young men in hooded sweatshirts perched motionlessly like malevolent Buddhas atop one of the boulders that studded the landscape. A woman with a baby carriage hurried for the exit before dark descended. There was not a squirrel in sight.

"Move in," said Kiki's voice in my earpiece. "Take your positions."

I inched down the steep path, checking behind every tree I passed and listening for the sound of footsteps behind me. When I was finally overlooking DeeDee's route, I crouched behind a patch of overgrown grass and raised my binoculars. I found Kiki kneeling in the shadow of a statue that showed a young faun taking refuge from a ravenous bear. Luz and Oona were close by, concealed in a bush. Betty, dressed as a sanitation worker, emptied garbage cans. When Kiki gave her the cue, Betty fished a copy of the *Weekly World News* out of a can and took a seat on a park bench.

"That's it. You're on, DeeDee," I heard Kiki say.

DeeDee entered the park from the north. With her handbag dangling from her arm, and iPod headphones in her ears, she danced down the wooded path, her dreadlocks swinging from side to side. The two young men on the rock watched her go by, their heads following while their bodies stayed still. After passing Betty on the park bench, DeeDee paused to dig through her handbag, pulling out a stick of chewing gum.

"That's right, take your time," Kiki encouraged her. I searched the surroundings but saw nothing of interest. As the sun faded and the streetlights beyond the trees began to flicker to life, I watched DeeDee blissfully bop all the way to the other side of the park.

"Good job, DeeDee," Kiki sighed in my earpiece. "Looks like we're out of luck."

"Hold on. There are men on the move near Betty," I heard Luz whisper.

I shifted my binoculars, but Betty's bench had been engulfed by shadows. "I can't see anything," I reported. "It's too dark."

"Your binoculars have night vision," Luz said. "Hit the button near your right pinky."

As soon as I pushed the button I saw the two figures that had been seated on the rock strolling straight for the spot where Betty sat alone on the park bench. Their hands were tucked deep in the pockets of their sweat-shirts, their heads bowed, and their faces hidden beneath hoods. Betty looked around frantically, but there was nowhere to flee. Too far away to run to her rescue, I watched helplessly from my perch on the hillside. As Kiki sprang from her hiding place, and Luz and Oona bolted from the bushes, a shrill scream bounced off the cliffs behind me. I knew in an instant it wasn't Betty. Two enormous black squirrels had leaped from the branches of a nearby tree and landed on the two hooded men.

As the men spun in circles, trying to pry the squirrels' sharp claws from their skin, a third squirrel bounced into Betty's lap before springing to the aid of its colleagues. I dropped my binoculars when I heard the sound of gravel crunching nearby and looked up in time to see a tall, lanky figure emerge from behind a tree and begin climbing the path to the top of the cliffs.

"Here," it said, stopping in front of me. "I believe you're looking for this." In the darkness, I could see it was a boy my age, but his face was so filthy it was impossible to know what he looked like. He handed me a black backpack. "Tell your friends to get out of the park."

"What? Why?" I didn't appreciate being ordered around by someone who smelled like a pet store.

"Those men down there aren't alone. Tell your friends to leave right now. I see your mouthpiece. I know you're all wired."

"Get out of the park," I told the Irregulars. "NOW," I added with urgency.

"Good," said the boy. He stuck two fingers between his lips and blew a deafening whistle. As he started back up the path, three large squirrels scampered up the cliffs and fell in line behind him.

· · ·

With a clap of her hands, Luz's work space flooded with light.

"You installed a Clapper?" DeeDee teased. "As seen on TV?"

"It's technology at its best," said Luz. "One clap switches the lights on, two claps makes me a cappuccino, and if I clap three times, the lasers come on and turn you all into toast. Make yourselves at home."

It was easier said than done. Limbless robots already claimed most of the chairs, and every flat surface in the workshop was heaped with wires, electrodes, and tools that would have thrilled a torturer. The five of us stood awkwardly in the middle of the room, trying not to touch anything that might leave us burned or brain damaged.

"So what was *that* about?" Kiki asked me. "I was planning to give those guys in the park something to remember us by."

"There were more of them than you thought. We weren't the only ones planning an ambush tonight."

"And you know this because . . . ," Oona said.

"Because the boy with the squirrels told me," I said. "He also gave me this." I held out the black backpack. Inside were the map and the motion detectors.

"How did he know it was ours?" asked DeeDee.

"I don't know," I admitted.

"You saw him? What's he like?" asked Betty.

"It was hard to tell in the dark. All I can tell you is that he was tall and dirty, and he stank like a yeti."

"Did you see the size of his squirrels?" asked Oona. "I thought Lopez was a pansy until I got a look at those monsters."

"Malaysian giant squirrels," said Kiki. "They're an endangered species."

"Are you all right? Did they hurt you?" DeeDee asked Betty.

"No, one just jumped into my lap. It dropped this." She reached into her pocket and pulled out a locket on a golden chain. "Weird, huh? It must have just stolen it from someone"

"Does it open?" I asked. "Maybe there's something inside."

"I haven't had a chance to look," said Betty, undoing the locket's clasp.

Inside the locket was a scrap of paper. Both sides were covered with tiny handwritten words. Betty walked over to a lamp to read, and the rest of us crowded around her.

"What's it say?" I asked.

Betty looked up at us, her face red with embarrassment. "It's a passage from an opera."

"Go on, give us a taste," said Kiki with a smirk.

Betty cleared her voice and started to read.

"O soave fanciulla, o dolce viso, di mite circonfuso
    alba lunar,
in te ravviso il sogno ch' io vorrei sempre sognar."

"You speak Italian?" DeeDee asked in astonishment.

"No, but I know what it means. It's from an opera I've seen a million times. *La Bohème*. My parents designed the costumes for the last production at the Met."

"Well?" said Luz.

Betty grimaced. "It's something one of the main characters says. I can't translate perfectly, but when he sees a girl named Mimi's face in the moonlight, he says he knows she can make his dreams come true."

"Wow," said Oona. "That's one smooth-talkin' squirrel."

"Last I checked, squirrels aren't fans of the opera. Betty's got an admirer," I said.

"Too bad he's a criminal," said DeeDee.

"Watch it! Some of my closest friends are criminals," noted Luz, gesturing toward Oona.

"I'm not a criminal. I'm a *business*woman," Oona insisted.

"Nobody's perfect," mumbled Betty. I could see she was flattered.

"He does seem sophisticated," I added. "But doesn't *La Bohème* end in tragedy?"

"Don't get carried away," Kiki cautioned. "I'm not saying you're not naturally irresistible, Betty, but even criminals don't usually fall in love so quickly. There may be something else going on here." Standing on tiptoe, she sniffed at Betty and couldn't hide her disgust. "Feet. I thought so. Isn't that the wig you were wearing yesterday?"

Betty frowned. "I washed it," she said. "I thought I'd gotten all the Eau Irresistible out. You think it was just the perfume that made him write this?"

"Come on, don't be disappointed," Kiki consoled her. "This is *good* news. If you're attracting boys without even trying, it could mean that Iris's special formula really does work."

"I'm sure you'd get plenty of love letters if you stopped wearing hairy moles and dressing like a freak," Oona remarked.

"Nice, Oona." DeeDee's voice dripped with sarcasm.

"I was just trying to say that she's pretty under all that crap."

"Thanks," said Betty. "But that crap is who I am. Why would I want someone to like me for anything else?"

HOW TO TAKE ADVANTAGE OF THE POWER OF SCENT

Most of us spend far too much time thinking—and worrying—about how people *see* us. I would recommend spending some of that time focusing on one of the other five senses—*smell*. I don't intend to waste your time by warning you of the dangers of body odor. (For that discussion, please refer to *Your Changing Body*, available at the Atalanta School Library.) Instead, I'll offer six handy tips for using your nose—and the noses of others—to your advantage.

Improve Your Memory

Cramming for a test? Scientists have discovered a simple trick that may improve your memory by up to thirteen percent. (Which could make the difference between a C and summer school.) As you study, periodically spritz the air with fragrance. (Rose is said to work well.) Then spray your pillow with the same scent before you go to sleep. The odor may help your brain retain more of what you've learned.

Be Your Own Bloodhound

First train yourself to recognize the fragrances of different soaps, detergents, perfumes, and shampoos. Then practice identifying people by their individual scents, which can be as unique as their fingerprints. Eventually you'll be able to walk into a room and know who's been there before you. (A handy trick if you suspect someone's been snooping through your bedroom.)

Appear More Trustworthy

Unless you're a chemistry prodigy or you hang around with Swiss scientists, it may be difficult to get your hands on some Fille Fiable. However, if there's someone whose trust you need to win, just do a little detective work. If you can find out what perfume her mother or grandmother uses, the smell should make her less likely to mistrust you.

Improve People's Moods

Who hasn't wished for the power to put a grumpy parent, teacher, or probation officer in a better mood? You should consult an aromatherapy guide to choose the ideal scent for your situation, but one of the most popular is lavender, which relieves stress and can lower blood pressure. Other fragrances may alter moods in different ways. The scent of citrus can increase productivity, for instance, while vanilla helps create a warm, cozy atmosphere.

Get Your Revenge

Nothing says *gotcha* like the odor of a well-hidden dirty diaper, deceased hamster, or rancid pork chop. Enough said.

Attract the Opposite Sex
Studies performed by such trusted sources as *Cosmopolitan* magazine have proven that fragrance can make almost anyone seem more attractive. A pleasant-smelling perfume, lotion, or shampoo will entice others to remain in your presence longer, giving you time to showcase your stunning personality. But be careful—too much of a good thing tends to make people nauseous.

CHAPTER FIVE

The Boy in the Box

The day after we recovered the map of the Shadow City, Betty Bent stepped out her front door to find a massive squirrel peering down at her. Painted in exquisite detail on the side of the building opposite hers, it wore a golden locket and a charming smile. The sign it was holding read WE'VE BEEN LOOKING FOR YOU.

"He knows where I live," Betty panted, running up to the rest of us as we loitered across the avenue from the Marble Cemetery, waiting for the sun to set. "He must have followed me home last night."

"*Who* followed you?" asked Luz.

"The squirrel boy!" Betty screeched as if the answer should have been obvious.

"You saw him?" asked DeeDee.

"No, I didn't *see* him!"

"Then how do you know he followed you?" Kiki asked, checking my reaction out of the corner of her eye. Like the other girls, I was finding the whole scene very amusing.

"First of all, he painted a giant squirrel across from my apartment. Then, just before I left to meet you guys, a squirrel dropped this through my window." Betty thrust a slip of paper at Kiki.

"*May I follow you home?*" Kiki read with a grin.

"That's kind of sweet," I said.

"He's a stalker," Oona announced, and Luz nodded in agreement.

"Stalkers don't usually *ask* for permission," DeeDee noted.

"Well, I guess the question is this," said Kiki Strike. "Do you *want* him to follow you home?"

Betty looked like she'd been poked with a stick. "I hadn't thought of it that way," she mumbled at last.

"Don't worry," said Oona. "He'll forget about you and go back to petty larceny once the perfume wears off." Kiki shot Oona a look that wasn't entirely friendly.

"What?" Oona exclaimed. "You guys have a problem with the truth?"

"You're hopeless, Oona," I sighed. "Let's just get started. It should be dark enough now."

• • •

Oona picked the lock on the cast-iron gate that stood squeezed between two buildings, and the Irregulars slipped inside the Marble Cemetery. Other than an elderly man with an eye patch who mowed the grass twice a month in the summer, we were the graveyard's most frequent visitors. Few in Manhattan even knew it existed, and aside from the bouquet of white calla lilies, which appeared without fail every Valentine's Day, we had seen no evidence of mourners. To an untrained eye, the cemetery looked like nothing more than an abandoned lot surrounded by a crumbling stone wall. But set deep in the grass were six mossy marble slabs that covered the entrances to dozens of underground tombs. The corpses of wealthy New Yorkers occupied all but one of the tombs. Inside an empty stone sarcophagus engraved with the name Augustus Quackenbush was a tunnel that led to the Shadow City.

A month had passed since the Irregulars had last been together in the Marble Cemetery, and it should have felt like old times again. But as the six of us carefully pried one of the marble slabs out of the earth and descended into the tombs below, I was already wishing the night was over.

"This place could really use some air freshener," Oona whined as we marched to the end of a marble hallway lined with mausoleums.

"Sorry, Princess, but the smell is only going to get worse from here," I snipped. "That reminds me—did somebody get more rat-repellent from Iris?"

"Picked it up this afternoon," said DeeDee. "She was upset that we didn't invite her to come tonight."

My right hand tightened into a fist when I heard Oona snort behind me.

"Iris knows we couldn't invite her," said Kiki. "Her parents are getting suspicious about all the time we've been spending in their basement. They want her to find friends her own age." The hallway reached a dead end, and Kiki stopped in front of Augustus Quackenbush's tomb. I caught a glimpse of the maze-dwelling monster carved into the side of the dead man's empty sarcophagus, and my skin erupted in goose bumps. "Okay. Everyone ready? Luz?"

Luz reached into her shopping bag and handed out packets of motion detectors.

"We have to split into pairs if we want to position them all tonight," Kiki explained. "DeeDee, you're with me. Luz, you and Betty are a team. Oona, you're going with Ananka."

"So how do these things work?" I examined one of the thin black disks, trying to hide my disappointment at being stuck with Oona for the evening.

"Simple. Each disk sends out an invisible infrared beam," Luz explained. "If someone—*or something*— passes through the beam, an alarm goes off. These are the receivers." We all were given small electronic gadgets that fit neatly in our palms.

"It looks like a GPS device," said DeeDee. "You bought six of them? That must have cost a fortune."

"I got them on eBay a while back. They were cheap 'cause they're old models, but they're easy to customize. They're programmed so that if one of our alarms goes off, the location of the tripped beam will flash on the screen."

"Where do you want us to put all the sensors?" asked DeeDee.

"I made maps of the Shadow City for each of us," I said. "Place a motion detector wherever you see a red dot. And whatever you do, don't forget to destroy your maps before we leave tonight." Even Oona nodded in agreement. In a town filled with homicidal princesses and kleptomaniac squirrels, keeping one map safe was hard enough.

We slid the heavy sarcophagus lid to one side. With her flashlight tucked into her waistband, Kiki climbed down the ladder that led from the coffin to a crude earthen tunnel below. Just as I started to follow behind her, Oona butted in front of me.

"I think you should let me go first," she announced in a superior voice. "Kiki may need help picking a lock and the rest of you are hopeless with your hands."

DeeDee let loose a quick, sharp stab of a laugh.

"Don't slip," Luz mumbled murderously. Betty offered me the sort of sad-eyed smile one gives a person who's about to have a limb amputated. It seemed even she pitied me for being paired with Oona, who was still livid about Iris's prank and punishing the rest of us for witnessing it.

One by one, the Irregulars descended blindly into the gloom. One by one, our boots hit dirt and we fumbled for our flashlights. Finally, there were six spotlights swirling around the cramped passageway that Augustus Quackenbush had built to smuggle stolen fabric from the graveyard to his nearby store. Never intended to survive to the twenty-first century, the passage was showing its age. Specks of earth sprinkled down from the ceiling, tree roots snatched at our hair, and by the time we reached the door to the larger tunnels of the Shadow City, we were already filthy. While Oona paused to brush herself off, I forged ahead. I figured the only way to survive the evening was to act like a professional and hope Oona took the hint. Hurrying through the tunnels, I planted our motion detectors as quickly as possible. Rather than help, Oona dallied and dawdled, rooting through crates and checking coat pockets for coins.

"Come on, Oona." I sighed when I caught her examining her nails in the beam of her flashlight. "I know you're mad, but we've got work to do. You can make me suffer when we're done."

"You should have brought Iris," Oona snapped without bothering to look up. "*She'd* never let you down."

"I'm sorry Iris embarrassed you. But you've got to admit, you deserved it." I could hear how cold my voice had become. "She's tired of being the butt of your jokes. And you know what, Oona? The rest of us are pretty sick of you, too. What kind of person picks on an eleven-year-old kid—or Betty, for that matter? It's like kicking puppies. And then you have the nerve to get offended when one of them fights back? I don't know what's wrong with you these days. You've always been a little rude, but lately you act like you were raised by wolves."

"You think I'm rude?" Oona's voice wasn't angry. She sounded surprised, as if the thought had never occurred to her. "I thought I was just being honest."

"People don't always need *you* to tell them the truth," I told her, though I was already beginning to regret it. I'd wanted my words to feel like a slap, but instead I'd delivered a punch. "Be a little nicer, would you? We're supposed to be your friends." I turned my back to her and started for the next location. It wasn't until I was almost out of sight that Oona began to follow me.

An hour later we placed our last motion detector inside the tunnel that burrowed beneath the Lower East Side. As I zipped up my empty backpack, the beam of my flashlight passed across Oona's face and I saw that her eyes were red and swollen.

"The room where we found the little Chinese statue isn't that far away." I tried to sound friendly. "Want to take a look?"

"Sure," said Oona quietly.

"I think this was a stop on the Underground Railroad," I explained once we stood in the room with the ten little beds. "There's an exit that leads to a synagogue on Bialystoker Place and a tunnel that stretches up to the riverbank. Someone was hiding slaves in the Shadow City and helping them escape to freedom." I pointed to the rumpled bed. "We found the Chinese statue wrapped up in those sheets. Kiki sat on it."

Oona's eyes skimmed across the bed, then came to rest on mine.

"I'm sorry I've been acting so awful. I know it's no excuse, but I've been under a lot of pressure."

"What's bothering you?"

"I need to tell you guys something," she confided. "But I haven't had a chance. First Kiki disappeared, then Luz got mugged, and then we found out someone's been in the Shadow City. Nobody's had time to listen to me. It's driving me crazy."

"I'm listening now," I told her.

"I think I need your help." She stopped. It was as if she'd admitted something shameful and had to work up the courage to continue. I saw her mouth open once more, but her voice was drowned out by a loud, insistent beeping. A bright red dot flashed on our receivers.

"Let's not worry about it," Oona pleaded once we'd switched off the alarms. "One of the other girls must have accidentally set off a sensor."

"I'm sorry, Oona. I know it's really bad timing, but we've got to check it out."

I'd never seen Oona appear so utterly defeated. "See what I mean?" she asked.

. . .

As we raced through the tunnels, all thoughts of Oona's confession were left far behind. According to our receivers, the tripped motion detector was under Chinatown, not far from a familiar storeroom. Once a passage had linked the chamber to an old opium den, but the Irregulars had destroyed the connection in June after the Fu-Tsang gang had used it to access the Shadow City. As we drew closer to the storeroom, Kiki and DeeDee joined us, and we sprinted together until we came to a sudden stop a few yards short of our destination. Luz and Betty were already waiting for us on the scene.

"Holy moly," whispered DeeDee. The storeroom was crammed with rats. Thousands of mangy creatures that hadn't been able to force their way into the chamber were crowded outside the door, craning their necks for a peek at what lay inside.

"I set off the alarm when we saw the rats," Luz

explained. "Something's going on in there. I thought we should all check it out."

"Good call. Ladies, it's time to freshen up." Kiki passed around a bottle of Iris's rat-repelling perfume, and the stench grew stronger than a freshly fertilized field on a hot summer day. "Okay, follow me." Kiki waded through the rodents, which squealed and scattered at the smell of her perfume. But though they kept a safe distance, this time they refused to run away.

Inside the storeroom, the biggest, most powerful beasts surrounded a cargo crate, gnawing at the wooden slats with superhuman concentration. A tiny hole had appeared in a corner of the crate, and one of the rats was on the verge of breaking through. He and his friends were not pleased to find six foul-smelling humans crashing their party. They backed away from the box and into the corners of the room, where they squealed loudly and gnashed their razor-sharp teeth.

"Whatever's in there must be pretty tasty," said Luz. "They were ready to eat right through the box to get to it."

"Let's see what we've got." Kiki pulled off the lid of the crate.

Curled up inside was a boy, his thin legs tucked up against his chest. His clothing was filthy and tattered, and when the beam of a flashlight passed across his face, he mumbled deliriously.

"He's not speaking English, is he?" asked Betty.

"Sounds like Chinese." Luz looked to Kiki and Oona. "What's he saying?"

"They speak more than one language in China," said

Kiki. "I understand only Cantonese and a little Mandarin. He wasn't speaking either of them."

"He was speaking Hakka." Oona's face was as gray as cheap porcelain. "He said he wants to go home."

"I'm sure he does," I said. "But how did he get down here in the first place?"

"If we don't get him out of here, we may never find out," said Kiki. "See the foam around his mouth? He's dehydrated. He may have been down here for days. We need to get him to a hospital."

"No!" Oona shrieked, startling the rest of us.

"What do you mean, *no*?" Kiki snapped. "You want him to die?"

"We can't take him to the hospital," Oona insisted. "He's an illegal alien. I'm sure of it. If you take him to the hospital, they'll send him back to China."

"Maybe that's what he wants," Betty suggested. "He did say he wants to go home."

"If we can't go to a hospital, what are we supposed to do with him?" I asked Oona.

"We'll have to take him to my house."

"Your house?" DeeDee's eyes were cartoon wide, but Kiki looked unfazed. She pulled Oona to the side.

"Are you *sure*?" Kiki asked quietly.

"Yes," Oona insisted. "Mrs. Fei and the ladies will know what to do."

"What ladies?" I asked, but they both ignored me.

"Everybody give your maps to Ananka and help me lift the boy out of the box," Kiki ordered. "Ananka, find us an exit near Catherine Street."

While I studied the map my mind remained stuck on one shocking thought. Kiki knew where Oona lived.

· · ·

We emerged from the Shadow City in one of the hot, hellish restaurant kitchens tucked beneath the sidewalks of New York. Pipes gurgling with sewage and steam hung so low from the ceiling that even Kiki was forced to stoop. In one corner, two freakishly fat cats shared a mouse entrée while cockroaches the size of parakeets danced on the countertops. We crammed all seven of our bodies onto a rusty metal platform, and DeeDee punched a red button on the wall. Slowly, the freight elevator rose out of the basement, through a metal grate, and delivered us onto the sidewalk above. The Irregulars' logo glimmered beneath the streetlight. It was one o'clock in the morning, and Chinatown was sleeping. Yellow tape printed with the word *caution* flapped in the glassless windows of an abandoned building across the street. A demolition notice was posted on the door and a debris-filled Dumpster concealed all but the tip of a golden *i*. Sadly, I made a mental note to revise the map. Another entrance to the Shadow City would soon be gone for good.

With Oona leading the way, we carried the boy to the stoop of a decrepit tenement building that was covered in artless graffiti. Oona rang one of the buzzers.

"It's awfully late," I whispered. "Don't you have your own key?"

"I don't need a key," Oona said. "Someone's always up." A few seconds later, a stunning woman in a tailored red suit and scarlet lipstick opened the front door. I thought I detected the outline of a pistol under her suit jacket. She greeted Oona with a smile that shriveled when she saw the boy. She didn't bother asking for an explanation. Instead, she peered anxiously in both directions before ushering us into a barren hallway. There, she and Oona exchanged a few nervous words.

"We need to take him upstairs," Oona announced to the rest of us.

"I thought Oona was an orphan," Betty whispered as Kiki and Oona carried the boy to the second floor.

"I'm not an orphan." Somehow, Oona had overheard. "But that woman isn't my mother. She's a bodyguard."

"Bodyguard?" Betty mouthed silently.

At the top of the stairs was a single door. Oona's bodyguard unlocked it, and we stepped out of the dingy hallway and into a palace. Precious rugs covered the floors, and mahogany furniture upholstered in silk sat solidly against the walls, which were painted the color of the sky and decorated with images of delicate willow trees and preening peacocks. In the middle of the room stood four Chinese women. The oldest was dressed in simple black pajamas, while the rest wore long, brightly colored robes and embroidered slippers. The younger three flew into action the moment we appeared, like birds fluttering about a beautiful cage.

"These are my grandmothers," said Oona. "Don't bother making small talk. They don't speak English."

"*She's* your grandmother?" I gestured to a woman who didn't look more than thirty years old.

"It's just an expression." Oona sighed. "It's not like they're related by blood."

Out of the corner of my eye I saw the oldest of Oona's grandmothers take a sharp breath as if she had received an unexpected blow. Recovering instantly, she knelt down by the couch where we had laid the sick boy. She was at least eighty years old, with silver hair wrapped in a bun and skin covered with rivers of wrinkles. As she felt the boy's pulse, I noticed her hands were unusually muscular and her fingertips rough and calloused. She pulled back the boy's eyelids before opening his mouth and examining his tongue. Then she turned and issued orders to one of the younger women, who disappeared into the kitchen.

"Mrs. Fei says his *ji* is too high," Oona explained. "He needs cooling tonics."

DeeDee and I exchanged a puzzled look. A minute later, the younger woman rushed back into the room with a pot of water and a platter filled with herbs. Mrs. Fei asked to be left alone with her patient, and Oona guided the Irregulars to the nearby dining room.

"Mrs. Fei seems to know what she's doing," said Kiki thoughtfully, taking a seat at the round wooden table.

"If she didn't, we'd all be dead by now," said Oona. "I've never been to an American doctor."

"What do you think we should tell her?" Luz asked. "She'll want to know where we found the boy."

"This isn't your house, Lopez," said Oona. "Mrs. Fei won't ask any questions. None of my grandmothers will."

"Who are these ladies?" asked Betty. "Why do you live with them?"

"They raised me," said Oona. "Now it's my turn to take care of them."

"But I thought you told us you aren't an orphan," said DeeDee. "Where are your parents?"

"My father owns factories in Chinatown. He smuggled these women into the country to work in his sweatshops. They were his slaves. I used the money from the manicure shop to pay for their freedom," said Oona. "I think the boy might belong to him, too."

"Your father sounds a lot like . . . ," I started to say.

"That's right," said Oona. "My father is Lester Liu."

· · ·

Secrets are like cough syrup—they can grow more potent with time. Keep one stored long enough and what might once have been harmless can wind up deadly. Two years earlier, Oona's secret would have inspired a few hours of gossip—but none of us would have held it against her. But the fact that she'd concealed the truth for so long made me suspect she had more to hide. And the one revelation she'd already made was shocking enough. Oona's father was a dangerous man. As leader of the Fu-Tsang gang, Lester Liu had grown rich smuggling counterfeit designer shoes and handbags into Chinatown. The Irregulars had destroyed his operation in June and sent most of his gang to jail. But Lester Liu had never been charged with a crime. He was still free, and Kiki Strike was at the top of his hit list.

"Why didn't you tell us?" I demanded.

Oona grimaced. "It's not the sort of thing I'd brag about."

The other girls were struck dumb. Luz didn't appear to be breathing. Betty was on the brink of biting off her lower lip. Only Kiki remained unshaken. I saw in an instant that she had known all along.

"I'm not a traitor," Oona muttered.

"Of course you're not," Kiki assured her. "Nobody thinks you are."

DeeDee caught my eye before turning to Oona. "You should have told us earlier," she said scientifically. "Is there anything else we should know?"

"No," said Oona.

"*I* think it was very brave of you to come clean." Betty put a hand on Oona's arm.

"It sure explains a lot," Luz added with a weary sigh.

"I need to think for a minute." I rested my head on the dining room table. A million memories were reshaping themselves in my mind. The room stayed silent as one of Oona's grandmothers set out a pot of tea and six little teacups. When the Irregulars were alone once more, Kiki took a sip and drew in a breath.

"Now that you've all had time for the news to sink in, let's talk business."

"Why do you think the boy we found belongs to your father?" DeeDee asked.

I saw Kiki give Oona a nod of encouragement.

"My father isn't just a smuggler. He's also a snakehead."

"What's a snakehead?" asked Luz.

"They smuggle people into the United States," Oona explained. "Poor people who need work. They promise a snakehead thousands of dollars to get them here, and when they arrive they have to pay off the debt. Until they do, they're practically slaves. My father makes them work all day and all night in his sweatshops."

"What if they refuse?" asked DeeDee.

"Sometimes they're beaten," said Oona. "Sometimes they're killed."

"Is your mother involved, too?" I asked.

"I don't know much about my mother, except that she was one of Lester Liu's clients. She died the day I was born. When my father found out that I was a girl, he didn't want anything to do with me. He gave me to Mrs. Fei. She and her friends at the sweatshop took care of me."

Luz was outraged. "What's his problem with girls?"

"In China, boys carry on the family name. It's their duty to take care of their parents when they get older. When girls grow up, they join their husbands' families, so many people consider them worthless. My father is very old-fashioned. To him, I was just a waste of money."

"You're joking!" cried Betty. "Has he ever met you?"

"A professional criminal couldn't hope for a better child," DeeDee added.

"I did meet him once," said Oona. "When I was ten, Mrs. Fei told me about my father. She said he was very rich, and I knew my grandmothers could barely afford to feed me. So every day, I'd put on the only dress I had and go out to look for him. I thought if he saw me, he might want me back. Then one day I found him standing outside one of his sweatshops. He was talking with two men about a secret shipment they were expecting that night. They knew I was listening, but they didn't care. They thought I was too stupid to understand. After they were done, I went up to Lester and introduced myself as his daughter. At first he laughed. Then he told me I was nothing until he said otherwise."

"That's terrible!" A tear dangled from Betty's false eyelashes.

"What a jerk," Luz agreed, though she didn't use the word *jerk*.

Oona continued. "It's okay. I got even. I went straight to the police and told them about the shipment. They raided the boat as soon as it entered the harbor. It was filled with statues that had been stolen from a temple in Cambodia. His men were arrested, but Lester Liu got away. He was on a flight to Shanghai before the police could question him. The day he left, he sent me a note. All it said was: *When I return, I will find you.*"

"I don't mean to rub it in, but you should have told us," said DeeDee.

"I was hoping I wouldn't need to," Oona admitted. "I thought he might have forgotten about me. It's not like I managed to hurt his business. He's done even better since he left for Shanghai. Half of Chinatown is here because of him."

"Maybe he *has* forgotten about you," Luz offered optimistically.

Oona frowned. "Wait here. There's something you should see." When she returned, she set a rectangular cardboard box in front of Luz. "Lester Liu sent me this. Go ahead, take a look." Luz peeked inside the box as if she were expecting to find a scorpion or a severed ear. Instead, she pulled out a dragon. It was a bronze statue of Fu-Tsang, the Chinese dragon that guards hidden places and the symbol of the fierce gang that bore its name. Someone gasped. It may well have been me. "Recognize it?" asked Oona.

We had all seen the dragon before. Several months earlier, I'd found it in a handbag that belonged to a kidnapping victim named Mitzi Mulligan. The ancient statue had provided the crucial clue that led us to the Fu-Tsang's lair where Sidonia Galatzina had been hiding the girls she'd kidnapped, hoping to lure Kiki to her death. The same night that police raided the hideout, the dragon mysteriously disappeared.

"You know what *that* means?" Oona was trembling.

"It means he knows you're a part of the group who busted his smuggling operation," I said. "You're in *big* trouble, Oona."

"Yeah," she agreed. "Which kind of makes me wonder why he invited me to dinner."

"What!" Luz exclaimed.

"He invited the rest of you, too."

"What?" It was Kiki's turn to be surprised.

"You were missing when the dragon came in the mail," Oona tried to explain. "I wanted to talk to you first, but by the time you were back, we were too busy hunting squirrels and searching for intruders."

"Are you saying that Lester Liu knows who I am?" Betty was almost swooning from the shock.

"I don't think he knows your name," said Oona. "The note just said *Kiki Strike and your talented friends are welcome.*"

"When's the dinner party?" asked Kiki.

"Friday," Oona replied.

"A day and a half." I could almost hear Kiki's mind whirling away. "I wish we had more time to prepare. In any case, I don't think all six of us should go. If it's a trap, we don't want to be in the same place at the same time. Ananka and I will be happy to escort you, Oona."

"Thanks for volunteering me," I said, wondering why I always got the unpleasant assignments.

"Don't mention it." Kiki winked.

"By the way," Oona added with a nervous smile. "The dinner is formal. You'll both need evening gowns."

Mrs. Fei poked her head into the dining room just as I let out a groan. The timing was so perfect that for a moment I suspected she'd been listening. She spoke briefly with Oona.

"The boy's awake," Oona announced.

As the other girls quickly filed out of the room, I pulled Kiki back. I jerked her arm a little too hard, and she turned to me with a tight smile that made it clear I'd come close to getting punched.

"You knew about Lester Liu, didn't you?" I whispered.

Kiki's ice-blue eyes studied me. "Yes," she said.

"How long have you known?"

"From the beginning."

"Don't you think you should have shared that information with the rest of us?" I pressed her. "We're supposed to be a team. We can't have secrets like that."

"You mean I should have told *you*, right? Don't take it personally, Ananka. It wasn't my secret to share."

Though Kiki made a good point, I hated to think that she and Oona had hidden the truth from the rest of us— as if we were too stupid or childish to handle it. I remembered a thousand little looks that had passed between them over the years, and I suddenly felt like a fool.

"How upstanding of you," I sneered. "But this wasn't some harmless little secret. In case you've forgotten, the Fu-Tsang helped your aunt try to kill us. If Lester Liu's daughter had decided to go over to the dark side, you'd be dead right now."

Kiki refused to bite back. "The first rule of being a team is trusting one another. And if you trust someone, you let her keep her secrets. When she's ready to tell you she will. You don't have to know *everything*, Ananka."

"Why not? Why should I trust Oona if she doesn't trust me? How do I know she's not hiding something even more dangerous?"

"Oona was worried that the rest of you would see her differently," Kiki bristled. "Don't prove her right."

. . .

In the living room, we found the boy sitting with his back against one arm of the couch, his legs stretched out in front of him. Mrs. Fei had tucked a blanket around him, and someone had washed his face and combed his black, chin-length hair. His thin head wobbled when he saw the six Irregulars enter the room, and his long, tapered fingers clutched the blanket. Oona pulled a chair beside the couch and spoke to him in Hakka. At first the boy merely gaped at her. He wasn't the first person I'd seen struck dumb by Oona's beauty. Finally he worked up the courage to reply in a hoarse voice.

"His name is Yu," Oona translated. "He's sixteen years old, and he's from Taipei. He wants to know where he is and who we are."

"Tell him he's in New York. Tell him we rescued him from the rats," said Kiki.

"And then ask him how he got into the tunnels," I added.

Yu's eyes passed over each of us before he spoke again.

"He says about a month ago he was kidnapped on his way to school. Two men grabbed him and took him to a boat. There were lots of kids inside—at least twelve, maybe more. He recognized one of the girls. She went to the same school. He wanted to talk to her, but the guards watched them day and night. The trip was very long, and many of the passengers got sick. When the boat stopped, they were tied up and put into large wooden boxes and driven to a building. He tried to escape, but he was caught and thrown into a room away from the others. That's where he discovered the door in the floor.

"He says he was lost in the tunnels for several days. He doesn't know how many. He couldn't find a way out. There was no one down there. Just giant rats and skeletons. He thought he had entered the underworld. When he was too exhausted to keep running from the rats, he crawled into a box and waited to die."

"What about the Chinese statue we found?" Kiki asked. "Where did he get it?"

"He says there were many wooden crates on the ship. A board on one had come loose. When he stuck his fingers inside, that's what he found. He kept it hidden in his schoolbag. If he ever escaped, he thought it might help the police identify the kidnappers."

"Once the ship got to New York, where did the men

take them? Can he describe the building?" If the building had an entrance to the Shadow City, I might be able to recognize it.

"He says that he never saw the outside of the building. It was too dark when they arrived. They were taken to a basement, and each person was put into a tiny wooden pen."

"What about the people who kidnapped him? Can he tell us what they looked like?" asked Kiki.

Oona listened and then turned back to us. "He says the guards had tattoos. Dragon tattoos. *See*, I was right. My father and the Fu-Tsang are behind this." Without waiting for us to comment, she spoke softy to Yu. He shook his head furiously in response.

"What did you just say?" I asked Oona.

"I told him I would pay to send him back to his family in Taiwan," she replied. "But he refused to go. He says he has to stay here to save the others."

"Tell him we plan to help," said Kiki. Oona relayed the message and Yu smiled, closed his eyes, and succumbed to his exhaustion.

"Well, one thing's for certain," I said as Oona stood up. "We'll have plenty to talk about over dinner with your dad."

WHAT TO DO IF YOUR SECRET'S REVEALED

It will happen to everyone at some point. A secret you've kept carefully hidden will be revealed at the worst possible moment. Your classmates may discover that you were born with a tail. Your mother may find out what you were *really* doing all those times you claimed to be babysitting.

Your next-door neighbor may learn that you enjoy entertaining large groups of people when your parents aren't home. Whatever your secret may be, you'll need to act fast to repair the damage.

I recently found myself turning to one of the best PR men in New York for his advice on a delicate matter of my own. A counselor to celebrities and politicians with some very sick secrets, he's a master at restoring reputations. Here's what he told me:

Don't Be Afraid to Say You're Sorry
If you've done something wrong, take responsibility and apologize. Nothing will defuse a situation faster than showing a little remorse. However, less upstanding readers may take a tip from the celebrity world and offer a *non-apology*. Rather than accepting blame for a terrible offense, apologize for a minor one. (For instance, instead of saying, *"I'm sorry I called that prosecutor a [fill in the blank],"* try *"I'm sorry I skipped lunch and let myself get so crabby."* See the difference?)

Be Careful What You Say and Do
These days, cell phone cameras and the Internet can take humiliation to a whole new level. So the moment your secret comes out, imagine you're living your life on camera—and act accordingly. That means no temper tantrums, no acting out, and no spontaneous confessions.

Never Let Them See You Sweat
Relax. If people think that they have the power to upset or embarrass you, they'll never leave you alone. Greet their taunts with a pleasant smile or a blank stare.

Shift Attention to Someone Worse Than You Are
This is what brothers and sisters were born for. It's not very nice to point out that your siblings' past crimes have been far more heinous, but it can make you look like a saint in comparison. Don't take this tack if your siblings are listening.

Become a Champion Do-Gooder
Show how misunderstood and maligned you've been by impersonating Mother Teresa. If you've been grounded, use your free time to do some

spring-cleaning around the house. If you've been labeled a bad seed, try volunteering at a local animal shelter. Everyone looks innocent when surrounded by puppies.

Ride Out the Scandal

Most people have the attention span of a dim-witted gnat. If you refuse to make a soap opera out of your secret, it will probably be forgotten faster than you think.

CHAPTER SIX

The Wild Child

Someone was banging on my bedroom door. I rolled over and pressed a pillow against my ears, hoping the noise would go away.

"Ananka, you're late for school!" my father yelled. "Get out of bed and unlock this door!"

In an instant, my eyes were open and I was fumbling for the alarm clock. It was 9:16. I leaped from my bed and ran for the door.

"Ananka!" my father bellowed again as the door swung open, and I caught the full force of his shout in my right ear. He cleared his throat and his voice assumed a normal volume. "Good. You're dressed." I looked down and realized I was still wearing the clothes I'd had on the night before. When I'd climbed back into my bedroom window at four o'clock in the morning, I hadn't had the energy to throw on pajamas.

"I've got to change," I mumbled, weaving down the hall toward the bathroom.

"You don't have time for that. Go on. Get going," my father snapped, failing to see that I was wrinkled and dirty. "If you're fast enough, you won't miss your second class."

My mother, still wearing her bathrobe, blocked my exit. Her eyes traveled from the Marble Cemetery mud caked on my boots to the dust that coated my black T-shirt. She grabbed her purse from the table by the front door and rooted around inside.

"Take this," she said, slapping a hairbrush into my hand. "And here's some reading material for the ride to school." She held out a glossy brochure. On the cover was a picture of a teenage girl milking a cow with one hand and holding a textbook with the other. "I'm making the call today," my mother announced as she pushed me out the door.

On my way uptown in the back of a taxi, I tried to stay calm. But one look at the brochure I'd been given made it perfectly clear that life as I knew it would soon be over.

—— THE BORLAND ACADEMY ——

Television. Video games. Drugs. With so much competing for our children's attention, it's no wonder that many young people today are failing to live up to their academic potential. At the Borland Academy, we have created a unique environment stripped of the distractions of the modern world. Located 130 miles outside of Burp, West Virginia, and set deep in the stunning Appalachian Mountains, the

Borland Academy is both a working farm and a well-respected academic institution. Students divide their time between classes developed to broaden their minds and farm chores designed to enhance their self-discipline. Freed from the negative influence of popular culture, students are able to spend their weekends acquiring a newfound appreciation for hard work and the simple pleasures of nature. The results of our approach speak for themselves. Last year, three Borland Academy students were accepted at Yale, and two of our handcrafted cheeses were awarded blue ribbons at the West Virginia State Fair.

Ideal for underachievers and children with a history of violence, the Borland Academy is designed to give each and every student the personalized attention he or she needs. Children are supervised twenty-four hours a day, and our professional nursing staff is authorized to dispense pharmaceuticals if necessary.

I had lived in New York City my entire life. I'd never seen a cow up close, and I had no intention of learning how to craft prizewinning cheeses. My mind was filled with a thousand plans at once. If I emptied my personal bank account, I could go into hiding. Get my own apartment. Attend public school. Fight crime at night, sleep late on the weekends. By the time my cab pulled up in front of the Atalanta School for Girls, I was convinced that it was time to assert my independence. I still had my share of the money the Irregulars had made from the treasures we'd found in the Shadow City. I would have gone straight for the bank if Principal Wickham hadn't been waiting for me on the sidewalk outside the school gates. As I slid out of the taxi, I wondered how a woman who weighed less than a sack of laundry and was older than the Empire State Building could make me feel like a naughty toddler with a soiled diaper.

· · ·

"Good morning, Ananka." The principal took in the sorry state of my appearance. "Your mother phoned to say you were on your way. She thought it might be a good idea if I escorted you to class."

"I'm sorry, Principal Wickham," I mumbled.

"So am I," she said, leading me up the stairs and into the school. "You know what this means, don't you?"

"Yes, I read about the Borland Academy on my way to school."

The principal laughed, though I saw nothing amusing about my plight. "I know the founder of the academy," she said. "Not a very pleasant man, but I'm impressed that he's finally found a way to combine his passions for academics and animal husbandry. Your mother seems to think that the Borland Academy offers the kind of environment you need, but I must admit that I'm not convinced."

"You're not?" I felt a second surge of hope.

"No. In fact, I'm planning to plead your case. Don't ask me why, but I believe you could be an asset to Atalanta. You *were* warned, however, so I will have to punish you. I think two weeks of after-school detention should suffice. You can stay until six each evening, working on an essay I assign you."

"Thank you, Principal Wickham," I gushed.

"Don't thank me yet." Principal Wickham delivered me to the door of the chemistry laboratory. "You have plenty of work to do if you intend to find your way back into *my* good graces. Your mother tells me you've read a great deal about New York. In two weeks' time, I expect you to deliver a twenty-page paper on one aspect of the city's history. Choose your subject wisely. It must be good enough to impress Mr. Dedly. Otherwise, I'm afraid you're heading for an F in his class, and if that should happen, I won't be able to save you from Borland. So report to the library after your last class, Ananka, and please . . . . do try to stay out of trouble."

· · ·

Inside the laboratory, I strapped on a pair of safety goggles and tied a black leather apron around my waist. My lab partner, a studious girl named Natasha with no talent for chemistry, was dumping liquids into a glass beaker and barely acknowledged my arrival. I stared at the wisps of sulfurous smoke that began to rise from the mixture and wondered how everything could have gone so wrong. My friends were keeping secrets from me, my mother was watching my every move, I couldn't seem to get any sleep, and I wouldn't even have time for lunch. In two hours' time, while my classmates ate (or pretended to eat), I would be on a reconnaissance mission in Central Park, across the street from Lester Liu's mansion. I was risking my freedom for a girl who couldn't be bothered to tell me the truth.

While Natasha scrambled to douse the flames that had started shooting from her beaker, I pulled a scrap of paper out of my pocket. There, in Oona's handwriting, was the address of Lester Liu's building on Fifth Avenue. I was tempted to bail and let Kiki, Oona, and Betty plan the operation on their own. But there was something about the address itself that had me intrigued. The epiphany came as my frantic chemistry teacher arrived with a fire extinguisher that belched mountains of snowy-white foam across the burning workbench. Lester Liu lived in the Varney Mansion.

· · ·

In August, the Varney Mansion had made the news when a piece of the building's marble facade had crashed to earth, taking out a taxicab and narrowly missing a prize Pomeranian owned by Mrs. Gwendolyn Gluck, one of the city's most prominent socialites. Before police could seal off the area, a second sheet of marble had flattened a mailbox, and the statue of a naked goddess that had guarded the doorway for a hundred years had slipped and shattered on the sidewalk. In the excitement that followed, the goddess's severed head had disappeared. Three days later it was found in Queens, affixed to the hood of a tricked-out Trans Am.

Had the building in question been any other, few people would have cared. Old and leprous, New York loses chunks of itself on a regular basis. But in the cafés and drawing rooms of the Upper East Side, it was whispered that the mansion on Millionaires' Row was being destroyed—not by time but by the ghost of Cecelia Varney.

When Cecelia Varney was born to one of New York's richest men, the newspapers labeled her *The Luckiest Girl in the World*. When she died ninety years later in her family's mansion, she was known to the city as *The Hermit of Fifth Avenue*. What happened in between has been the subject of two TV movies and an off-Broadway musical, but nobody knows for sure. At age thirty-four, the stunning socialite suddenly divorced the third in a series of gold-digging playboys. She then shocked her famous friends by dumping them in favor of little-known psychics and frequenting séances rather than nightclubs. On the morning of her thirty-fifth birthday, without any warning, Cecelia Varney locked herself up in the mansion with two trustworthy servants and a pair of six-toed cats (a birthday present from her friend Ernest Hemingway). She never left the house again, and it was said she was still there, buried somewhere in the basement. The one servant to survive Ms. Varney was spotted hailing a cab as the undertaker arrived. It was the last time anyone saw her.

The day Cecelia Varney's obituary ran in the *New York Times*, real estate brokers began stalking the mansion like hungry hyenas. Not only was the house among the most magnificent in New York, it was said to be filled with Ms. Varney's priceless collections. Over the course of fifty-five years, she'd spent her family's entire fortune without ever setting foot inside a store. Men who were sworn to secrecy—and paid well to keep their word—made deliveries in the dead of night. Rumor had it that Ms. Varney had hoarded countless artworks long thought to be lost or destroyed, and everyone in town wanted a peek at her treasures. Unfortunately, her will made it clear that neither the house nor its contents could be disturbed. Everything belonged to the seventy-six cats (all descendants of the original pair) that roamed the rooms at will.

So it came as some surprise when the building changed hands just weeks after Cecelia Varney's death. The cats, it seems, had disappeared without a trace. Not even the latest batch of kittens could be located. Without the heirs around to claim it, the mansion was auctioned off. A mysterious billionaire purchased it all. Before the building had started to crumble, one of my classmates at Atalanta swore she'd seen a small, dapper man in a pale gray suit open the door to the mansion. I should have known when she mentioned the cane that it was Lester Liu.

. . .

I found Oona and Betty waiting for me in Central Park, across the street from the Varney Mansion. Even though Betty was the one in disguise (blond hair, black suit, brainy glasses), it was Oona who seemed unfamiliar. Overnight, she had transformed from a trusted friend into Lester Liu's daughter.

"Hey." Oona glanced my way and then back across Fifth Avenue. "What do you think?" I felt my excitement wither as I surveyed the mansion. Beneath its brace of metal scaffolding, the building looked lifeless, its stone so white, it could have been carved out of ice. Every window was dark—blocked by shutters that sealed out the city. Most of the mansions on Millionaires' Row were ostentatious monuments to the men who had built them. The Varney Mansion was a mausoleum.

"You know we'll be some of the first people inside," I said. "I wonder what he's got in there."

"Probably a dozen Taiwanese school kids," said Oona. "I bet he makes them polish the floors. By the way, can you believe he lives *here* while I spend all my free time in a nail salon?"

"How's Yu?" I asked, hoping to remind her that life could be worse. "Is he getting any better?"

"I guess. He seems pretty healthy to me, but Mrs. Fei says he's got to stay in bed for a few days. I think she just wants to keep him around. He's the sweet, lovable child she never had. And he's a boy, too, so she must think she hit the jackpot."

"It's the twenty-first century," I said. "I can't believe some people still prefer boys over girls."

"Uh, guys," said Betty. "Sorry to interrupt, but how long are we going to wait for Kiki? I have to get back to school."

I checked my watch. Only twenty minutes were left until lunch was over. "Okay, let's get started," I said, taking charge. "Oona, if the house was just sold, I bet the real estate company still has a floor plan in their computers. Do you think you can get to it?"

"No problem," said Oona. "I'll hack in tonight."

"Betty, can you ask Luz to whip up a few bugs?"

"What are you going to do with whipped bugs?" Betty asked.

"*Listening devices*," I corrected her. "Small ones we can plant around Lester Liu's house."

"Ahh, right." Betty smiled at her mistake. "I should sew some hidden pockets into the dresses I'm making for you. That way you won't get caught if your bags are searched."

"Perfect. Can you also talk to Iris and DeeDee and see if we can use some of their trustworthy perfume?"

"Hey," said Oona. "Aren't *you* going to do anything?"

"I can't," I snapped. "I've got detention until six o'clock, and after that I'll be trying to explain to my mother where I was last night."

"You got caught?" gasped Betty.

"Yeah. I'll tell you the whole story when it seems a little less tragic. Now, last thing. How many people live in the mansion with Lester Liu?"

Oona shrugged.

"Okay." I sighed. "I guess somebody's going to need to watch the place over the next twenty-four hours and see who goes in and out. Any volunteers?"

"I'll do it," said a voice behind us. Betty squealed as a squirrel jumped up on her shoulder and nuzzled at her neck.

A tall, thin boy dressed in camouflage stepped out from behind a tree. His face and neck were smeared with dirt and his hands were covered in paint. He may have been fifteen or sixteen, his hair may have been red, and he may have been good-looking. It was almost impossible to tell.

"Get that squirrel off of her," I insisted.

The boy whistled and the squirrel bounced back to him.

"He wasn't attacking her," said the boy. "He likes her."

"I hope they don't like her as much as they liked our friend Luz. Your little monsters really scratched her up." Few people could withstand Oona's snarl, but the boy stood his ground.

"Yes, I'm sorry about that. They get a little excited sometimes. I'm trying to teach them better manners. We don't want to hurt people; we just want their money." His voice was cool and crisp. Every word was perfectly enunciated. It was as if he were an extraterrestrial who'd learned English *too* well.

"Have you been following me?" asked Betty.

"Yes," the boy freely admitted, taking us all by surprise.

"Who *are* you?" I asked.

"You can call me Kaspar."

"Like the friendly ghost?" Oona snickered.

"Be nice," said Betty.

"I think it's more like Kaspar Hauser," I said, recalling a book I'd once found in the tiny section of my parents' library devoted to child-rearing manuals. "He was the original *wild child*. He was discovered in Germany a long time ago."

"Smart," said Kaspar. His smile revealed teeth as white as freshly scrubbed subway tiles. He hadn't been living in the park for long. "Who are *you*?"

I checked with Oona and Betty.

"Go ahead," said Oona. "It may give us an excuse to kill him in the future."

"I'm Ananka Fishbein. That's Oona Wong. And the girl you've been stalking? Her name is Betty Bent." I wondered if the boy was blushing under all that dirt.

"Where are your three other friends?" he asked. "The

little white-haired girl, the mean-looking one, and the girl who was meant to be squirrel bait?"

I peered down at my watch. Where was Kiki?

"Aren't you clever?" I said. "Maybe you should tell us a little bit more about yourself before we invite you to join our club."

"What would you like to know?" Kaspar leaned causally against a tree trunk like an old-fashioned swash-buckler.

"What's up with the squirrels?" I asked. "Why did you teach animals to steal?"

"I didn't teach them. They taught me," Kaspar said without a hint of humor. "I'm afraid it isn't a very pleas-ant story."

"Unpleasant stories are my favorite kind," Oona goaded him. "I'd love to hear yours."

"If you insist," Kaspar said. "A few years ago, I woke up and discovered that my parents had abandoned me. I still don't know where they went, but they took every-thing of value in our apartment. When I couldn't pay the rent, the landlord kicked me out. So I came to live here in the park. One morning I was digging through a Dump-ster for food when I noticed some men delivering cages filled with unusual squirrels to the back door of a pet store. I remember thinking that the animals looked even more miserable than I felt. They deserved to be free, not sitting in a cage where idiots could gawk at them.

"While the back door was open, I crammed a rotten potato in the lock. When the men left, I snuck into the store and set the squirrels free. Some of them ran off, but these three stuck with me. After a while, they started bringing me presents. Chocolate bars, ten-dollar bills, diamond tennis bracelets. At first I didn't realize they were stealing them. I was just happy I had money to buy food. But when I found out, I knew I had to put their skills to good use. With the money we made, we could set more animals free. No living creature should be kept in a cage."

Betty was blinking back tears and even Oona seemed uncharacteristically touched. But as far as I was concerned, his story didn't ring true.

"Now that you know my secret, how about sharing one of yours?" Kaspar asked. "Where did you get that map? The moment I saw it, I knew it was important. I suspected the girl we mugged would come back for it. I didn't expect her to bring such charming friends."

I refused to be flattered. "We can't tell you about the map."

"I understand. You would need to ask the white-haired girl first. She's your leader, I assume."

"We don't need *anyone's* permission," snapped Oona. "We just don't trust squirrel-loving thieves."

"You *are* a criminal," said Betty softly. "And we don't really know you."

"Perhaps there's a way I can earn your trust." Kaspar looked past Oona and me to Betty. "Did I hear you say that you need someone to watch this building?"

"*Perhaps*," Oona said, mocking his peculiar way of speaking.

"I'll keep an eye on it. I'll stay here all night, and I won't even ask why. Maybe I'll even solve the mystery of the Varney cats. But I have one condition. Betty must agree to have dinner with me."

"No way," I said. "That's too much to ask. We don't use our friends as bargaining chips."

"It's okay, Ananka," Betty said. "When all this is over, if that's still what he wants, I'll do it." I could see that Betty didn't believe she'd have to honor the deal. Somehow, she thought that one whiff of Eau Irresistible could still have Kaspar hooked.

"Betty . . ." I tried to warn her.

"My mind's made up," she announced. "But I have one condition, too. No more pet store raids and no more muggings, okay? I don't date delinquents."

"Excellent. Then we have a deal." Kaspar flashed his movie-star smile and began to climb an oak opposite Lester Liu's mansion. "Meet me here tomorrow evening, and I'll give you my report."

We left Kaspar perched on a limb of the tree and hurried back to class. The nearest subway station wasn't far from my school, and the three of us walked briskly in the same direction.

"Where was Kiki?" fumed Oona. "I stuck with her last time, and that sadistic cousin of hers nearly killed me. Now my own father wants to murder me, and she doesn't even show up."

"Something must have happened. Kiki would never blow off a reconnaissance mission." Although I was worried about Kiki, I couldn't help but feel pleased that she and Oona were on the brink of falling out. "Do you think one of us should drop by her house after school?"

"I'll do it," said Betty. "But then I'm going straight uptown to see DeeDee. I've got to find a way to get this perfume off."

"Yeah, about the perfume, Betty. I think you just made a mistake with squirrel boy back there. No perfume on earth lasts *this* long," I told her.

"Why else would Kaspar want to help us? I feel bad, even if he is a criminal. It's like I'm taking advantage of him."

"I've got a better idea," said Oona. "Why don't you save yourself the trip to DeeDee's and take a good look in the mirror?"

"What do you mean?" asked Betty.

Oona looked over at me and rolled her eyes. "And you all say *I'm* hopeless?"

· · ·

The four o'clock bell set off a stampede of schoolgirls. As I sullenly pushed my way through the herd toward my first afternoon of detention, it occurred to me that I might soon find myself in the presence of greatness. Every school has its celebrities, and at the Atalanta School for Girls, Molly Donovan topped the A-list. Molly's fame had little to do with the fact that her actress mother had been awarded two Oscars or that her father, a plastic surgeon, was responsible for half the noses at Atalanta. Most Atalanta girls were rich and many were famous, but few could claim to have *earned* their success. Molly was celebrated for having been sentenced to detention more times than any other girl in the history of the school. I'd heard that on her two hundredth visit she intended to commission a commemorative tattoo.

Molly and Mrs. Fontaine were alone in the library

when I arrived to serve my sentence. Though renowned as the strictest of disciplinarians, Mrs. Fontaine bore the curse of a pea-sized bladder. Each morning, students of all ages placed bets on the number of times she would bolt for the bathroom during the course of the day. The money that changed hands every week could have bought Mrs. Fontaine her own gold-plated Porta Potti.

I tried to gather the books I'd need to write the essay Principal Wickham had assigned, but the Atalanta library couldn't hold a candle to the one I had at home. (Though it did boast an impressive number of books devoted to *Your Changing Body*.) I was snickering at one of the titles when I saw Mrs. Fontaine shifting her considerable weight from side to side and grimacing as if she were about to burst. As soon as I chose a study desk two rows behind Molly, our jailer warned us to keep our mouths shut and sprinted for the door.

"Pssst."

I peered over the top of my desk. Molly was kneeling on her chair, staring back at me. Though she wasn't exactly the picture of a troublemaker, with her chipmunk cheeks and Pippi Longstocking freckles, Molly was notorious for contributing to the delinquency of others. I looked down at my books and tried to ignore her.

"Pssssssssssst."

Molly refused to give up. I lifted my head above the divider. Molly smiled sweetly and twisted a red ringlet around her finger.

"You've never been here before," she said. "What'd you do?"

"I was late for school this morning."

"Oh," said Molly, clearly disappointed. "Is that it? I was hoping you were the stink-bomb girl."

Hearing footsteps in the hallway, I dropped back into my seat and buried my head in a book. Molly's reflexes were not quite as fast.

"Molly, sit down and get to work!" screeched Mrs. Fontaine. "If I see you bothering Ananka, I'll make sure you're here all month."

"I've already got detention till the end of October," Molly pointed out.

"Then let's talk *November*," said Mrs. Fontaine.

I pulled three sheets of paper out of my notebook and began my essay. I had planned to write about the grave-robbing incident that had sparked the Doctors' Riot of 1788, but instead, another subject took hold of me.

Beneath Bialystoker Synagogue on the Lower East Side lies a hidden room . . .

Fifteen minutes later, I heard Mrs. Fontaine leave the room. I felt warm breath on the back of my neck, and I jolted upright, nearly head butting Molly Donovan.

"Interesting essay," said Molly. "Your spelling's terrible."

"Go away," I whispered, keeping one eye on the door. "You're going to get us both expelled."

"I can't get expelled," said Molly. "I've been trying for years. It doesn't matter what I do. My parents just donate more money to the school."

Suddenly I was interested. "Why do you want to be expelled?"

"I hate it here. I'd rather be anywhere but New York."

"Really?" I asked in astonishment. "Why?"

"It's my parents. They won't leave me alone. They think I'm *special*."

"But I always heard you were quite smart."

"Not *that* kind of special. *Gifted* special."

"Oh yeah? What's your gift?" I asked.

"My mom calls me the human calculator. I can do complex math equations in my head. My parents used to bring me out at cocktail parties to entertain their guests. When I was eleven, I decided I wasn't going to be their monkey anymore. I even got a D in geometry last year," she said, sounding terribly proud.

"Congratulations," I said. "What's the square root of 7368?"

"You, too?" Molly sighed. "85.837. Are three decimal places enough?"

"Sure, but I can't check it. I don't have a calculator."

"Then I guess you'll just have to trust me. Oops, here comes the fountain. Don't tell anybody what I just told you. It would ruin my reputation."

"Okay," I whispered, as Molly slid back into her seat.

• • •

Another fifteen minutes passed before Molly returned.

"Isn't this fun?" she asked.

"It's better than I thought it would be." I was actually starting to like her.

Molly sat on the edge of my desk. "I love detention. It's my favorite time of day. You get to meet such interesting people. It's too bad I have to see my shrinks after this; otherwise, I'd invite you to dinner. My cook makes a fabulous bouillabaisse."

"Shrinks?" I asked. "You have more than one psychologist?"

"Sure, I'm *gifted*, remember? It's a husband-and-wife team. I see them three times a week. They specialize in dealing with exceptional children."

"What's it like?" I asked.

"Terrible. They give me lots of tests and make me talk about how it feels to be so smart. Sometimes I get to perform for an audience of experts. It's like being one of those chickens at the carnival that play tic-tac-toe."

"That does sound pretty bad," I agreed.

"Of course it does. I don't know why my parents send me to see them. Their own son ran away. I heard he lives in the park now. They tried to catch him for a while, but he's *gifted*, too. Kept getting away. Uh-oh, here she comes again."

· · ·

I spent the next fifteen minutes counting the nine hundred seconds until Molly was back.

"Hey there," she said. "Where were we?"

"That boy. The one you said ran away. What's his name?"

"Phineas Parker. Why?"

"What does he look like?"

"No idea. I've never seen him. Why do you want to know?"

"Just curious," I told her.

"If you know where he is, you could claim the big

reward his parents have offered. But I doubt you're cruel enough to turn him in."

"Not after what you've told me. By the way, what's *his* gift?"

"Art," said Molly. "His parents have his paintings all over their office. Supposedly they sold one a while back for something like thirty thousand dollars."

"Listen, Molly. Do you think you might be able to get me a picture of Phineas?"

"Probably," she said. "What would I get in return?"

I thought for a moment. "If you get me a picture, I'll get you expelled."

"Promise?" said Molly, her eyes gleaming.

"I promise," I assured her.

"Molly!" Mrs. Fontaine took us both by surprise. "That's it! You're here through *November*."

"Great!" Molly exclaimed as she bounced back to her seat.

. . .

On my way home from school, I took out my phone to call Kiki, only to discover two missed calls from my house. It was not a good sign. When I walked through the front door, I found my mother waiting in the hallway, clutching a stopwatch like a sadistic track coach. She glanced down at the clock and then back up at me.

"It's forty-seven minutes after six. Why are you late? I checked online. There's nothing wrong with the subway."

"Actually, I walked home." Her tone had me scared, and I desperately wished for a little Fille Fiable. "I'd been sitting down for hours. I needed some exercise."

"Exercise is the least of your concerns right now. Your father and I would like to talk to you in the next room." I was too shocked to move. "Now!" my mother ordered.

The floor of the living area remained covered with fallen books. Only a small circle surrounding the couch had been cleared of debris. I took a seat across from my parents and tried to ignore a book entitled *Central American Temples of Doom* that was calling to me from across the room.

"Would you like to tell us why you had such a hard time getting out of bed this morning?" my mother asked.

"I was tired?"

"That's the best you can do?" My explanation had been rejected and my mother looked disgusted. "I had just finished talking to the head of the Borland Academy when your principal rang," she said. "She seems to think she can get you back in line. Though it's against my better judgment, I agreed to give her a chance."

"Thank you," I muttered.

"Not so fast. The Borland Academy is still expecting you in December. I've already written the check. Sleep late again, and you'll wake up on a bus to West Virginia."

"We don't want to punish you, Ananka," said my father, looking a little uncomfortable. He always preferred to play the good cop. "We just want to help you succeed. If you do well in school, then one day you can do whatever you want. You can study giant squid or join the FBI or dig up old bones around New York. But you'll never be able to do all of that if you don't get through geometry first."

"Your father may not want to punish you, but *I* do,"

my mother declared. "We have given you our trust and your privacy, and you have abused them both. That's why we've felt the need to take a few precautions. Your father and I have spent the day finding all the books you'll need for your studies. They're in your room now. Everything else in the library is temporarily off-limits until you learn how to focus.

"Every day for the next two weeks, you will come directly home from detention and begin your homework. During this time you will stay away from Kiki Strike. Do you understand?"

"Yes." It's easy to sound humble when you think you have an ace up your sleeve.

"Fine. Then it's time to get started. And, Ananka?"

"Yes?"

"Tomorrow you'll take the subway home."

I hurried to my room to inspect the damage. My desk drawers had been rifled, and many of my favorite books had been confiscated, but my collection of New York history books hadn't been touched. My copy of *Glimpses of Gotham* remained, along with the map that was tucked between its pages. I almost breathed a sigh of relief until I happened to notice the windows. Both were secured with brand-new padlocks. I was trapped inside. I lay down on my bed, fully prepared to have a good cry, when there was a knock at the door and my father stuck his head inside.

"It's really not that bad," he whispered. "Just get an A on your next test and she'll forget everything. You can do it!"

"Thanks, Dad." I sniffled.

"By the way, something came by messenger for you

today. I think it's from one of your friends. Don't tell your mother I gave it to you."

"Okay," I agreed. He tossed a small manila package onto the bed.

"If you need any help on your homework, just let me know."

"I will," I promised, wiping my eyes.

I ripped open the package and dumped the contents out onto the bed. There were two padlocks identical to the ones on my windows, a miniature hammer and chisel, and a small leather case. The case contained a metal test tube that was cold to the touch and labeled *Liquid Nitrogen*. I fished inside the envelope and found a note.

> Sorry I stood you up today. Heard you got busted.
> It's not as bad as it looks. If you can't pick the locks,
> you can use this kit. Coat one of the locks with nitrogen
> and let it sit for a minute or two. When the lock
> freezes, just shatter it with the hammer and chisel. (Be
> careful! Nitrogen freezes fingers, too.)
>
> See you tomorrow night.
>   Kiki

CHAPTER SEVEN

Sleeping Beauty

Friday morning, I pushed through the front doors of the Atalanta School a full forty-five minutes before the first bell. The halls were practically empty. I raced past a few scholarship students and a suck-up or two on my way to the bathroom. I'd downed a triple espresso while walking to the subway, and the effects were becoming unpleasant. As I struggled frantically with the buckle of my belt, I heard someone slam the door of the neighboring stall.

"Psst! Ananka." The whisper bordered on a shout. I looked down and saw a freckled face grinning at me from under the divider.

"Molly?" I groaned. The girl really needed to work on her boundaries. "What are you *doing*?"

"Come over here," she insisted.

"What? No!"

"Come over here. I've got something for you."

"Don't you think that would look a little *weird*, Molly?"

Molly scowled. "I'm serious. Do you want it or not?"

"Good God, Molly. Can it wait a minute? I'm about to explode."

"No, it *can't*. In case you've forgotten, I have every teacher in school watching me. I don't have much time."

I took a deep breath and unlocked my stall. I didn't have a chance to check for eavesdroppers before Molly pulled me into her stall. We stood nose to nose over the toilet.

"This is very strange," I told her. "Why all the secrecy?"

"I got you a photo of Phineas Parker." Molly unzipped her backpack. It was empty aside from a picture in an enormous silver frame.

"I just needed the photograph, Molly, not the frame. This is from Tiffany's. Your shrinks are definitely going to know it's missing."

"Like I care? I'll tell my dad to add a hundred bucks to their next check. Ooooh! Or maybe they'll make me find another doctor. That would be fantastic! So what do you think?"

I had a hard time pulling my eyes away. Phineas Parker had auburn hair, hazel eyes, and the face of a Greek god. An enormous squirrel sat perched on his shoulder.

"Yeah, that's what *I* thought," Molly cackled. "Who knew he was such a looker? If he ever decides to move back home, maybe I'll get his parents to set us up."

"Molly," I said with a smile, "by that time, you're going to be hundreds of miles away from New York."

"So you're really going to do it?"

"A promise is a promise. Nothing's going to happen immediately, but one day soon, you're going to get expelled."

Molly threw her arms around me and smothered me with a hug so powerful that I nearly lost control of my bladder. Two girls giggled when Molly and I stepped out of the stall, but I didn't care. Never in my life had I made anyone so happy.

. . .

That evening, only hours before Lester Liu's dinner was set to begin, I took the subway home from school, walked straight past my mother with my head held high, and locked myself in my bedroom. Shortly before seven o'clock, my father knocked at the door and asked if I cared for a little bread and water. I politely informed him that I'd already eaten and requested that he leave me to my studies. At seven fifteen, I carefully cracked one of the padlocks and tiptoed down the fire escape. By seven thirty, I was outside Betty Bent's building. I didn't feel an ounce of guilt.

My fingers had just brushed the bell when Betty opened the door and dragged me inside her dark basement apartment. Before I could say a word, she lifted one finger to her lips.

"I'm glad you came early," she whispered, taking a quick peek over her shoulder. "There's something you should see."

"Is anyone else here?" I asked.

"Just Oona. Come on." She weaved around the mannequins and headless dressmakers' dummies that crowded the living room. Her parents were designing costumes for a new opera that appeared to be set on Mars.

"Hold on just a second. I've got something to tell you,"

I hissed at Betty's back. "I discovered your boyfriend's secret identity today."

Betty slowed her stride but refused to turn around. "Boyfriend?"

"You know who I'm talking about. He loves the outdoors, enjoys working with animals, and hasn't seen a bar of soap in a while." Betty stopped walking. "His real name is Phineas Parker. His parents are psychologists. He ran away a few months ago. Want to see a picture?"

Betty nodded mutely, and I passed her the picture I'd removed from its frame.

"Not bad, huh?" My grin faded when I saw Betty's face. "What's the matter with you?"

"Nothing. I just wish Iris had never made that love potion. Look—maybe you shouldn't tell anyone else about this."

"Why not?" My fine detective work had been rewarded with a first-class piece of gossip. Keeping it to myself would be like winning the lottery and losing the ticket.

"He hasn't given us any reason to sell him out. Let him keep his secret for now."

"Don't tell me you have a crush on the wild child of Central Park."

Betty shrugged. "What if I do? What difference would it make?"

"But he's been following you around like a lovesick baboon," I argued. "Obviously, he likes you, too."

"Maybe. But thanks to Eau Irresistible, I'll never know for sure," she said with a sigh. "Now hurry up or you'll miss the show."

Betty bustled toward her bedroom at the back of the

building. Light flooded into the living room through the open door.

"Okay, stand here." Betty shoved me into a shadow and pointed into the bedroom. "Take a look."

Gazing into three full-length mirrors was Oona, wearing a magnificent dress composed of multiple layers of pale, dove-gray silk and chiffon. Whenever she moved, hundreds of beads sewn along the hem of the gown sparkled like morning dew.

"What an amazing dress. Did you design it?" I asked Betty.

"No. Oona brought it with her. In a huge box with a big red bow."

"A present from Daddy?"

"Uh-huh. It was delivered to her house this morning. She had to try it on here. She said her grandmothers wouldn't approve if they knew she was accepting gifts from Lester Liu."

"I take it you don't approve, either?" I asked. Betty shook her head. "It *is* a little strange, I suppose. But it's only a dress."

"It's *not* just a dress. See all the little sparkles on the bottom? Those are *real*. They're diamonds."

"They can't be real," I scoffed. "There are *tons* of them."

"I know, but they are. I tested one. And there wasn't just a dress in the box she brought. Did you see her new jewelry?"

Still unaware we were watching, Oona stopped twirling for the mirrors and reached into a giant box that lay open on the bed. A thick diamond bracelet flashed on her wrist as she pulled out a silver fur stole and draped it around her shoulders. She struck a movie star pose and blew a kiss at her own reflection. I suddenly felt as if I were spying on a stranger. The Oona I knew had her faults, but her dignity wasn't for sale. Not only would she have refused Lester Liu's gifts, she'd have set the box on fire and tossed it into the street. This was a person I'd never seen before. An impostor, perhaps. An evil twin. Or maybe, it occurred to me, this was the *real* Oona— the side of herself she'd kept hidden from the rest of us.

"She does look great," I muttered, afraid to share my suspicions with Betty.

"She's *gorgeous*. That's the problem," Betty whispered. "Her father's found her weakness. Who knows what he wants, but he thinks he can buy her trust. I'm starting to get worried, Ananka."

"Me, too," I admitted. If the Irregulars' safety depended on the girl in the mirror, we were all in grave danger. The buzzer rang.

"I'll be right back," said Betty.

"Hi, Oona." I stepped into the light of the bedroom. Oona waved at my reflection.

"Well, what do you think?" she asked.

"Your father has excellent taste," I noted dryly.

"He does, doesn't he?" Oona spun around once for her own amusement before she saw the expression on my face. "Don't look at me like that," she snapped. "If he sent something, I have to wear it, don't I? What would he think if I showed up in one of Betty's old rags?"

I didn't know what to say. As Betty returned to the bedroom with Luz, DeeDee, and Iris in tow, I finally put a finger on what bothered me. Oona's argument made perfect sense. It just wasn't something my friend would have said.

"Your parents are letting you hang out with us again?" I asked Iris as she walked through the door.

"Yeah, they finally figured out that it's better to have older friends than no friends at all." Iris reached out to brush her hand against Oona's silk dress. "You look amazing, Oona," she gushed.

"Tell me something I don't know, munchkin," Oona replied haughtily as she twirled out of Iris's reach.

"Pretty on the outside," DeeDee grumbled under her breath. "Where's Kiki?"

"Looks like she's going to be late," said Betty. "Have a seat."

"I brought your bugs." Luz dropped onto Betty's bed with a thump. She pulled a flat, nickel-sized object out of a paper bag and held it pinched between her thumb and index finger. "There are twenty of them, and you can put them anywhere you want. There's adhesive on the back if you need to stick one under a table or behind a painting."

"You're a genius," I told her.

"It's been said before," Luz replied.

"Iris and I brought some Fille Fiable." DeeDee placed three small spray bottles on Betty's vanity. "Just remember that it stays strong for only a few minutes. You may need to reapply it several times."

"You're telling *me* how it works?" Oona asked. "In case you've forgotten, I got a personal demonstration from your vertically challenged sidekick."

"Okay!" Betty refused to let Oona's comment do damage. "Time to get you dressed, Ananka. Want to come, Iris?"

"You bet!" Iris chirped, eager to escape from Oona.

· · ·

As costume designers for the Metropolitan Opera, Betty's parents spent their days designing Viking costumes for men with small bones and transforming plump prima donnas into starving French peasants. On countless occasions, I'd seen the evidence of their work lying half stitched in the living room, but I'd never been invited to visit their studio.

"Ever wonder why we live in a basement?" Betty asked Iris, her hand poised on the knob of a door posted with *keep out* signs. "This is why." She opened the door to reveal an enormous work space packed with costumes of every imaginable description—donkeys, Romans, sultans, and geishas. "We'd never get this much space above ground, and sunlight destroys the color of the fabrics."

"You could make a fortune on Halloween," Iris marveled.

"My parents would never loan this stuff out. In fact, they'd probably kill me if they knew what I was doing." Betty walked over to one of the clothes racks and began rifling through the hangers. "How do you like this, Ananka?" She held out a pink costume with gossamer wings.

"Very amusing," I droned.

"Can I try it on?" Iris's hazel eyes twinkled.

Betty peered down at the girl in confusion. "I don't think it's the right size for you. Besides, you're almost twelve. Why would you want to dress up like Tinker Bell?"

Iris stared at her green ballet flats. "I was just thinking that I could use an outfit like that in case you guys needed my help again sometime. You know, when you need someone to look like an innocent little kid."

"I doubt we'll have any need for a fairy. How about a little mermaid? You could do surveillance from fountains." I was the only one laughing.

"You've been spending too much time with Oona," Betty scolded. "Looking young isn't the only thing you're good at," she told Iris. "If *some* people want to treat you like an eight-year-old, that's their problem. Don't forget that you've already saved their butts once. With your brains, I'm sure it won't be the last time."

"She's right," I admitted. "I apologize, Iris."

"I'm over it," said Iris. "Let's get back to work."

"Want to see Kiki's dress?" Betty pushed a devil to one side and revealed an elegant dress of satin and lace. "I thought she'd want to stick with black, so I had to make it myself. All of the adult dresses are way too big for her and most of the kids' dresses are sherbet colored."

"It's great, but I'd kill to see Kiki in bubble gum pink."

"You might have to. Oh, and here's yours." She pulled out a long silk dress in a deep burgundy. "My mother designed this for a modern interpretation of Medea. Bloodstains won't show on it."

"Good to know," I said. "Do you really think I'll look okay in that?"

"Are you kidding? You're going to be fabulous," Betty

insisted. "And see," she said, sticking a hand into the folds of the skirt. "Hidden pockets for the bugs—just like I promised."

· · ·

With my new dress on, I sat at Betty's vanity, my back to her collection of fake noses while she finished the last touches on my makeup. Iris stood to one side as Betty gave her instruction.

"One of Ananka's eyes is just a teensy bit bigger than the other, so we're going to add a little extra liner to the small one . . ."

"What time is it?" Oona butted in. Having finally grown bored of staring at her own reflection, she was re-arranging Betty's wigs, which rested on dozens of Styro-foam heads lined up against the wall. Luz was sprawled out across the bed, staring at the ceiling. She checked her watch.

"Almost eight fifteen," she said.

"Where's Strike?" Oona growled. "It's going to take us thirty minutes to get uptown and we've got to be there by nine. If Kiki stands us up for this one, I swear I'll kick her butt."

"Good luck," snorted Luz. "I'll give you fifty dollars to try."

Iris started to titter and then thought better of it.

"Kiki will be here," DeeDee said just as the buzzer rang. "See?" She jumped up to answer the door.

When DeeDee returned, her face was grim. Kiki's looked like a still from a horror film.

"Sorry I'm late," she said.

"No problem. Are you feeling all right?" Kiki's complexion was more cadaverous than usual and her eyes were bloodshot and swollen. She looked as if she hadn't slept in days.

"Verushka was sick again. I had to find a new doctor."

"I thought she was feeling better," said DeeDee. "What's the problem now?"

"It's her leg. There's still something wrong with it."

"Do you think you should be here?" I asked. "Shouldn't you be at home with her?"

Oona cleared her throat in protest, but the rest of us ignored her.

"She didn't want me to miss this," Kiki said. "The doctor's with her now."

"Are you sure you're feeling up to a dinner party?" asked Betty. "One of us can go in your place if you need to stay at home."

"*Excuse me?*" Oona whined. "I love Verushka as much as any of you, but this is serious, too."

"I'll be fine," Kiki assured us with a weak grin.

"Then hop up, Ananka," Betty told me. "You're finished, and I've got fifteen minutes to do some serious damage repair."

"Nice dress, Oona," Kiki said as she took my seat at the vanity. "A present, I assume?"

"Yeah, her father's really got her number, doesn't he?" DeeDee said.

"I hope you're talking about my dress size, Morlock," Oona barked.

. . .

As our taxi sped up Madison Avenue, Oona, Kiki, and I studied the floor plans of Lester Liu's mansion. Two blocks south of our destination, we jumped out of the cab and walked toward the park. A group of tourists strolling down Fifth Avenue stopped to ogle us. In her pale gray dress, Oona resembled a marble goddess sprung to life, and Betty had worked wonders on Kiki. With her colorless hair, startlingly white skin, elegant black dress, and red lips, she could have been queen of the vampires. Even I looked presentable, though I struggled to walk gracefully in my heels.

Kiki glided beside the wall that separates Fifth Avenue from Central Park. Slipping past the Children's Gate at Seventy-sixth Street, she approached two men who were sitting on the ground, enjoying a feast of Vienna sausages and cold beans.

"Kiki Strike," she said, holding out her hand to the elder of the pair.

"Howard Van Dyke." The man reached up to shake her hand. He was short, portly, and unusually hairy—like a garden gnome gone to seed. "Care for a cocktail weenie?" he asked.

"No, thank you," Kiki declined politely. "I'm allergic."

"I'm Kaspar," said the younger man, jumping up and shaking Kiki's hand. "I've read about you in the papers. Oona, Ananka," he said with a little bow in our direction. "You're both looking splendid this evening."

"Thanks, squirrel boy. Ow!" Oona yelped when I elbowed her.

"Hi, Kaspar," I said.

"Betty told me you've been very helpful," said Kiki. "Thank you for watching the mansion."

"It's been a pleasure," said Kaspar. "Howard kept me company."

"Thanks to you, too, Howard," said Kiki. "So what have you seen?"

"There hasn't been much activity," Kaspar noted. "There's a butler who comes and goes throughout the day. He's an unusual character. Looks a little like Genghis Kahn with a bad toupee—you can't miss him. There's also a cook, but he left a few minutes ago. I think there may be only one servant in the house at the moment. There were a couple of visitors this morning. A tall man in a bespoke suit showed up around nine. Well groomed, but a little flashy. He stayed for only a few minutes. The second was a deliveryman who unloaded a container of snakes."

"Did you say *snakes*?" I asked.

"That's what it looked like," Kaspar confirmed. "Are you sure you want to go inside?"

"Snakes or no snakes, we don't have a choice," Oona said, giving me the evil eye. "We were invited to dinner."

"Then I'll wait here to make sure you come back out again."

"That's very gallant of you," said Kiki. "But we can take care of ourselves."

"I'm sure you can. But you see, my social calendar is empty this evening. I don't have anything else to enter-tain me," said Kaspar, displaying a remarkable skill for diplomacy. "If you don't mind stopping by after dinner, I'd be curious to hear about the snakes. As your friends may have told you, I am something of an animal lover."

"In that case, maybe we'll bring you some leftovers," said Kiki with a grin.

"And perhaps a bottle of Châteauneuf du Pape?" asked Howard. "It's the best wine for weenies."

"I'll see what I can do." Kiki laughed as we started for the exit.

"I like Kaspar," Kiki announced as we crossed Fifth Avenue. "I wonder why he ran away from home."

"How did you know?" I asked in astonishment.

"His teeth looked a little too perfect," said Kiki. "If he'd been living in the park for that long, they'd be growing moss by now."

· · ·

Lester Liu's butler stood aside and waited silently as the three of us entered the mansion's foyer. Tall, dark, and oddly coiffed, he studied the space above our heads, though I sensed he saw everything. I avoided the snow-white pelt of a Siberian tiger, which lay flat against the floor, its head lifted in a savage welcome. Beneath a crystal chandelier lit with dozens of flickering candles, Oona's diamonds came to life, issuing little sparks as she glided across the marble. Kiki's eyes circled the room, taking note of escape routes, and possibly searching for snakes. On the ground floor, there were two tall doors on either side of the foyer. The door to our right had been hastily boarded over. Each piece of wood was studded with nails that were gnarled and bent.

"We're here to see my father." Oona's voice, always a little too loud, ricocheted off the marble walls. Without uttering a word, the butler turned his eyes to the grand staircase. A small man in a tuxedo was descending from the second floor, the tip of his cane tapping each step. In profile, his face looked cold, but as he navigated the last curve of the stairway, he broke into a charming smile.

"My dear Oona." Lester Liu spoke with the spit-polished accent of a newly titled English lord. With his free hand, he took his daughter by the shoulder and planted a kiss on both cheeks. "You are even more stunning than your mother. From now on, you must always dress like this." I expected Oona to squirm or launch an insult in his direction. Instead, she gaped at her handsome father, unable to speak.

"These must be your friends." Lester turned first to Kiki. "Miss Strike, I presume," he said, reaching for Kiki's hand. "You are every bit as impressive as I imagined you would be."

"You flatter me, Mr. Liu." Kiki's arched eyebrow made it perfectly clear what she thought of his opinion. "Are you keeping someone out—or in?" she asked with a smile, pointing to the blocked doorway.

Lester Liu matched Kiki's smile and upped the ante. "That is a touch of Ms. Varney's decorating. She was quite frugal in her later years. Rather than heat the entire mansion, she shut off the east wing to lower the gas bill.

"But how can I focus on these trivialities with such a charming young creature standing in front of me?" he asked, extending a hand in my direction.

"Annie Fisher," I lied. If Lester Liu didn't know my name, there was no point in giving it to him. "It's a pleasure to meet you, Mr. Liu." His hand was as cool and as dry as a statue's.

"The pleasure is all mine," he insisted. "Would you

care for a tour of the house? I'm afraid I haven't had many visitors and I'm eager to share my treasures." He glanced at Oona as he said this, and a chill crawled down my spine.

Lester Liu held his arm out to me, and I shocked myself by taking it. Beneath his jacket, I could tell he was thin but muscular. He steered me with surprising ease through a door and into a maze of cold, dark chambers, each cluttered with the treasures of Cecelia Varney.

Apparently, once Cecelia Varney had discovered that money couldn't buy happiness, she had set out to purchase everything else. We started our tour in an empty room lined with tall mirrors. Reflected in the glass, I saw Kiki's eyes darting into every corner while Oona's remained fixed on her father's back. Lester pulled a remote control from his jacket pocket and the room filled with light. The mirrors turned translucent, revealing shelves crammed with thousands of delicate porcelain figurines. Imprisoned behind the glass were maidens dancing jigs, young girls teasing cute little kittens, and pretty lasses whispering to their sweethearts.

"The Staffordshire Room," Lester Liu announced with a hint of disgust in his voice. Even porcelain girls seemed to give him the willies. "Ms. Varney's taste was good, but not always consistent. These will be sold at auction next week. I expect they will pay for some of the renovations I have planned. Though getting rid of these little monsters will be one of the finest improvements I could make." The lights dimmed, and I felt Lester Liu's arm pulling me through another dark doorway.

"I believe you will find this room amusing, Miss

Strike." The lights flashed on so suddenly that a sharp pain shot through my head and I wobbled on my heels. When I stopped blinking, I found myself in a bedroom furnished with ostentatious antiques. Beside a canopy bed draped in richly embroidered cloth was a bureau inlaid with gold. A leather-bound book stamped with a golden crown lay open near the foot of a silk-covered chaise longue. In the center of the room, on a squat marble pedestal, sat a plain golden box. "This is Marie Antoinette's bedroom," said Lester Liu. "It is almost exactly as she left it the evening she fled from a crowd of torch-wielding peasants. The French government has been trying to recover these items for centuries. Of course they still have no idea where to find them."

"What's in the box?" asked Kiki, moving in for a closer look. "It's not quite as old as the rest, is it?" Her hand gripped the side of the pedestal, and I knew she had planted the first of her bugs.

"You have an excellent eye," said Lester Liu with a serene smile. "The box is a later addition to the room. It contains a head. In 1955, a rather unscrupulous antiques dealer convinced Ms. Varney that it had once belonged to the queen herself. The DNA tests I've commissioned have been unable to tell me *whose* head Ms. Varney purchased, but it was certainly not Marie Antoinette's. Most likely it belonged to some lesser member of the French royal family. Given the unusual size of the nose, I would say—" He was interrupted by a loud crash that came from Staffordshire Room. The headless torso of a porcelain milkmaid flew through the doorway and landed at my feet.

"What was that?" I gasped.

"Do you have someone following us?" Kiki demanded. She rushed to the doorway and was swallowed by the darkness.

"I assure you there is no one there, Miss Strike," Lester Liu called out halfheartedly.

"The room's empty," Kiki announced when she returned. Her icy eyes fastened on Lester Liu. "I should inform you that our friends know where we are. If we're not home by midnight, the police will be called."

"I would hope so." Lester Liu frowned and patted my hand, which was still trapped in the crook of his arm. "Come along, ladies. There's much more to see."

· · ·

Oona's father led us through more than a dozen dim chambers, each a bizarre museum devoted to one of Cecelia Varney's unusual passions. Even the halls were cluttered with paintings hung from the floor to the ceiling. Lester Liu pointed out works of art long believed to be lost, including a van Gogh portrait of a sullen redheaded man, while I checked all the paintings for moving eyes, certain we were being watched. I grew increasingly jittery as the tour continued, expecting to be set upon at any moment by venomous snakes, Fu-Tsang thugs, or a lethal combination of the two. As I stood in front of a glass case in which an enormous yellow-green diamond labeled *The Florentine* was the only item on display, I thought I detected the sound of something panting behind me. When I turned to find myself alone in the room,

I nearly sprained an ankle rushing to catch up with the others.

I limped past Russian icons, astronaut PEZ dispensers, and a men's urinal inscribed with the signature *R. Mutt, 1917*. It was as if we had wandered into the most expensive flea market on earth, and I could see that Oona was tempted to do a little shopping. When she lingered in front of a pair of platinum and emerald cuffs that had once belonged to the Duchess of Windsor, Lester Liu unlocked the cabinet and offered them to her. Kiki and I shared a worried look when Oona took a little too long to refuse.

When we reached the final room on Lester Liu's tour we found it empty but for a large glass coffin.

"At last," said Lester Liu. "Allow me to introduce you to my own Sleeping Beauty."

Inside the coffin lay a thin female form clothed head to toe in a shroud of jade squares bound together by thin gold wire. Kiki knelt to study the figure; then her milky eyes snapped up to Lester Liu's face.

"It's a Chinese mummy," she noted. "Who is it?"

"Very astute, Miss Strike," said Lester Liu. "This is the finest of Cecelia Varney's possessions. The woman you see before you is known in China as the Traitor Empress. She's almost two thousand years old. Grave robbers looted her tomb in the 1940s, and Ms. Varney secretly purchased its contents with the assistance of a corrupt government official. Only a handful of people know that the Empress ever left China."

"So there's really a body in there?" I asked.

"Certainly. When they found her, she was perfectly preserved. Perhaps the most beautiful mummy ever discovered. Her skin was still soft, and there was blood in her veins. They say the condition of her hair was remarkable. Like a river of black silk. But once they removed her from her tomb, the Empress started to age. Ms. Varney spared no expense constructing this airtight coffin. Were it ever to be opened, the mummy would quickly crumble to dust.

"I've been told that Ms. Varney spent a great deal of time in the Empress's company. It seems she was quite taken with her story."

"Why do they call her the Traitor Empress?" I asked.

Lester Liu gazed down at the woman in the coffin, his expression cold.

"She betrayed her family, Miss Fisher, and for the Chinese, there is no greater crime. But then again, she was born a barbarian. Her treachery was to be expected." Leaning on his cane, Lester Liu addressed the three of us.

"The story is only a legend, but most legends begin with a grain of truth. It is said that many centuries ago, the Chinese Emperor sent his heir to make peace with the leaders of the tribes that lived to the west of his lands. There, the foolish boy fell in love with a barbarian princess. She was beautiful, but hopelessly wild. She possessed none of the feminine virtues that were prized in China, yet he was determined to take her as a wife. When the tribes' leader noticed the young man's feelings for his daughter, he was pleased. One day China would have an empress with barbarian blood.

"The Emperor agreed to the union. A blood alliance

with the barbarians was better than a never-ending war. But when he laid eyes on his son's bride-to-be, he knew she could never be Empress. Her cheeks were chapped, and her hands were hard from holding the reins of a horse. Worse still, she was stubborn and insolent and refused to abide by the rules of the court. Yet the Emperor loved his son, and his son loved the girl. He tolerated her until the day she added treason to the list of her offenses. His guards intercepted secret correspondence between the girl and her relatives. The letters revealed a plot to murder the Emperor and his heir.

"The Emperor had little choice but to have the girl executed. But he couldn't bear to break his son's heart. The girl was given a poison, which made her fall into a deep sleep, and the son was told she had died of fever. She was buried alive in the most magnificent tomb ever constructed for a female. But tales of her betrayal were whispered in court until finally the whole empire knew the terrible truth.

"They say that as the tomb was closed, the girl's barbarian servant placed a curse on the Emperor and his court. One day, she said, the Traitor Empress would awaken and have her revenge."

Oona spoke at last. "Don't you think it's a little sick to keep stuff like this in your house?" It was as if the story had broken a spell. While Lester Liu's eyes were on his daughter, I saw Kiki slip a bug inside a wall sconce. "Mummies, severed heads, what else do you have in here? Jimmy Hoffa?"

"I'm pleased to see you've recovered from your shyness, my dear. As a matter of fact, I don't intend to keep the Empress. The treasures from her tomb have been donated to the Metropolitan Museum of Art, and an exhibit will open next month. It will be the most impressive collection of ancient Chinese artifacts ever seen outside of China. The mummy is too fragile to move at the moment, but she will be the centerpiece of the show.

"Of course the opening gala will be spectacular. And nothing would please me more than to have my only child by my side."

Oona's short, obscene response was interrupted by another loud crash and a faint moan. The three of us whipped around, expecting someone to emerge from the dark room we had only recently exited. Oona and I were content to peer into the gloom from a safe distance, but Kiki again decided to investigate.

A minute later she returned with a puzzled look. "One of the paintings fell from the wall."

"Please do not concern yourself, Miss Strike," Lester Liu advised calmly, brushing invisible dust from the Empress's glass coffin. "The butler will see to it."

"What's going on?" Oona tried to disguise her fear, but the diamonds on her wrist flashed as her hands trembled. "What the hell are you trying to pull?"

Her handsome father offered an infuriating smile. "How amusing. One rarely hears such colorful language issue from the mouth of a lovely young girl. It's much like watching a monkey sing opera. I assure you that I am not *pulling* anything, my dear."

"Stop calling me that," Oona snarled. "I'm not *your* anything."

The butler entered from the far side of the room and stood as still as stone.

"Ah," said Lester Liu. "Dinner is served."

• • •

The wood-paneled dining room was dimly lit. A fire flickered at the end of the room and a single candelabrum glowed in the center of a long mahogany table. The butler guided me to a chair that seemed miles away from my friends. Across the room, Lester Liu's face was hidden in shadows. From where I sat, I could see little but the white of his shirt.

I felt the butler at my side and looked up to see him dipping a ladle into a deep tureen. The dancing dragons painted on the bottom of the bowl in front of me were drowned in a dark orange liquid. I stirred the soup with the tip of a silver spoon and a row of sharp, black spines broke the surface. My head snapped up in astonishment, and Lester Liu chuckled from across the table.

"It isn't an assassination attempt, Miss Fisher," he said. "It's sea urchin. I think you'll find it's delicious."

I blushed and brought a spoonful of the liquid to my lips. It tasted like a murky tidal pool. I thought I saw the butler smirk when he passed by on his way to the kitchen with the empty tureen. When the kitchen door closed behind him, we heard the sound of china shattering, as if he'd thrown the dish against the wall. The spoon dropped from my hand and splattered soup across the front of my dress.

"Oh dear," sighed Lester Liu. "I hope that wasn't the

second course. It's a rare Chinese delicacy—baby cobras in chili sauce."

"Is your butler always so clumsy?" sneered Oona.

"That wasn't the butler." Lester Liu paused to sip his disgusting soup. "That was my ghost."

HOW TO KNOW IF YOUR HOUSE IS HAUNTED

Just because you haven't *seen* a ghost doesn't mean that there isn't one watching *you*. According to parapsychologists, not all ghosts reveal themselves as readily as a poltergeist. Some spirits simply lurk in the shadows, content to inspire goose bumps and a creeping sense of unease in their human housemates. Others make strange noises in the dead of the night or shift objects when no one is looking. But if you suspect that you're sharing your home with the dead, there *are* some steps you can take to find out for sure.

Catch Your Ghost on Film

Experts agree that ghosts are more active at night (surprise, surprise). So when your house is suitably dark and eerie, take multiple pictures of the rooms you believe to be haunted. When examining the photos, don't discard any *bad* pictures. Cameras can record things that the human eye can't detect, and any professional ghost hunter will tell you that those strange glowing orbs, inexplicable mists, or shafts of light that *ruined* your photos may in fact be ghosts.

Log Your Observations

Whenever you hear, see, or feel something strange, jot down the time and a description of your experience. This will allow you to spot patterns to your *visitations* and may help you discover that the creepy hissing noise you hear every day at four o'clock is only the sound of sprinklers turning on in your neighbor's front yard.

Consult Your Compass

Apparently, most compasses fail to work in the presence of ghosts. When you're near a spirit, the needle may be unable to fix on a point.

Instead, it will spin around the dial or simply refuse to give an accurate reading.

Set Up a Video Recorder

Ghosts have an annoying tendency to avoid anyone who's looking for them. So instead of sitting up all night with your camera in hand, set up a video recorder and get a good night's rest. If possible, switch your camera to infrared mode, which can capture heat signatures. In the morning, watch the tape while you're eating your cereal and see what all that thumping around in the dark was about.

Keep Track of the Temperature

Many residents of haunted houses report unexplained temperature fluctuations. One spot in their otherwise toasty home may feel like Antarctica on a winter's day. Another may be unbearably hot. So keep a few indoor thermometers in key places. If nothing else, weird cold or hot spots may help you figure out where best to set up your video recorders.

Monitor Any Movements

Do you hear mysterious footsteps at midnight or wonder why the refrigerator door is always standing open in the morning? Set up a few cheap motion detectors around your home. They'll alert you to any movement and help you determine whether your house is haunted—or your sister just enjoys a forbidden midnight snack.

Invest in an EMF

Most professional ghost hunters turn to an Electromagnetic Field Detector (EMF) to help them detect unusual energy sources. Higher than normal readings may indicate the presence of a ghost (or a refrigerator, so be careful). EMFs can be purchased for as little as twenty dollars, but a compass (see above) may work just as well.

CHAPTER EIGHT

The Hungry Ghost

Most people, when they want to get to know someone better, rely on the same set of boring questions. "What do you do for a living?" they'll ask. "Where do you go to school?" "What were you doing at 9:45 p.m. on August the fifth?" While the answers to these questions may shed some light on a person's financial status, educational prowess, or homicidal tendencies, they can't really tell you what makes her tick. So whenever I meet a person for the very first time, I like to wait for the right moment and then ask if she believes in ghosts. It's a little odd, I'll admit, but that one simple question has spared me from untold hours of mind-numbing chitchat. If my new acquaintance laughs at such a silly thought or offers a condescending shake of her head, I'll soon invent an excuse to go my own way. But I'll know I'm in luck if she answers with a resounding "Yes." It makes no difference if she seems mousey, morose, or mentally unhinged. Any person who believes in ghosts has at least one good story to share.

That evening, I took one look across the table at Oona Wong and knew she was a believer. She didn't snicker at her father's assertion. Like the rest of us, she simply lowered her spoon to the table and prepared for the story she knew would follow. Lester Liu slid his soup to one side and leaned in to the candlelight. His charming smile had vanished. He wore a somber expression—a mixture of dread, grief, and fear that added years to his face.

"Cecelia Varney must not like strangers living in her house," Kiki Strike said casually, as though a haunted mansion were no more unusual than a bad bed-and-breakfast.

Lester Liu shook his head slowly. "Ms. Varney is resting in peace. The mansion didn't come with any ghosts. I'm afraid that *I'm* the one who is haunted. That's why I invited you to dinner this evening. I am hoping Oona will agree to help me."

Oona's tongue was tied so Kiki spoke for her. "Why Oona? What you need is an exorcist."

Lester Liu ignored her advice and addressed his daughter instead. "My dear," he said softly, as if preparing her for difficult news. "Have you ever heard of a hungry ghost?" Oona's eyes widened, her lips parted, and a little gasp passed between them. She seemed to know the story he was about to tell. Even Kiki was temporarily silenced.

"What's a hungry ghost?" I asked, not certain I was ready for the answer.

Across the table, Lester Liu's eyes disappeared beneath the shadow of his brow. "In China," he began, "it is said that when a person dies in a state of great anger, her soul remains on earth, trapped by a hunger for vengeance. The angrier the soul, the more powerful the ghost. Of course, the problem can grow worse if the dead person has not been provided with the things she needs in afterlife. It is under such conditions that a soul may become a hungry ghost."

A series of muffled crashes and bangs came from beyond the kitchen door.

"I have seen my ghost countless times. Her face is still beautiful, but the rest of her is nothing but bones, skin, and hair. Over the years her power has grown, and now she follows wherever I go. That is why I rarely leave this house. It is why none of the servants will stay. I find I have no choice now but to give my ghost what she desires."

Oona's face was white with terror, and even Kiki looked stricken. I was still confused. "Why is she so angry? What did you do?"

"I abandoned her child. I gave it away because it wasn't the boy I wanted. I have not been a good husband or father, Miss Fisher. Nor have I been a good man. But that must change. It is time to make amends to the people I have injured. That is what Oona's mother has been trying to tell me."

The butler emerged from the kitchen, holding a silver tray. As he made his way toward Lester Liu, I noticed that the back of his suit was dripping with slime, as if he'd been attacked by a giant slug. He whispered softly in his boss's ear.

"I'm sorry to report that we must skip directly to the third course," Lester Liu announced. "The second has not survived. It's a pity. Baby cobras are so difficult to come by in New York. Americans possess such pedestrian palates, and I am forced to import them directly from Thailand."

The butler circled the table, dropping two deep-fried crabs onto each of our plates. Mine were locked together in an embrace, as if they'd been consoling each other as they prepared to meet their fate. As soon as the servant had returned to the kitchen, Oona shoved her plate away and glared at her father. I was pleased to see the anger in her eyes.

"You want *me* to get rid of your ghost? Why should I help you? While you lived like some third-world dictator, with your creepy servants and your baby snakes, I lived in a run-down apartment with four women who could barely afford to feed me. They had to steal fabric from *your* sweatshops to make my clothes. We shared a bathroom with thirty other people and lived without heat in the winter. I had to teach myself English. I didn't even go to school until I was eight. All because I was a *girl*?" Oona was screaming now, her face ugly with rage. "You expect me to feel sorry for you now, you pathetic old man? Trapped in a mansion on Fifth Avenue with a hungry ghost? How many people have died because of you? How many people are still slaving away in your factories? It's your turn to suffer."

I wondered if Oona had gone too far. Lester Liu remained calm, but his nostrils were flared and his teeth clenched. We hadn't planted all of our bugs or uncovered any clues about the missing Taiwanese children, and if Lester Liu gave us the boot, we might never have another chance. I knew the same thought was passing through Kiki's mind. She politely excused herself and left the dining room, presumably headed for the powder room. That left me alone to witness the battle between Oona and her father.

Lester Liu addressed his daughter coolly. "In China, a child would never say such things to her father. Respect for one's parents is the most important virtue."

"Does this look like China to you?" asked Oona. "I was born *here*. I'm an American. And you're just a criminal."

"Oona," I whispered, trying to calm her.

"It's all right, Miss Fisher," said Lester Liu with a weary sigh. "My daughter has spoken the truth, I'm afraid. As you're no doubt aware, I have done terrible things. However, I am not the only criminal in our family." He turned to Oona. "I know how you afford to live as you do, my dear. I know about the forgery and the nail salon. I am sorry you were forced to abandon your morals. Your mother must be heartbroken. She was a simple woman with strong principles. That is why I have invited you here. To ask if you would, in honor of your mother, renounce the criminal life. I have already done so myself. Since you and your friends destroyed the Fu-Tsang, I have been living the life of a legitimate businessman."

"Do legitimate businessmen kidnap Taiwanese school kids?" I wanted to kick her when she said it. Leave it to Oona to put our plans in jeopardy just so she could make a point.

Lester Liu looked confused. "I'm at a loss for words, my dear. This isn't a Dickens novel. What use would I have for schoolchildren? You must know that there are many men left in Chinatown who have not made the resolutions I have made. Crime did not stop when I stopped committing it.

"I have earned more money than I could possibly spend, Oona. The factories will be closed. Debts will be forgotten. I purchased the Varney Mansion with the intention of donating most of her treasures to museums. Marie Antoinette's room will be sent back to France. The paintings will be displayed where others can see them. I will become one of the most important philanthropists in the city. A man who is admired, rather than feared. I want you to be with me. As my daughter you will finally receive the attention you deserve. New York's rich and famous will line up to meet you."

Suddenly I felt a frigid breeze on my bare shoulders. The flames of the candles were blown from their wicks, and the blaze in the fireplace surged and then vanished as if it had been sucked up through the chimney. The room went black, and a wail that might not have been wind made me faint with fear. We were not alone in the room. I fumbled blindly for the knife I had seen sitting next to my plate. Gripping it like a dagger, I waited for something to happen. I heard footsteps approaching from behind. A hand suddenly gripped my wrist, and a breathy whisper filled my ear.

"I finished upstairs. Go do the ground floor." A quick scratch and a single flame lit a ghostly face. Kiki Strike held her match to one of the candles and then used it to light the others.

"Maybe *you* prefer to dine in the dark, but I like to see what I'm not eating," she said, sitting down in front of her untouched plate.

"Excuse me," I mumbled, rising from the table and practically running for the door.

. . .

Outside the dining room, I took a tiny crystal bottle from my pocket and refreshed my Fille Fiable just as a large hand gripped my shoulder.

"Allow me to show you to the powder room," the butler droned in a deep, flat voice.

"Thanks, but I've been going to the bathroom by myself for years now." I leaned toward him and hoped the perfume would work its wonders. "If you could just point me in the right direction."

The butler paused in midbreath as if his brain were at war with itself.

"It is the third door on the right." He pointed down an unlit hallway and returned to the kitchen. I began to breathe a sigh of relief until I remembered I was in a strange mansion with a ghost on the loose.

Even in phantom-free environments, I don't care much for the dark. Like anyone with an imagination, I see shapes in the shadows and figures crouching in corners. A midnight trip to the bathroom will leave me trembling in terror, and a power outage can be practically life threatening. So while I was fairly certain that Lester Liu's ghost had no bones to pick with me, I knew if I looked I would see her everywhere. I rushed blindly through the six rooms on the hall. I vaguely remember a library, a study, a few bedrooms and a bathroom. I left bugs behind books, under chairs, and behind a toilet. (Probably not the best idea, I realized later.) In ten minutes, I was

finished. I straightened my dress, refreshed my Fille Fiable, and walked back to the dining room. It was empty,
but for the butler who was cleaning up the remains of a
roast duck that were strewn across the room and oozing
down the legs of the table. I thought for a moment that
I'd seen him smiling.

"Your friends have decided to leave, miss. They are
waiting for you in the foyer." He set down the tray of
mangled meat and led me to Oona and Kiki. Oona's
beautiful dress had been splattered with sauce and Kiki
was removing grains of rice that clung like lice to her
long black hair. Lester Liu stood with Oona's stole in his
hand, an embarrassed look on his face.

"What happened?" I asked.

"The butler claims he was pushed," said Kiki. "The
fourth course landed on Oona."

"Please accept my apologies," Lester Liu pleaded.
"The ghost usually reserves her punishments for me. I
hope you will still consider my offer?"

"Why don't you hold your breath and see what happens." Oona glowered as she grabbed her stole.

"One more thing before you go?" Lester Liu put a
hand on his daughter's arm. "Your mother would want you
to have this. It's the only picture left of her." He pulled a
photo from the inside pocket of his jacket. I caught a
glimpse of a pretty young woman in an old-fashioned
dress.

Oona snatched the picture from his hands and stormed
out the door.

"Where are you going?" I called, running to keep up
with her as she headed straight for the street, one arm

raised high in the air. A taxi on the other side of Fifth Avenue swerved across a lane of traffic and came to a halt in front of her.

"I need to be alone." Oona opened the door of the cab and jumped inside.

"Wait . . . ," I started to say, but Kiki grabbed my arm, and I let the door slam.

"Let her go," she said, lifting her hand to hail a cab. We heard a shrill whistle from across the street. Sitting on the rock wall that rings Central Park was the wild boy.

"That was fast," Kaspar remarked as we approached. "Where did Oona go? Looked like she was in a hurry."

"She had a date with a dry cleaner," I said. "She's a very messy eater."

Kaspar accepted the explanation but didn't pretend to believe it. "Did you see the snakes?" he asked.

"They were on the menu," Kiki told him. "Baby cobras in chili sauce. According to our host, they're a delicacy in China."

I shuddered at the thought. "I'd rather eat dirt from a dog run."

Kaspar wasn't amused. "Did you say *cobras*? Most cobras are endangered. You can't buy them anywhere in New York. Did your host mention how he came by them?"

"He said he imports them from Thailand," said Kiki. "You should probably know that you've spent the past day and a half watching the home of one of the most infamous smugglers in New York. There's nothing he wants that he can't get."

"Why were you were having dinner with a smuggler?"

"He wanted to introduce Oona to his ghost," I said. "And no, I'm not joking."

For a boy with his own wild stories to share, Kaspar seemed remarkably surprised. "Who *are* you guys?" he asked. "You have maps of strange places. Smugglers invite you to dinner. And I don't even know what to think about the ghost."

"It's a long story for another time," said Kiki. "I have a feeling we'll be seeing more of you. But now I've got to get home; a friend of mine is very ill."

"I'm sorry to hear that." He really did seem to be sorry. "May I ask one favor before you go?"

"Sure," said Kiki.

"Please say hello to Betty," said Kaspar. "And tell her I'm looking forward to dinner."

. . .

As our taxi sped downtown, Kiki and I sat quietly. There was too much to talk about, and neither of us knew where to start.

Finally Kiki sighed. "You smell really bad."

"I went a little overboard with the Fille Fiable right before we left. I ran into that creepy butler."

"You weren't gone for long. Are all of your bugs in place?"

"Yeah. There weren't as many rooms to cover with the east wing blocked off. So do you think there's really a ghost?"

"I don't know. Oona seems convinced."

"I feel sorry for her," I said. "The dead mother she's

never met comes back from the grave and expects Oona to become an upstanding citizen."

"I didn't buy that part. Lester Liu is after something. I just don't know what it is. I wish I could think more clearly." Kiki rested her head against the cab window and sank into silence.

"Kiki?" I asked. "Is everything okay?"

"Of course everything's not okay. I just told you that Oona's father has something up his sleeve."

"That's not what I mean. You keep missing meetings or showing up late. It's not like you. How sick *is* Verushka? Is there something I should know?"

Kiki rubbed her eyes, smearing her mascara. She took a deep breath, and I realized she was inhaling Fille Fiable.

"I made a stupid mistake," Kiki admitted. "Verushka may be dying. And even if she doesn't die, we're both in a lot of trouble."

I was too shocked to cry. Too shocked to say anything other than, "Can I see her?"

· · ·

Ten minutes later, I stood in the doorway of Verushka's room, my feet refusing to move any farther. If it hadn't been for the slow, steady rhythm of the heart monitor, I would have been the first to call an undertaker. Kiki knelt beside the bed, holding one of her guardian's lifeless blue hands and brushing her hair out of her face. Verushka's eyes fluttered and her lips moved. Kiki leaned in to listen.

"I couldn't keep it a secret forever," she replied with a tremor in her voice. "Ananka was worried about you. The others would be, too, if they knew the truth." Verushka weakly motioned for Kiki to bend forward so she could whisper in her ear.

"I won't tell her unless I have to, Verushka. I know you're right. She needs to be able to deal with her father. And I'll make sure she doesn't get herself into trouble. It's not going to be easy, though. Now there's a ghost involved."

A middle-aged man in a white coat pushed past me and busied himself at a table, preparing a syringe of colorless liquid. He held the syringe to the light and tapped it to remove any air bubbles. A stream of liquid shot from the tip of the needle.

"What are you giving her?" Kiki asked as the doctor inserted the needle into Verushka's left leg. The old woman's eyes fluttered and shut.

"You wouldn't understand," the doctor replied.

"I might," Kiki insisted, standing up and fixing her eyes on the doctor. "I'm young, not retarded."

"Look," he said, peering down imperiously at Kiki. "I have more than ten years of higher education. I'm not even sure you've been alive that long. So why don't you stop pestering me and let me do my job. You hired me to save this woman, not to provide you with a medical degree."

Kiki's eyebrow shot toward the ceiling. "Go ahead. Do your job. If you do it well, I'll forget this conversation took place," said Kiki. "But if anything happens to her, I'm going to hold *you* responsible."

The doctor rolled his eyes as Kiki stomped out of the room.

"What a jerk," I said once we were out of earshot.

"I didn't hire Dr. Pritchard for his bedside manner,"

said Kiki. "He's good and for the right price, he's willing to keep his mouth shut. Unfortunately, I'm stuck with him."

"You're not stuck with him. Let's call an ambulance and get Verushka to the hospital."

"We can't. I took her there last week. That was my big mistake. The doctors traced the problem to the bullet lodged in her leg. It was releasing cyanide into her system. I guess my aunt and her henchman had a backup plan. If the bullet didn't kill Verushka, the poison eventually would.

"When the doctors removed the bullet, I thought they'd saved her life. But then they reported the bullet wound to the police. When I caught a nurse taking Verushka's fingerprints, I smuggled her out of the hospital. I thought she'd recover, but the improvement must have been temporary. The poison is still in her system. It's killing her."

"If it's so serious, why are you worried about fingerprints?" I asked.

"Verushka is still wanted for my parents' murder," said Kiki. "And the proof of her innocence is in Pokrovia. Even if the hospital saved her life, she'd only end up in jail. I know Verushka. This is what she would want."

"Do you really think Dr. Charming can save her?" I asked.

"Personality aside, he's one of the best doctors in the city. I've spent every penny we had to make sure he has everything he needs. I'll probably have to make another kung fu film to pay the bills."

"No, you won't," I told her. "The rest of us will help. I still have the money I made from the Shadow City gold. It's all yours."

"Thanks," said Kiki, as our cell phones began beeping.

A text message had arrived for each of us. "*Golden Lotus. Tomorrow. Noon. Oona.*"

"You have bigger problems than Lester Liu," I told Kiki. "Stay with Verushka until she's better. I'll take care of the meeting tomorrow."

• • •

I crawled back through my window before the clock struck midnight. As I changed out of my fancy dress, I listened at the door of my room. My parents were still awake. I could hear the faint sound of angry German voices and the *rat-a-tat* of machine-gun fire coming from the living room. If they were relaxed enough to enjoy a movie, my activities must have gone undiscovered. Exhausted as I was, there was still one thing left to do before I lay down to sleep. I opened my door and tiptoed down the hall to the guest bedroom.

At 11:00 the next morning, after my father had left for his Saturday study group, I approached my mother as she poured herself some coffee. As much as I would have liked to wait until she'd consumed her third or fourth cup, my mission couldn't be postponed.

"I need to go to the library," I informed her.

"Sure you do." For someone fairly new to sarcasm, she was getting quite good at it.

"I'm serious." I held up my notebook and showed her the beginning of the essay Principal Wickham had assigned. "I'm writing an important paper on the Underground Railroad. It could keep me from getting an F in Mr. Dedly's class, but we don't have two of the books that I need to finish it."

My mother was bemused. "Our nineteenth-century American history books are in the closet in the guest bedroom. You know that. If you're looking for something we don't already own, I doubt you'll find it at the library."

"We used to have the books, but they're not there anymore. Dad must have taken them," I said. "You know how he's always loaning stuff out."

My father's lending habits were my mother's pet peeve. "Which books do you need?" she asked. I handed her a scrap of paper with two titles listed on it. "Let's have a look, shall we?"

I waited patiently for half an hour as my mother searched the guest bedroom closet. Unless she checked under my mattress, she had no hope of finding them.

"I wish your father wouldn't treat our house like the New York Public Library." She finally sighed and consulted her watch. "You've got two hours, Ananka. If you're not back by one thirty, I'm coming to get you. And you better be sure that I'll make a scene."

· · ·

The Golden Lotus nail salon, ten blocks north of the library, was closed for business for the first time in over a year. A sign was clearly posted on the door, yet I arrived to find a woman in a mink coat and sunglasses peeking through the window, searching for signs of movement and finding it hard to believe that she might have to wait a whole day for a pedicure.

"Excuse me," she said in the same tone of voice she must have used when addressing other people's maids. "Do you work here? Do you speak English?"

I looked around, wondering if she might be talking to someone behind me. There was no one there. "No," I informed the woman as I rapped on the door. "I don't speak English."

"Do . . . you . . . give . . . man-i-cures?" she inquired, enunciating each word as if she were speaking to an idiot rather than a foreigner.

"Can . . . you . . . read?" I asked, tapping at the *closed* sign on the door.

The woman stood back in shock as DeeDee unlocked the door to the salon and let me in.

"Go do your own nails," I told the woman before I slammed the door behind me.

• • •

On the floor of the salon's front room, a mosaic depicted an ancient Greek oracle lost in a trance. Luxurious manicure stations lined walls, and the chairs and tables were covered in crisp white linen. In the back of the building, at the end of a long row of waxing rooms, was Oona's office. One of the doors in the narrow hallway stood open, and I caught a glimpse of Yu sleeping on a table.

"He's been working all morning," DeeDee explained. "But he's still a little weak. Oona made him take a nap."

"Oona put Yu to work? What's wrong with her?"

"No, Yu wanted to do something nice for Oona. He insisted. Wait till you see what he's done."

"Did Oona tell you about last night?"

"Yeah," said DeeDee. "Creepy, huh? Luz is setting up her equipment. She's got recordings from all the bugs. We'll find out what Lester Liu is up to."

I opened the door to Oona's office and stopped dead in my tracks. On the wall behind her desk was the top half of a mural that showed the six Irregulars engaged in a valiant battle with the rats of the Shadow City. The image looked so real that it might have been a photograph. I could even make out individual whiskers on each of the rats.

"Yu painted this?" I asked. "He saw the rest of us only once. How did he remember our faces so well?"

Oona shrugged. "I guess somebody kidnapped the most talented kid in Taiwan. He's been painting Mrs. Fei's portrait, too, and now she's his biggest fan. It's always Yu this and Yu that. It's all so sweet that it makes me want to vomit. So is Kiki coming?"

"She said she'd catch up with you later. So what do you think about last night? Is your dad still on the wrong side of the law?"

Oona nodded. "I'll admit he had me going for a while, but when I woke up this morning, I knew it was all a scam. The ghost, the mummy, the exhibit, everything. I can't wait to listen to the bugs."

"Oona?" I said, my eyes suddenly drawn to the jewelry on her wrist. "Where did you get those bracelets?" She was wearing the same platinum cuffs she'd been admiring at Lester Liu's house.

"You mean *these*?" Oona asked, trying to make light of the situation. "They came by messenger this morning. I guess they're my father's way of apologizing for last night."

"You *are* going to return them, aren't you?"

"Who do you think you are—my probation officer?"

snapped Oona. "I haven't had time. Besides, who's it hurting if I wear them around the office for a little while?"

"You," I said.

"Okay, guys, I'm all set up, so postpone the catfight. We're ready for business." Luz Lopez had been watching from the hallway, with her hands shoved deep into the pockets of her jumpsuit. She motioned for us to follow her into one of the waxing rooms, where her laptop computer was open on the table. Betty, acting as Luz's assistant, handed out cordless headphones.

"Betty and I went through all of last night's feeds," Luz said. "Most had nada. One kept recording a toilet flushing and a few other things you probably don't want to hear. But we did get some interesting stuff. I'll play the best part first."

Betty turned to Oona. "This might be hard for you. Are you sure you want to listen?"

"Whatever it is, I can take it," Oona assured her.

We inserted the headphones into our ears and gave Luz the thumbs-up. The recording began suddenly with the sound of footsteps on a marble floor and what I imagined were ice cubes tinkling in a glass.

"Thank you, Sukh." It was Lester Liu's exhausted voice. "That will be all for tonight."

"I apologize for the disturbances this evening, sir," said the butler in his distinctive monotone.

"You're not to blame. How could I be anything but grateful to you? You're the only servant who's stayed. Such loyalty is rare in this world."

"It has been an honor, sir."

"That will be all, Sukh."

"Yes, sir."

Luz fast-forwarded through several minutes of silence. The recording started again with the sound of a glass shattering and a shriek.

"Get back!" Lester Liu screamed. "Don't come any closer." In the background, I could hear panting—quick, shallow breaths like those of a rabid animal. It was the same sound I had heard in the mansion.

"I tried!" he pleaded. "You frightened her away, but I tried. Don't I deserve one night of peace?" The panting slowed and became labored, as if the creature were struggling to breathe. A wail started softly and rose to a deafening pitch.

"Please," begged Lester. "Please. I will do what I can tomorrow. I'll do anything to stop this. Anything! No! No!" The last word was delivered at top volume and followed by the thump of a body hitting the floor. The recording stopped.

"That's pretty much it," Luz explained. "The butler comes back and helps him to his room, but then there's nothing more for hours. I can check the stuff that's been coming in this morning, if you're interested."

"I don't need to hear any more." Oona's face was ashen, and her eyes mesmerized by the computer screen.

"You know, Oona," Luz began. "I can't believe I'm going to suggest this. I mean, it goes against everything I believe as a scientist, but there may be someone who can help you."

"Who?" asked Oona.

"My mother goes to see this guy. He's a medium—you

know, he says he can talk to dead people. Anyway, my mom's convinced that he's been in touch with her sister who died in Cuba fifteen years ago. I always thought it was a scam, but now I don't know. It makes her feel better at least. It might help you to talk to him."

"Oh, come on, Luz," I moaned. "You *can't* be serious."

"Give me the address," said Oona.

CHAPTER NINE

The Gifted One

In Manhattan you can always tell a tourist by the angle of her head. Though most of the city belongs to the sky, New Yorkers rarely look up. We're more likely to stare straight ahead as we shove through the crowds—or fix our eyes on our feet as we weave around steaming dog piles and treacherous subway grates. Most of us take the familiar for granted, but in a city like New York, nothing stays familiar for long. Those who don't mind being mistaken for tourists will find gargoyles leering down at them, cat burglars inching across ledges, or window washers dangling from thin metal wires. All it takes is the curiosity to stop and see the world from a different perspective.

The address Luz had given us belonged to an old office building near Madison Square Park. Oona and I stood in front of it with our heads tilted back at an uncomfortable angle. The overcast sky hid the top of the structure from view.

"Are you sure this is it?" asked Oona. "I was expecting something a little more . . ."

"Mysterious?" I offered as the clouds thinned and we caught a glimpse of the upper floors. On top of the otherwise ordinary building sat a penthouse designed to resemble an ancient Greek temple. A wisp of smoke from a nearby chimney weaved between the sturdy stone columns that supported the structure. Painted on the triangular pediment beneath the building's roof, a single green eye looked out over Manhattan.

"Is that what you had in mind?" I asked.

"Pretty much," murmured Oona.

Inside the lobby, we scanned a list of the building's businesses. Tucked between *Norton's Custom Taxidermy* and the *Proctology Association of Manhattan* was *Oskar Phinuit, Liaison to the Spirit World.*

"Looks like we're going to the penthouse." I felt a pleasant twinge of excitement in my belly. Oona merely looked nauseous.

. . .

An old-fashioned elevator delivered us to the twenty-fifth floor. Tall windows lit a room that was empty but for a single desk. Behind it sat an elderly woman wearing a tweed suit that must have been purchased before the Second World War. The waves in her ebony hair looked hard to the touch, and the bud of a black rose was pinned to her lapel.

"We bought two dozen chocolate bars from your schoolmates yesterday." She spoke in the clipped, crisp voice of a 1940s movie star. "Come back tomorrow. We may have need for more then."

"We're not here to sell candy." I felt a little annoyed. At certain times of the year, it was hard to go anywhere in the city without adults expecting you to force chocolate on them. "We have an appointment with Mr. Phinuit."

"*Monsieur* Phinuit, if you please. And your name is . . ."

"The appointment is for my friend. Her name is Oona Wong."

"I see." The woman peered over the rims of her glasses. "Does Oona Wong speak?"

"Too much." My joke landed with a thud. "She's just a little nervous," I added.

"In that case, please come forward." The woman retrieved a clipboard from a desk drawer.

"Oona would like to reach—"

"No, no, no!" The woman wagged a finger at me. "Don't tell me. And for heaven's sake, don't tell Monsieur Phinuit. If the person you're trying to contact would like to be reached, Monsieur Phinuit will know. Now, there are a few questions I must ask you. Are either of you prone to fainting?"

We both shook our heads.

"Do you have any imaginary friends or hear voices in your head? Good. Are you currently taking any medication or abusing any controlled substances? Good. Have you visited a medium in the past? No? That's fine. Have you ever had a near-death experience in which you saw a bright light at the end of a tunnel? No? Well, I suppose you're both still young. Last question. Did you happen to bring any food with you? No? Excellent. It would interfere with Monsieur Phinuit's ability to concentrate."

She made a few notes on her clipboard and shoved it back inside its drawer.

"Please follow me, and I will take you to Monsieur Phinuit. Remember, it's important that you speak as little as possible. Answer any questions he may ask, but do not volunteer any information." The receptionist rose from her chair and with one quick yank, straightened her long, tight skirt. She moved quickly across the wooden floorboards in impossibly tiny steps and stopped in front of the room's only door.

"May you reach the other side," she said.

. . .

Beyond the door lay a larger room. Three of its walls were entirely glass, and for a moment, I experienced the sensation of floating in space. A dense, gray fog pressed against the windows, swirling and churning. What appeared to be faces and figures formed in the clouds but dissolved before my brain could make sense of them. My ears detected a faint hiss—the sound of a crowd whispering in the distance.

"*Bonjour.*" Near the far windows, an enormous man filled a wooden chair big enough to serve as a park bench. "Please. Come closer." As we obeyed his command, a weak beam of sunshine briefly pierced the fog, and Oskar Phinuit's black suit shimmered like snakeskin. His dainty hands rested on top of his spectacular stomach, and the emerald ring on his left pinky rose and fell with his breath. His face wore an oddly sated expression, like a python that's devoured an entire sheep. I wondered if he had eaten everything in the room.

"Have a seat." He motioned to two metal folding chairs positioned in front of him. "I apologize if you find my furniture uncomfortable. I must keep my surroundings free of clutter. Even ordinary objects emit psychic signals that can interfere with my ability to channel the spirit world."

Recalling the receptionist's warning, Oona and I took our seats silently. Oskar Phinuit examined us with two green eyes that floated like olives in a sea of pasty flesh.

"May I be so rude as to ask your age?"

"Fourteen." I would have preferred to add a few years, but it's best to be honest when dealing with psychics.

Oskar's eyes opened and shut in one lazy blink. The rest of him remained motionless. "And you would like to talk to the dead?"

"Yes."

"I see. That may be difficult to achieve. Most children have not lived long enough to forge many contacts in the spirit world. It would be far easier to tell you about your past lives. After all, it was not so long ago that you both were enjoying other existences. Your friend, I believe, was a woman of high standing. You may have known each other."

The last thing I needed was to hear that I had been Oona's maid in a previous life.

"That would be fascinating, I'm sure, but my friend needs to reach someone."

"Didn't my secretary tell you? It makes no difference if the young lady is trying to reach the dead. We must see if they are trying to reach *her*."

"She thinks she's already been contacted—by the person's ghost."

"Oh? She's seen a ghost, has she?" Oskar's mouth opened to release a breathy chuckle, and I was unnerved to see no evidence of teeth. "Let me guess. It wasn't the best-behaved spirit. It threw things, didn't it? Made a bit of a mess?"

At last Oona spoke. "How did you know?"

"Poltergeists—noisy ghosts—often appear in the presence of girls your age. For some reason, they aren't quite as interested in boys or adults. No one knows why. Some of my colleagues claim that the troublesome spirits are mere hoaxes—naughty little girls teaching their elders a lesson. But I am of a different opinion. It is my belief that adolescence is a time of great power. It may be that the spirits flock to feast on that energy. Or perhaps poltergeists are powers inside of the girls that have yet to be harnessed."

"You're saying that Oona could be causing the haunting?"

"It is within the realm of possibility. But before we draw too many conclusions, let's see if there is indeed a spirit on the other side who would like to speak with your friend." Oskar's eyes rolled back and his head fell forward until it rested on his multiple chins. "There is someone here with us." Oskar's voice was garbled, and I wondered if he was finding it difficult to breathe. Behind him, the clouds pressed against the windows as if we were racing through the sky. "A lovely woman of Asian decent. She died many years ago, but she has not found peace." I glanced over at Oona, who was sitting bolt upright in her chair. "She insists that you change your laundry detergent."

"Are you kidding? Laundry detergent?" Oona muttered.

"Silence!" Oskar roared. "The spirits say what they need to say. Umm-humm? Umm-humm. She wants you to know that you are not alone. Someone is always listening."

Oona leaned over and whispered in my ear. "Do you think this spirit writes for Hallmark?"

"Oona, shut up," I mouthed, hoping Oskar hadn't heard her.

"There's something more," he continued. "You have found yourself faced with a decision. You must choose what to keep and what to let go. If you choose wisely, you will have everything you've always desired."

Oona was serious once more. "Can the ghost tell me about my father? Does he really want me as his daughter, or is he trying to lure me into a trap?"

A deep crevice appeared in the fat on Oskar's forehead as he concentrated. "The message is not entirely clear," he said. "The spirit says that you must not look to your father for answers. You will find them only inside yourself. The time has come for you to grow up and do your duty. When you accept someone's love, you accept a great responsibility. Now the spirit is fading. She has said her piece."

"That's it?" Oona couldn't believe it.

"Wait a moment. There's another spirit entering the room. An older woman with dark glasses. I believe she may be blind. She has a message for the other girl in the room."

"Really?" I blurted. My great-aunt Beatrice had met her end in August shortly after entering the record books as the first sight-impaired senior citizen to reach the summit of Mount Everest. Later that month, two climbers had come across her corpse sitting upright in the snow, a radiant smile on her frozen lips.

"She says you should be doing your homework," Oskar announced. "Wait a moment. I suspect she may be joking. It's very difficult to tell with the dead sometimes. She wants you to know that the answer to your dilemma lies under the temple. Now she, too, has vanished." Oskar's eyes rolled down and he blinked rapidly as they adjusted to the light. "The spirits are fickle today. At times they'll ramble for hours and hours. Other days, it's a merely a word or two. Did you hear what you needed to hear?"

"Maybe." Oona's voice lacked emotion.

"Thank you for your time," I said as Oona bolted for the door.

. . .

As soon as we were in the elevator, Oona grasped my wrists like a castaway clutching a life preserver.

"We have to go the Shadow City," she insisted.

"You mean right now?" Her grip was tight enough to leave bruises, but I managed to wriggle free.

"I need to know if my father's behind the kidnappings. We've got to get Kiki and take Yu down to the tunnels. Maybe he can lead us to the other kids."

"Oona, Yu's still weak. And Kiki won't be able to come. I'm not supposed to tell you this, but Verushka may be dying. Kiki needs to stay with her."

The doors of the elevator slid open, and I stepped out, but Oona didn't budge.

"Verushka's dying?" she uttered as the doors began to close. I shoved my arm between them and received a painful pinch before they opened once more.

"The bullet in her leg was poisoned."

"We've got to get Mrs. Fei over to their house right now! She'll know how to save her."

"Kiki's already hired a doctor. He's got the personality of a Gila monster, but he's supposed to be good."

Oona's breathing began to sputter and her eyes wouldn't settle. "Oh my God!" she wailed. "Everything's falling apart!" I suddenly realized why Verushka had kept her sickness a secret. I'd just pushed Oona over the edge.

"Calm down," I urged, feeling a little panicked myself. "There's still a chance that Verushka could recover. And you having a nervous breakdown isn't going to help anyone."

"But what should I do? I don't know if my father wants to spoil me or kill me, and now some porky medium tells me I have to *do my duty*? What if Lester Liu hasn't gone legit? What if he *did* kidnap those kids? Am I still supposed to play his doting daughter? Do I owe him something just because we're related?"

"Are you sure that's what the spirit was trying to say? It was all a little confusing, if you ask me."

"My mother's ghost said that if I made the right choice, I'd have everything I ever desired. Don't you think that means I should accept Lester Liu's offer?"

I hoped not. If Lester Liu gave Oona everything she desired, what would that mean for the Irregulars?

"I think she said that you should already know what to do."

"Well, I *don't*. Who knows—maybe Oskar Phinuit made the whole thing up. Some of that stale old mumbo jumbo could have come straight from a fortune cookie. And that stuff about the laundry detergent—what was *that* about?"

"I don't know, Oona, but I think you should listen to what he said. The second spirit did sound a lot like my great-aunt Beatrice."

"Yeah, and the answer to all your problems *lies under the temple*. Where's the answer to *my* problems? It's not in the detergent aisle at the grocery store, I know that much for sure. Please, Ananka. Can we just have a quick look around the Shadow City?"

I checked the clock on my cell phone. At eleven thirty I'd told my mother I'd be gone for two hours, and now it was almost four o'clock.

"All right, Oona. Let's go back to the salon. If Yu is feeling up to it, we'll take him down to the tunnels."

"Thank you." Oona sighed with relief. I couldn't remember if I'd ever heard her use those two words before.

· · ·

Betty and DeeDee pounced on us as soon as we entered the Golden Lotus.

"I'm so glad you're back!" Betty couldn't stand still. She had been pacing the floor and was finding it difficult to stop.

"Where's Yu?" asked Oona, barreling past her.

"He was working too hard," DeeDee explained, as Oona frantically checked the waxing rooms. "He nearly fainted. Luz took him home in a cab."

"Oona, come back," Betty called. "Something's happened." It was then that I nearly sat on a Malaysian giant squirrel that had curled up in one of the manicurists' chairs.

"Did he come to pick you up for your date?" I teased.

"What's that thing doing here?" Oona snapped. "This isn't a zoo. Get your boyfriend's beast out of my salon."

"He's *not* my boyfriend. Would you listen? I'm trying to tell you something. The squirrel snuck through the door while we were helping Yu into the taxi. It came to deliver *this*."

Betty handed me a scrap of paper that was still damp with squirrel spit. On it were written the first few lines of a love letter that ended abruptly with one scrawled word: *Help*.

"I think Kaspar's in trouble," said Betty. "The squirrel won't leave. We've tried to let him out, but he won't go."

"Squirrel boy lives in Central Park. If he didn't know how to take care of himself he'd be buried with all the John Does on Hart Island by now," said Oona dismissively. "He's probably just trying to get your attention. It doesn't matter, anyway. We don't have time to worry about him right now. I need your help."

"Oona," I said in my most soothing tone. "We've got to look into this right away. We can go to the Shadow City later. Yu isn't even here. What do you expect us to do?"

"I *expect* you to get your priorities straight. Who's more important, Ananka? Me or some kid who let a bunch of squirrels attack Luz?"

"Of course you're more important," DeeDee tried to

explain. "And if you were in trouble, we'd drop everything. But if your problem can wait for a little while, we've got to help Kaspar."

Oona's energy disappeared in an instant. "Whatever. Do what you want. What good are you guys, anyway? You're never around when I need you. Kiki doesn't even show up half the time, and the rest of you are more interested in a kid you barely know. So go ahead, get out of my salon."

"You're kicking us out?" Betty muttered in disbelief. "You're not going to help us find Kaspar?"

"I've got my own problems," Oona announced, stomping toward her office. On the wall behind her desk, the mural of the Irregulars was almost complete. "I've always had to do things on my own, and I guess I always will." With that, Oona slammed the door. Betty, DeeDee, and I traded incredulous glances.

"Impressive temper tantrum," said DeeDee.

"She's just stressed out," I replied. "She'll come around."

"Always the optimist." DeeDee didn't believe it for a minute.

. . .

Our first stop was Central Park. Not far from Lester Liu's mansion we heard someone sobbing. The noise appeared to be emanating from an azalea bush the size of a MINI Cooper. I peeked between the branches and found Kaspar's friend Howard Van Dyke huddled in the hollowed-out center of the bush, cuddling a plump, red-feathered chicken. Curled up next to him were two giant squirrels and a kitten. Howard's tears stopped when he saw me.

"Have you come to take me away?" he asked, wiping his nose on the sleeve of his jacket.

"No, Howard. It's me, Ananka. Kaspar introduced us, remember?"

"Oh yes!" Howard was suddenly cheerful. "This is April," he said, holding up the chicken. "She's the only friend I have left. I saved her from an evil chef at Tavern on the Green, and we've pledged eternal friendship."

"It's nice to meet you, April," I said, trying to sound social. "Howard, have you seen Kaspar lately?"

Howard began to cry again. His chicken squawked when he hugged it to his chest.

"Kaspar's gone. They've taken him back to his cage."

"What do you mean? Can you remember who took him?"

Howard thought for a moment. "I remember . . . I remember this morning we were eating beans right over there."

"Okay, that's a good start. Do you remember anything else?"

"I remember a man with shiny hair. He was wearing one of my old suits."

My hope faded a little. "How did he get one of your old suits?"

"I don't know. But it was one of the suits I used to wear when I worked on Wall Street."

"So you're saying it was nice?"

"Three-button Prince-of-Wales-check worsted wool."

"What did the man in the suit do?"

"He hit me very hard. When I woke up, my friend Kaspar was gone."

"Do you have any idea why he took him?"

"Yes. They want to make him do tricks like the seals at the zoo."

"They?" I asked. "You mean his parents?" Howard nodded. I looked back at Betty and DeeDee. We had the information we needed.

"Howard?" Betty poked her head into the bush. "Are you hungry?"

"That man spilled my beans," sobbed Howard.

"We'll help you get something to eat. Can you step out of the bush for a minute?"

Howard crawled out on all fours, then stood up and brushed himself off. April the chicken stayed loyally by his side.

"Here's some money," said Betty. "Go get some food and I'll be back to check on you later."

Howard looked down at the twenty-dollar bill in his hand. "Can I have a chicken salad sandwich?" he asked with excitement.

"Sure," said Betty. "Just promise me that you won't share with April."

. . .

"Where are we going?" DeeDee asked once we were out of earshot. I was leading them to the other side of the park. Three large black squirrels scampered alongside us.

"I think we need to see some shrinks," I said.

"What?" DeeDee exclaimed, hurrying to catch up with me.

"We're going to see Kaspar's parents," Betty explained. "His real name is Phineas Parker. His mom and dad are psychologists."

"How do you guys know that?"

"I had detention with one of their patients," I informed DeeDee. "She told me about Kaspar."

"You think his parents kidnapped him?" DeeDee asked.

"There's only one way to find out." I pointed above the trees to the top of a building. Jagged towers of stone rose along its edges like the battlements of an enchanted castle. "Their office is in there."

When we reached the edge of Central Park West, Kaspar's squirrels took one look at the Parkers' building and bolted back through the trees. As cold as the park must have gotten at night, they still weren't ready to leave.

Drs. Parker and Parker shared a space on the first floor of 55 Central Park West. We were buzzed inside and greeted by a young woman dressed in designer jeans, a hoodie, and a Che Guevara T-shirt. Her glasses were self-consciously cool and her highlighted hair pulled back in a playful ponytail. She was clearly paid to put children at ease. It wasn't working.

"Hey, guys!" she sang as if she were overjoyed to see us. "I'm Shiva. Are you here to see Jane and Artie?"

"Who?" I asked. Shiva frowned.

"Do you have an appointment?" she demanded in a far less friendly tone.

"No," I said. "We're looking for the parents of Phineas Parker. We're friends of his."

"Hold on." Shiva turned her back to us and spoke

quietly into a walkie-talkie. "*Artie*, there are three girls here who say they know Phineas. . . . Okay . . . May I take them to the waiting room? . . . Oh, *Artie*, you're so brilliant. . . . Okay . . . Thank you, *Artie*." The way she said *Artie* made me nauseous. I wondered what *Jane* thought about it.

When Shiva spun back around, her fake smile had returned. "Follow me, guys, and I'll show you to the waiting room. Jane and Artie are with a client right now, but they'll be out soon."

She guided us down a hallway that had been painted a child-pacifying shade of green. Dozens of paintings lined the walls, each a perfect copy of a masterpiece, only with a detail or two altered to amusing effect. Rembrandt's famous self-portrait showed the artist with a finger shoved up his nose. The *Mona Lisa* wore a pair of brass knuckles. *The Girl with a Pearl Earring*'s upper lip was curled into a snarl.

"Here you go." Shiva held a door open for us. "Have a seat. It will be a couple of minutes. Just make yourselves comfortable."

We entered a cluttered, windowless space. Wooden chairs in primary colors huddled around three little tables. Each of the tables was piled with books with titles such as *The Burden of Genius, Einstein's Tears, Coping with Mediocrity,* and *The Fountainhead.* A chalkboard with a long mathematical equation scrawled from top to bottom stood in one corner of the room. Two little feet peeked out beneath it.

"What kind of shrinks are the Parkers?" Betty asked before she knew we had company.

"They specialize in helping gifted children," I said. "There's one hiding behind the chalkboard."

I rolled one side of the chalkboard away from the wall and peered down at a young boy crouched in the corner, hugging a stuffed bear with his legs folded against his chest.

"Hi there," I said. "My name is Ananka. Why are you hiding?"

The boy looked up at me with big brown eyes that were neither sad nor scared. He said nothing, but blinked rapidly for half a minute.

I tried again. "Why don't you come out and sit with us? There's nothing to be frightened of. We're all very nice."

The boy dropped his bear and made a series of lightning-quick signs with his hands.

"I think he may be deaf," I told DeeDee and Betty.

The boy sighed with frustration and pulled a pen and a scrap of paper from his shirt pocket. He scribbled furiously for a few moments, then handed me a note.

APPARENTLY YOU DO NOT UNDERSTAND
MORSE CODE OR SIGN LANGUAGE. I AM
NOT HIDING FROM YOU, NOR AM I DEAF.
I AM UNDER SURVEILLANCE. THE ROOM IS
EQUIPPED WITH TWO VIDEO CAMERAS. THIS
IS A SOCIAL EXPERIMENT. MY DOCTORS
WANT TO OBSERVE MY INTERACTIONS
WITH NORMAL CHILDREN. I HAVE NOTHING
AGAINST YOUR KIND. I'M SIMPLY NOT IN
THE MOOD TO BE STUDIED TODAY.
                              GEOFFREY

"Lovely penmanship," I said softly. "Where are the cameras?"

Geoffrey pointed to two small boxes mounted near the ceiling. They looked quite innocent aside from the cluster of wires that led from the back of the boxes into the wall.

"Hey, DeeDee," I said, walking toward one of the boxes. "Give me a leg up." DeeDee shot me a suspicious look but bent down with her hands locked together. When she lifted me into the air, I grabbed hold of the wires and yanked them out of the box. "One more," I told her, heading for the other corner.

"They won't be pleased," warned Geoffrey from behind the chalkboard.

"I don't care if they're pleased," I said, speaking directly into the second camera. "It's illegal in New York to video-tape people and record their conversations without their permission. And I don't recall being asked to sign any re-lease forms." With that, I pulled the wires from the second box.

"You can come out now," I told the little boy. "The cameras are off."

"Thank you." Geoffrey looked as relieved as a dog let out for its morning walk. "But I'm afraid their experiment was useless anyway. Given your knowledge of New York State law, I can see that you're hardly *normal*. Your IQ must be well above average."

"I'm not a genius," I said. "I just read a lot."

"How do you think geniuses become geniuses?"

"Do the doctors experiment on you often?" asked Betty.

"It's Shiva. She's the worst. I'm her graduate school project. It's my own fault, really. I wanted to fit in with other people my age, but my parents think it's abnormal to want to be normal. This is my punishment. I'll be here until I can accept that I'm different."

"That's terrible," Betty commiserated. "Why don't you pretend to be cured?"

Geoffrey sighed. "Nobody needs to tell me I'm different. I've known it all my life. But I refuse to let Shiva think she's won. She'll never graduate if I have anything to do with it."

Shiva barged into the room, and Geoffrey scurried back to his hiding place.

"Those cameras were expensive, you little brats!"

"That's the price of breaking the law," I said. "Who do you think you are, anyway, Jane Goodall?"

"I'd *rather* work with gorillas. They have better manners," Shiva snarled.

"Yeah, and they can't stand up for themselves. Look. We didn't come here to take part in your sick experiments. Are we going to see the Parkers or not?"

"Fine," Shiva growled through clenched teeth. "Follow me. I'm through with you anyway."

· · ·

Drs. Parker and Parker shared an office that resembled an art gallery. The walls were painted a blinding white and decorated with a series of paintings that showed animals staring mournfully from behind bars.

"Hello," said a man with a closely trimmed red goatee. He was wearing the sort of outfit that was meant to look thrown together but was probably assembled by a team of experts and cost more than an average car. "I'm

Dr. Arthur Parker. This is my wife, Dr. Jane Parker." His wife stepped forward to shake our hands. Everything about her appearance—from her belted sweater to her colorful glasses—was meant to convey warmth and trustworthiness. But something in her manner made me suspect that she didn't care much for children.

"Shiva tells us you know Phineas," the male Parker said. "Do you mind if we ask how you met him?"

"His squirrels attacked one of our friends in Morningside Park," I replied.

"Oh." Dr. Parker frowned. He walked to the other side of his desk and pulled out a checkbook. "How much do you need to cover the damages?"

"We're not here for money," said Betty. "We're here to find Phineas. We're worried about him."

"Why would *you* be worried about *him*?" asked Kaspar's mother as if it were the most ridiculous statement she'd ever heard.

"Someone kidnapped him from Central Park this morning," I informed them. "We're wondering if you had anything to do with it."

"First of all," said Kaspar's father, as if he were trying to talk some sense into a dim-witted goat, "if we were responsible, it wouldn't be kidnapping. We *are* his parents."

"We spoke to a friend of his a few minutes ago," I said. "He saw Phineas being dragged away by a man with slicked-back hair and a fancy suit." An epiphany followed the image that flashed through my mind, but I didn't dare share it.

Kaspar's parents traded a secret smile. "Yes, that's how he ran away from home. He hired a homeless man to make his disappearance look like a kidnapping. It was a month before we discovered he was living in the park. You see, Phineas is different. He's not like you. He's *special*."

Kaspar's father jumped in with a phony smile. "Now, Jane, I'm sure they're all special in their own ways. It's just that our son is gifted in ways that you wouldn't understand."

"Try us." DeeDee was sick of having her intelligence questioned.

"*Dear . . .* ," warned Arthur Parker.

"If you insist," said Kaspar's mother, as if she'd been hoping we would ask. "Look around you. Our son is responsible for all of the paintings in this room. Others in the same series have been sold at auction for more than thirty thousand dollars. Impressive, wouldn't you say?" We all agreed. "Okay. What if I told you they were painted when he was five?"

I focused on one of the paintings. It showed a monkey slumped forlornly in the corner of a cage. Its limbs were limp and its head rested against its chest. Outside the cage, a leering crowd had gathered. A burly man's arm was pulled back as he prepared to hurl a peanut at the little creature. It was an impressive piece of work for a five-year-old.

"I'd say it makes me want to cry," said Betty. It didn't take much to make her cry, but I was feeling a little teary eyed myself.

Kaspar's mother beamed. "Yes, it can be painful to find yourself faced with such superior talent."

"Our son first began to show promise as a toddler,"

said Arthur Parker. "He was little more than two when he used his crayons to copy the Picasso drawings we have hanging in our home. Some have even suggested he improved on Picasso's work. After that, scholars from all over the world traveled to New York to observe him. Asia's foremost expert on gifted children spent more than six months with Phineas, testing the limits of his talent. According to his report, there are no limits."

"That's what inspired us to leave our jobs in advertising and help other children like Phineas realize their potential," said Jane Parker. "Coping with genius isn't easy. Phineas has always been more sensitive than other children."

"Yes," her husband agreed. "These paintings, for instance, were done after an outing to the zoo. While the other children giggled and pointed at the animals, Phineas cried. He couldn't bear to see the animals being gawked at in their cages."

"He's always adored animals," said Jane Parker. "That's why we gave him the squirrels. Other children have dogs and cats, of course. Phineas needed something a little more unique. But he refused to keep his pets locked up. He insisted they run wild. You should see what damage a giant squirrel can do to an antique coatrack." She and her husband chuckled at the memory.

"The point is," Arthur Parker said, "we want our son back. If he remains in the park, the loss to science will be incalculable. But please, let *us* worry about him. Don't search for him yourselves. I don't want you to be hurt if you discover he doesn't want you to find him. He's always had young women chasing after him. Some of them have even been geniuses in their own right."

"What my husband is saying is that if you keep chasing Phineas away, we may never be able to bring our son home," Jane Parker told us.

"You're both insane, aren't you?" asked DeeDee. She had been fuming throughout the entire speech, and by the time it was over I'd never seen her so angry. "We just told you that your son's in danger, and you act like we're a bunch of silly groupies?"

Kaspar's father smiled placidly. "You see, Jane, I knew they wouldn't understand. I think it's time we got back to work. You girls can leave now."

"Well, you know what you can do?" DeeDee started. I grabbed her arm and dragged her out of the office

"You can go to . . ." Betty finished DeeDee's thought in a calm, clear voice before she closed the door behind us.

· · ·

"Can you believe those people?" DeeDee raged as we slipped back into the park. "No wonder the kid lives in the park! No wonder he sets all the animals free!"

"Calm down, DeeDee," I said.

"Calm down?" she shouted. "I was trying to help their brilliant son, and all I got in return were a bunch of veiled insults."

"Maybe his parents were right," Betty mumbled. "Maybe Kaspar is avoiding us. What if the Eau Irresistible wore off and he decided he didn't want to make good on our date?"

"Howard *saw* Kaspar get kidnapped," I argued.

"Howard's sweet, but he hangs out with a chicken. He might not be the most credible witness," Betty said.

"He's a lot more reliable than those two kooks. I suggest we start thinking about what to do next," DeeDee insisted.

"I thought of something when I was describing the guy who took Kaspar," I said. "Slicked-back hair, fancy suit, sadistic tendencies. You know who that sounds like?"

Betty looked at me and DeeDee and shook her head. "Who?" she asked.

"Sergei Molotov."

"Livia's henchman? The guy who shot Verushka? Why would he want to kidnap Kaspar?"

"I don't know," I admitted. "But I've got to talk to Kiki. I'm going down to her house right now."

"We'll come with you," Betty said.

"I'm sorry," I told them. "I need to go alone."

"Why can't we come?" DeeDee demanded to know.

"It's a . . . secret." I didn't have to look at them to know how they felt about my answer.

HOW TO SUMMON A POLTERGEIST

Is there someone in your family who could use a good scare? Then why not summon your own poltergeist? If you're looking for a quick prank, the classic *walkie-talkie under the bed* trick should suit your purpose. However, if one night's fun isn't enough for you, here are some simple tricks that can convince your loved ones that they're being haunted. Being a good ghost takes time, dedication, and subtlety—but the results are bound to be priceless.

Make a *Discovery*

Plant an old, creepy item somewhere around your house and pretend to discover it. Your object could be anything—a picture, a strange toy, or a chilling letter. If you live in an older building, you can say you found it under a floorboard or behind the radiator. If your home is new, claim you dug it up in the yard. Speculate about who might have owned it and what might have happened to her. Then drop the subject for at least a day before moving on to your next trick.

Use the Power of Suggestion

If you're a good actor, this can be your most effective trick. One morning, ask your family if they heard *the noises* the previous night. Don't go overboard. You don't need to convince them of anything—only to plant the idea in their heads. A couple of days later, you might ask if they've ever seen anything strange in the basement or attic. If you're asked for a description, just shake your head and insist it must have been your imagination.

Make the Familiar Unfamiliar

Nothing frightens people more than when the familiar suddenly seems unfamiliar. Rearrange the kitchen cabinets in the middle of the night. Use black shoe polish to put an *X* across every mirror (no matter how small). Flip photos and artwork around so they all face the wall. Purchase an old dress or shirt from a flea market and hang it in one of the closets. Leave stacks of pennies in strange places.

Strange Noises

No haunting would be complete without a few unexplained noises. Unfortunately, it's easy to get caught in the act of producing them. Don't go for the obvious moans and wails. Hide a small tape player in different places around your house and have it play a simple recording—maybe a child's giggle or an old man's grunt.

Have Some Fun with Your Photos

Remove family photos from their frames and make color copies. (You can also single out an individual, if you choose.) Take the copies (not the originals!) and carefully rub out the faces of the people shown. Put the originals somewhere safe and place your creepy copies in the frames.

Send Them a Message from Beyond

As your haunting escalates, you may want to leave a few messages for your family. Use ChapStick to write *help* on the bathroom mirror. (It will be obvious only when the mirror steams up.) Or use lemon juice to scrawl *get out* on a wall above a radiator. (This works only in the winter when the radiator's heat will eventually turn the invisible message brown.)

CHAPTER TEN

Secrets, Lies, and Double-Crossing

It's a simple fact of human nature. If you have a secret to tell, you won't find a single soul who doesn't want to hear it. Warn people it will ruin their lives, break their hearts, or bring down the government—they'll still grit their teeth and insist that you spill it. While it's a weakness we all share in common, the irresistible urge to listen to secrets would do little harm if most of us weren't so eager to share them. Every day, seemingly harmless secrets slip past our lips, and sometimes it isn't till later that we realize the damage that one of them has done.

The sun was beginning to set, and the west-facing greenhouse felt as bright and as hot as the face of the sun. Kiki's face was hidden beneath a wide-brimmed hat that shielded her delicate skin as she watered Verushka's orchids. The older woman hadn't regained consciousness all day, and Kiki was channeling her nervous energy into chores. I watched as she tenderly brushed a layer of black Manhattan soot from the leaves of a butterfly orchid.

"I told Oona that Verushka might be dying." It felt strangely good to confess. "She wanted to go to the Shadow City today to look for Yu's friends. I had to explain why you couldn't go."

Kiki kept her eyes on the orchid. "You've got a big mouth, Ananka. If I hadn't inhaled so much Fille Fiable, I never would have told you. Verushka was worried that Oona might find out." She paused as if she were summoning the energy to continue. "Look. I know Oona seems tough, but it's all an act. She's far more fragile than you think. She has a ghost and a deadbeat father to deal with. The last thing she needed was something new to worry about."

Kiki's reproof stung. "I know, and I'm sorry. I made a mistake. Oona's already cracking under the pressure. We listened to the feeds from Luz's bugs this morning, and it seems like the ghost might be real. Oona even dragged me to see a medium this afternoon. He said that if Oona did her duty she'd have everything she desired. Now she's desperate to find proof that her father is lying. I think it's because she's starting to believe him."

"Did you take her to the Shadow City?"

"No. Something else came up. I told Oona she'd have to wait, and she pitched a fit. I'm worried it may have pushed her over the edge."

"What happened?"

"One of Kaspar's squirrels delivered a message to Betty while Oona and I were on Twenty-seventh Street talking to the dead. He's been kidnapped."

Kiki's milky eyes flashed. "Did you go see his parents?"

"You know about his parents?"

"A kid who speaks like a college professor doesn't disappear without someone noticing. I did a little research after I met him. Phineas Parker, right?"

"Wow. You're good."

"I own a computer and I can type. That's really all it takes. Did his parents capture him?"

"I doubt it. They're totally bonkers. They basically called us groupies and suggested that Kaspar staged his disappearance to get away from us. But I don't believe it. Kaspar's friend Howard saw the kidnapper. The man's not going to win any awards for mental health, but I swear, Kiki, the person he described sounded just like Sergei Molotov."

Kiki squashed a tiny worm that had emerged from the bud of a ghost orchid. "It's not impossible," she finally said. "I have a hunch that Livia and Sidonia are planning something. They know about the poisoned bullet. I wouldn't be surprised if Molotov stayed in New York to wait for Verushka to die. If she does, I'll be more vulnerable than ever."

"But why would Molotov kidnap Kaspar? It doesn't make sense."

"I don't know," Kiki admitted. "Maybe I need to be more careful about who I'm seen with. Okay. Here's what you need to do." She stopped and looked at me quizzically. "Are you going to write this down?" I grabbed a notebook out of my bag. "Where Kaspar's concerned, all we can do right now is check the parks in Manhattan, just to make sure that he isn't avoiding us. And keep an eye out for new giant squirrels. As for Lester Liu, ask Luz to make some of those surveillance cameras that look like pigeons and station them across from his mansion. That way we can keep track of everyone who comes and goes. Keep listening to the recordings from the bugs, and as soon as Yu's feeling better, take him down to the tunnels. I'll go with you if I can. In the meantime, tell Oona to be patient. If her father's up to something, we'll find out eventually."

"Patience isn't one of Oona's strengths," I reminded Kiki. "Lester Liu's smart, and he's found his daughter's weaknesses. I'm worried she's going to fall for it all."

"Go talk to her," Kiki counseled. "I've tried to make it clear that I'm on her side, but she needs to know that the rest of you are, too."

. . .

My cell phone showed five missed calls from home, and I didn't bother to check the messages. The two hours I'd said I'd be gone had turned into six, and I knew I was begging for trouble. But I couldn't go home without speaking to Oona. I hopped on the subway to Chinatown, and when I emerged on Canal Street it was already dark. A row of roasted ducks hanging in a restaurant window reminded my stomach that it hadn't been fed since breakfast. I paused to gaze longingly at the dumpling soup being sipped by a man with a wart on the tip of his chin. Reflected in the glass, I saw a silver Rolls-Royce glide by behind me. My hunger vanished as I watched the car turn down Oona's street.

When I reached her building, I found the Rolls parked outside. Lester Liu's butler waited behind the wheel, staring straight ahead at the street in front of him.

Climbing the stoop, I saw Oona dashing down the stairs, with Mrs. Fei in pursuit. Even with the door closed, I could hear them shouting in Chinese. Oona burst outside, nearly knocking me over the railing.

"What are you doing here?" she demanded

"I went to see Kiki. . . ." I paused, taken aback by the dress she was wearing. I remembered admiring it in the window of Bergdorf Goodman, and I knew the price must have been astronomical. And when Oona lifted her arm to scratch a patch of red skin beneath her collar, I spotted the platinum cuffs that Lester Liu had given her. "You're still wearing the bracelets."

"And your point is?" Oona snarled. Mrs. Fei arrived on the stoop, out of breath from the sprint down the stairs. Her hair had come unfastened, and it flowed down her back like a silver waterfall. She took Oona's hand and appeared to plead with her. "I've got to go," Oona said, breaking free from her grandmother and hurrying toward the Rolls-Royce.

"Go where?" I asked.

"I'm having dinner with my father."

"You can't!" I cried. "It's too dangerous. At least wait until one of us can go with you. We all want to help you."

Before Oona ducked inside the car, she turned back to me. "It's too late. I don't need your help anymore. I figured everything out." The door slammed in my face.

"Wait!" I begged, but the car was already peeling away from the curb.

"She is gone." I looked down in surprise at Mrs. Fei, who was resting on one of the steps, watching the Rolls-Royce disappear around the corner. "I tell her to stay home. Her father is a very bad man. But I am not her real mother. She won't listen to me."

"When did you learn English?" I took a seat beside her on the cold concrete.

"Long time ago. I teach myself," said Mrs. Fei. "So I could keep Wang out of trouble. She always speaks English when she don't want me to understand."

I smiled at the thought of Oona's tricks turned against her. "Your secret's safe with me, Mrs. Fei. But why do you call her Wang?"

"Wang is the name I gave her when she was born." There was grief in her voice, as if she were speaking of someone who'd died. "She says it is the name of a peasant. Not a name for the daughter of a rich man. She always want everything to be new and beautiful. She don't want to live in Chinatown with a poor old lady."

"That's not true," I tried to assure her, but when I heard the uncertainty in my voice, I thought it best to change the subject. "How is Yu?"

"He is a good boy. Wang is mad because I don't let him look for the children today. But it is my job to make him better, not let him get worse. I tell her that, and she call Mr. Liu. She said in English that she believes there is a ghost in his house."

"She did?" I barely choked out the words.

"Wang is in big trouble," said Mrs. Fei. All I could do was nod in agreement.

•   •   •

The following week, fall landed hard on New York. In the little park across the street from my house, I saw the last leaf flutter down from above, only to find itself pinned to the windshield of a passing car. I spent hours with my nose pressed against the cold glass of my window, waiting for something—anything—to happen. Since returning from Oona's house at seven thirty in the evening without a reasonable excuse to account for my eight-hour absence, I had been placed under house arrest. Convicted ax murderers are allowed more freedom than I was.

Not that it mattered. There wasn't anything I could do. Luz and DeeDee were leading what was left of the Irregulars. Iris, dressed as a cookie-selling Girl Scout or a trick-or-treater, smuggled updates to me whenever she could, but there was never much to report. Kaspar was still missing, and Betty spent every free moment searching the island's parks and scanning the newspapers for signs of giant squirrels. But even the city's intrepid reporters had no idea what had become of the vigilante and his three furry sidekicks. Luz's pigeon cameras showed regular deliveries of exotic yet edible animals to Lester Liu's mansion, as well as frequent visits from Oona, who was barely speaking to the rest of us. But thanks to the bugs in her father's mansion, we knew how she spent much of her time. She and Lester Liu were busy preparing for the Empress's coming-out party at the Metropolitan Museum of Art. Enormous blood-red banners announcing the exhibition hung from the entrance of the museum, and across the city, bus stop ads and billboards reminded New Yorkers that it wouldn't be long before *The Empress Awakens*. With the lavish opening gala little more than two weeks away, Lester Liu and his beautiful daughter had become the city's most famous philanthropists.

DeeDee and Luz tried their best to break Lester Liu's hold on Oona. They took Yu to the Shadow City, but he failed to guide them to the missing Taiwanese teenagers. They called the ASPCA to report Lester Liu's unusual deliveries, but the inspectors were either charmed or bribed by the dapper old gentleman and left without checking his refrigerator. After those and other disappointments, Luz and DeeDee spent days with their eyes glued to the surveillance tapes, searching for any sign of illegal activity. All they witnessed was a tearful Mrs. Fei being turned away twice from the mansion's front door.

Only Kiki remained in contact with Oona, who called her every few days to check on Verushka. There had been no progress on that front either. The doctor had prevented Verushka's condition from deteriorating, but her health hadn't improved. Somewhere in the city, Sergei Molotov was patiently waiting for her to expire. Whatever he and Livia had planned remained a mystery, and I dreaded the day that we would find out.

It was two weeks into my sentence, on a cold, wet Sunday at the beginning of November, when I heard a strange sound issue from one of my desk drawers. Inside, I found an old GPS device vibrating like a Mexican jumping bean. A motion sensor had been tripped in the Shadow City. Several seconds later, a text message arrived on my phone. *"Iris's house. ASAP."* It was from Kiki Strike.

My heart was racing, but I managed to appear calm as I bargained with my mother for an early release. For weeks, I'd impersonated the perfect child. I had put my parents' library back in order without being asked, and I'd cleaned the oven—twice. When the boredom got bad enough, I'd even finished my homework and turned in the essay that Principal Wickham had assigned. I hoped to have earned enough goodwill to be allowed an un-chaperoned stroll, but at first my request was denied. It took a humiliating amount of groveling before I was fi-nally granted a couple of hours outdoors.

· · ·

"Hi, Ananka!" Iris ushered me into her house. She was wearing a tiny white lab coat with her initials embroi-dered on one of the pockets.

"You're looking very professional today, Iris. What's the occasion?"

"A package just came in the mail. It had three of these coats and a chemistry set in it. I think I have a se-cret admirer."

I started to crack a joke, but held my tongue when I remembered the scolding I'd gotten from Betty. "I hope he's handsome."

"Me, too," Iris said dreamily. "How much do you think delivery boys make?"

"I have no clue. Why do you want to know?"

Iris blushed. "Never mind. You better get down to the basement. I told the nanny I've got diarrhea, and she ran out to get some medicine. She could be back any second."

I scrambled down the stairs and found the Irregulars waiting impatiently.

"What took you so long?" asked DeeDee.

"I had to make a deal with my warden. Where's Oona?" The other girls traded glances.

"How should *I* know?" DeeDee said. "She won't return my calls."

"She's been busy. Spending Daddy's money is hard work." Luz sounded bitter, and even Betty didn't rush to Oona's defense.

"I guess she's not coming," said Kiki, handing me a bottle of Iris's rat-repelling perfume. "Go ahead and freshen up. We'll just have to go without her."

"Should *you* be here?" I asked. Kiki had lost weight since I'd seen her. Her black pants looked three sizes too big, and they remained above her hips only with the help of a tightly cinched belt. "Shouldn't you be at home with Verushka?"

"The doctor says she's in stable condition. Sitting around the house isn't going to make her any better," said Kiki. "At least here I might do *somebody* some good."

"In that case, we should get started," said DeeDee. "Unless we want Iris's nanny tagging along."

"Do we know where we're going?" I asked.

"Underneath Chinatown," Luz answered.

. . .

Inside the Shadow City, Luz led the way through the dark tunnels toward the location of the tripped alarm. As soon as we were under Chinatown, we began to hear shrieks, screams, and what sounded like cursing in an unfamiliar language. I felt a warm body brush past my ankles as a rat scampered past me to join the mob of ravenous beasts that had assembled outside a thieves' den.

We waded through the rodents and found a girl standing on top of a rickety table, gripping a candle that was little more than a stub of wax. The rats were taking turns clambering up the table's legs. As each one made it over the side, the girl punted it across the room. A ball of greasy fur flew past my head as we entered the chamber, hit the wall, and then quickly lined up for another chance at a meal. One of the Irregulars screamed. My eyes followed the finger that Luz was pointing. The girl looked as though she were rotting. The skin of her arms and legs was covered with oozing green blotches and speckled with what looked to be blood.

As the scent of our perfume filled their nostrils, the rats parted, leaping out of our path and snarling at us from the sidelines. The girl on the table froze when she saw Kiki. Judging by her starstruck expression, she would have been less surprised to see Jackie Chan coming to her rescue. As DeeDee sprayed her down with rat-repellent, the girl coughed and lashed out, nearly knocking the bottle from DeeDee's hands. But when the rats retreated, she began to understand. She let Kiki take one of her arms and examine it under the flashlight.

"Don't touch her!" shouted Luz. "She could be contagious!"

"Relax," Kiki told her. "She's covered in paint."

"Yes. Paint," the girl agreed, bobbing her head up and down. Her black bangs had grown over her eyes, and she held them back with one hand so she could get a good look at Kiki.

"You speak English?" Luz asked.

"No," replied the girl, then sensing our disappointment, "Little."

"How did you get here?" Kiki asked. The girl shook her head in confusion. Kiki asked again in Cantonese and Mandarin, but the girl shook her head each time. "Looks like she speaks only Hakka." Kiki noted. She tried again. "Ladder?"

"Yes. Ladder." The girl pointed to a ladder in one corner of the room that led to an exit from the Shadow City.

"Come on, Ananka," said Kiki. "Let's see what's up there."

"Why me?" For some reason, I always got stuck with the dangerous jobs.

"It's for your own good. You've been cooped up too long. If you don't get a jolt of adrenaline soon, you're bound to go soft."

Seventy feet above the thieves' den in the Shadow City, we pushed open a trapdoor and pulled ourselves into a dungeonlike space. A splinter from the ragged floorboards slipped beneath the skin of my palm, and I stumbled into a wall of jagged rocks. After two weeks of house arrest, I was already out of practice. Kiki put her ear to the room's only door.

"Hear anything?" I whispered.

"It's quiet. I think we're alone."

Beyond the dungeon lay a maze of hastily constructed cubicles. We crept through the corridors, peeking into cramped pens that had recently housed human beings. Each was empty but for a single mattress, and the concrete floor was splattered with paint. Multicolored footprints led in circles, and we found a small, bright red palm print on one of the plywood walls.

"Looks like we're too late," said Kiki. "The kids have been moved."

"What do you think they were doing here?"

"Given the evidence, I'd say they were painting."

"Your powers of deduction astound me," I teased. "Any idea *what* they were painting?"

"Well, the splatter seems to be concentrated in a corner of each cubicle. They were probably working at easels." Kiki dropped to one knee to study a single smear of blue paint on the floor. "Ultramarine. It's a pigment made from crushed lapis lazuli, and it isn't cheap. The kids weren't just painting to pass the time. We should check upstairs and see where we are."

A flight of rickety stairs led to the ground floor. When we reached the landing, we saw the sun pouring through massive holes in the roof. Aboveground, the building was nothing more than a hollow shell. The floors and windows had been ripped out, and only four crumbling brick walls kept the structure standing. Pigeons cooed from a hundred nooks and crannies. Their feathers and droppings had transformed the ground into modern art. Kiki tried the front door of the structure, ramming her shoulder against the wood when it refused to open. A man passing by was startled by the ensuing bang, and the bucket he'd been carrying slipped from his fingertips. Foul, gray sea cucumbers flopped out on the sidewalk. I stared past the construction zone tape at the scene in front of me. We were just down the street from Oona's house.

"Coincidence?" I asked Kiki, knowing what her answer would be.

"There's no such thing. Let's go get the girl. Since we're already here, we might as well ask Oona to translate."

. . .

Oona's brightly dressed bodyguard stormed down the stoop without giving a second look to a miniature thug spray painting his tag on the side of the building. She was lugging a bulky suitcase, and she wasn't smiling.

"Is Oona home?" Kiki repeated the question in Mandarin when the woman ignored her.

"No," the woman replied rudely in English. "She's having lunch with her father."

"She's at *lunch*?" DeeDee's blood boiled.

"Do you mind if we wait upstairs for her?" I asked.

"Do what you want. I don't work here anymore." The woman shoved past us and disappeared down the street.

"Why would Oona get rid of her bodyguard?" Betty wondered.

"Why do you *think*?" Luz huffed.

Looking up at the second floor, I saw Mrs. Fei watching from a window. I gave her a wave, and she came down to greet us. We hadn't made it past the foyer before Mrs. Fei grabbed the girl we'd found in the tunnels and scratched at the paint on her arms. Then she took her patient by the chin and studied her tongue and eyeballs. Once she was satisfied, Mrs. Fei led us upstairs and dragged the girl to the bathroom, where we heard water running in the tub. When she returned, Mrs. Fei spoke with Kiki in Mandarin.

"The girl is healthy," Kiki translated. "Just dirty. Mrs. Fei wants to know if we'd like some tea while we wait for Oona."

Oona barged through the door. "The wait is over." She was wearing a short sable jacket over a gray pencil skirt. Her long black hair was twisted into a chignon and pinned with a diamond-encrusted comb. At the base of her neck, the skin was red and covered in tiny bumps. "Long time no see. I didn't know you guys wanted me in your little club anymore."

"What's wrong with you?" Luz demanded. "The alarms in the Shadow City went off two hours ago. You should have been with us."

"They did?" Oona looked genuinely surprised. "What happened? Why didn't somebody call me?"

"We *did* call you," DeeDee told her. "You didn't bother to pick up."

Oona was in no mood to be taken to task. "What is this, some sort of intervention? I was having lunch, and it was loud in the restaurant. I must not have heard the phone ring."

"Or maybe you just didn't want to interrupt your afternoon with Daddy," I said. "You two sure are spending a lot of time together, aren't you?"

Oona reached under her jacket and scratched furiously at her neck. "Like I have a choice? While you guys have been running around looking for squirrel boy, I've had to do my own detective work."

"Detective work?" Luz scoffed.

"I've never seen a detective wear sable," Betty muttered softly. It was a powerful blow, and Oona looked stunned.

"Well, I guess you've all made it clear how you feel," she said.

"What are we supposed to think?" DeeDee stated matter-of-factly. "You won't answer our calls, and you spend all of your time shopping and going to lunch with a man who might want to kill us. You even fired your bodyguard. What's up with that, by the way? Don't need the protection anymore?"

"For your information, I gave her the boot 'cause she has sticky fingers. I found one of my best rings stuffed under her mattress. Kiki, how much more of this crap do I have to take?"

Kiki was quiet for a moment.

"You're in over your head, Oona," she said at last. "Whatever you're trying to do, you *have* to let us help. Something big is going down. Think about it. Your father shows up after all this time; then Kaspar disappears and Sergei Molotov is spotted in town. I know it all looks random right now—but there could be a connection.

"And that's not all. We just found a Taiwanese girl in the Shadow City. She led us to the basement where she and the other kids had been locked up. Guess where it was?"

"Where?"

"In the abandoned building down the street from your house."

"Really?" Somehow, Oona didn't sound shocked. She seemed *happy*.

"And you say you didn't see *anything*?" DeeDee couldn't hide her skepticism.

"I saw construction workers going in and out all the time."

"Did you notice anything strange *today*?" asked Kiki.

I could see a memory flicker through Oona's mind. "They woke me up this morning. They were hauling a bunch of crates out of the building. It couldn't have been past eight o'clock."

"That must have been when they moved the kids to another location," I said.

"What did the girl say?" asked Oona. "Did she know who kidnapped her?"

"She doesn't speak much English," said Kiki. "That's why we're here. We need you to translate."

Oona scowled. "Of course. I should have known that's why you came."

We suddenly heard two cries of joy in the hallway and found Yu and the Taiwanese girl locked in an embrace.

"Looks like they're happy to see each other," Luz observed.

"Friends usually are," Oona snipped. She listened to their conversation for a moment. "Her name is Siu Fah. She and Yu were schoolmates."

The girl saw us watching and pointed at Kiki. Yu gave Kiki a once-over and both of them giggled.

"What did they just say?" I asked.

"They were talking about how much Kiki resembles the star of a famous kung fu movie called *Cute Little Demon Girl*." Oona couldn't help but grin.

"Tell them it's just a coincidence," Kiki said. "Then ask Siu Fah how she escaped."

Oona questioned the girl. "She says her captors told her that Yu had died, but she never believed them. She knew he'd found a way out, so she snuck into the room where he'd been kept. She searched whenever she could, but it took her more than a week to find the trapdoor."

"What did her kidnappers look like?"

We waited impatiently for Oona to translate. "They were mostly Chinese. She says she saw their boss only once." Oona hesitated and looked around at the rest of us.

"Go ahead. Ask her," Luz demanded.

Siu Fah spoke for two full minutes before Oona began to translate. "She says he was a pale man with black hair. He was always dressed in a suit. She thinks he spoke Russian with some of the men." I couldn't tell from the look on her face if Oona was relieved or disappointed.

"Molotov," Kiki spat.

"What were they painting?" I wanted to know.

"Painting?" Oona repeated pensively before posing the question to Siu Fah. "She says she doesn't know what the other kids were painting. She was never allowed to look. But she was ordered to copy a work she'd never seen before. It was a picture of a fat lady looking into a mirror that was held by a little boy. She finished it a couple of days ago and they took it from her. She thinks it's been sold."

Kiki's brow furrowed. "Sounds like a painting by Peter Paul Rubens. *The Toilet of Venus*. I think they were copying famous works of art."

"Ask her if she has any idea where they took the other kids," said DeeDee.

Siu Fah's voice grew sad. "She doesn't know. She was trying to save them, but she failed," said Oona.

I felt a tug on the back of my jacket. Mrs. Fei waved me into the kitchen. I waited until no one was looking and slid inside.

"The building you talked about. It belongs to Lester Liu," Mrs. Fei whispered.

"How do you know that, Mrs. Fei?"

"We lived there when Wang was a baby."

"Does she remember?" I asked.

"I don't know," said Mrs. Fei.

"Where's Ananka?" I heard Betty ask in the hallway. Mrs. Fei put a finger to her lips.

"Just getting a glass of water," I called.

· · ·

Five of us left Oona's apartment and filed out onto the sidewalk. A few blocks away we stopped for a quick consultation.

"I guess we didn't get the goods on Lester Liu," Luz said.

I had to tell them. "He owns the abandoned building. Don't ask me how I know that. I just do."

"Just what we need—more secrets." DeeDee sniffed.

"But Siu Fah described Sergei Molotov," said Betty.

"Do we really know that for sure?" DeeDee asked solemnly. "How do we know our translator was trustworthy?"

"You think Oona was lying?" The possibility hadn't occurred to me, and I chided myself for being so gullible.

"I'm just saying that none of us speak Hakka," said DeeDee. "We have no idea what that girl really said. She could have described Lester Liu to a T and we wouldn't have known the difference."

"Oona's definitely up to *something*," Luz insisted.

"That fur she was wearing cost a fortune," Betty added.

"Do you think Yu and Siu Fah are safe with her?" asked DeeDee.

"Shut up! All of you." It had been a while since I'd seen Kiki lose her temper, and I'd forgotten how terrifying she could be. Her eyes were wolflike and her hair wild. Bright blue veins throbbed beneath the skin of her forehead. "Is this how you talk about your friends? None of you have any idea how hard this has been for Oona. Do any of you know what it's like to grow up without a family? Of course you don't. Maybe Oona *is* tempted. Maybe she wants to have a father like everyone else. As far as I'm concerned, there's only one thing that matters. Right now we don't have a single shred of evidence that she's done anything wrong. So what if she's Lester Liu's daughter? I knew that when I invited her to join the Irregulars, and in the past two years she's done nothing to make me question her loyalty."

"I was just trying to be logical," DeeDee defended herself.

"This is *life*. It isn't a science experiment. People don't always act *logically*."

"They don't tend to change, either," DeeDee said. "Don't forget—Oona's spent a lot of time on the wrong side of the law."

"She's right," I added softly.

Kiki stared at us all with disgust. Then she spun around and marched toward Canal Street, leaving us standing in shock on the corner.

"*Somebody's* a little sensitive," said Luz.

"Kiki doesn't have parents either," DeeDee pointed out. "She thinks she knows how Oona feels. She can't see what's really going on."

· · ·

That night, I received two urgent e-mails. Both were addressed to four of the Irregulars. Oona's and Kiki's names hadn't made the list. The first message came from Betty and contained a link to the *New York Society Journal* Web site. There I found three pictures taken at a posh party the previous Saturday night. They showed Lester Liu arm in arm with Oona. Both were smiling for the cameras. The caption beneath the photos read *Philanthropist Lester Liu and his stunning daughter.*

Luz had sent the second e-mail. According to her surveillance equipment, at exactly 8:00 p.m., all the bugs in Lester Liu's mansion had stopped working. Fifteen minutes later, the pigeon cameras had gone dark.

CHAPTER ELEVEN

Assassin on the Loose

At seven o'clock the next morning, the bitter odor of burning coffee wafted into my bedroom. I threw on my robe and tiptoed to the kitchen to investigate, expecting to find a bushed burglar or an undersized princess. Instead, I discovered my mother sitting at the table, sipping from a PBS mug. She said nothing when I offered a hoarse "good morning," but continued to study a copy of the *New York Daily News* that lay open in front of her. Even with the paper upside down, I had no difficulty identifying the woman whose picture graced page two. It was Livia Galatzina, the exiled Queen of Pokrovia and Kiki Strike's aunt.

Adrenaline pumped through my system. My hands quivered as I poured coffee into the last clean dish in the house and took a seat at the table. My mother pushed the paper toward me and stood up to refill her cup. The headline read *Assassin at Large in Manhattan*.

AUTHORITIES HAVE CONFIRMED that a woman sought
in connection with the fourteen-year-old murder of
Crown Princess Sophia of Pokrovia has recently
been seen in New York. In early November, a sixty-
year-old woman was admitted to St. Vincent's Hospital, where she was treated for an infected bullet
wound. In accordance with New York City law,
nurses fingerprinted the patient and reported the
incident to police. The fingerprints were later identified as belonging to Verushka Kozlova, a former
member of the Pokrovian Royal Guard who al-
legedly poisoned the country's royal family more
than a decade ago, before vanishing without a trace.

According to police reports, Ms. Kozlova disappeared from St. Vincent's before her arrest could be
secured. Witnesses claim she was in the company of
a small, unusually pale girl who gave her name as
Trixie Drew. Some have suggested that the teenager
bore a strong resemblance to the now legendary
Kiki Strike. Unfortunately, the hospital's security
cameras show no sign of Kozlova's companion, and
a nurse who photographed the girl with a cell phone
camera later discovered that the image had been
mysteriously erased.

While the teenager's identity remains unknown,
one remarkable possibility has been suggested.
Reached for comment in St. Petersburg, Russia, the
exiled Queen of Pokrovia rejoiced in the news that
her sister's murderer has finally surfaced. Queen
Livia also speculated that Ms. Kozlova's companion
might be her niece, Katarina, Sophia's only child.

Though it has long been thought that the child was murdered along with her parents, Queen Livia now admits that Princess Katarina disappeared the day of the assassination. "If my beloved niece is still alive, I urge her to return to her family. I will treat her as my own daughter and ensure that she is recognized as the rightful heir to the throne of Pokrovia."

Queen Livia has offered a $100,000 reward for any information leading to the capture of Verushka Kozlova."

On the opposite page, I spotted a short article about the mysterious disappearance of New York's giant squirrels, but there was no time to read it. I glanced up to see my mother staring at me, and I knew my acting skills would determine my fate. I tried to look bored as I tossed the paper back across the table.

"So every pale girl in the city is Kiki Strike now? This is nuts, Mom. I've got to get ready for school."

"Then you won't mind if I phone Principal Wickham this morning and check that you've made it there?" my mother asked. I was ready for my close-up.

"Be my guest." I sniffed sarcastically. I took one last swig of my coffee and headed for the bathroom.

. . .

Of course, I had no intention of going to school. I turned on the tub faucet and tried calling Kiki, but only got through to her voice mail. I took the fastest shower on record, and as soon as I was a reasonable distance from my house, I bought all the New York newspapers and hailed a cab. When I rang Kiki's bell, she answered immediately. For the first time since I'd known her, I saw real fear in her face.

"I thought you were Dr. Pritchard," she said. "He should have been here ages ago. Verushka's had a rough morning."

"Haven't you heard?" I felt my first rush of panic and my heartbeat pounded in my ears. Kiki read the newspapers religiously, and I'd expected her to be ready with a plan. My cell phone rang. Betty's number flashed on the caller ID. "I'll call you back in a minute," I told her. As soon as I hung up, Luz's number appeared on the display.

"Heard what?" Kiki asked. I passed her a copy of the *Daily News*. Her eyes flew over the type. "Where did that old hag get a hundred thousand dollars?" she scoffed. "Call the Irregulars and ask them to get over here. We need to clean the place out. Tell them to leave the weapons. Just take our personal belongings. I'm going to get Verushka."

"What about the doctor?" I asked. "How will he know where to find us?"

"The doctor's a rat," Kiki shouted as she sprinted for the bedroom. "I bet he's already spent Livia's reward."

"What are we going to do with Verushka?" I called, though I already knew there was only one option. But if Lester Liu and Sergei Molotov were connected somehow, it didn't seem wise to take Verushka to Oona's house. "Kiki, do you really want to—" I started to say.

Kiki barged back into the living room like a gunslinger entering a saloon. "I thought I made myself clear last night, Ananka. Whatever you're thinking right now, you should keep it to yourself."

. . .

Luz, DeeDee, and Betty arrived as we were rolling Verushka's wheelchair out of the bedroom. They took to their work like professionals, moving efficiently and talking little. It wasn't the previous night's argument that was still on their minds. Behind their vacant expressions, I could see they were hurt. They were cleaning up the consequences of a secret that no one had shared with them. Luz and DeeDee silently dumped clothing and papers into plastic trash bags. Betty pulled two wigs from her oversized purse, along with a nurse's smock, a pair of glasses, and a fake nose. In less than a minute, she transformed Kiki and Verushka into an elderly African woman and her private nurse. With Verushka mumbling incoherently, we couldn't risk public transportation, so Kiki and I swaddled her in blankets and speed-walked the mile to Chinatown. Not far from Fat Frankie's, I spotted two policemen eyeing us from across the street. If Dr. Pritchard had gone to the authorities, the NYPD would be on the lookout for an elderly woman with a blue tinge to her skin. Even with makeup on, Verushka's appearance remained remarkably odd. As the cops crossed over to question her, I sprayed the three of us with a mist of Fille Fiable. Whether it was the disguises, the perfume, or the foul stench of body odor that saved us, I'll never know, but the police let us by without any hassle.

. . .

When we reached Oona's building, Kiki and I hauled Verushka's limp body up the stairs to the second floor. Kiki had phoned in advance, and all four grandmothers stood ready for action. They had transformed the dining room into a makeshift hospital and helped us gently lay Verushka down on a cot. Then Mrs. Fei began barking orders, and the younger women scattered in three directions.

"Is she your mother?" Mrs. Fei inquired as she checked Verushka's pulse.

"She might as well be." Kiki didn't seem surprised to hear Oona's grandmother speaking English. "She's taken care of me since I was a baby."

Mrs. Fei's expression quickly hardened. "If you care so much you should have come earlier. Cyanide, right? The poison is eating her. Your friend could die," she scolded.

"I thought I'd found a good doctor," Kiki explained.

"American doctors." Mrs. Fei grunted. "They know machines and chemicals. They don't know the human body. I make you a deal. I save your friend, and you save Wang." It wasn't hard to see where Oona got her bluntness.

"What makes you think Oona needs to be saved, Mrs. Fei?" Kiki asked.

"Because I listen to her when she speaks to her father. She thinks he wants her back, but I know he is going to break her heart. I tried to go see him and beg him to leave her alone, but he won't talk to me." She pointed at a beautifully wrapped package sitting by the door. "See that? Every day something new comes. Wang thinks presents are the same thing as love. Every day she goes to his house. Sometimes she don't come home till late at night."

Mrs. Fei's warning meant more to Kiki than anything I could have said. "I promise—we'll watch out for Oona," she assured the old woman.

"*Please*. Or one day Wang will never come home."

"You speak excellent English." None of us had heard Oona arrive. Though she appeared oddly composed, the rash on her neck was livid. "How long have you been spying on me, Mrs. Fei?"

"Not spying—listening. I want to help you." Mrs. Fei's voice was free of guilt, but I could barely stand to watch the exchange.

Oona slowly shifted her eyes to Kiki and me. "So what have you guys been discussing with my grandmother?" She offered an artificial smile when we didn't answer. "Never mind. It doesn't matter. How's Verushka?" Oona knelt by Verushka's cot and took one of her blue hands.

"Mrs. Fei thinks she can save her."

"You'll have to stay here until she gets better," Oona told Kiki. "You can take my room."

"Where will you sleep?" I asked.

"At the mansion," Oona replied coldly. "I'm moving there tonight."

Mrs. Fei gasped, and her entire body seemed to shrivel.

"I don't think that's smart," I warned Oona. With Luz's bugs out of commission, the Irregulars had no way to ensure her safety.

"We're finalizing the plans for the Empress's party tonight. My father wants me to be at the museum at six. Why would I come all the way back to Chinatown if he lives just down the street? At least I'll have a little privacy there."

"I won't listen!" Mrs. Fei pleaded. "Stay here. This is your home."

"It's not where I belong," Oona said, not unkindly. "I need to be where I can take care of my responsibilities."

Mrs. Fei wrung her gnarled hands, but said nothing in response.

"What about the ghost?" I tried. "Aren't you scared?"

"The ghost will be happy if she gets what she wants. Besides, if it *is* my mother, why should I be frightened?"

I saw Mrs. Fei catch Kiki's eye.

"I'm going with you to the museum tonight," Kiki announced.

"That's funny. I don't remember inviting you. There's no way I'm letting you leave Verushka."

"Then I'll go." It sounds courageous in retrospect, but I had to force the words out.

"I'm not helpless," said Oona. "I don't need a chaperone."

I spoke without thinking. "That's not the point."

"Oh, I get it." Oona's nostrils flared like her father's, and her rash turned scarlet. She scratched violently at the skin of her neck until a drop of blood stained her white collar. "You both think I've drunk the Kool-Aid, don't you? You think I'm Daddy's little girl now, right?"

"No, you're *not* right." Kiki bristled. "I've just trusted you with the most important thing I have. Do you think for one second I'd have brought Verushka here if I thought you weren't loyal? What other proof do you want?"

"What about you, Ananka?" Oona watched my face

closely as I struggled to come up with an answer. "Yeah, I thought so. Come to the museum if that's what you want. I don't have anything to hide. Now, if you don't mind, I need to pack."

"Oona?" I couldn't take my eyes off the blood on her shirt.

"What? What are you staring at?"

"I think it's time to switch laundry detergent."

Oona slapped her hand to her neck and gazed at the blood that came away on her fingers. Then without a word, she left the room.

· · ·

As a truant and a fugitive from parental justice, I couldn't go home. Instead I spent most of the frigid November day with Yu and Siu Fah, hunting down herbalists as we gathered the items on a five-page shopping list that Mrs. Fei had prepared. On every street in Chinatown, hundreds of round bodies wrapped in down coats grazed, bumped, and bounced off one another as each of them waddled toward warmth. But somehow the cold, harsh winds didn't bother me much. Though we shared only a few words in common, Yu and Siu Fah were surprisingly good company. I'd forgotten how contagious happiness could be, and for the first time in weeks, I felt optimistic. But when we returned to Oona's apartment after sunset, I switched on Channel Three and got a strong dose of reality. The local news opened with a shot of Kiki's house. The front door stood open, and cops streamed in and out of the building as the lights on their squad cars silently spun. Adam Gunderson, Channel Three's top reporter, had made his name earlier that year by exposing Kiki Strike as a hoax. Now he was in front of her house, dressed in an Arctic-ready parka with a microphone in hand. Next to him stood a short, oddly feminine man of indeterminate age. I was certain it was Betty Bent in disguise.

> "Good evening, Janice. I'm here in Chelsea, where police have discovered the hidden lair of one of the world's most notorious assassins. For fourteen years, Verushka Kozlova has been wanted in connection with the murder of the Pokrovian royal family. An anonymous tip early this morning led authorities to this carriage house on Eighteenth Street. Inside the booby-trapped building, they discovered a veritable arsenal of martial arts weapons. Fingerprints taken from the scene confirm that Ms. Kozlova once lived here, although her whereabouts are currently unknown.
>
> "Virgil Krull, a neighborhood resident, says he's often seen Ms. Kozlova's companion entering and leaving the building. Mr. Krull, is it true that the girl bears a resemblance to the fictional Kiki Strike?"

Virgil Krull squinted into the camera and spoke with a high-pitched Southern accent.

> "I don't know much about this Kiki Strike everybody keeps talkin' about, but the girl I saw was a plump little thing with one leg shorter than the other. I don't know how much trouble she could cause, what with her infirmity and all."

"So you doubt that Ms. Kozlova's companion could be a teenage vigilante?"

"I reckon not. She seemed kinda slow, too. I figured she had a touch of the 'tard if you know what I mean."

Hiding his smile with his microphone, Adam Gunderson quickly moved on to the next question.

"How does it feel to have lived across the street from a known assassin, Mr. Krull?"

"I gotta say, it's pretty exciting. You don't come across those sorts back in Mississippi. Makes me glad I moved to New York."

"Well, that's one way of looking at it, I suppose. Thank you, Mr. Krull.

"Janice, the other neighbors I've spoken with don't recall ever having seen the building's residents, and security tapes from nearby houses mysteriously disappeared this morning. Sources inside the police department say the authorities are baffled. For now, Verushka Kozlova remains at large, and the residents of downtown Manhattan won't sleep soundly until she's captured. Reporting live from Chelsea, this is Adam Gunderson for News Channel Three."

"Good old Betty." Kiki was standing behind me. "That should confuse everyone for a little while."

"Everyone but Sergei Molotov. Do you think you'll be safe here?"

"As safe as I would be anywhere." The edge in Kiki's voice told me not to linger on the subject.

"I should get started for the museum," I said, pretending to check my watch. "It's almost six"

"You may need this." Kiki handed me a vial of Fille Fiable. A tiny amount of amber liquid sloshed around in the bottom of the bottle. "It's all we have left. I'll ask DeeDee to make some more. I have to call her and the others tonight anyway."

"To find out where they've stashed your stuff?"

"To apologize," said Kiki. "I should have told them about all of this earlier."

· · ·

My cab turned west on Eighty-first Street, and I saw the museum looming large at the end of the block like a temple built to appease a powerful god. Golden light streamed from its windows, and high above the museum's main entrance, three bloodred banners flapped in the breeze. Beneath them stood Lester Liu, dressed in a fur-collared coat and surveying Fifth Avenue like a king watching over his kingdom. His silver hair remained perfectly still as the wind moved around him. I waved to Oona, who was dashing up Fifth Avenue. She joined me in front of a lifeless fountain, her expression as cold as the rainwater that had collected and frozen inside it. Together we climbed the stairs to greet her father, and I prayed that the Fille Fiable I'd applied in the cab hadn't worn off.

"Good evening, Miss Fisher. How delightful to see you." Lester Liu knew how to say one thing while making it perfectly clear that he meant another. He offered Oona an insincere smile. "I wasn't expecting company this evening, my dear."

"She invited herself," Oona replied bluntly. It was nice to feel wanted.

"I've been dying to see the museum at night ever since I was a little girl." I tried to sound chipper while Lester Liu's cold eyes held me captive.

"Well then, this should be quite a treat for you. Come along. Oona and I must see to the Empress."

· · ·

Without hundreds of tourists chattering in dozens of languages, the Great Hall of the Metropolitan Museum of Art was eerily quiet, and everything seemed larger in the after-hours gloom. The vaulted ceiling felt as high as the heavens. Junglelike flower arrangements sprouted from recesses in the walls, and an ancient sphinx crouched between two marble columns, guarding the treasures that lay inside.

"Ah! Mr. Liu!" a dapper, white-haired gentleman in a perfectly tailored suit called out. Freakishly tall, with a spine as stiff as a steel rod, he appeared to cross the vast room in less than ten strides.

"Mr. Hunt." Lester Liu reached up to shake the man's hand. "Allow me to introduce my daughter, Lillian, and my new assistant, Miss Fisher. Ladies, Mr. Hunt is the director of the Metropolitan Museum."

"Here to help with the arrangements for the gala, girls?" Mr. Hunt asked, though he didn't pause for an answer. "I'm told almost everyone on our list has returned an RSVP," he bragged to Lester Liu. "I can't say that I've ever seen such an acceptance rate! The opening party for *The Empress Awakens* is bound to be the event of the season." He then proceeded to bore us with a long list of famous names who would be in attendance, including two teenage movie stars I was certain had never seen the inside of a museum.

"Why did he call you Lillian?" I whispered to Oona as Mr. Hunt yammered away.

"He thinks Lillian Liu has a nice ring to it," she said. "What do I care what he calls me? I made Oona Wong up."

"Girls?" Mr. Hunt interrupted. "Would you like to see the exhibit? I've just a few more telephone calls to make this evening before we get started, and I thought you might enjoy a sneak peek at the show."

"It would be a pleasure," Mr. Liu answered for us.

"James!" Mr. Hunt called to a sullen security guard who was loitering by the coat check. "Would you please make yourself useful and escort Mr. Liu and his companions to see the new exhibit? I'll be with you shortly, Mr. Liu."

Oona and her father walked in step behind the security guard while I trailed behind. As we neared the broad staircase that led to the second floor, my eye fell on a figure lurking in the darkness of one of the side galleries. I paused, waiting for it to move.

"It's a statue, Miss Fisher," I heard Lester Liu say. "No need to panic. The museum is full of them." Oona snickered and I felt myself blush.

· · ·

Upstairs, we strolled past dimly lit rooms and portraits of people long dead. The farther we plunged into the building, the stronger I felt the urge to flee. Only a horror film heroine would find herself alone in the Metropolitan Museum of Art with a smuggler and his slippery daughter. I tried to take note of the route that we took, but without a trail of bread crumbs or a ball of string to mark the path, I knew I'd be hopelessly lost in the museum's maze. My eyes darted from side to side, and I couldn't resist checking over my shoulder to see if anyone had crept up behind us. As we approached the southern end of the building, the sound of hammers grew deafening. A workman appeared as if out of nowhere and disappeared into a dark red room at the end of the hall. Our journey had come to an end.

"Don't leave the exhibition without a guide," the security guard shouted over the banging. The guard's eyes never left my face, and I realized the warning was for my benefit. He must have noticed me lingering behind and mistaken my agitation for mischievousness. "The alarms and motion detectors are activated in the galleries. If you want to look at the paintings, come back when the museum is open. If you want to leave, please contact us at security and we'll take you to the exit."

"Thank you, James." Lester Liu oozed charm. "If all the museum's guards are as diligent as you are, I know I can feel perfectly confident that my treasures will be safe."

When the guard turned to leave us, I felt stripped of my last defense. But while my mind screamed for him to stay, I quietly followed Lester Liu into the exhibition space. The first gallery was in chaos, with wooden crates leaning against the walls. A birdlike man with a tangle of yellow hair shouted orders at a team of muscle-bound workers in white gloves. Four of the men were carefully lowering a large painting into an open crate while two of their coworkers were busily sealing another with nails.

"Stop, stop, stop!" shouted the man when he saw us. The hammering halted, and the man rushed over. "Mr. Liu," he said, whipping off his glove and holding out his hand. "We're honored to have you here, sir."

"Dr. Jennings," Lester Liu said. "How is the work progressing?"

"The other galleries are in order, sir. This is the last room to be renovated. We're just removing the final works from the previous exhibition. They should all be gone within the hour."

"Where are you taking them?" I asked, gesturing to the crates and feeling my courage slowly return. The little man seemed shocked I could speak.

"My new assistant," Lester Liu explained.

The man's eyes flickered back and forth between the two of us as if wondering how to respond to my question.

"Some will be put into storage, and others will be sent back to the museums that loaned them. The two that belong to the Met will be returned to their original galleries. Does that answer your question?"

"Why pack them so carefully if you're just moving them to another part of the museum?"

One question was bad enough, but two was unheard of. The little man looked stunned, and Oona rolled her eyes. I was in danger of pushing too far.

"These are priceless works of art. Even the frames are worth millions. My colleagues are often less conscientious, but *I* would be this careful if I were merely moving them across the room. Now, Mr. Liu, may I show you the rest of the exhibit?"

While Dr. Jennings, Oona, and Lester Liu forged ahead, I paused to watch the workers finish preparing the crates. As a beefy man bent over to hammer a last nail, his shirt came untucked from his pants, exposing a spectacular plumber's crack—and the tattooed head of a cross-eyed dragon. It was Fu-Tsang. I spun around to see if anyone else had noticed and found Oona staring at me from across the room, her eyes daring me to speak.

"Are you coming?" she growled.

. . .

Had my mind not been dancing with dragons, I might have been struck with the same awe the grave robbers must have felt when they first entered the tomb of the Empress. I stepped into a dark room that featured brightly lit glass boxes set on tall black pedestals. Inside each, a miniature world appeared to float four feet above the floor. There were perfect porcelain replicas of ancient palaces, mansions, and courtyards—each so detailed I could see the tiles on the roofs. Another case displayed a sprawling farm inhabited by bite-sized pigs, chickens, and ducks. These were the Empress's supplies for the afterworld. Anything a woman of her rank might have needed had been carefully copied and buried alongside her. Peeking into the next gallery, I saw an army of foot-high clay servants, all still awaiting orders from their mistress. Each room of the exhibit was designed to guide visitors deeper and deeper into the Empress's tomb, until at last they reached the magnificent chamber where her mummy would be on view.

"The Empress is due to arrive on the day of the gala," I heard Lester Liu announce. "I apologize for the delay. She and her coffin are extremely fragile. I have taken Mr. Hunt's advice and hired a team of experts to transport her from my home to the museum."

"Of course, Mr. Liu. The Empress's room will be ready when she is," Dr. Jennings assured him. "Shall we take a look?"

"Oh, Lillian!" Lester Liu called out. Oona shot me a warning look and hurried off in pursuit of her father. When at last she was out of sight, I slipped back to the entrance and watched the workmen load one of the crates onto a dolly. The tattooed man wheeled it away. As his coworkers shifted their attention to the next work of art, I followed the crate out the door.

I've done dumber things, but not many. Despite countless lessons from Kiki, my tailing abilities remained laughably bad, and I had only two drops of Fille Fiable to save me from the trouble I knew I was stirring. As the man pushed the crate through the empty hallways of the Metropolitan Museum of Art, I kept a safe distance, ducking behind columns and accidentally groping a statue or two. My brain was working at double speed, and things were beginning to make sense to me. Rather than attempting to deactivate the museum's motion detectors and silent alarms, the Fu-Tsang were stealing paintings as they were moved from place to place. And there was no longer any doubt in my mind that Oona was involved.

The man turned a sharp corner, and I waited several seconds before peeking around the bend. The painting was nowhere in sight, and I could hear the creak of the dolly's wheels growing fainter.

"It's about time!" I heard someone exclaim. The voice seemed to come from the last of several galleries on the hall. "I've been waiting all night. Let's go!" I inched down the hallway, begging my shoes not to betray me. A floorboard creaked, and I froze in midstep. I slid off my flats, tiptoed to the gallery's entrance, and slowly poked my head around the corner. The crate lay open and the Fu-Tsang thug and three other men were hoisting the painting into the air.

"Now take it over there." A man stood in the center of the room, directing the action with the self-importance of a pharaoh commanding an army of slaves. "Let's try to get it on the wall before dawn, shall we?" My head spun. The painting hadn't been stolen. It had only been moved. Once it was flat against the wall, I could see a plump nude with a massive derriere lounging in a Turkish setting. But there seemed to be something peeking over her shoulder—something that seemed out of place. When I shifted my stance, the object vanished. There was no way to get any closer. I'd have to return in the morning.

I slinked back down the hall and tried to remember which way I'd come. Bad luck struck, and the turn I chose led me straight to Mr. Hunt.

"Who are you?" he demanded as if he'd never laid eyes on me. "Come here this instant. Where in God's name are your shoes?"

I walked over to the man, hoping to get close enough to give him a whiff of my perfume.

"I'm Mr. Liu's assistant, sir. I was just looking for the bathroom, and I got lost." I prayed the perfume could compensate for my pitiful excuse.

"You are no longer in my employ, *Miss Fishbein*." I shriveled when I heard Lester Liu's voice. He'd come to look for me. "Mr. Hunt, would you mind asking security to deal with this troublemaker so that I can return to my work?"

"Not at all," replied Mr. Hunt, with far more enthusiasm than the situation merited.

Given the choice, I would have preferred to spend the night in jail. Instead, the museum security staff called my mother. As I waited by the coat check for her to arrive, Oona and her father passed me on their way out. Lester Liu refused to acknowledge my existence, but once her father was out the door, Oona couldn't resist having the last word.

"What did you think you were doing?" she snarled. "This isn't a game. If it weren't for me, you'd be dead by now."

"Don't do me any favors," I spat back at her. "I don't associate with traitors."

TEST YOUR DETECTIVE SKILLS

A good detective never lets even the tiniest detail slip past her. When solving crimes and saving cities, even the name of someone's pet chicken could provide a vital clue. (Though it doesn't in this book.)

The following test will help you determine whether you're ready for action—or could use a little more practice. Keep in mind—in real life, there are no multiple-choice questions.

1. **What is the name of Howard Van Dyke's pet chicken?**
   a. Nugget
   b. April
   c. Thelma
   d. Extra Crispy

2. **What time did your next-door neighbor leave his house this morning?**
   a. Exactly ten minutes and eleven seconds later than yesterday
   b. Who knows? I decided to sleep in
   c. I would *never* intrude on someone's privacy!
   d. Come to think of it, I haven't seen him in weeks. Maybe I should knock at his door

3. **Which of the following *cannot* be found in your trash?**
   a. The identity of your secret crush
   b. Your best friend's unlisted phone number
   c. Several empty jars of Marshmallow Fluff
   d. That rather unpleasant note from your principal

4. **Which statement best describes the hot dog vendor on the corner of Fourteenth Street and Sixth Avenue?**
   a. Purveyor of the tastiest processed meats in Manhattan
   b. Spy for the Mongolian government
   c. Criminal wanted for crimes against the animal kingdom
   d. Friend of the squirrels

5. **Which of the following will prevent you from seeming mysterious?**
   a. Scar- and tattoo-free skin
   b. A name like Tiffany
   c. A big mouth
   d. The lack of a criminal record

6. **Finish the following sentence: Based on what I've read so far, Oona Wong is a . . .**
    a. Dastardly double agent
    b. Sweet-tempered girl with a heart of gold
    c. Poltergeist
    d. Pseudonym

Extra Credit

Create a disguise that's good enough to fool an acquaintance using only the contents of your handbag or backpack.

You've been caught snooping on a suspicious relative (for the second time). Craft an appropriate non-apology. (Feel guilty later, if you like.)

Pull on some rubber gloves and remove the trash can from your sister's room. Examine the items inside and compose a list of her activities over the past two days.

ANSWERS:
1) b
2) a
3) If you've been paying attention, none of this should be in your trash.
4) c
5) c
6) d—You haven't read ahead, have you?

CHAPTER TWELVE

. . . .

Prisoner of Cleveland Place

I've always admired movie heroines who, when captured by the enemy, refuse to divulge their secrets. Threaten, torture, or taunt them, and all you'll receive in return is a soul-stirring speech about honor, integrity, and the high price of freedom. In the end, they either escape from their tormentors or die heroically, leaving behind a handsome, heartbroken lover and inspiring an entire nation with their courage. As I waited for my mother to drag me home from the Metropolitan Museum of Art, I promised myself I would behave with the utmost dignity. There would be no crying or pleading or begging for mercy. (And tragically, no devoted heartthrob to witness my bravery.) I carefully crafted the single response I would give to my mother's questions: One day you'll understand.

The problem was, there weren't any questions. And one glimpse at the disappointment on my mother's face reminded me that she wasn't the enemy. She was the mother of a sneaky, lying, untrustworthy girl who couldn't or wouldn't explain her actions. On the ride home from the museum, there were no lectures and no talk of boarding school. My mother stared silently out the window, watching Fifth Avenue fly past. I saw what my secrets had done to her, and I wished I could tell her the truth. But I knew I had waited too long.

I felt slightly less sympathetic when I found two large suitcases on the floor of my bedroom, along with a note informing me that the next two days would be my last at the Atalanta School for Girls. My phone was confiscated, and my computer was missing. Even the windows had new locks. There was no way to contact the Irregulars. Until I could break free from Fishbein Fortress, Oona's treachery would remain a secret.

· · ·

The next morning, things only got worse. When I started for school, I found my mother dressed and waiting by the door.

"You're not!" I uttered in disbelief.

"How else can I be sure that you get to school?" She smirked, holding the door open for me.

There are few things in life more humiliating than being escorted to school by your mother. What annoyed me most was that she had managed to foil the only escape plan I'd devised. She sat next to me on the subway and watched me out of the corner of her eye as we passed several newsstands hawking the morning papers. *Assassin at Death's Door!* screamed the cover of one. *Hero Doctor Tells All!* shouted another. When my mother delivered me to the front door of the Atalanta School, several witnesses started to titter. Fortunately, Molly Donovan had been lingering outside, waiting for another chance to be tardy. With one look from Molly, eyes were averted, lips were zipped, and I was allowed to walk into the school with what little was left of my self-esteem.

"Whaddya do this time?" Molly and her curls bounced along beside me.

"I got caught sneaking around the Metropolitan Museum last night."

"The museum? You're kidding!" If I hadn't had her respect before, I certainly earned it then.

"I wish."

"You must be telling the truth. You're being watched, you know. They probably have you down as a flight risk."

"Who's watching me?"

"Shhh. Just look around. Don't be too obvious. Let them have their fun. This is the most excitement these teachers have all day. Makes 'em feel like Nancy Drew." One quick glance to both sides proved she was right. Every teacher we passed was stalking me with her eyes. I began to understand what it was like to be Molly Donovan.

"Maybe we shouldn't be seen together right now," I murmured, trying to keep my lips from moving.

"Yeah, I guess hard-core gangsters like you can't afford to be seen slumming around with two-bit criminals like me," Molly jested.

"Sorry. I don't know what I was saying. It doesn't matter anymore if I get expelled."

"Funny, that's just what I wanted to talk to you about. You know that promise you made me? Do you think you could speed things up a bit? I'm getting a little desperate.

I've attracted the attention of a graduate student who works for my shrinks. She seems to think I'm her ticket to fame and fortune."

"Her name wouldn't be Shiva, by any chance?" I asked.

"You've met the she-beast?" I nodded. "Well then you know what I'm talking about. My parents let her put cameras in my bedroom so she can study me in my *natural environment*. So you better act fast, 'cause if this goes on for long, I may have to kill her."

"I don't know, Molly. I'm a little overwhelmed right now."

"You have time to break into the Metropolitan Museum, but you don't have time to help out a friend?"

"Believe it or not, I have other friends who are in worse trouble than you."

"Let's see what you think at the end of the day," Molly challenged me, holding open the door of my first-period class. "There's nothing worse than losing your privacy. Have you ever heard of the observer effect?"

"No."

"Don't you *ever* listen in class? The observer effect is one of those weird scientific phenomena. When people are put under observation, their behavior changes. It's like when you go into a store and a security guard starts following you. *You* know you're not going to shoplift anything, but you start feeling guilty, and then you start acting suspiciously. That's the observer effect. So here's my question. How can you know who you really are if you're being watched all the time?"

· · ·

I didn't need the whole day to get Molly's point. When first period ended, I caught myself slinking through the hallways like an escaped convict on the run from the law. By second period I was clinically paranoid. Wherever I was, I could feel a thousand eyes crawling all over me. If I went to the bathroom, I'd emerge to find a teacher loitering outside. If I happened to pass within fifty feet of the school's exit, the sound level would dip as if people were holding their breath to see what would happen. I might have started hearing voices by third period, but when I took a seat in Mr. Dedly's classroom, the day began to look a little brighter.

The person sitting behind the desk at the front of the room didn't possess Mr. Dedly's copious nose hair, pained expression, or penchant for mismatched tweeds. Instead, it was a pretty Indian woman dressed in a shimmering turquoise sari. A tiny diamond set in her left nostril sparkled, and her gold bangles tinkled like a wind chime when she rose to address the class.

"Mr. Dedly was called away this morning. I am Ms. Mahadevi. I will be your substitute teacher today. Before I begin the lecture, I must speak with one of the students in this class." She studied the roll book, her finger scrolling down the list until she stopped somewhere in the middle. "Ananka Fishbein. Please come to the front of the room. The rest of you may talk quietly amongst yourselves."

My classmates were too busy gossiping to notice the strange new teacher take me by the arm and lead me out the door.

"Ananka," she whispered without any trace of a Bombay accent. "It's me."

"Betty?" I started to laugh till she shushed me. "What did you do with Mr. Dedly?"

"A couple of hours ago, the Amateur Archaeologists of Manhattan got a tip that a construction crew in Coney Island had discovered the remains of a pirate ship and were trying to hide the evidence. Your teacher's the president of the club, so he had to go check it out. Pretty good, huh? It was Luz's idea. We heard what happened at the museum last night. Kiki asked me to come see you. She thought you'd be under strict surveillance."

"That's the least of it. My mother's shipping me to a boarding school in West Virginia on Thursday. Don't worry," I added when Betty's face fell. "I'll come up with a plan. Who told you guys about the museum?"

"Oona. Who else? She said you got caught snooping around. I've never seen her so mad. I thought she was going to start foaming at the mouth."

"Oh really? Did she tell you *why* I was snooping around?" Betty shook her head. "Yeah, I thought she might have left that part out. I was *snooping around* because there were Fu-Tsang at the museum."

"No!" Betty's bracelets jangled as she clapped a hand over her mouth.

"*Yes.* I saw a guy with a dragon tattoo on his butt. He was moving the paintings from an earlier exhibit. I thought he might be stealing them, so I followed him."

"Was he?"

"No," I admitted. "Turns out he was just taking them to another part of the museum. But I swear there's something weird going on over there. And the worst part is—Oona's got to be in on it. She saw the guy with the tattoo just like

I did. She knows the Fu-Tsang are involved, and she didn't tell anyone. I think she's stepped over to the dark side."

Betty winced. "I wish I could say I was surprised. I'll call Kiki as soon as class is over."

"Somebody needs to visit the museum, too. I'd go myself, but they said I was banned."

"I'll go. My next period is free, and the museum's only a few blocks away. What do you want me to do when I get there?"

"Have a look at the painting I saw being moved last night. I'll find out what it's called. There was something strange about it, but I can't put a finger on what it was. It was a picture of a naked woman lying with her back to the painter. It looked like there was something peeking over her shoulder."

"Sounds creepy. We should go online and look up the name of the painting as soon as I finish my lecture."

"Perfect. So does that mean you're really planning to teach this class? Do you know anything about New York history?"

"There's one thing I know pretty well." Her voice had already begun to adopt the mellifluous rhythm of an Indian accent. "Let's go inside. We'll talk again after class."

. . .

The classroom grew quiet as Betty approached the podium. She held up a portrait of a hideous woman whose fleshy jowls sported a faint five o'clock shadow. Judging by the woman's curly black wig and blue silk dress, the painting dated from the mid-eighteenth century. I suddenly knew the subject of Betty's lecture, and I couldn't help but smile.

"Can anyone identify this unfortunate-looking woman?" Betty asked, her accent perfect once more. No one raised a hand. "Very well. This is a former governor of the British Colony of New York. *His* name was Edward Hyde."

The class burst into laughter.

"Not only was he a poor excuse for a governor, Mr. Hyde loved to dress like his cousin Queen Anne. Unfortunately, as you can see, he did a very poor job of that as well. Today we will be reviewing a few techniques Mr. Hyde might have used to make his costume more convincing."

For the first time that day, I was almost beginning to enjoy myself when the door opened and a lemurlike fourth grader passed a note to the substitute teacher.

"Ananka Fishbein," she said with a touch of pity in her voice, "you have been summoned to the principal's office."

· · ·

Molly Donovan had just returned from walking the plank. I saw her shuffling out of the principal's office with her head hung and her spirit crushed. I took her arm and guided her around the corner.

"What's wrong?" I whispered. "What just happened?"

"I'm never getting out of here," Molly moaned. "I told my calculus teacher where she could stick her protractor, and all I got was a ten-minute lecture. Wickham said my parents' donations don't make any difference to her. She says I'm still here 'cause I have potential."

"I'm so sorry, Molly. Maybe you should tell her why you want to get expelled."

"You really think *that* would help?" Molly despaired.

"These people are all the same. If they think you have potential they want to suck it right out of you."

"I don't know if the principal's like that," I argued. "She might want to help you."

Molly snorted. "Face it, Ananka. I can't trust adults. You're my only hope."

. . .

The principal was at her computer when I entered. I could see the screen's reflection in her glasses. She was looking at the file of an Atalanta student. I didn't need to ask to know it was mine.

"Please close the door, Ananka," she ordered. "I wasn't aware that you're friends with Miss Donovan."

"You heard us talking?"

Principal Wickham looked up and smiled slyly. "My sight may be failing, but my hearing's as sharp as ever. So am I to understand that Molly *would like* to be expelled?"

"She wants to get out of New York. She says her parents think she's special."

"But Molly *is* special," said the principal.

"Special enough to be brought out at parties to entertain her parents' guests? Special enough to see her shrinks three times a week and have cameras put in her bedroom?"

"Oh dear." Principal Wickham took off her glasses and nibbled on the frame. "I'll have to think about what to do with Miss Donovan."

"I hear the Borland Academy's accepting new students." If I had to go, maybe I could take Molly with me.

"I appreciate the information, Ananka. But I didn't

ask you here to discuss Molly Donovan. I would like to have a little chat about *you*."

"Yeah, about that . . ." I grimaced as I said it. "I'm sorry for skipping school yesterday. I know you tried to help me. I apologize for letting you down."

"Yes, it was very disappointing, Ananka." Somehow her voice didn't match her words.

"And I'm sure my mother told you about the museum incident. Everyone's been watching me like I'm going to make a run for Mexico."

"Your mother seems to think you might leave school a little too early today. But that's not why I wanted to talk to you. I've just finished reading your essay, and I thought it merited a discussion."

I hadn't thought of the essay in more than a week, and I was mortified to remember what I had written. "I'm sorry for that, too. I'm sure it wasn't what you were expecting."

"That is true. But it's nice to know that after fifty years at Atalanta I can still be pleasantly surprised."

"You liked it?" I had never suspected she might take my work seriously.

"It's a remarkable piece of research. When Mr. Dedly returns, I'm certain he'll be pleased. In fact, I wouldn't be surprised if you receive an A for the semester. But tell me, how did you happen to find the Underground Railroad stop beneath Bialystoker Synagogue?"

"I do a little exploring here and there," I managed weakly.

The principal laughed. "You lead an interesting life, Ananka. You know, when I was a child, my grandfather used to tell stories about hidden rooms beneath Manhattan. He claimed to have visited some in his youth, though

I doubt he was on any noble mission. Apparently he was a bit of a rogue."

"He must have been one of the few who survived the plague," I said.

"I'm sorry? Which plague was that?"

"That's a whole other essay, Principal Wickham."

"Well, I'd love to read it when you're finished. I believe we might be able to have this one published."

"No!" I said it a little too quickly. My heart skipped when I thought of Kiki's reaction. "I wrote it for *you*. I don't want anyone else to read it."

"It's your essay, Ananka, but I urge you to reconsider. Information like this should be shared with the whole city. But I do believe we've discovered the source of your academic woes. You have a gift that has been ignored. We may need to take another look at your schedule."

It was nice to know I was gifted, but I didn't think it made much of a difference. How many IQ points does it take to milk cows and make cheese?

"But, Principal Wickham, tomorrow's my last day at Atalanta. Didn't my mother tell you? I'm leaving for the Borland Academy on Thursday."

Principal Wickham frowned. "This is all news to me," she said, picking up the phone. "I must have a word with your mother. Would you mind excusing me?"

"Sure," I said. Whatever she had planned, it wasn't going to work.

. . .

When I hit the hall, I knew one thing for certain. In forty-eight hours, I'd be in West Virginia. There was no point in fighting it. As soon as the Irregulars knew the truth, there would be nothing left to keep me in New York. In a stunning display of recklessness, I had confessed a secret to someone I barely knew, thinking nothing could possibly come of it. Now the Shadow City was once more in danger of discovery, and it was all my doing.

I couldn't face Betty, so I ditched class and made my way to the library. I took a seat at a computer terminal, intending to type out my confession. My elbow hit the mouse, and the screen illuminated. An earlier visitor had been reading the daily gossip columns online. An item in the *New York Post* announced that Queen Livia of Pokrovia would soon return to the city to search for her long-lost niece. I signed on to my e-mail account, and with my fingers poised above the keys I paused to think. My disgrace was inevitable, but though the Irregulars wouldn't be my friends for long, I had to help them while I could. I e-mailed the gossip column to Kiki, brought up a new Web page, and typed in the URL of the Metropolitan Museum of Art.

The Empress Awakens had replaced an exhibit entitled *From Venus to Vargas: A Celebration of the Female Form.* I had no doubt that it had been quite popular. It took little searching to identify the painting I had seen being moved. *Odalisque in Grisaille* was even lovelier than I remembered. But when I printed out a color copy, I saw no evidence of anything but a pillow behind the woman's shoulder. Paging through photos of the other works that had been on display, I found nudes lounging on sofas, nudes enjoying picnics, and nudes prancing through parks. Judging from the artwork, there seemed to be no shortage of things one could do without clothes. As I stifled a yawn, I happened upon a painting of a large blond woman gazing into a mirror. I didn't even need to read the name of the artist. It was the painting Siu Fah had described. It was the one she had copied.

I had barely finished printing out images of the paintings in the exhibit when the bell rang. Racing through the crowded halls, I managed to catch Betty before the next period started.

"You shouldn't have skipped my class," she huffed when I found her. "You might have learned something."

"Sorry, but I was making good use of my time. I brought you copies of the paintings from the exhibit that *The Empress Awakens* replaced. Have a look at these two—they're still at the Metropolitan Museum. See if you notice anything strange."

"Want to give me a hint?"

"Not yet," I said. "I'm just working on a hunch. I want you to see them with fresh eyes."

"Okay. I'll meet you in the girls' room during lunch." She took the printouts and tucked them away in her bag. "By the way, I heard a couple of your classmates gossiping about Oona."

"You did?" I'd been too busy to pick up on the latest gossip.

"Uh-huh. I guess Oona's the prize guest these days. All the rich girls' parents are desperate to have Lester Liu's daughter over for dinner."

"Figures."

"Yeah, but here's the thing. It sounds like Oona hasn't accepted any of their invitations. She keeps snubbing them all."

"She's smart. Turning them down once or twice will make her even more irresistible. There's nothing these girls respect more than someone who snubs them. It's all part of her plan."

"Yeah, I guess that makes sense. It just hurts to think that Oona would really turn traitor," Betty said miserably.

A few hours earlier, I might have replied with a catty remark. Now I kept quiet. Oona wasn't the only one who'd betrayed the Irregulars.

. . .

When the lunch bell rang, I grabbed a hummus sandwich from the cafeteria and it exploded when I took my first bite. I was washing the nasty stain out of my sweater when Betty walked into the bathroom, looking like she'd seen a ghost. Her eyes were glassy, her long black wig was askew, and her diamond nose ring was missing. A seventh grader on her way to the sink stopped to gawk at Betty as if she couldn't figure out what was wrong with the picture.

"Fix your hair," I ordered under my breath.

"Huh?" It was as if I had woken Betty from a dream.

"Look at yourself in the mirror," I demanded. "What's wrong with you?" I asked while she adjusted her costume.

Betty gazed into the distance, and I wondered if I should slap her like they do in the movies.

"You can leave now," I informed the seventh grader, who had finished washing her hands.

"I saw *Odalisque in Grisaille*," Betty finally said.

"Yeah? And?"

"You were right. There's something in it that isn't supposed to be there. Behind the woman's shoulder. You can't see it if you look straight at the painting. You have to be standing in just the right place."

"Anamorphosis." I was pleased to know I hadn't been hallucinating at the museum.

"Ana-what?"

"That's what those hidden images are called. They're optical illusions. You can see them only from certain angles. So what was it?"

"A squirrel."

We stood in silence, watching each other in the mirror. The painting I'd seen showed a woman in a Turkish setting. There was no reason for a squirrel to be there. I didn't even know if they *had* squirrels in Turkey.

"Are you sure?" I asked.

"I'm sure. There was another painting from the exhibit with a hidden squirrel. It was called *Venus and Adonis*. The squirrel was sitting on a tree branch."

"Do you think . . ."

"I don't *think*, Ananka. I *know*. Those are Kaspar's paintings." And then she started to cry.

· · ·

During last period I planned a daring after-school escape. My fate might have lain in the mountains of West Virginia, but I had to find a way to postpone it. At four o'clock, I bolted for the exit without waiting for Betty. I didn't know where I would go, but as soon as I was safe,

I'd contact the Irregulars. I hurried down the path that led to the school gates only to find my mother leaning against a parking meter.

"Going somewhere?" she asked.

"Home?" I sighed. It was time to admit defeat.

The subway was crammed with home-bound students, but only one had a parental escort. To hide my humiliation, I practiced the vacant stare of the jaded commuter, my eyes skimming the ads that ran along the top of the train. The most disturbing featured side-by-side pictures of an anonymous man's head. The *before* head was little more than a barren patch of scalp, while the *after* sprouted thick, luxurious hair. A brand of synthetic spray-on hair took credit for the improvement. For sixty blocks, I read and reread its tagline: *They'll never know the difference!* Hidden within those words, a mystical meaning eluded me. By the time the train doors opened at Spring Street, I knew what it was.

That evening, I sat in my room, staring at the wall for hours on end, without any means of contacting the outside world. I hadn't bothered to fill the two suitcases that still sat on the floor of my room. I didn't care if that meant leaving town with just the clothes on my back. I was the only person who knew that a terrible crime had been committed. I couldn't stop dwelling on five simple facts:

1. Lester Liu was a crook.
2. Oona Wong was a traitor.
3. So was I.
4. Something bad was about to happen.
5. There was no way I could leave New York.

The door to my room opened, and someone stepped inside.

"Go away," I said. "I'll pack later."

"I hear West Virginia's lovely this time of year." I turned to see Kiki sitting at my desk, looking completely at home. She unbuttoned her long black coat and threw one boot-clad leg over the other. "Send us some gouda when you get settled in."

"Do my mom and dad know you're here?"

"Shhhh. Of course not. But they couldn't lock *every* window in the apartment."

"How's Verushka?"

"She's awake and looking a little more human. It's too soon to say for sure, but I think Mrs. Fei may have saved her."

"That's wonderful." I smiled weakly. "Did you get the story I e-mailed you? Livia's coming back to New York."

"We'll worry about that later. How are you?"

"Miserable. This may be the last time I see you till summer."

Kiki raised an eyebrow. "I'm not going to hand you over to the cows just yet. I heard you had an interesting time last night. Want to tell me what happened?"

"Didn't Betty tell you?"

"I missed her first call. By the time I finally reached her, she was too upset to make much sense. Besides, I figured it would be far more entertaining to hear it from you."

"Well, when I went to see the Empress exhibit with Oona there were still some workmen in one of the galleries. They were packing the paintings from the previous exhibit. One of them bent over, and I saw he had a

Fu-Tsang tattoo. When he loaded a painting onto a dolly, I followed him to see where he was taking it. But he didn't steal it. He just delivered it to another part of the museum. I watched them hang the painting, and I thought I saw something strange, but I couldn't be sure.

"So this morning I went online to check out the paintings from the earlier exhibit. All of them were nudes. One was *The Toilet of Venus*—the same painting Siu Fah was copying before she escaped. Betty went to see two of the others this afternoon. She said they both had squirrels where there shouldn't be squirrels. She's convinced that Kaspar painted them."

"Yes, she managed to get that much across. What do *you* think?"

"I figured it out, Kiki. I know what's going on. Lester Liu and the Fu-Tsang have stolen some of the paintings from the naked lady exhibit. He used the Empress to get into the galleries when the alarms were turned off. Somehow they switched the artwork. The ones the workers put up last night—or shipped back to other museums—are all fakes. That's why the Taiwanese kids were kidnapped. He was forcing them to make reproductions. Now that they're finished, there's no telling what he plans to do with them. And I think Betty's right. I think Kaspar is with them. Who else would add a squirrel to a Rubens painting? It was a secret message for us."

"Excellent work, Dr. Watson," said Kiki. "But I know something you don't."

"What's that?"

"You saw Cecelia Varney's art collection the night of

the dinner party. If Lester Liu already owns enough art to fill a museum, why would he need to steal more?"

"Good question." She was right. It didn't make sense.

"Did you ever consider that he might not be stealing the paintings for himself? Remember when we heard that Livia and Sidonia were staying with that Russian gangster?"

"Oleg Volkov?"

"That's the one. I did a little research when you told me. You say the stolen paintings are all nudes?" I nodded. "Since he made his fortune, Volkov's become one of the biggest art buyers in the world. He's been on a spending spree for quite some time. But his taste is very specific. He doesn't care about style or period. I don't even think he cares if the art's any good. He only purchases paintings of naked women. The bigger the ladies, the better, it seems."

"You think Lester Liu stole the paintings for Oleg Volkov?"

"How else could Volkov complete his collection if the paintings he wants aren't for sale?"

"What about Sergei Molotov? Where does he fit in?"

"He must be in on it, too. Maybe he's not in New York just for me."

"What do you think they all want?"

"Money, power, revenge—or some mixture of the three. I suspect we'll find out soon enough."

"There's one other thing, Kiki. You're not going to like it. Oona knows what's going on. She saw the Fu-Tsang guy at the museum, but she didn't do anything. She's got to be in on the scheme."

Kiki's icy eyes glimmered. "I suppose you *could* come to that conclusion."

"You still don't believe it, do you? What does Oona need to do? Write a confession?"

"She's been our friend for years, and she's never let us down before. Before we condemn her, we owe her one thing."

"What?"

"The opportunity to defend herself. That's why we're all meeting at noon tomorrow at Lester Liu's house. Looks like you'll have to cancel your travel plans."

"But how am I going to do *that*? Everyone's watching me."

"We'll have to create a diversion. It doesn't have to be anything major, just enough to let you slip away."

It was then that I experienced one of my life's few moments of genius.

"Do you have time to make a delivery tonight?" I asked.

HOW TO FORGE A WORK OF ART

I would never advocate a life of crime, but the truth is, it's often easier to *forge* a work of art than it is to *expose* a fake. That's why there are forgeries hanging in some of the finest homes and museums around the world. In fact, some even claim that the *Mona Lisa* displayed in France's Louvre is merely a counterfeit copy of the original. So when it comes time for you to purchase your first masterpiece, it's best to know what you're up against. Here are some of the steps an accomplished forger may be taking to swindle you.

She'll Choose Her Subject Carefully

It's unusual (but not unheard of) for a forger to re-create an existing work of art. Most prefer to produce a *new* painting and pawn it off as a lost work of a respected, dead artist. However, a good forger will think twice before manufacturing a Picasso or a van Gogh. The more famous the artist, the more likely those pesky, microscope-wielding people known as "experts" will get involved.

An Artist Is Hired

It doesn't matter if a forger can't paint—there are plenty of people who can. Unfortunately, any American painter willing to do a forger's bidding is likely to charge an exorbitant fee. (Or worse, demand some of the profits!) Fortunately for the criminal community, many countries, such as China, have highly trained young artists who are willing to work for cheap. Most of the time, they don't even need to be kidnapped.

Another Painting Must Be Sacrificed

A forger can't just go to the local art supply shop to pick up supplies for her painting. A brand-new canvas is a sure sign of a fake. Often, she'll simply purchase a bad work of art that's the same age as the painting she's reproducing—and paint over it. The fraud can be detected with an X-ray, but she'll ensure that no one looks that closely until her money's in the bank.

She Does Her Homework

Experts often detect forgeries by examining the paints and brushes used to create it. A good forger will research the pigments and tools the original artist would have employed and stick to them—even if it means grinding up a few cochineal bugs to get the right color of red (carmine).

The Art Must Suffer the Ravages of Time

As a painting ages, fine cracks (called craquelure) appear on its surface. Unless a forger wants to wait a decade or two for these fissures to begin to appear, she'll have to re-create them herself. She may expose the painting to heat, etch the surface with a pin, or mix egg whites into her pigment. There's no fail-safe technique, but any of the three—if done well—will fool most eyes.

A Clever Story Is Invented

A forger can't just claim she inherited the painting from her grandma in Topeka. She must invent what's called a "provenance." This is a history of the work that traces its owners over the decades or centuries. Buyers should be particularly wary of romantic stories that involve ancient, aristocratic families who've fallen on hard times.

Fingers Are Crossed

Even when a forgery is detected, it's often swept under the carpet. The wealthy are loath to admit they've been duped, and even museums will sometimes leave a fake hanging on the walls simply to avoid embarrassment.

CHAPTER THIRTEEN

Runaway

At precisely 8:18 the next morning, a stink bomb was tossed into the teachers' lounge of the Atalanta School for Girls. Twenty-two more were ignited in quick succession and left to do their dirty work in the building's classrooms, broom closets, and lavatories. The final bomb was detonated in the school's main lobby as students and faculty fled, many retching and squealing with disgust. The culprit stood in full sight of the evacuating crowds, laughing maniacally at the chaos she'd caused. Though a gas mask hid most of her face, there was no mistaking Molly Donovan's bright red curls.

The wail of sirens drilled at my eardrums. Three police cars screeched to a halt in front of the school, and a SWAT team jumped from the back of an unmarked van. Molly didn't put up a fight—after all, it was she who had placed the call to 911. As she was handcuffed and dragged from the building, I slipped through the mesmerized mob and walked briskly away from the school.

Though my plan had proven a stellar success, I didn't feel like celebrating. My life was a mess, and it seemed easier to flee than to stay put and engage in a little spring-cleaning. I'd told too many lies for my parents to forgive me. There was no going back. Protecting the secret of the Shadow City had cost me my home. Sharing that secret would cost me the Irregulars.

I hung out in a magazine shop for an hour or so, catching up on my celebrity gossip, until the owner rudely informed me that he wasn't running a library. Back on the streets, my paranoia returned. Cop cars seemed to slow as they passed me. Shopkeepers watched from their windows. Finally, I purchased a cup of coffee and a bagel and headed for Central Park to wait for the Irregulars. A few lonely snowflakes drifted down from the clouds above. A square-jawed man in a tracksuit raced by, his fists punching their way through the icy air. A bleary-eyed dog walker waiting for a poodle to finish its business was forced to leap out of the jogger's path. I turned off the trail near Seventy-eighth Street and headed for the trees across from Lester Liu's mansion. A pair of battered wing tips stuck out from under a bush and I heard the soft clucking of a chicken.

"Who's there?" a frightened voice called out from between the leaves. "What do you want?"

"Howard? Is that you?"

"Maybe" was the cautious reply.

"It's Ananka. Remember me? I'm a friend of Kaspar's."

Howard Van Dyke's head popped out of the bush. With his beard festooned with twigs and leaves, he might have been a spirit of the forest.

"Well hello," he said merrily. "How kind of you to pay

me a visit. Would you like to come inside?" He shoved the branches apart, and I ducked into the bush. The clearing at the center was surprisingly spacious, with enough room for me, Howard, his chicken, Kaspar's squirrels, and a kitten. A week's supply of Vienna sausages and canned beans sat stacked on one side.

"Looks like you're well stocked," I said.

"Yes, it's very strange. Different people bring me groceries every day. On Monday it was a Chinese movie star. Yesterday it was a lovely Indian lady in a splendid dress."

"That was Betty," I said, though I couldn't recall seeing her dressed as a Chinese movie star. "They were all Betty. She likes to travel in disguise."

"I see." Howard nodded as if it all made perfect sense. "She said that I shouldn't live in the park. She told me I need to go home."

"Where is home?" Howard's kitten scrambled onto my lap, and I ran my fingers through its soft black fur.

"I lived over there." He pointed toward the west side of the bush. "I had a wife and two children. I see them sometimes, but they don't see me. They don't know who I am anymore."

"Why not?" I asked. "Why don't you live with them?"

"I made a mistake." Howard tucked his face into his beard and began to cry. "I bought bad stocks and lost all our money. I thought I could hide the truth, but my wife found out when they took the furniture away. That's when I decided to live in the park. I couldn't go home. My family is better off without me."

"How do you know that? Have you ever *asked* them how *they* feel?"

Howard looked up in surprise. "That's just what the movie star said."

"And what did you tell her?"

"I'm scared."

"You can't hide forever, Howard. You've got to go home sometime. Maybe they'll forgive you. Maybe they won't. But you need to give them the chance. It's only fair." Just saying it made me feel guilty. I looked down at the kitten purring in my lap. "Howard? Where did you get this kitten?"

"That's Kaspar's kitty. He found it the day he went to save the snakes."

"What do you mean, *save the snakes*?"

"He didn't want any more snakes to be eaten, so he went to save them. Then the man in the suit came and took him away."

I heard a Vespa in the distance. Kiki had arrived on the Upper East Side.

"Howard, I want you to listen carefully, okay? Take very good care of this kitten. Don't let it out of your sight, and don't let it get lost. In a couple of days, Kaspar will be back to get it."

"He will?" Howard was overjoyed. "You're going to save Kaspar?"

"Yes. And he'll be very happy if you still have this kitten." I looked back down at the kitten and counted again. There was no mistaking it. The animal had six toes on each foot.

· · ·

While I'd been visiting with Howard, the first blizzard of the season had begun. Fat flakes hurled themselves at the city. They clung to branches and stuck to the sidewalks, transforming New York into a scene from a black-and-white movie. The sounds of the city were muffled, and traffic lights swung in the wind, their bright green orbs the only color left on Fifth Avenue. In this silent, frozen world, Lester Liu's hulking white mansion loomed over Fifth Avenue like the Fortress of Solitude.

Kiki Strike chained her Vespa to a park bench across the street from Lester Liu's house, while Betty, DeeDee, and Luz converged on our meeting spot from three different directions. Nobody was smiling.

"A million dollars to the first person who can guess what I found in the park," I told the group.

"I'm not in the mood for games," said Luz. "And you don't have a million dollars."

"Just tell us, Ananka." DeeDee's eyelids drooped with exhaustion.

"Fine," I huffed. "I just had a chat with Kaspar's friend Howard. He's been sharing a bush with the heir to the Varney fortune."

"Howard has a six-toed cat?" Kiki's eyebrow touched the edge of her black knit cap.

"Yep. Kaspar found it the day he was kidnapped."

"Kaspar?" Betty's eyes sparkled at the mention of his name. The girl had it bad.

"Does that mean we can get New York's first family of crime kicked out of their fancy mansion?" Luz smirked.

"I thought we were trying to keep an open mind, Luz." Kiki sighed.

"Right now, I'm just trying not to freeze to death." DeeDee shivered and shook the snowflakes from her dreadlocks. "Can we get started? I was up all night making more Fille Fiable." She reached into her coat and brought out a large perfume bottle. "If I don't get some rest soon, I'm going to collapse."

"Go home if you're tired," Kiki offered. "You've done enough for today."

DeeDee shook her head. "No way. I'll sleep a whole lot better when I find out what's going on."

"Sure you want to know?" asked Luz.

"Don't start again," Kiki warned.

· · ·

I got the feeling we'd been expected. The butler opened the door and silently stepped to the side. Lester Liu greeted us in the lobby, a cane in one hand and a monogrammed handkerchief in the other. His head suddenly pitched backward and then slammed forward in a violent sneeze. He daintily wiped his nose and tucked the hanky into his breast pocket.

"Good afternoon, ladies." His normally smooth voice was raspy and nasal. "My daughter suspected you might drop by today. Forgive me for not shaking hands. I have a terrible cold, I'm afraid. I wouldn't want to endanger you."

I glanced at DeeDee, and I knew from the terrified look on her face that Lester Liu's cold had rendered our Fille Fiable powerless.

Kiki cut straight to the point. "Is Oona here?"

"She is indeed. She's in her room, being fitted for the dress she'll wear to the gala tomorrow night. I would be happy to take you to her." Lester Liu paused to give me a patronizing smile. "As long as Miss Fishbein promises not to wander off again."

Kiki spoke for me. "We'll all stay right behind you, Mr. Liu."

"Then please—follow me, ladies." He gestured toward a door riddled with nail holes. It was the same one that had been barricaded the first time I visited the mansion. The other girls slipped into the gloom on the other side, but I hesitated at the threshold. The air in the east wing was thick with dust. Tiny particles sparkled in the thin strips of daylight that squeezed through the slats of the shutters. The sparsely placed furniture appeared to be up-holstered in matted gray fur. I found it hard to believe that Oona Wong would spend much time in a part of the man-sion that looked and smelled like a mausoleum.

"You may stay here if you prefer, Miss Fishbein." I could hear the humor in Lester Liu's voice. "Sukh will see that you stay out of trouble."

I had no desire to hang around with Genghis Kahn's badly coiffed double. I hurried over to Betty, Luz, and DeeDee, who were huddled together in the center of the room.

"You've opened the east wing," Kiki noted calmly as she took everything in. "Not worried about the heating bill?"

Lester Liu guided us into an empty living hall. "I be-lieve I can afford all the necessary modern conveniences, Miss Strike. Now that my daughter has come to live with me, I needed the additional space. This wing of the man-sion will serve as her private quarters. As you can see, we still have some decorating to do." My eyes passed across the faded wallpaper decorated with interlacing lotus flowers and patches of oozing black mold. If the house wasn't haunted, it was missing an excellent opportunity. Kiki must have had the same thought.

"How's your ghost?" she asked. "Has she finally disappeared now that Oona's here with you?"

Lester Liu chuckled, which brought on a sneeze. "No. The ghost is still with us. I don't expect she will ever go away. Do you know what ghosts *are*, Miss Strike?"

We wandered through a garden room, its domed glass roof covered in snow. A tangle of dead plants crunched under our shoes. As we stepped over the petrified trunk of a palm tree, I felt Luz yank on my sleeve. We both knew Oona would never have gotten so far without turning back. It was obvious that Lester Liu wasn't taking us to see her, but Kiki seemed not to notice. I tapped on her shoulder, but she chose to ignore me.

"Does anyone know what ghosts are, Mr. Liu?" she asked.

"*I* do. Ghosts are how the past stays alive. No one can escape from his past, Miss Strike. Not me. Not you. Not even Cecelia Varney. Do you know why Ms. Varney locked herself away in this mansion? She believed she was haunted. She discovered that her fortune hadn't come from potato farms as she had always been told, but rather from her father's gun factories. A medium convinced her that the spirits of the people who'd been killed by those weapons would one day have their revenge. She gave the spirits an entire wing of her mansion in the hope of appeasing them, and she tried to squander her fortune so that no human heirs would inherit her guilt."

"So she *wasn't* concerned about the heating bill."

"No, Miss Strike. Ms. Varney understood that the past never goes away. Unless we take action, everything we do will someday come back to haunt us."

Beyond the garden room lay an enormous wood-paneled ballroom. Light spilled out from under a door at the far end. We were now deep inside the vast, empty wing of the mansion. The sharp click of Lester Liu's cane on the parquet floor suddenly stopped.

"Ah, here we are," said Lester Liu. "You'll find what you're after inside that room."

"I think I'll stay here," Luz mumbled.

"Me, too," DeeDee agreed. Betty wouldn't budge.

"Come, come ladies, what's to be frightened of?"

Kiki gave me a sharp nod. While I stepped toward the door, she stayed behind, standing within arm's reach of Lester Liu. I knew she could take him out with a single punch. I twisted the handle of the door, but it seemed to be stuck.

"It won't open." My mouth was dry and I felt light-headed.

"Then I suggest you turn the lock," Lester Liu advised.

I felt the lock click between my fingers, and I held my breath as I opened the door. There, sitting on the floor of a dusty room, were more than a dozen people, their hands and feet bound, their eyes blindfolded, and gags stuffed in their mouths. I could see nothing but the top of their heads. All but one had black hair.

"Surprise!" called a familiar voice.

Sergei Molotov slid into view with a pistol in his hand. I tried to slam the door in his face, but Molotov grabbed my arm and pulled me into a headlock, the gun jammed into my temple. I heard him sniff at my neck.

"Do you bathe? You smell disgusting. Like armpit." He had just gotten a nose full of Fille Fiable.

"Let me go. I'm a double agent," I whispered. "I've been working for Mr. Liu."

"You have?" Sergei sounded confused, and I felt his grip weakening.

"What *are* you doing, Mr. Molotov? Put the girl with the other children," Lester Liu ordered. While he was distracted, the Irregulars attacked. But before Kiki could land a punch, Lester Liu drew a long dagger from his cane. The tip rested in the hollow of Kiki's throat. The other girls froze.

"It looks as if your past has returned to haunt you, Miss Strike."

"Hello, Princess," Molotov sneered at Kiki. "How nice to see you again. And how is my old friend Verushka Kozlova? Is it true what the newspapers say—that she may already be dead?"

Kiki ignored him and turned to Lester Liu. "You trust this man? You're aware that he has a nasty habit of murdering his employers, aren't you? Who knows what he'll do to you."

"That might be a cause for concern if Mr. Molotov were in my employ." Lester Liu lowered his dagger and offered Kiki a smug smile. "But he takes orders from the head of this operation—your dear aunt Livia. I can see no reason for her to harm me when our arrangement has proven so mutually beneficial. She will provide her patron, Oleg Volkov, with some artwork he desires, and Mr.

Volkov will generously fund Livia's return to New York. She, in turn, will give me your map of the underground tunnels. As a bonus, I will be able to enjoy my revenge.

"Now, ladies," said Lester Liu, as charming as ever. "Would you mind joining Miss Fishbein? I apologize if your quarters feel a bit cramped, but we don't intend to have you as guests for long. Mr. Molotov, would you please immobilize the girls? I'd rather not have any disturbances this evening."

"You're going to kill us, I suppose," said Kiki as Molotov tied her hands behind her back.

"Oh, heavens no." Lester Liu chuckled. "I am a businessman, not a murderer. I don't intend to *kill* your friends. I plan to *sell* them. There are countries where people your age demand very high prices. As for you, Miss Strike, you are no longer my concern. Your aunt may do whatever she pleases with you, though I can't help but hope that her plans include a great deal of pain."

"What about Oona?" Kiki asked.

Lester Liu licked his lips as if savoring a delicious thought. "I have a special punishment in mind for the girl who calls herself my daughter. I must admit I'm both impressed and appalled by her greed. I bought her trust at a bargain price. I can't tell you how easy it was to turn her against you. She wanted nothing less than the wealth of an Empress. I think you'll agree that it's only fitting she should share the Empress's fate."

"You know, there's a problem with your plans," said Kiki. "Livia's map of the tunnels is worthless. Your men would be eaten by the rats in minutes."

"That is no longer a problem, Miss Strike. Why do you think I worked so hard to win my daughter's trust when I could have just killed you all? She has told me your little secret. I have what I need to keep the rats at bay. Now, if you'll excuse us, there's a party to plan."

Molotov flipped the light switch and left us in the darkness. I tried to wriggle my hands free, but the rope burned my wrists.

"Hey, Kiki. Would this be the wrong time to say I told you so?" It was DeeDee's voice.

"Would this be the wrong time to say that Oona's dead if I get out of here before her father has a chance to kill her?" Luz added.

"Kaspar! Kaspar? Are you in here?" Betty whispered.

"Umm-hum," said a muffled voice.

"Do you think anyone will hear us if we scream?" I asked.

"Do you want them to gag us, too?" Kiki asked. "Stay calm. We've got to find a way to save Oona."

"Save Oona?" Luz spat. "In case you've forgotten, she's the reason we're in this mess. That greedy little traitor even told her daddy about the rat-repelling perfume. I say we save our own butts and let Oona get what's coming to her."

"You'd let her die in an air-tight coffin? You'd let her corpse lie on display at the Metropolitan Museum of Art?" Kiki asked. "Whatever she's done, she doesn't deserve *that*."

"What do you mean?" Betty whispered.

"Don't you get it? That's what Lester Liu meant by *sharing the Empress's fate*. That's what he plans to do to her."

"Oh, come on," Luz said. "He's not going to kill her. How would he explain his own daughter's disappearance?"

"That's a good question," I noted.

"Entombed forever in the Metropolitan Museum of Art. That's pretty bad," DeeDee said pensively.

"I don't care," snapped Luz. "It's still better than ending up somebody's slave."

"Nobody's going to die or be sold into slavery." It was a familiar male voice.

"Kaspar!" Betty cried.

The shutters on the windows opened just enough to dimly light the room and reveal a relatively clean and startlingly handsome Phineas Parker.

"Hello, Betty." Kaspar beamed as he loosened her restraints. "Did you find my squirrels?"

"That's how we knew the paintings in the museum were forgeries," she said. "I'm so glad I found you. I—I mean *we*—have been looking for you for weeks."

"I'm glad *you* found me, too." I could see that his feelings for Betty hadn't changed.

"So, Kaspar, how did you end up getting kidnapped?" I asked, feeling somewhat embarrassed to be a captive witness to their reunion. "Howard said you were trying to save some snakes?"

"I guess you could say that," Kaspar replied with a laugh. "The morning after your dinner party, Howard and I were having breakfast when I saw a delivery van from a company called Tasty Treasures pull up in front of the mansion. I was certain it was the same one I'd seen deliver the snakes. So when the driver went inside the mansion, I snuck over to see what was inside his van. I found cages crammed with snakes and monkeys and lizards. I couldn't let them loose in the streets—I'd given Betty my word. I was trying to come up with a plan when the deliveryman came back. I heard him speaking with a Russian man about a shipment of cats that had been shipped to Malaysia. I guess six-toed cats are considered lucky there. The deliveryman admitted that he'd kept one for himself. I looked down and saw a kitten curled up on the floor of the van. I didn't know what else to do, so I grabbed it and ran. Of course the Russian saw me and followed me into the park. Howard managed to trip him, which gave me just enough time to scribble a note to Betty. I don't know what would have happened to me if I hadn't had some of my drawings in my pocket. When he realized I was an artist, he locked me up in that basement with the other kids."

Kaspar turned to Betty. "Were you worried about me?"

"*Very,*" Betty whispered.

"Enough with the lovey-dovey crap," Luz interjected. "How did you just break free?"

"A present from Oona." Kaspar held up a tiny X-Acto knife. "You should have a little more faith in your friends."

DeeDee's eyes narrowed. "Why would Oona give you a knife?"

"To help us escape. If it weren't for Oona, we'd all be crammed in a shipping crate right now. One of the Taiwanese girls disappeared after we finished our paintings, and the guards decided it was too risky to keep us in the same place. They were planning to ship us out of New York, but Oona convinced her father to bring us here in case any more work needed to be done.

"Last night, she brought me the knife and a set of lock-picks. She told us to sneak out tomorrow evening while everyone is at the opening of the exhibition."

"Would this be a bad time to say I told you so?" Kiki asked DeeDee.

"Just because Oona spared Kaspar doesn't mean she's a saint," DeeDee responded tersely. "She still helped Lester Liu steal those paintings."

"Wrong again," Kaspar said. "Oona's never been in league with her father. She's going to expose him tomorrow at the party. We figured out where he got the names of the kids he kidnapped, and Oona knows where all the paintings are hidden. She wants to humiliate him."

"Why would she tell you that?" Luz scoffed. "You're practically a stranger."

"Who was she supposed to tell?" Kaspar said. "From what I've heard, none of you believed her."

"We might have, if she had confided in us," Betty mumbled.

"Oh my God, what have we done?" DeeDee whimpered as the truth began to sink in.

"Does Oona know what kind of danger she's in?" Kiki asked.

"No," said Kaspar. "She thinks her father's fooled."

"Untie me," Kiki demanded.

"I will if you insist, but Molotov will be back to check on us later. We don't have any chance of escaping tomorrow if anyone's missing when he returns."

"Untie me," Kiki repeated. "And untie Ananka. We know the layout of the mansion, and somebody has to find Oona before it's too late."

HOW TO PREDICT THE WEATHER

For years I was convinced that New York's meteorologists were all out to get me. Each morning I watched their forecasts. I laughed at their cheesy jokes, admired their superwhite teeth, and believed everything they told me. As a result, I've been buried in blizzards, drenched by rainstorms, and baked alive during heat waves. That's why I've learned to rely on my own senses for signs that foul weather may be on the way.

Bees Buzz Lower

When a storm is approaching, the air becomes thick with moisture, which means insects (and the birds that eat them) will often buzz about closer to the ground. Other animals, including cats and dogs, have been known to predict tornados and earthquakes, so if Rover starts acting like he's been possessed, it may be time to take cover.

Sound Becomes Sharper

No, you aren't developing superhuman powers. The fact that you can hear those men in masks whispering from a block away indicates that a low-pressure front is moving in. Prepare for a day or two of nasty weather.

Smoke Sends Signals

Look up at the chimneys around you. If the smoke rises straight into the air, go ahead and plan your picnic, stakeout, or rocket launch. If it flattens out or lingers in the sky, you'll probably need a rain check.

The Sky Changes Color

As any professional shepherd could tell you, a red sky in the evening is a good predictor of fair weather, while a red sky in the morning means rain is on the way. But if you happen to see a rainbow in the west, don't bother with the fabled pot of gold. Search for your umbrella instead.

Grandpa Begins Complaining

The elderly can be excellent weather forecasters. Their aching joints often signal a drop in barometric pressure, which means rain is coming.

Stenches Start to Linger

There are days when New York City smells like the inside of an outhouse. When bad weather's approaching, smells often become much stronger. If your home is surrounded by flowers and trees (rather than garbage cans, dog piles, and sewer drains), this might not be such a bad thing.

CHAPTER FOURTEEN

Scavenger Hunt

tay right behind me and do what I do," Kiki ordered. She picked the lock on our door and crept silently along the walls, pausing from time to time to listen for signs of movement. Dressed in black, Kiki could fade into the shadows. But though I'd traded my crimson sweater for Luz's army jacket, I still felt conspicuous, and I scolded myself for not being better prepared.

We had just dipped our toes in the pool of light from the mansion's foyer when the doorbell rang, and we heard footsteps descending the grand staircase. Kiki slid back into the darkness. When I tried to follow, I stumbled over my own feet and landed on my butt with a soft thud. The footsteps in the foyer came to a halt. Kiki stuck out a hand and with one swift pull yanked me upright. We flattened ourselves against the wall as the steps drew closer and the butler appeared in the doorway. Sukh stood motionless, listening, while his eyes slowly scanned the room. We were right beside him, no more than three feet away. I closed my eyes and tried not to faint when I realized what was hanging from his arm. It was the Empress's jade shroud.

"Forget what just happened," Kiki whispered in my ear once Sukh had returned to the foyer. "Forget about it right now, or none of us will ever make it out of here."

The front door opened. "May I help you?" we heard the butler say.

"Hi!" My head whipped around to face Kiki. It was Iris's voice. "I'm looking for my friend Oona."

"Aren't you a little *young* to be friends with Miss Liu?" Sukh sounded skeptical.

Iris was offended. "I'm just short for my age. Can I see her?"

"Miss Liu is indisposed at the moment. Perhaps you could return another time."

"Is something the matter with her?" I could tell Iris knew something was wrong. "Is she sick?"

"Miss Liu is fine," the annoyed butler replied. "But she's not seeing visitors today."

"Have any other girls stopped by?"

"Not to my knowledge. Good day, miss."

"Please tell her Iris was here!" Iris shouted as the door closed.

"What was she doing?" I whispered to Kiki as Sukh's footsteps grew fainter. "Shouldn't she be in school?"

"Shouldn't you?" Kiki asked.

When at last the coast was clear, Kiki turned the corner and stole toward the stairs. I would have given at least one minor appendage to stay behind in the abandoned wing of the mansion. Beneath the dim glow of the crystal chandelier, there was nowhere to hide. We might as well have been cardboard targets at a shooting range. At the top of the stairs, we found ourselves standing at the end of a long hallway. There were eight closed doors to pick from. Our lives depended on how well we chose.

"Most of these rooms weren't being used when I planted the bugs," Kiki whispered. "Oona's got to be in one of them." She tiptoed toward the first door, listened with her ear to the wood, and then peeked through the keyhole. "This could be it," she said, ducking into the room.

The shutters were open, and a pale, silvery light washed over a magnificent bedroom. Outside, the air was thick with snow, and the afternoon sun a dim blur. Against the far wall sat an antique four-poster bed with its green velvet curtains drawn shut. My steps muffled by a priceless Persian rug, I bolted across the room and heaved the heavy fabric to one side. Someone lay sleeping on top of the covers, her glossy black hair spread out over the pillow.

"Oona?" I whispered. When there was no response, I poked the body. It felt cold and stiff beneath my fingers. "There's something wrong with her," I told Kiki. Without thinking, I yanked the drapes back farther, and the light fell upon a gruesome sight. Kiki's hand clapped over my mouth, stifling the scream that was trying to escape. Lying on the bed was a corpse clothed only in a red silk robe. We were too late. Oona was dead.

"Ananka. Ananka, listen to me. It's not Oona." Kiki refused to remove her hand until I opened my eyes for another look. The person on the bed was the same size as

Oona, and even in death it was easy to see that she, too, had once been a beauty. But now her leathery skin was stretched tight over her cheekbones. The tip of her nose was crumbling and her mouth hung open in an endless scream. It was the mummy.

"*That's* the Empress? How old *was* she?" I managed to mutter once I'd stopped hyperventilating. I had always imagined the Empress as an older woman, but the body on the bed looked remarkably youthful.

"Hard to tell," Kiki replied. "She must not have been much older than we are when she died. I'm starting to feel sorry for the poor thing. She gets murdered, her grave is robbed, and then her mummy's dumped in a bedroom on the Upper East Side."

"What do you think Lester Liu will do with her?"

"Whatever he has in mind, I doubt it'll be fit for an empress."

The thought of a two-thousand-year-old mummy buried beneath the refuse on a garbage barge or decorating the den of an eccentric collector was too bleak to bear.

"We've got to save her," I told Kiki. "Even if she was a traitor, she doesn't deserve this."

"We'll try," Kiki agreed. "But the living have to come first."

· · ·

Back in the hall, Kiki cautiously approached a second room. We were inches away when the door opened a crack, and we heard a familiar laugh on the other side. I froze in terror. In seconds I would have come face-to-face with Lester Liu if Kiki hadn't snatched my hand and hauled me down the corridor. A door swung open as we passed. Oona sat alone on the floor of an enormous bedroom, dangerously close to a blazing fireplace big enough to roast a prize-winning pig. Kiki and I slipped inside and quietly closed the door behind us. I heard Oona talking softly, as if to an invisible companion. She had propped up her mother's photograph on the floor in front of her and surrounded it with tangerines, apples, and limes. In her lap lay a pile of brightly colored paper that looked from a distance like money. Every few seconds, Oona took a handful of cash and flung it into the flames. I was certain she had lost her mind and I started to speak, but Kiki put a hand on my shoulder. "Wait," she mouthed silently.

When the last scrap of paper had been transformed into ash, Kiki and I approached the fireplace. Hearing our footsteps, Oona glanced over her shoulder before returning her eyes to the fire.

"Does she have what she needs now?" Kiki asked softly.

"It's only the beginning." Oona's cheeks were flushed from the heat. "I have fourteen years to make up for."

"What were you doing?" I asked.

"Sending my mother ghost money for the afterworld. She'll need it when she finally gets there." Oona smiled sadly when she saw the confusion that must have been written on my face. "In China, many people believe that what you burn in this world will belong to your ancestors in the next. I should have made these offerings a long time ago, but I've been a terrible daughter. If my mother's a hungry ghost, it's all my fault. It was my duty to take care of her and punish Lester Liu." She stood up and brushed the ashes from her clothes. "The door was locked. Did you pick it?"

Kiki raised an eyebrow. "No, it opened as we ran by."

Oona nodded. "The ghost must have let you in. But that doesn't mean you should stay. It's too dangerous for you guys to be here right now."

"Too late," I told her, letting the ghost comment pass. "We've already been kidnapped. We just saw Kaspar downstairs. He let us in on your plan. Why didn't you tell *us*? We could have helped."

"You were busy, and it was my responsibility—not yours. I had a hunch my father was up to something, but I couldn't figure out what it was. I had to get close to him and make him believe that he'd won me over. So I took his gifts and spent his money and played his game. After a while, I convinced him. Turns out I'm a better actress than I thought, 'cause I ended up convincing you guys, too. But then again, the minute you found out I was Lester Liu's daughter, you were all willing to believe the worst of me."

"Kiki wasn't. She always trusted you. But you're right about the rest of us. I promise it will never happen again." It hurt to admit that I'd been such a fool, but I knew telling the truth was the only way to keep Oona's friendship.

"Don't worry. I forgive you," Oona said sadly.

"So all this time you've been trying to avenge your mother's death? If you'd just told us what your father had planned . . ."

"I didn't know. I had my suspicions after I met Siu Fah. But I didn't know he was stealing paintings from the museum until I saw the Fu-Tsang guy the night you got caught. After we left, I told my father I'd figured it all out and said I wanted to help. It was the only way to find out where he was hiding the Taiwanese kids before something terrible happened to them. But I had to give him a secret if I wanted to make him believe I was on his side."

"We know." I couldn't help but sound disappointed. "You told him about the rats. That wasn't very smart, Oona. What if something goes wrong? If he gets his hands on a map of the Shadow City, the whole city's in danger."

Oona's temper flared. "Do I *look* like an idiot? I didn't tell him about the *perfume*. I gave him my old Reverse Pied Piper. If he ever gets the map, his men are going to be rat food the minute they enter the tunnels. But that's just plan B. If I have my way, Lester Liu won't get that far."

Kiki waited a moment for Oona to calm down. "I understand that you're doing this for your mother, but do you really think she'd want you to put yourself in danger? And what about Mrs. Fei? She'd be heartbroken if something happened to you."

"You're talking about the person who's been spying on me for years?" Oona huffed.

"She loves you, Oona. She was only listening so she could help you. She's always taken care of you and treated you like a daughter. What about your duty to *her*?"

Oona started to speak but stopped. She sat down on the side of her bed and put her head in her hands. It was as though she'd found a fatal flaw in her plans. "You're right. I've been so stupid. That's what the medium was trying to tell me, but I heard only what I wanted to hear. I ignored all that stuff about laundry detergent and someone listening. I misunderstood the whole message. But it doesn't matter. I can't stop now. I've come too far. There's no going back."

"Yes, there is!" I insisted. "We can all get out tonight. We'll find a way."

"Lester Liu is going to kill you," Kiki said bluntly.

"I'm sure he'd like to." Oona looked up with a triumphant smirk. "But after tomorrow, he'll be in jail."

"No, Oona. He's going to kill you *tomorrow*," said Kiki, and panic flickered across Oona's face. "We had a little chat with him earlier. He said he wants you to die like the Empress. I'm pretty sure that means two things: First, he's going to switch your body with the Empress's. Ananka and I just found the mummy in a room down the hall. They must be getting the coffin ready for you. Second, he wants you to be buried alive just like she was. My guess is you'll be given a drug that paralyzes you. Then he'll let you smother to death inside the mummy's airtight coffin while everyone at the party watches. You'll be covered with the jade shroud, so nobody will ever know the difference. Sound like fun to you?"

I shivered at the thought, but Oona stood firm. "I'll just have to come up with another idea."

"Here's one. Get out of here while you can and go to the police," I said.

"No." Oona put her foot down. "Lester Liu could escape—just like last time. I'd have to watch my back for the next thirty years. So would the rest of you. I've got to find a way to end this for good." She turned to Kiki. "Isn't that what you'd do if you were in my shoes? Would you give Livia and Sidonia another chance to get away?"

Kiki took a deep breath. "Maybe there *is* a way," she said thoughtfully. "But you can't do it on your own. You have to let the rest of us help."

"Have you both lost your minds?" I asked.

· · ·

Minutes after Kiki and I returned to captivity, Sergei Molotov arrived to check on his prisoners. He slinked into the room like a debonair demon and flipped on the lights, temporarily blinding us all. His slicked-back hair gleamed like motor oil and drew attention away from his unhealthy complexion and needlelike nose.

"Are you comfortable, my little princess?" Molotov thrilled at the sight of Kiki bound and tied. "I spoke with Queen Livia this afternoon. She and Mr. Volkov will be in America soon, and she is looking forward to seeing you. She said she hopes to arrive in time for the funeral of Verushka Kozlova. What is the English phrase—*She will spin on her grave?*"

"Spit," said DeeDee.

"Yes, thank you," said Molotov. "She will spit on the grave of Verushka Kozlova."

Kiki stared at the wall as if she hadn't heard a word. The ropes around her wrists and ankles were only for show, and if it hadn't been for our friend upstairs, Kiki would have coldcocked Molotov in no time. When she didn't answer, Molotov drew closer. I caught a whiff of his rank aftershave.

"You don't speak? I have ways to make people speak. I was told not to hurt you, but maybe Mr. Liu would not mind if I damage one of your friends? Maybe this one?" He kicked me in the shin hard enough to make me yelp.

"You're a monster, Molotov." Kiki's voice was thick with anger. "You want me to speak? Then let me ask you a question. What's going to happen when Oleg Volkov doesn't get his paintings? What do you think he'll do to you? I hear he can be very creative."

When Molotov smiled, his thin red lips stretched taut across a row of gray teeth. "What nonsense. The paintings are absolutely safe. Queen Livia will deliver them to Mr. Volkov herself. The question you should be asking is how will *she* deal with *you*? I hope her plan is as brilliant as Mr. Liu's."

"You're a slow learner, aren't you, Molotov? You'll never keep me locked up for long. And this time, I'm not going to let you and that wicked old witch get away."

"Who is going to set you free, Princess? The ghost?" Molotov rolled his eyes back and waved his long, pale arms in the air. "Woooooooo . . ." I might have laughed if the wail hadn't been the same one we'd heard on the surveillance tapes. Lester Liu had known about our bugs all along.

Molotov had started to take his performance to a whole new level when we all heard a thump outside the room. Then another. And another. They might have been the noises that old houses make. They could have been the storm outside—or a tree branch banging against a window. But they sounded like footsteps. The Taiwanese kids sat up straighter. The Irregulars trained their eyes on the door. Sergei Molotov stopped midwail and perked up his ears.

"Maybe she will," Kiki said with an impudent grin.

"This old house is falling apart," Molotov pronounced. "The spirits are not coming to save you. The Chinese girl's mother is no more a ghost than your mother is. I am the only ghost here. *I* throw the food. *I* make the noises."

"Are you making those?" Luz laughed. "'Cause if so, I'm really impressed."

The thumping grew louder and louder. Someone—or *something*—was coming closer.

"Who said it was Oona's mother?" Kiki taunted him. "Maybe Cecelia Varney's still hanging around. She can't be too happy about what you did to her cats."

Molotov pulled his gun from his waistband and waited. The thumping stopped right outside the door. As frightened as I was, I couldn't help but enjoy Molotov's terror.

"You know, Molotov, a wise man once told me what ghosts really are." The quiver in Kiki's voice didn't match her expression. "They're the past returning to settle the score. In China they have hungry ghosts, but in Pokrovia we have Likho. Remember her? The one-eyed hag, the spirit of misfortune that everyone knows not to tempt. What if she's finally come for you? After all you've done, didn't you think she'd catch up with you sooner or later?"

Molotov could no longer bear the suspense. He flung open the door and pointed his gun into darkness beyond. There was nothing there.

"See, Princess," he said, recovering his courage. "No ghosts. It was only the house making noises."

"Remind yourself of that when you're walking back through the dark," Kiki said with a snicker.

. . .

I had no idea what time it was. Somebody's head was on my shoulder, and a few people were snoring. I sat staring into a room so dark that it didn't make much difference whether my eyes were open or shut. I should have been making plans, but instead I was thinking of the hidden room beneath Bialystoker Synagogue when a sliver of light slid under the crack of the door. I heard a click and the door began to creak open. A thin figure in a long white nightdress floated into the room. The candle in its hand lit a pale face framed by dark hair that flowed over two thin shoulders. For a moment, I was certain it wasn't Oona, but her ghost.

"Molotov's gone and everyone else is asleep," she whispered.

"Good." Kiki had stayed awake, thinking. She shook Betty and prodded Luz with the toe of her shoe. "Get up," she urged everyone as Oona untied us one by one. "Time to go to work."

"Where am I?" mumbled Luz.

"You're tied up in a homicidal smuggler's haunted mansion," I informed her.

"Right. I remember now. My mom's going to be *pissed*."

"That's Luz Lopez for you," Oona quipped as she removed DeeDee's restraints. "Fearless in the face of death, but terrified of her own mother."

As soon as she was free, DeeDee stood up and threw

her arms around Oona. The logical scientist had disappeared, and a sentimental sap had taken her place. "I'm so sorry for thinking you were a traitor. I really got carried away. I hope you can forgive me."

"Me, too," Betty said, wiping both sleep and tears from her eyes.

"Make that three of us. I can't believe we were all so stupid," said Luz. "Now can we rescue you and get the heck out of here?"

Oona gave Luz's ponytail a friendly yank. "Apologies accepted, but you can't leave. The alarms are on. If you try to open one of the doors or windows they'll go off, and it will be the Fu-Tsang and not the police who answer the call."

"Who cares?" Luz moaned. "I'm dead either way. My mom really is going to kill me."

"At least you'll get to suffer in New York. I'll be milking cows in West Virginia," I pointed out.

"You're both always welcome in the park." It was hard to tell if Kaspar was serious.

"Okay, okay. Can we focus, please?" said Kiki Strike. "We'll save everybody one at a time. Oona gets to be first."

"It's about time." Oona pretended to complain.

"Don't push it, Wong," Kiki cracked. "I've got a plan, but we're going to need some supplies. Since we're stuck in this mansion, we'll just have to make use of the resources at our disposal. And, Oona, if we can't get everything we need, we're getting out of here tonight. Understood?"

"Understood."

"All right. First things first. Kaspar, untie the other kids. They must need a good stretch by now. Oona, explain to them what's happening. DeeDee, how much Fille Fiable do we have left?"

"There was a whole bottle in my coat pocket. I don't think they took it."

"Great. We got lucky. Now for the hard part. Lester Liu wants to bury Oona alive, so he's going to need a drug of some sort—one that will paralyze her so she won't move around in the glass coffin. Whatever it is, we have to find it and replace it with something harmless. DeeDee, you're coming with me to look for it. If we can't find the drug, the whole deal's off."

"It could be one of the drugs they use to paralyze people during surgery," DeeDee said. "I say we start in the kitchen. Something like that would probably be kept refrigerated."

"Keep an eye out for snakes," I warned.

"That goes without saying," said Kiki. "Okay, Betty, you and Kaspar need to find some dresses for us to wear to the party tomorrow. Since we can't go home to change, we'll have to make do with whatever Cecelia Varney has in her wardrobe—"

"Wait, wait, wait," Luz interrupted. "We're going to the opening of the exhibit? Are you nuts? Lester Liu would recognize us in a second—and Ananka's probably banned from the museum for life."

"Just till I'm eighteen," I corrected her.

"We'll just have to be careful and hope that the Fille Fiable does the rest."

"But I don't understand your plan," said Betty. "How are we going to keep Oona from ending up inside the Empress's coffin?"

"We're not," Kiki told her.

"But she'll smother!" DeeDee argued.

"Not if Luz finds a way to let air into the coffin."

"So we're going to let Lester Liu think he's won?" Luz was intrigued.

"And we'll be at the exhibition to witness Oona rise from the dead and send her father to jail."

"That's one way to get everyone's attention." Oona sounded pleased with the plan. "What do you want me to do?"

"You and Ananka are going to hide the Empress," Kiki said.

"What for?" Luz asked. "She's already dead."

"Because it's the right thing to do. Otherwise they're going to get rid of her, and Ananka and I agree that she's had it rough enough."

"Where are we going to hide her?" I asked.

"I know a place," said Oona.

· · ·

We parted ways in the mansion's foyer. Oona, Betty, Kaspar, and I slunk upstairs to Cecelia Varney's bedroom, expecting the alarms to go off at any moment. The house was quiet and though all of us had removed our shoes, our footsteps sounded like thunder to my ears. At the top of the stairs, Oona passed the room with the mummy and opened the fourth door on the hall. The moonlight fell on a single twin bed covered with a ratty brown blanket. There was no other furniture in the room. The walls were bare and the floorboards naked. Nothing offered any pleasure to the eye or touch. It looked as if Cecelia Varney had lived the life of a medieval nun. Oona lit her candle and floated across the chamber.

"There's nothing here," whispered Betty. "I don't even see a closet."

"Maybe you're not looking hard enough." Oona stopped in front of a fireplace that dwarfed the massive one in her room. She tilted an andiron and pushed the back wall of the firebox until there was an opening big enough to squeeze through. "I'm the only person who knows about this."

"How did you find it?" I marveled.

"The ghost showed me the first day I was in here alone," she said. "She wanted me to see it."

"So you really believe there's a ghost?" Kaspar asked.

"Of course there's a ghost," Oona replied as if it should have been obvious to everyone.

. . .

The first thing I saw when I entered the cramped room behind the fireplace was someone looking back at me. A young blonde in a black lace gown stared out from a portrait on the wall with a cold, haughty expression on her beautiful face. I recognized Cecelia Varney from the photo that had accompanied her obituary, but it was hard to believe it was the same woman who had spent her last fifty-five years hiding from the rest of the world. Lining the room were racks of beautiful gowns, most in styles that had been the height of fashion in the 1940s and '50s. A wall of shelves held black velvet boxes filled with sparkling jewels. It was as if the old hermit had imprisoned the dazzling socialite inside a secret chamber. Adding to the eeriness, every item was in pristine condition, and there wasn't a speck of dust in the room.

"Can you believe it?" Oona picked up a diamond necklace and let it twinkle in the candlelight. "Cecelia Varney had all this and it only made her miserable. She got to the point where she couldn't figure out who loved her and who loved her money, so she started to think that her fortune was cursed. She figured if she could spend every last dime before she died she could keep the money from hurting someone else. Sounds crazy, but maybe she was right."

"How do you know all that?" I asked.

"My father found her journals. I read as much of them as I could stand. It was some pretty depressing stuff. You know her last husband stole a million dollars from her and ran away to Venezuela? After that, who *would* you trust? I'd probably leave all my money to a bunch of cats, too.

"So what do you think, Betty? Does Cecelia Varney have what we need?"

Betty examined the dresses on one of the racks.

"They're a little old-fashioned, and they're all size six. I'll have to make a few alterations, but I think I can come up with something. It's not going to be pretty, though." She pulled out a shimmering beaded black dress that looked smaller than the others. "She couldn't have been more than a teenager when she bought this. I think I know who gets to wear it tomorrow."

As Kaspar and Betty ransacked the clothes racks, Oona and I tiptoed to the mummy's chamber and wrapped the body in a sheet. Carefully, without bending or bumping the Empress, we brought her back to Cecelia Varney's bedroom. We were just outside the hidden room when muffled voices reached our ears.

"I don't understand, Betty." Kaspar's voice lacked its usual confidence. "I thought we had a deal. If I watched the mansion, you would have dinner with me."

Betty sighed. "Yes, that was the deal. But a deal's worthless if one person isn't thinking straight when it's made."

"Why weren't you thinking straight?"

"I'm not talking about myself. You were under the influence when you made me the offer."

Kaspar was indignant. "Under the influence? You can call me a criminal if you like, but I don't drink and I don't do drugs. I may have eaten a few too many Vienna sausages that morning, but I was thinking very clearly."

"No. No, you weren't. You see, a friend of ours made a perfume—a love potion. It spilled all over me the day before you saw us in Morningside Park. That's what made you develop a crush on me. Then I took advantage of you."

"Let me see if I understand. You were wearing this perfume the night you went to Morningside Park. Somehow I inhaled it and fell instantly in love. Then you took advantage of my unfortunate state to make me do your dirty work. Is that right?"

"I'm so sorry," Betty whispered, and Kaspar started to laugh. "Shhh!" Betty pleaded.

"All right, all right," Kaspar said, trying to control himself. "It's just so ridiculous."

"It's true! I know it's hard to believe, but DeeDee and our friend Iris are very good chemists. They can make anything."

"Oh, I don't doubt they're capable of making a love potion. But let me ask you a question. Remember the note that I wrote you that night? Did the words sound familiar?"

"I know them by heart. It's a passage from *La Bohème*. I've seen that opera a hundred times. My parents are costume designers."

"Did you happen to be at the opera to see *La Bohème* on the night of August eighteenth?"

"Maybe." Betty paused to think. "Yes, it must have been the eighteenth. It was the weekend before my father's birthday."

"And did you wear a white dress and a curly black wig?"

"Yes," she admitted. I could tell Kaspar had caught her by surprise.

"Did you cry when Mimi died?"

"I always cry at that scene."

"And were you wearing any perfume that night?"

"No. How do you . . ."

"I was sitting across the aisle from you. It was a week before I ran away. I thought you were the most fascinating girl I'd ever seen. I tried to introduce myself, but you disappeared backstage before I had a chance. When I saw you again that night at the park, I couldn't believe my luck."

"Really?"

"I rest my case."

There was a long silence. Oona winked at me and smooched the back of her hand. I tried to muffle my giggling.

. . .

When we carried the mummy through the fireplace and into the hidden room, we found Kaspar and Betty just inches apart, their faces beet red.

"Where should we put the Empress?" I wondered, trying to act casual, though I couldn't stop smiling.

"Let's lie her down on this." Kaspar spread a fur coat out on the floor.

"Did you guys—um—hear anything just now?" Betty asked nervously.

"We've been busy rescuing a mummy," Oona replied, balancing on the edge of the truth.

"So this is the Traitor Empress?" Kaspar bent down beside the mummy. "Mind if I have a peek? Is she decent?"

"Yeah, she's dressed." I laughed. When Kaspar pulled back the sheet, both he and Betty flinched.

"You know, Oona, if she still had a nose she'd kind of look like you," Betty remarked once she'd recovered from the shock.

"What's she wearing?" I asked. What I'd thought was a robe was actually a long strip of red silk painted with golden words. "Can you read it, Oona?"

"That writing's two thousand years old. How would *I* know what it says?"

"It's definitely some sort of message," Kaspar noted.

Oona's spine suddenly went rigid. "Everybody shut

up!" she whispered frantically. Someone was walking past Cecelia Varney's bedroom. "They've come to get me!" A door creaked open in the hallway.

"She's gone." Though the voice was faint, it clearly belonged to Sukh.

"They found out that I'm not in my room. I've got to go."

"No!" I insisted. "We don't know if Kiki replaced the drug they're going to use. You could die."

"It doesn't matter," Oona said. "If they don't find me upstairs, they'll go to the east wing. If you guys are missing, there's no telling what they'll do. I won't let a dozen people suffer to save me."

"Kiki will think of something!" Betty whispered.

"I can't take that risk. Hide here until the coast is clear. Maybe I'll see you tomorrow. But whatever happens, thanks for helping. You're the best—the only—friends I've ever had." With that, she scurried out of the hidden room.

"Oona, come back!" Betty called, but this time there was no answer.

· · ·

The sun was already rising when Kaspar, Betty, and I made it back to the east wing of the mansion with our arms filled with finery. The other Irregulars hurried toward us as we crept into the room. The Taiwanese kids noticed that Oona was missing and began whispering amongst themselves. I felt terrible. None of us could tell them what had happened.

"What took you so long?" Kiki insisted. "We were about to organize a search party."

"They came for Oona," I said, though I could hardly believe it. "We had to hide."

"She gave herself up to save us," Betty told the group through her tears. "They came to get her while we were upstairs, and she knew if they didn't find her they'd look down here."

"Oh, Oona!" Luz moaned.

"Looks like I made a bad bet," Kiki confessed. "I was gambling on our search coming up short. That way we might have convinced Oona to leave the mansion tonight."

"Did you find the drug they were going to use?" I asked DeeDee.

"Tubocurarine." DeeDee shook off the shock. "It's a plant toxin from South America. Tribes there once used it to poison dart tips, and for a while doctors used it to keep people still during surgery. But now it's considered too dangerous. There's no reason for Lester Liu to have it. We found it sitting on the counter in the kitchen. We replaced it with tap water."

"You found it on the counter? Are you sure you switched it in time?"

"I think so." DeeDee didn't sound as confident as I'd hoped.

"Betty," Kiki said, taking charge of the situation, "do we have outfits for tomorrow?"

"They're a little old-fashioned and may not fit, but if we drench ourselves with perfume we might get through the front door."

"Good enough. Ananka? Is the Empress safe for now?"

"She is," I reported.

"Luz?"

"I chipped out a small corner of the coffin. It was all I could do with the tools I had. But it's enough to let air in, and I don't think anyone will notice."

"Then nobody panic. The plan's a go."

CHAPTER FIFTEEN

The Empress Awakens

By seven o'clock the following evening, the Irregulars were ready for the ball. Betty had done her best with the contents of Cecelia Varney's closet, but none of us were destined to make the night's best-dressed list. The lumpy bust of DeeDee's strapless blue dress was stuffed with several pairs of stockings. Luz refused to wear high heels and paired a fifties-style dress with her own scruffy combat boots. Betty had pinned a rose-colored gown to my less-than-adequate form. If one pin popped, the entire ensemble could fall to the ground. Betty wore a bright yellow frock that Luz had refused, and the color made her look sickly—though Kaspar didn't notice. Only Kiki's beaded black dress seemed to suit her, though it was clearly several sizes too big. The rest of us would have to depend on our Fille Fiable to convince the doormen that we belonged anywhere other than an asylum.

Kaspar would not be attending the gala. Cecelia Varney hadn't owned a tuxedo, and her dresses were much too small for him to go in drag. So while the rest of us waited for the Empress to awaken, Kaspar would take the Taiwanese artists to Oona's house. He was happy to do his part, but he insisted on returning to Central Park to search for his squirrels. Everyone knew it was an excuse to be near the museum in case Betty needed assistance. Kiki tried to convince him to stay in Chinatown, but he simply refused to hear of it.

Shortly before seven, Kiki and Luz left us to scope out the mansion. At seven fifteen they returned with word that everyone had left for the gala. With Kiki leading the way, all seventeen of us moved quickly through the darkness of the mansion's east wing. We reached the foyer without any trouble and were almost at the door when we heard a low chuckle from above. Sukh waved at us from the second-floor landing but seemed loath to give chase.

"What are you waiting for? Get the door!" DeeDee shouted.

"Going somewhere, Princess?" Sergei Molotov emerged from the Staffordshire Room and pointed the barrel of his gun directly at Kiki.

"What are you doing here?" Luz demanded. "We saw you both leave."

"We drove Mr. Liu to the gala. It is only a few blocks away. You did not think Mr. Liu would leave children home alone, did you? That would be very irresponsible."

"So what are you going to do, Molotov? Shoot us?" Kiki spat. "Go ahead and try. Your gun doesn't have enough bullets."

"You are correct," Molotov sneered. "I have only six

bullets. I tell you what. You choose the five friends you would like me to shoot. The last bullet I will keep for you. Whoever is left can do as they like." Molotov smiled. He knew we couldn't afford to fight him. Kiki might have taken chances with her own life, but she wouldn't let harm come to the rest of us.

"You aren't allowed to hurt us," Kaspar pointed out.

"Nor am I allowed to let you escape. It is a dilemma, no? What do you say we make this easy for everyone? You go back to the room, and you will not be shot. Sukh, please show the children to their chamber."

"Certainly, Mr. Molotov," the butler replied.

I heard two footsteps, a heavy thud, and a moan. My eyes snapped to the staircase where Sukh lay sprawled on his back, the expression on his face a mixture of pain and confusion. He picked himself up and limped slowly down the stairs. Only ten steps from the bottom, his large body lurched forward. With his arms stretched out in front of him, he appeared to have taken flight. Then gravity reasserted itself and brought him crashing down to earth. He bounced off three stairs before landing in a motionless lump at the bottom. To those of us who'd been watching, one thing was obvious. The butler had been pushed. But there wasn't anyone behind him.

Kiki was not among the witnesses. While most eyes had been trained on the spectacle, hers had remained locked on Sergei Molotov. With his attention momentarily diverted, she sprang into action. A shot rang out and glass shattered. Molotov scrambled for his gun, which Kiki had kicked into the Staffordshire Room. Kiki, Kaspar, and Luz bolted after him. Before they made it to the door, a tremendous crash sent a tremor through the foyer and left the chandelier swaying. Then everything was strangely still. Kiki, Kaspar, and Luz stood frozen in the doorway.

"What just happened?" Betty finally asked.

"Umm. . . ." Kaspar searched for a way to explain what he'd seen. "A cabinet full of figurines just fell."

The rest of us rushed for the doorway. Shards of glass and porcelain littered the floor of the Staffordshire Room. One of the tall wooden cabinets that had stood against the wall now lay facedown on the floor. Two carefully polished Italian shoes stuck out from beneath it. The feet inside them weren't moving. Beside the toppled cabinet stood the one figurine that had escaped undamaged. It was a girl playing with a kitten.

"How could it fall on its own?" DeeDee asked.

"It couldn't," Kiki replied.

· · ·

A wide strip of burgundy carpet ran like a river of blood from the edge of Fifth Avenue to the entrance of the Metropolitan Museum of Art. Limousines, Bentleys, and Rolls-Royces waited in line to disgorge their fabulous passengers at the curb. Despite the snow piled in the gutters and the arctic breeze whipping through the trees, there was scarcely a coat to be seen. Celebrities and socialites offered prim poses for the crowds of paparazzi who toed the edge of the carpet. Occasionally, the flashes would pause to allow a stiff-backed old lady or a bespectacled nerd to saunter past. Though their faces were unknown to New York's tabloid readers, these were the gala's most important guests—people so fabulously wealthy that they felt no need to mug for the cameras.

The Irregulars watched the action from across the street while Luz's teeth chattered like castanets and my skin turned an alarming shade of purple. Our midnight scavenger hunt in Lester Liu's mansion may have turned up ball gowns and poisons—but none of us had thought to grab coats.

"Everyone ready?" As pale as an ice sculpture brought to life, Kiki seemed perfectly at home in the cold. Unable to speak, the rest of us nodded stiffly, and Kiki passed around the bottle of Fille Fiable. "Don't go easy on it. Getting through the door is going to be the hardest part."

Reeking of body odor, the Irregulars bypassed the red carpet and hurried straight for the entrance of the museum. A muscular guard in a tight black suit nudged his companion and started to snigger as we climbed the stairs. Both men stepped forward, using their formidable bulk to block our path. Kiki took the lead. Even in heels, her head reached no higher than the guards' chests. They peered down at the tiny girl with amusement. Like most New York doormen, they lived for the chance to keep rabble like us away from their rich and beautiful bosses.

"Invitations," one barked.

"We don't need invitations," Kiki said confidently. "We're personal guests of Lester Liu."

The men's laughter trailed off as our Fille Fiable finally reached their nostrils.

"What's that god-awful stench?" asked one guard, smelling the air.

"I believe it's you two." Kiki pinched her nose. "Forget your deodorant this morning, gentlemen?"

Betty giggled as both guards attempted subtle sniffs of their armpits.

"Pretty bad, huh?" Kiki said. "Most monkeys smell fresher. But I'm afraid I don't have time to give you a lesson in personal hygiene. Lester Liu is waiting for us."

One of the guards whipped out a walkie-talkie. "I'll just check with Mr. Hunt."

"I wouldn't bother the director," Kiki advised. "What if he decides to greet us himself? One whiff of you guys and you're out of a job."

"She's right, Lenny," the other guard said in a low voice. "Maybe we should just let them in."

"I think that's probably best for everyone," Kiki agreed.

"Please don't say anything," the first guard pleaded as he opened the door of the museum to let us inside. "I need this job to pay for calf implants. Otherwise I'll never be able to wear shorts."

"Don't worry," said Kiki. "I'd never think of coming between a man and his shorts."

Inside the museum's Great Hall we found New York's rich, famous, and fabulously dressed milling around crab apple trees dripping with thousands of brilliant red blooms. Projected onto the museum walls, an image of a cross-eyed Fu-Tsang dragon circled the guests like a predator patiently choosing a victim from the herd.

"Teeheehee." Behind us, two girls were whispering to each other. They made no effort to hide the subject of their conversation. I recognized them immediately. They were both famous for playing sweet, innocent characters on film and living debauched off-screen lives.

"What?" demanded Luz. "Do you find something amusing?"

The blonde giggled again. "We were wondering who your stylist is," she sneered. "She must be very dedicated. I bet she had to dig through a dozen Dumpsters to find those boots."

"At least my friend doesn't dress like an over-the-hill showgirl," Kiki countered. "I'd hang on to that outfit if I were you. The way your career is headed, I have a feeling you'll be wearing it again soon."

The smiles on the girls' faces shriveled. "What are you, some kind of albino midget?" snarled the brunette before turning to her friend. "Why are we wasting time with these freaks? Let's go find the party." As they pushed past us with their noses in the air, Luz casually placed one heavy combat boot on the train of the brunette's sequin gown. A loud rip could be heard over the chatter in the hall. The brunette squealed when she felt a cool breeze on her exposed backside. She clenched her fists and started for Luz.

"You've got to be kidding!" Luz laughed. "Bring it on, sister."

Kiki grabbed the brunette's thin arm and forced her to inhale a little Fille Fiable. "You should go home before something very unfortunate happens," she counseled. "And next time you go to a party, don't forget to wear underwear."

"That was fun," I said as the brunette hurried for the door while her friend watched in shock. "Let's have another celebrity showdown. How about that sleazy little actor who's always bragging about his revolting love life? He's over there, bothering some poor lady at the bar."

"We're not here to have fun," Kiki reminded me. "No more brawls tonight. We need to find Oona as quickly as possible."

· · ·

A plush jade-green carpet flanked by white flowering crab apple trees led up the stairs from the Great Hall. Guests grouped in twos and threes were beginning to follow the path to the Empress's exhibit. The Irregulars tried our best to blend into the crowd, but heads still turned at our unusual outfits, and more than a few people sniffed at us with undisguised disgust. We were just about to pass the second-floor ladies' room when an elderly woman in an understated dress emerged. I ducked behind a crab apple tree only to find that it offered little in the way of cover. Principal Wickham squinted at me through the branches. I was frantically preparing an explanation when she turned and charged down the carpet toward the exhibit. I had no idea if she'd seen me, and I prayed I could avoid her for the rest of the evening. Otherwise, saving Oona would cost me my freedom.

I caught up with the Irregulars as they forged ahead into the exhibit. Imperial dragons floated on the walls while guests mingled and marveled at the Empress's treasures.

"All this for a traitor," I heard a woman say, and my flesh turned to ice. For all I knew, Lester Liu was thinking the same thing about Oona.

"Those Egyptians really knew how to send a girl out in style," a man remarked to his companion as they barged past me for a closer look at a tiny replica of an Imperial palace.

"Walter, you're *such* a cretin," his friend whispered. "This stuff isn't Egyptian; it's *Japanese*."

"Actually, it's all Chinese," Betty politely informed them.

"Do you see her dress?" The first man tittered. He hadn't even waited for Betty to walk away. "If *anything* belongs in a museum . . ."

"Don't," DeeDee warned me when she saw the fury on my face.

. . .

Past the gallery that showcased the Empress's miniature kingdom, we entered the room with the army of clay servants. For the first time I noticed that each face was unique, as if the figures had all been modeled after real people.

"Interesting," Kiki murmured with her nose almost pressed against the glass. "The statue in the Shadow City—the one Yu found on the boat. It must have been one of the Empress's servants."

"It couldn't have," I whispered. "Lester Liu said that the contents of the tomb were brought to New York in the 1940s."

"There are a couple of problems with your analysis. Let's start with *Lester Liu said* . . ."

"You mean the Empress wasn't one of Cecelia Varney's treasures?"

"No. She must have come over on the boat with Yu and Siu Fah. Everything here was smuggled out of China this year."

"Time to move on," Luz warned us just as the museum's director entered the room with Lester Liu.

We plunged deeper and deeper into the Empress's tomb, past the embroidered silk wardrobe she was to take to the afterlife and the four interlocking coffins made of stone and lacquer, which had once held her mummy. Finally we entered a cavernous room with dozens of dinner tables circling the perimeter. A podium and a microphone stood at one end. People were starting to gather for dinner, and most seemed far more fascinated by the seating arrangements than they were by the glass coffin at the heart of the room. Only three people were examining the jade-clad mummy. One was Iris McLeod, dressed in a frilly purple dress that made her look like a gigantic grape. As we approached the Empress, the odor of armpit grew overpowering.

"Did you see that?" A man who'd been standing near Iris jumped back from the coffin.

"See *what*, George?" The woman beside him sounded annoyed.

"The mummy just twitched!"

The woman looked around to see who had heard him. "No more wine for you!" she answered in an angry whisper. "Remember what happened at the last gala? That statue you decided to take for a twirl was priceless. I'm surprised they let us in the door this time."

"I know what I saw, Jocelyn. That mummy *moved*! Did you see it?" the man inquired of Iris. Before she could respond, his wife grabbed his arm and dragged him away from the Empress.

"You scared that little girl!" she scolded. "The poor thing will probably have nightmares for months!"

"I think you're overreacting, dear. She seemed quite mature to me."

"What's she doing here anyway?" the woman continued. "It's getting so that you can't go anywhere in this city without being harassed by oddly dressed children."

"Iris!" DeeDee whispered, tapping the girl on the shoulder.

"There you are!" Iris seemed overjoyed to see us. "Where have you guys been? There are missing-person posters with Ananka's picture all over Greenwich Village, and when I stopped by Oona's house, that weird butler wouldn't let me see her. I thought something bad must have happened. I figured if I didn't find you here, I'd call the police when I got home."

"We got tied up for a little while. I'll tell you all about it later. How did you get in?" I asked.

"My parents are consultants for the museum. They're always invited to these things." She tilted her head toward a scholarly looking pair seated at a table near the entrance. "I talked them into bringing me this time."

"Smells like you had to use a whole bottle of Fille Fiable," said Kiki.

"Half. The other half is hidden in my tights. By the way, where's Oona? I've got to thank her."

"Thank her for what?" Luz asked.

"A few days ago, somebody sent me three new lab coats and a huge chemistry set. I tracked down the store they came from and used my perfume to make the owner tell me who bought them. Turns out it was Oona. She must have spent a fortune. So where is she?"

Kiki's eyes glanced down at the mummy and then back up at Iris.

"No!" Iris gasped. "Is she okay?"

"We'll know in the next few minutes," Kiki told her.

"Is there anything I can do?"

"Just enjoy the show," I said. "We've got it all under control."

"Are you sure?" Iris sighed with disappointment. "I wore this stupid dress just in case you needed me."

"You know, ladies, it wouldn't hurt to have a backup plan," Kiki conceded. "Keep your eyes on me, Iris. If anything goes wrong, I'll give you a signal. Run out to the park and look for Kaspar—he's a tall boy with red hair. He'll know what to do."

"Great!" Iris chirped. "I promise I won't let you down."

· · ·

When most of the guests were finally seated, the museum's director stepped up to the podium. The five Irregulars were stationed in the corners of the room, far beyond the light of the lamps that glowed in the center of each table. I tucked myself into the corner farthest away from Principal Wickham, who was dining with the artist I'd seen in the photo on the wall of her office.

"Good evening." Mr. Hunt surveyed the crowd of beautiful people. "Welcome to the opening of *The Empress Awakens*. You have been the first to see some of the most remarkable Chinese treasures ever gathered in the

Western Hemisphere. It gives me great pleasure to introduce the man whose unparalleled generosity has made this exhibition possible. Ladies and gentlemen, I give you Mr. Lester Liu."

Thunderous applause filled the room as Lester Liu took the stage. It was Oona's cue, but nothing happened. The body beneath the mummy's jade shroud didn't budge. As my anticipation turned to terror, I tried to signal Kiki, only to find her head turned in Iris's direction. She nodded once, and Iris excused herself from the table and made her way to the door. I had to appreciate Iris's acting. Even from a distance, her body language screamed bathroom emergency.

Lester Liu's voice was still raspy and hoarse, but he basked in the admiration of the crowd. "Thank you, Mr. Hunt. I am not a man of many words, but I am pleased to offer the Traitor Empress to the city that has given me so much over the years. Now that I have retired, I intend to dedicate my days to making more gifts of this sort. Assisting me in my philanthropic endeavors will be my beloved only child. She has spent the past five years at school in Switzerland, but she has kindly agreed to return to New York to help her father. I would like to take this opportunity to introduce Miss Lillian Liu."

A stunning girl in a black dress joined Lester Liu at the podium. She couldn't have been more than fifteen years old, and from where I stood, her resemblance to Oona was uncanny. Without thinking, I lurched forward for a better look. As I did, I felt several pins pop, and I grabbed the top of my dress before it could slide to the floor.

"Teeheehee." I looked over to see the blond actress pointing at me from a nearby table. I ducked back into the shadows, but not before Lester Liu's eyes had darted in my direction.

"Thank you very much," he croaked into the microphone. "I hope you enjoy the festivities." As the guests clapped, Lester Liu ushered the girl he'd called Lillian to an exit and motioned to a security guard. Scanning the room, he identified each of the Irregulars. The guard pulled out his walkie-talkie, and soon five burly, uniformed men were cautiously weaving among the tables toward each of us, trying not to upset the diners. I sniffed my wrist. The smell of Fille Fiable was growing weaker, and I hoped there was still enough to save me. I searched for the escape route that I should have identified earlier. Both exits were blocked by security.

"Will you come with me, miss?" It wasn't a question. The guard grabbed me by the arm and his meaty fingers dug into my flesh. I started to struggle. If the Irregulars were kicked out of the party, there would be no one left to save Oona.

A bloodcurdling scream rang through the room, and I felt the guard's grip loosen. When several more screams joined the chorus, I managed to break free. At first, I couldn't tell what was happening. Food was flying, crystal was shattering, and an old man fell into a faint. I was starting to wonder if the museum possessed a poltergeist of its own when a giant squirrel leaped onto the table in front of me. It snatched a toupee from the scalp of an aging movie star and knocked a bottle of red wine into the lap of the blond celebrity. Elsewhere, the squirrel's two friends were also gleefully working the room. The guard who had come to escort me out of the building ripped the cloth off a table and tried to fashion a squirrel net.

I spotted Kiki in the middle of all the excitement with a chair raised above her head. With one swift movement, she brought it down on the coffin. The glass rained down on the jade-covered figure inside. For a moment, the pandemonium paused and time stood still. Then people began to rush for the exits, only to find them barricaded from the outside. Iris and Kaspar had secured the room. No one was leaving till the excitement was over.

"What's she doing!" someone shouted as Kiki tore the shroud off Oona's body, exposing a thin figure wrapped tightly with strips of blue-striped fabric. The room grew silent. Even the most dim-witted celebrities at the gala understood that ancient Chinese mummies don't come wrapped in twenty-first-century sheets.

"Thanks," Oona said when Kiki removed the gag that had been stuffed in her mouth. "I could really use some water."

"Don't let him leave!" I shouted, pointing to Lester Liu, who was skulking toward an exit. "And watch out for his cane!"

The museum's director, a Broadway actress, and the CEO of a computer company stopped Oona's father at the door. Socialite Gwendolyn Gluck snuck up behind Lester Liu and grabbed his cane just as he tried to remove the dagger concealed within it. Once his escape had been thwarted, I pushed through the crowd to Kiki's side and found her fumbling with Oona's restraints.

"Looks like the girl's tied down to the base of the coffin," noted an onlooker. The entire room had gathered round to witness the excitement.

"This really is the event of the season!" someone exclaimed.

"Pass the little pale girl a knife," someone else demanded. Kiki cut Oona free with a steak knife. Beneath the strips of fabric, Oona was barefoot and wearing a sleeveless white nightgown. Her skin was covered in red welts from the wrapping. She grabbed a bottle of water off a table and gulped it down. Then the crowd parted as Oona made her way to the podium to address the audience.

"I think that's the girl who does my nails," a woman whispered. "What's she going to say? She doesn't speak any English."

I couldn't have felt prouder as I watched Oona take the microphone. The same girl who once would never have left the house without her diamonds and designer handbag was standing in front of New York's most fashionable crowd wearing only her nightie.

"Hello, everyone. I'm really tired, so I'll make this short. My name is Oona, and Lester Liu is my father. Fourteen years ago, he abandoned me because I wasn't a boy, and tonight he tried to kill me because I know the truth. Everything you've seen in this exhibit was illegally smuggled out of China earlier this year. You see, that's what my father does. He smuggles artifacts, he smuggles people—he even smuggles endangered species.

"Lester Liu is no philanthropist. He offered these

items to the museum for one reason only. He needed access to the galleries in order to steal five priceless paintings, which he had promised to a perverted Russian gangster. The paintings were cut from their frames and smuggled out of the building while the Empress's exhibit was being designed. They were replaced with forgeries created by twelve young artists who he had kidnapped from their homes in Taiwan. He got their names from a pair of New York psychologists and an Asian expert on gifted children. The original artworks are hidden in that man's apartment." All eyes focused on Dr. Jennings, the assistant curator I'd met during my last visit to the museum. The birdlike man instantly broke down in tears. "Now," Oona continued, "I assume the police have been called. I'm willing to answer any questions they might have."

As soon as Oona's speech was over, cell phones were whipped out of purses and pockets, and the flash of cameras lit the room. Out of the corner of my eye, I spotted Kiki slinking toward an exit. I caught up to her just as she rapped at the door.

"I'm coming with you," I told her. "I'm not ready to go home yet."

"Hey Iris, you can open up," Kiki called through the door.

"Did everything go okay?" Iris's purple dress was ripped and covered in grass stains.

"Thanks to you," I said. "You're getting pretty good at saving our butts."

"Somebody's got to." Iris beamed.

"Listen, I shouldn't be here when the police come," Kiki told her. "Tell Kaspar and the other girls to meet us at Fat Frankie's at nine o'clock."

Kiki and I were halfway down the jade-green carpet when I heard someone calling out to me.

"Oh, Miss Fishbein." I felt my heart stop. "Don't tell me you were going to leave without saying hello to me."

"Hello, Principal Wickham," I muttered as I turned around.

The principal walked up to Kiki and held out her hand.

"Miss Strike. It's nice to see you again. It looks as if you turned out to be dangerous after all."

"You remember." Kiki was impressed.

"I would never forget a student," said Principal Wickham. "Particularly one with such unusual ambitions. Now, Ananka, I imagine this incident tonight has something to do with your disappearance yesterday morning?"

I couldn't think of anything to say, so I nodded.

"That girl on the stage is a friend of yours, isn't she?" I nodded again.

"Well, then, given that you just helped foil a major art heist, I think we can excuse your absence from school. I'll see you bright and early Monday morning. Mr. Dedly is eager to discuss your discovery. But now, I suggest you hurry up and run home. Your parents have half the police department searching Manhattan for you."

"I can't go home, Principal Wickham. If I do, I'll be on the next bus to West Virginia. I can't risk being sent to boarding school."

"Ah." Principal Wickham thought for a moment. "I'm

afraid I can't risk losing you, either. You see, I've told too many people about the hidden room beneath Bialystoker Synagogue. I'd hate for them to think I was finally becoming senile. What would you say if I were to come to your house tomorrow afternoon and explain a few things to your parents?"

My heart was racing. I couldn't bear to look at Kiki. "Okay," I gulped.

"Excellent! I'll see you tomorrow at noon. And good job this evening, Ananka. Miss Strike, if you ever care to return to Atalanta, I would be happy to arrange a scholarship."

A group of policemen rushed past us, and Kiki and I hurried for the exit of the museum. I said nothing until we were on the front steps.

"I can explain . . . ," I started to say.

"Save it," Kiki snapped. "We'll discuss this as a group."

HOW TO CRASH A PARTY

A good detective never needs an invitation. Don't let a velvet rope prevent you from foiling a crime or digging up a few clues. Whether you're tailing a suspect to a bat mitzvah or an Oscar party, there are countless ways to get through the door.

Do Your Homework
Who's been invited? Is there anyone on the list who won't be attending? Could the press make an appearance? Will food be served? The more you know, the easier it will be to choose a course of action.

Confidence, Confidence, Confidence
It's not just dogs that smell fear. Any good doorman can detect nervousness and anxiety from a block away. If you want to get in, you have to

believe you belong. And always have a good story prepared long before you show up.

Make It a Challenge
Most unsuccessful party crashers do it for all the wrong reasons. Whether they're social climbers or star stalkers, they tend to care too much. Remind yourself that the world won't end if you don't get in—you'll get what you're after one way or another. The less you care, the better your chances.

Use a Costume
Why risk being stopped at the velvet rope if you can breeze through the back door? A waitress's uniform, cook's apron, cleaning lady's smock, plumber's tool kit, or fire marshal's badge will get you past most service entrances. Make sure to bring a change of clothes, or you could end up serving hors d'oeuvres or plunging toilets all night.

Adopt an Entourage
This time-honored trick takes a bit of finesse. Wait somewhere inconspicuous until a large group of people approaches the door. Then simply join the mob. The doorman's unlikely to give each person a grilling—particularly if there's someone important leading the way. But make sure you look like you belong with your new friends. If you're dressed head to toe in J.Crew, you'll probably stick out in a crowd of goth Lolitas or motorcycle chicks.

Take Advantage of Your Age
Unfortunately, this works only if you're under fifteen and the party isn't adults only. Muster up a tear or two and tell the doorman you're looking for your parents, your wallet, or one of your mother's pearl earrings. If you're escorted inside, simply give your companion the slip. Odds are, he won't waste his time hunting down an innocent kid.

Ask for the Bathroom
This ruse works best at bigger, fancier parties. Before the ball, dress your best, but use your powers of disguise to look under the weather. Hurry toward the entrance when the doorman's busy (but not overwhelmed) and

ask him directions to the bathroom. If your request sounds urgent—not over the top—you'll be ushered inside. No one wants vomit on the red carpet.

Don't Be a Wallflower
Once you're inside, be sure to mingle. You're less likely to get bounced if you've made some new friends.

CHAPTER SIXTEEN

. . . .

Secret's Out

The Irregulars were crowded into a booth at Fat Frankie's. Iris, who'd slipped away from her parents in all the confusion, was feeding french fries to the three large squirrels hidden underneath the table while Kaspar and Betty flirted with abandon. A tower of empty plates was evidence of the ferocious hunger that had overcome the group when we'd arrived at the restaurant. Kiki and I sipped coffee as the others crammed their mouths with an array of greasy delights. Luz had single-handedly inhaled two gyros, a hamburger, and a hot-fudge sundae. I hadn't eaten in more than thirty-six hours, but the hunger pangs I should have been feeling had been smothered by fear.

As we waited for Oona to finish with New York's finest, the others chatted, mostly about the mysterious girl who'd been introduced as Lester Liu's daughter. Luz insisted she was Oona's twin. Betty couldn't be sure. DeeDee didn't believe they were any relation. When asked for her opinion, Kiki shrugged and refused to join the debate. Bets were being waged as Oona entered Fat Frankie's. Luz subtly tucked her cash back into her pocket and pulled another chair up to the table.

Perhaps because of our own ridiculous attire, none of us had considered what Oona would wear to the after party. She arrived sporting a plastic police-issue rain poncho over her cotton nightgown, and her feet flopped around in a pair of oversized Converse sneakers. Somehow she made the outfit look chic. And despite the burden of goose bumps and synthetic fibers, she seemed happier than I'd ever seen her.

"Hello, shorty," she said, plopping down next to Iris. "Cute dress. Who'd have thought I'd be saved by a bunch of squirrels and a talking plum?"

Iris struck back with a smile. "You're welcome, Wong. I see your brush with death hasn't done much for your personality."

"Haven't you heard? I'm hopeless." Oona laughed. "I suggest you get used to it."

"How did everything go with the police?" Luz asked.

"Let's just say that Lester Liu won't be bothering any of us for a very long time. The police are at the mansion right now. Along with kidnapping, attempted murder, art theft, and smuggling, it looks like they're planning to charge him with eating endangered animals and keeping a corpse in his house. I guess that's illegal in New York—who knew? And they found Molotov and Sukh—you guys really did a number on those two."

"Are they dead?" whispered Betty.

"No, but they probably wish they were. I heard the

paramedics say that Molotov would be in a body cast for months. We should go to the hospital and stick chili peppers up his nose."

"What about the other girl?" I asked. "Did you find out who she is?"

"Lillian Liu? She's long gone," Oona said. "And Lester's not talking. I never got a chance to see her. Was she cuter than I am? Just joking. No really, what'd she look like?"

"Um," Luz said nervously. "You know, it's funny. She looked just like *you*."

Oona took the information in stride. "I guess she'd have to look pretty similar for my father's plan to work. I wonder where he found such a remarkable specimen of feminine beauty."

"No, seriously, Oona. She looked *exactly* like you," Luz insisted. "Are you sure you're Lester Liu's only child?"

"Luz needs glasses," DeeDee butted in. "I didn't think she looked *that* similar. So what went wrong with the plan? Why did they decide to tie you up?"

"Just bad luck, I suppose. Sukh gave me an injection, and when I didn't feel anything happen, I figured you guys had switched the drug. I tried to stay still, but it's a lot harder than you'd think. Just when they were putting me into the coffin, my nose really started to itch, and Molotov caught me in the middle of a scratch. I guess they didn't have time to try any other drugs, so they just held me down and wrapped me up. I'm really lucky you all made it into the party. If you hadn't been there, it could have gotten really boring inside that coffin."

"You can joke now, but you shouldn't have risked your life," Kaspar told her. "If something had gone wrong, we couldn't have forgiven ourselves. But thank you for protecting us."

Oona frowned. "You don't have to thank me. I owed it to these guys. I made it really hard for them to trust me, and they still showed up to save the day." She turned to the rest of us. "I should have told you about Lester Liu years ago. I'm sorry I put you in danger."

"We're sorry for doubting your loyalty," DeeDee told her. "We should have had more faith in you."

"Then I suggest we all stop feeling sorry. Everything turned out okay in the end, didn't it?" Oona grinned.

"I'm just looking forward to a little peace and quiet." Betty sighed.

"And some sleep," added Luz.

"Don't expect any right away." Kiki spoke at last, and the Irregulars fell silent. "Ananka has a confession to make."

All eyes turned to me. It was the surprise in them that made me feel ill. No one ever expected *me* to break any rules. "When I got in trouble at school, my principal assigned me an essay as punishment. I wrote about the Underground Railroad."

"Perhaps you'd like to be more specific?" Kiki goaded me.

I took a deep breath and let the words flow out on the exhale. "I wrote about the Underground Railroad stop beneath Bialystoker Synagogue. The one Kiki and I found in the Shadow City."

"You did *what!*" Luz leaped to her feet and a plate shattered on the ground, spraying a chair with catsup.

"Oh, Ananka!" Betty was horror-stricken. "*Why?*"

"What is she talking about?" Kaspar whispered to Iris. "What's the Shadow City?"

"I can't tell you," Iris whispered back.

"I guess I didn't think that the stop should be a secret," I told Betty. "But I never thought the principal would take it seriously. I thought she'd laugh it off. I'm not exactly Atalanta's star student. But it turns out the principal believed every word of it."

"And she's told other people," Kiki added. "Ananka has put the Shadow City at risk of discovery. We need to decide what to do. We need to decide *tonight.*"

"You mean decide how to keep people out of the tunnels?" asked Iris.

"Yes. And decide whether Ananka should remain a member of the Irregulars."

I stared down at the table, unable to meet anyone's eyes. The stunned silence was excruciating.

At last, DeeDee cleared her throat. "Ananka, I don't know why you thought the principal wouldn't believe you. That's just stupid, if you don't mind my saying so. But I'm curious—why do you think that the room under Bialystoker Synagogue shouldn't stay a secret?"

"Well . . ." The truth was, I hadn't really thought through my actions. I'd only followed my gut. "I guess I'd been thinking a lot about secrets and how it's hard to know which ones to keep. No offense, Oona, but your secret ended up causing a lot of trouble. And then

I made things even worse by opening my big mouth and spilling a secret that Kiki had asked me to keep. But there's one thing I'm pretty sure of. I don't think a secret should be kept if sharing it could do the world some good. Whoever built that room with the ten little beds risked her life to help other people escape from slavery. And the people who passed through were brave enough to do whatever it took to make it to freedom. Everyone in New York should know what they did. The Underground Railroad isn't like the Shadow City. Keeping it to ourselves would just be selfish. But I realize the decision wasn't mine to make. I should have spoken to the rest of you."

DeeDee watched me with a blank, scientific expression. I felt certain I hadn't convinced her.

"I agree with Ananka," she said. "People should know about the Underground Railroad stop."

"I think so, too," Betty said.

"*The answer to your dilemma lies under the temple,*" Oona quoted. "I still don't know what that means, but I vote to let people know."

"What did you just say?" asked Luz. "Never mind. I agree with the rest of them. And I'll also add that Ananka hasn't been the only person keeping secrets around here, Miss Strike. But what are we going to do? Are we going to open up the Shadow City to the public? Is it all over?"

"Hold on. Let me think for a second." DeeDee bent her head and let her fingers trace the scar on her forehead. "The room was at the end of a tunnel, right? What if we set off an explosion and block the passage? We could even give people access to that storeroom with all the pickled oysters. We'd just make it look like the tunnel was never meant to go any farther. Nobody would ever know the difference."

"I like it!" said Luz. "We haven't had a good explosion in a long time."

"It does seem like a reasonable solution," Kiki admitted. "So I guess we're all in agreement. Ananka stays and the Underground Railroad goes public. Any questions?"

Kaspar raised his hand. "I have one. Have you guys been talking about some sort of subterranean city?"

The entire table howled with laughter.

· · ·

The Irregulars unanimously voted to let Kaspar in on our secret. Kiki even promised him a tour of the Shadow City. On one condition.

"As Luz pointed out, there have been quite a few secrets floating around. I think it's time for all of us to come clean. So if anyone's been keeping information to herself, now's the time to share it. I'll start. I'm sorry I didn't tell some of you how serious Verushka's illness had gotten. My intentions were good, but you all deserved to know. I'd also like to recommend that we use Fille Fiable only in the most dire emergencies—and promise never to use it on one another. Everyone agree?"

"Agree!" cried the table.

"Okay, Kaspar, it's your turn."

"Well . . ." Kaspar glanced nervously at Betty. "This is harder than I thought. My name isn't Kaspar, it's Phineas

Parker. I ran away from home a few months ago. My parents are . . . well, they're hard to describe."

"I know," said Betty. "I've met them. We went to see them after you disappeared."

"You did?" Kaspar's face flushed with embarrassment. "Whatever they said to you, I deeply apologize. They can be quite cruel."

"You don't have to apologize," Betty assured him. "We don't hold people responsible for their parents anymore."

"Were they the psychologists Oona mentioned at the gala—the ones who gave Lester Liu the names of the Taiwanese kids?" DeeDee asked.

Kaspar nodded. "I'm sure I saw Oona's father at my parents' office before I ran away. I doubt they meant to do anything wrong. They're not the best parents in the world, but I don't think they're criminals. Now, do you mind if we move on? I'm curious to hear what secrets Betty has hidden."

"My secret? Okay, here goes. I want all of you to know that I've decided to honor my deal with Kaspar. I'm going to have dinner with him—if that's still what he wants."

"What about the . . . *you know what*?" Luz asked.

"What?" Betty asked in confusion.

"Eau Irresistible?" Luz whispered.

"My turn." Oona quickly raised her hand. "Ananka and I *happened* to overhear a conversation about the first time Kaspar saw Betty. It was about a month before she spilled the Eau Irresistible." Kaspar and Betty turned matching shades of red.

"I wouldn't say it's a secret, but there's something I probably should have told the rest of you earlier," DeeDee broke in. "Iris did some more tests without me. The love perfume doesn't work. It never did."

"I've got a crush on a boy who makes the deliveries for a falafel shop," Iris admitted. "I practically took a bath in Eau Irresistible and he never looked twice at me. And I'm a really big tipper!"

"That's your secret?" Oona laughed.

"I'm eleven. Give me time," Iris said.

"You know, one day soon, you're not going to need any perfume," Kaspar told her, and Iris squirmed with pleasure.

"Luz?" Kiki prompted. "Anything you'd like to share?"

"Um, well, my name isn't really Luz Lopez. It's Amber White. I'm a forty-five-year-old dental technician from Toledo, and in my spare time I enjoy dressing up as Disney characters. I joined the Irregulars because I really like hanging around with fourteen-year-olds. I hope you guys won't hold it against me."

DeeDee laughed so hard that coffee spurted from her nose.

"Okay, Luz," Kiki said. "We get it. No secrets. Oona, anything else you'd like to tell the group?"

"Don't look at me, I'm one hundred percent clean. You guys know everything now."

"Oh really?" Iris sang. "What about the lab coats? And the chemistry set?"

"Look who's a girl detective now," said Oona. "Those aren't secrets. I figured I owed you a gift or two after I'd been so nasty. But you can send your thank-you note to Lester Liu—he paid for them."

"All done?" Kiki asked. "Anyone got anything else on her chest?"

"There is something you should know, Oona," I said softly. Everyone looked nervous. "When we broke out of the mansion, I think we had a little help."

"Are you talking about the ghost?" Oona asked. "She's pretty handy to have around, isn't she? I wonder if Mrs. Fei would let her come haunt us."

"Yeah, but there's something else. Sergei Molotov told us he threw all the food that night and made the noises for our bugs. If the mansion really does have a ghost, I don't think it's your mom."

"Of course it isn't," Oona said. "It's Cecelia Varney."

"You know?" Betty asked.

"Sure. I figured it out when she showed me the secret room. I don't think she wanted me to end up the way she did—rich, lonely, and paranoid. I wish there was something I could do for her."

"I think I know how to thank her," said Kiki.

. . .

We left Fat Frankie's at ten p.m. Iris hailed a cab and sped off toward home, hoping the last of our Fille Fiable would help convince her parents that she'd gotten lost in the madness at the museum. The rest of us headed for Oona's house. There were still two tasks to finish before we went home to face our punishments. After all, those of us with parents might not see daylight until the new year. Most of the Irregulars put on a brave face, but Luz lost all color every time she thought of what her mother might have in store for her.

The smell of dumplings filled the stairwell of Oona's building, and we could hear people laughing inside the apartment. Yu, Siu Fah, and the other kidnapped kids were celebrating their freedom in the living room. They applauded as we entered the apartment and barraged Oona with questions. While she answered each one in Hakka, Kiki and I went to look for Verushka. We found her in the kitchen, hacking up a chicken. Though she leaned heavily on a crutch, Verushka was out of her wheelchair and her skin, while pale, looked remarkably human. Mrs. Fei's herbs had brought her back from the brink of death.

"Kiki! Ananka!" Veruskha put down her cleaver, limped across the room, and threw her arms around both of us. "The children told us about the mummy and the museum. Did everything go as planned?"

"Does anything ever go as planned?" I asked. "I'm happy to see you looking so healthy, Verushka. Do you feel as good as you look?"

"Oh yes," Verushka confirmed. "Mrs. Fei is an excellent doctor. But I am thinking it would be better to be dead." Kiki looked horrified and started to object, but Verushka silenced her. "Listen to me, Katarina. If Livia believes I am dead, we will have the advantage again."

"The element of surprise?" Kiki asked. "I hadn't thought of that."

"We must find a way to let people believe I am gone."

"But you don't have to worry about Livia and Sidonia," I said. "They won't be coming back to New York now that we've destroyed their plans."

Verushka patted me on the shoulder. "We must teach you to play chess soon," she said. "That way you will learn to think ahead. We must always worry about Livia and Sidonia. They have made their move, and now we must make ours. We will force them to return to New York."

"Why?" I asked, just as Mrs. Fei emerged from the pantry with her arms filled with cans.

"Where is Wang?" the old woman asked anxiously when she saw us. "Is she safe?"

"She's in the living room," I assured her. "And Lester Liu is in jail."

"Talking about me again?" Mrs. Fei's mouth snapped shut as Oona pushed through the door. "Go ahead, Mrs. Fei, practice your English." Oona folded her arms across her chest and waited for the old woman to speak.

"I am sorry. I learned English because you never tell me anything. I just wanted to keep you safe."

Oona dropped her arms and picked a carrot up off the counter. She bit off the tip and chewed casually.

"You would like us to leave?" Verushka asked.

"No, you can stay. I don't have anything to hide anymore. You know, Mrs. Fei, a ghost once told me that someone was always listening. It took me a while to figure out she meant you."

"A ghost? You spoke to your mother?" Mrs. Fei whispered.

Oona thought for a moment. "I'm not sure if it was my mother," she confessed. "I'm not even sure it was a ghost. But whoever it was knew what she was talking about. She said I had to make a choice to leave something behind. If I did, I'd have everything I ever desired."

Mrs. Fei looked confused. "But Ananka says that Lester Liu is in jail. How can he give you everything you want?"

"I don't want more money or a mansion. I don't even care about all the fancy clothes and jewelry anymore. Those were the things I chose to leave behind. I realized all I ever wanted was for someone to want *me*. I wasted too much time hoping it would be my father."

Mrs. Fei attempted to console her. "I tried to warn you. Lester Liu is a bad man."

Oona nodded. "I think I always knew that. I was confused for a little while, but deep down I always knew he couldn't have changed. When the ghost told me that I had to do my duty I thought that meant putting Lester Liu in jail. But that's not what she meant at all. She wanted me to do my duty to *you*."

"To me?" Mrs. Fei asked.

"You're the only mother I've ever had. You're the best mother I could have had. You didn't have to take care of me. You did it because you wanted to. I should have figured that out a long time ago. That way I might have spent less time feeling sorry for myself for what I *didn't* have and more time appreciating what I *did*. I'm so sorry. You deserved a better daughter."

Tears coursed down the old woman's wrinkles, and Oona bent down and wrapped her in a hug. "You are a good girl, Wang," Mrs. Fei sobbed.

"I'm glad you think so, but I still prefer Oona."

"Blunt as ever," I laughed.

"Where do you think I get it from?" Oona asked. "By the way, I have one question, Mrs. Fei. There was a girl at the museum tonight. Lester Liu introduced her as his daughter. Is that possible? Could she be related to me?"

Mrs. Fei blew her nose and wiped the tears from her face. "The other baby died."

"Other baby?"

"Your mother was very sick. The babies came too early. Lester Liu did not want to call a doctor. His house was filled with things he had smuggled. I was the only person who knew what to do. I tried to save you both. But Lili didn't survive. When I took you, I left her with your mother."

Oona steadied herself against the counter. "I had a twin sister?"

"Lili?" Kiki asked.

HOW TO KNOW WHEN TO SHARE A SECRET

It's not always easy to know which secrets need to be shared—and which should be kept at all costs. Since I'm prone to confusing the two, I consulted the most ethical people I know and put together this handy guide. Now, whenever I feel a secret dangling on the tip of my tongue, I just ask myself these seven simple questions.

Want to try it out? Take a moment and think of the biggest secret you know . . .

1. **Is the secret nice and juicy?**

    It doesn't really matter. I was just curious. No, don't tell me. Just move on to question 2.

2. **Will sharing the secret bring down an evil dictator, solve a dastardly crime, or put a bad guy behind bars?**

   If your answer is *yes,* you should definitely share it. But be sure to confide in the right people. There are spies everywhere.

   If your answer is *no,* proceed to question 3.

3. **Will harm come to you or someone else if the secret is kept?**

   If the answer is *yes,* any self-respecting heroine would find the courage to spill the beans.

   If *no,* go to question 4.

4. **Will someone be harmed if the secret is told?**

   There's too much pain and suffering in the world as it is, so if your answer is *yes,* odds are you should keep your lips sealed.

   If *no,* keep going to question 5.

5. **Could good things come from sharing the secret?**

   If the answer is *yes,* a virtuous person would let the cat out of the bag. In some situations, keeping a secret that should be shared can be as bad as blabbing one that shouldn't.

   If the answer is *no,* go to question 6.

6. **Does the secret belong to another person?**

   If you've gotten this far and your answer is *yes,* you should seriously consider keeping your trap shut.

   If *no,* please continue.

7. **Is your secret likely to be revealed?**

   This is a trick question. All secrets will be revealed someday. You'll have more control over the situation if you go ahead and share your secret before someone else beats you to it. Keep in mind that the longer a secret is kept, the more damage it can do.

8. **Is your secret particularly embarrassing?**

   If *yes,* you can take your chances and keep it to yourself. (But always keep question 7 in mind.)

If you've reached the end of this questionnaire and your answer is *no*, you probably have a pretty dull secret, unless . . .

9. **Have you discovered a hidden treasure, alien spacecraft, or lost city?**

   If *yes*, feel free to share your secret with me.

CHAPTER SEVENTEEN

Someplace Like Home

Early the next morning, while the sluggish winter sun inched above the East River, the Irregulars said our good-byes on the slippery, ice-coated stoop of Oona's building. Kaspar, Betty, and I set off to find Howard Van Dyke and the six-toed kitten. Kiki and the others were on their way to the Marble Cemetery. DeeDee had spent the evening crafting a batch of her trademark explosives, and before the day was over, the Shadow City would be just a little bit smaller.

I stopped off to pick up some breakfast for Howard, but when we reached the park and shook the snow from his hideout, we found it deserted. Kaspar's squirrels raced inside to feast on a half-eaten can of beans, stirring a storm of feathers and leaves.

"I don't understand." Kaspar's eyes scanned the nearby trees as if expecting to find his friend perched on a branch. "Howard's always here in the morning. He likes to sleep in."

"You didn't see him last night when you came for the squirrels?" I asked. I wished we had checked on Howard earlier. The weather had gotten far too cold for a feral stockbroker.

"No, but I wasn't surprised. He watches his family in the evenings. When the lights go on in their house, you can see their every move. Howard calls it hobo TV. The squirrels prefer to stay in the park. They have bad memories of the Upper West Side."

"Howard has family in Manhattan?" Betty asked. "Why doesn't he live with them?"

"But I thought you . . . ," I started to say before it finally hit me. There was one other person who could have had the heart-to-heart with Howard. I should have realized sooner that the benevolent Chinese movie star who'd urged him to go home had been none other than Oona Wong.

"His wife and kids live on Seventy-fifth Street," Kaspar said. "He ran away from them last summer. He always cried when he talked about it, but he never told me why he left."

"He told *me*," I said. "And I have a hunch that Howard's gone home."

. . .

Howard's family lived on a charming, tree-lined street in a picture-perfect brownstone with a big bay window. An impish little boy stood with his nose pressed piglike against the glass. Betty waved to him, and he stuck out his tongue. When we rang the bell, a plump, pretty woman in pearls came to the door. The boy peeked out at us from behind her skirt, his face contorted into a hideous gargoyle grin.

"Mrs. Van Dyke?" Kaspar inquired.

"Yes," she answered cautiously, rubbing her hands together to stay warm.

"Hello, ma'am. My name is Kaspar." He didn't have a chance to explain any further before Howard's wife flew outside and wrapped her arms around him. Betty giggled with surprise.

"Kaspar!" the woman cried. "Howard's told me all about you. Thank you for keeping him alive all this time. I've been frantic for months!"

"You have?" Kaspar's voice was muffled by the woman's sweater.

"I nearly died of joy when I saw him," Mrs. Van Dyke said. "I was beginning to think he'd never come home."

"So you're not angry at him anymore?" I blurted before I realized I was getting a little too personal. "I'm sorry. It's just that Howard told me that he lost all your money."

Mrs. Van Dyke released Kaspar and checked over her shoulder to see if anyone was listening. When she caught her son making faces at us, she shooed him inside and gently closed the door. "I was mad at first," she said softly. "But I'll tell you all a little secret. I knew when I married Howard that he wasn't the world's best stockbroker. And believe me, that isn't his only fault. He's a tremendous slob, too. I found his dirty underwear in the bread box once, and he goes through a case of those vile Vienna sausages every month. But he was the most wonderful man I'd ever met. So I did what I had to do. I stashed money away every month, just in case something happened, and I never told him about our savings. With the interest I earn, we'll get along just fine."

"But I heard they took your furniture away," I said.

"They came for it, that's true. But I took care of the bill on the spot."

"So Howard ran away for nothing," Betty marveled.

"If only I'd known . . ." Kaspar groaned.

"You're not to blame," Mrs. Van Dyke assured him. "Howard didn't have his pills with him the day the men came for the furniture. Otherwise, I don't think he'd have hidden for so long. As you may have noticed, he gets a little confused without his medication. He suffered a rather nasty head injury a few years back. He was showing off and dove into the kiddie pool at a resort in Acapulco," she confided. "But that's enough ancient history for today. I imagine you three came to see Howard, not me."

. . .

In the Van Dykes' living room, we found a man sitting on the floor less than ten feet from the television. If April the chicken hadn't been by his side, I might not have recognized Howard. Clean, beardless, and odor free, he was wearing a natty blue blazer and striped Harvard tie.

"Hello there!" He jumped up when he saw us and shook our hands. "I can't believe what I've missed! I've been catching up on the news for two days straight. Did you hear about the two-headed calf in Minnesota? Wait one second . . ." He stopped and sniffed the air around us. "Kaspar, you smell practically human! Have you gone home as well?"

"If my home were like *this*, I would have gone back ages ago," Kaspar told him. "But I'm still on my own. Well . . . not exactly." He winked at Betty.

"This must be the young lady you used to rattle on about," Howard noted. "Has she come round at last?"

"I think so," said Kaspar.

"I have." Betty blushed.

"Glad to hear it! Who needs a home when you have a good woman? Have a seat, all of you. Anyone care for some sausages?"

"Actually, Howard, this isn't a social call," Kaspar explained. "I would love to catch up, but we have something urgent to see to today."

"Does it have anything to do with Cecelia Varney's cat?"

"So you've heard?"

"My wonderful wife kindly saved the newspapers from the past four months. She knows how I like to keep up on current events. I'm almost up to September now. I was petting little Fang when I read about the missing heirs to the Varney fortune. Oh—I hope you don't mind that I named him. A tough-guy name might bolster his self-confidence, don't you think?"

"Seems reasonable," Kaspar agreed. "Is Fang still here?"

"Of course! But he stays in the bedroom most of the day. He's terribly afraid of April. She can be a little snippy at times. By the way, what do you intend to do with him?"

.   .   .

Lester Liu's mansion was mobbed with reporters, sightseers, animal rights activists, and mummy lovers. Television vans had blockaded Fifth Avenue and traffic was backed up for blocks. Kaspar, Betty, and I watched as Adam Gunderson from Channel Three News filmed a report.

> "*Good evening, Janice. I'm here on the Upper East Side of Manhattan where, just last night, a wealthy philanthropist was unmasked as one of the most brazen criminal masterminds this city has ever seen! Lester Liu, whose mansion you see behind me, was charged this morning with an appalling list of misdeeds, including kidnapping, art theft, and attempted murder. Channel Three has also uncovered evidence that Mr. Liu is the secret leader of the Chinatown Fu-Tsang gang, a band of bloodthirsty smugglers who've terrorized lower Manhattan for decades.*
>
> "*While the Fu-Tsang gang is said to have smuggled everything from counterfeit handbags to illegal drugs, people smuggling appears to have been the primary source of Lester Liu's wealth. Police have already closed seven illegal sweatshops owned by Mr. Liu, and just hours ago, ten Taiwanese*

teenagers appeared at the Fifth Precinct police station in Manhattan, claiming they were smuggled into the country and held captive by Mr. Liu and a man named Sergei Molotov. Once their statements have been taken, the teenagers will be returned to their parents overseas.

"But perhaps the most remarkable aspect of this story is the person who brought Mr. Liu to justice— his fourteen-year-old daughter, Oona Wong. Miss Wong has not been available for interviews, but witnesses at last night's gala describe her as an attractive if poorly dressed girl with an excellent grasp of the English language.

"For the full story and latest revelations, tune in at five for a Channel Three Special Report. For now, this is Adam Gunderson reporting live from Fifth Avenue."

"That was wonderful, Mr. Gunderson! My name's Tiffany Thompson, and I'm your *biggest* fan," I gushed.

Adam Gunderson lowered the mirror he'd been using to check his hair and offered me a smug smile. "Thank you. It's great to know there are still a few kids watching the news these days." He made it sound as if most young people spent their evenings mugging old ladies and vandalizing graveyards instead of enriching their minds with his reports.

"Oh, I watch you every single night. That's why I wanted to make sure you were the *first* to know what I found in the park."

Adam Gunderson's eyes glazed over. "I appreciate it, young lady, but I'm quite busy right now. We're filming a special report on Lester Liu. Why don't you stand over there out of the way while I tape this next segment?"

"Maybe this can be a part of it?" I held out the kitten. When its fur brushed his suit, the reporter leaped backward.

"Somebody get me a lint brush!" he screeched. "I've got cat hair all over me. Would you please take that thing away?" he hissed.

"But I thought you might want to have a peek at its toes," I whined. "They're very unusual. Aren't cats supposed to have only five?" In an instant, Adam Gunderson's face went from annoyed to ecstatic. He snatched the cat out of my hands and examined its toes.

"Where did you find this animal?" he asked, trying to hide his excitement.

"Right here in the park, across the street from that big house. I saw a bunch of cats being loaded into a delivery van, but this little one snuck out."

"Do you remember the name on the delivery van?" the reporter inquired. His lips moved silently as he waited for my answer, and I knew he was praying.

"Sure," I said. "It was from a company called Tasty Treasures."

"Somebody get me an address for Tasty Treasures!" he shouted.

As a frantic assistant pushed past me, I happened to glance up at the Varney Mansion. One of the shutters on the second floor swung open, and a hazy figure briefly appeared in the window. I'll be the first to admit that it could have been the glare of sunlight on the glass, or one of the many police officers still roaming the building. In fact, there are hundreds of possible explanations that all make perfect sense. But I'd like to think it was Cecelia Varney.

· · ·

"That should do it," I told Kaspar and Betty. "You can always depend on Adam Gunderson. He's not very bright, but he's incredibly persistent. He'll make sure the cat gets the mansion and the animal smugglers get a cage of their own."

"So now that we've done our good deed for the day, where to?" Kaspar asked as the three of us strolled down Fifth Avenue. "Should we drop in to the Carlyle Hotel for a spot of tea?"

"Very amusing," I said, though the thought of a cucumber sandwich was very enticing. "It's time for me to go home and take my punishment." Since we'd come from Howard's house, I was almost looking forward to it.

"Me, too." Betty sighed.

"Why don't you guys come stay in the park with me?" Kaspar offered. "We could start our own colony."

"You can't live in the park forever," Betty told him. "You have to go home sometime."

"If only to shower," I advised.

"Howard went home and look how well that worked out," Betty tried.

"I will never go back to my parents' house," Kaspar declared. "It's not my home. It's just a laboratory with overpriced furniture. You know, just because I'm related to Arthur and Jane doesn't mean I belong with them. They've spent my whole life trying to make me into the perfect child, and I'm tired of being their guinea pig.

"I guess meeting Mrs. Van Dyke settled it for me. She doesn't care if Howard's less than perfect. She's crazy about him anyway. You know what my mom would do if she found my underwear in the bread box? She'd call in a team of experts to analyze my aberrant behavior."

"I'm sorry." Betty reached for Kaspar's hand and his dark mood instantly brightened.

"So am I," I said. "But I refuse to let my friends date vagrants. We've got to find someplace for you to go."

"I think you both have your own problems to worry about. You'll probably be grounded for the next decade or two."

"We'll see." I was feeling strangely optimistic. "When I ran into my principal at the museum last night, she promised to talk to my parents. If anyone can save me, she can. So why don't you tag along with me? There's an extra bedroom in our apartment. If I don't get shipped off to boarding school maybe my parents will let you stay till you figure things out."

I didn't want to get anyone's hopes up, but I already had a plan.

. . .

Every lamppost in my neighborhood was plastered with the same missing-person poster. The unfortunate girl in the picture looked bloated, pasty, and slightly cockeyed. Kaspar was kind enough to assure me that I was much better looking in person. We hid in a doorway across the street from my building and waited for Principal Wickham to arrive. At 12:00 on the dot, a taxi pulled up and the tiny old woman hopped out. We rushed across the street to greet her before she could buzz my apartment. The squirrels stayed behind, rummaging through a neighbor's trash can.

"Thank you for coming, Principal Wickham. But before we go inside, I'd like to take a second to introduce you to my friend Phineas Parker."

The principal took off her glasses and studied Kaspar.

"It's a pleasure to meet you, Mr. Parker," she said. "You look a great deal like your father. How are Arthur and Jane?"

"You know my parents?" Kaspar couldn't hide his distaste for the subject. "I'm sure they're doing well, but I haven't seen them in months. I've been living alone."

"In Central Park," I added.

Principal Wickham's brow wrinkled with concern. "My, that sounds rather unpleasant," she said. "Were things that bad at home?"

"Worse," Kaspar admitted.

"I wanted you meet Phineas because I think you may be a fan of his artwork. He was the one who painted the squirrels all over town."

"Is that right? I miss seeing your creatures. They added a certain spark to my day. Why did you stop?"

"I was kidnapped by Lester Liu and forced to replicate two of the paintings he stole."

To her eternal credit, the principal didn't blink. "Which ones?" she asked.

"*Odalisque in Grisaille* and *Venus and Adonis*."

"How interesting. I had an opportunity to view the forgeries this morning. Mr. Hunt, the museum's director, is an old friend of mine. The anamorphosis in those two paintings is very impressive indeed. But I must confess. I've long been familiar with your art, Mr. Parker. In fact, I have one of your paintings at home. An early work, I believe. It was a gift from the parents of one of my pupils. I haven't been able to display it, however. It's much too sad."

"Is it from the zoo series?" I asked.

"Yes, as a matter of fact. It's a painting of a rather beleaguered panda. May I ask what your inspiration was, Mr. Parker?"

"One of my parents' patients," Kaspar admitted.

"That's why I was hoping you could help him," I said. "He can't stay in Central Park, but he can't go home, either. His mom and dad are nuts."

"Ananka!" Kaspar blushed.

"It's true, isn't it?" I demanded.

"I see." When Principal Wickham raised her eyebrow, she looked like an elderly Kiki Strike. "It just so happens that I'm having lunch with a former Atalanta student today. She's a rather well-known artist, and she owns a small art academy outside of the city. She was with me this morning at the museum and judging by her reaction to your work, I believe she might be persuaded to offer you a scholarship, Mr. Parker. Would you mind waiting here while I have a word with Ananka's parents? I should be finished in a few minutes, and then, if you're not busy, perhaps you could join my friend and me for lunch."

"See?" I whispered to Kaspar as Principal Wickham rang the buzzer. "You've just got to know when to tell the truth."

. . .

"Ananka!" my mother yelped when she opened door. "Where have you been?"

"Ananka?" My father's head popped out of the living room, and then he sprinted down the hall. Both my parents smothered me with hugs, and several minutes passed before they realized that Principal Wickham was watching.

"You must have brought her home." My mother's voice was cracking with emotion. "I can't tell you how grateful we are. Where on earth did you find her?"

"The Metropolitan Museum of Art," the principal replied.

My father gulped as my mother's face turned to stone. "You went back there?" she growled.

"Perhaps we should talk," Principal Wickham said calmly. "Would you mind if we have a seat?"

Like every first-time visitor to our home, Principal Wickham marveled at my parents' library. Unlike most adult visitors, however, she didn't seem nervous walking past the precariously balanced stacks of books that lined every wall.

"I can understand why Ananka hasn't been interested in her schoolwork," she said. "Your daughter could receive a wonderful education by simply staying home." She took a seat on the sofa and peered down at the newspapers on the coffee table.

ART HEIST FOILED BY FOURTEEN-YEAR-OLD! cried the *Post*.

ANCIENT MUMMY FOUND IN MANSION! shrieked the *Daily News*.

My eyes lingered on a headline on the front page of the *New York Times*. VERUSHKA KOZLOVA PRESUMED DEAD, DOCTOR'S INCOMPETENCE MIGHT BE TO BLAME. I forced back a smile. The previous night I'd heard Kiki on the phone before I drifted off to sleep in my makeshift bed on Oona's floor. Apparently she'd managed to kill off Verushka and get her revenge on Dr. Pritchard with one quick call.

"Have you read today's papers?" the principal asked my parents.

"We've been a little preoccupied," my father said.

"I think you might want to take a look." The principal pointed to the cover of the *New York Post*. The photo showed Oona behind the podium at the gala. "Recognize anyone?"

"That's Ananka's friend!" my mother gasped. "The one who's always picking our locks!"

"Take a closer look," the principal advised. In the background of the picture stood a geeky girl in a terrible dress. I barely recognized myself.

"Ananka?" My father looked as if he might collapse. "Is that *you*?"

I waited too long to speak.

"I can't help you if you won't help yourself," Principal Wickham warned.

"It is," I admitted.

"That's where I found her," the principal informed my parents. "I was a guest at the gala. Your daughter and her friends foiled the largest art heist in the history of the Metropolitan Museum."

My parents gaped at me as if I were a visitor from a distant planet. I knew their brains were busy reassessing everything that had happened over the past three months.

"Why don't you explain how it happened," Principal Wickham urged me. "I'm quite curious to hear for myself."

"Well, I guess it started with the giant squirrels . . . ," I began. I told them about everything. The kidnapped Taiwanese kids, Lester Liu and the hungry ghost, Kaspar's disappearance. I skipped only one part of the story—the Shadow City. Keeping one secret wasn't going to kill anyone.

"That's why you kept sneaking out of the house?" my father asked.

"And falling asleep during class?" my mother added.

"And running away?"

"Yes, yes, and yes," I said. "I apologize for lying to you, but I had to help my friends. I couldn't go to West Virginia before everything was settled."

My father snuck a look at my mother.

"We weren't going to send you to the Borland Academy." He sighed. "We just wanted to scare some sense into you. Your mother was convinced you were well on your way to becoming a juvenile delinquent, and to be quite honest, I didn't know what to think."

"I—I—*all right,* that's true," my mother said. "I'm willing to admit I was wrong. I just wish you'd confided in us. If nothing else, we might have been able to help. You're only fourteen years old, Ananka, and you have to trust us to know what's best sometimes. And even if you *are* some kind of girl detective, I won't let you neglect your education. With all the time you've missed, I wouldn't be surprised if you fail most of your classes this semester."

"I thought you might be concerned about that, Mrs. Fishbein," said Principal Wickham. "That's why I came along today. Every year, I choose one promising Atalanta freshman to be my personal protégé. This year, I've chosen Ananka. Her predecessors have gone on to become some of the most accomplished women in the country. I believe your daughter may have the same potential."

"You do?" My mother pressed one hand to her heart as if she were expecting the organ to sputter to a stop.

"I do. I also want to assure you that Ananka will be allowed to make up all the work from the classes she's missed. With a little tutoring, she should end the year with reasonable grades. In fact, she's already earned an A in one class."

"I have?" I asked.

"Yes. In light of your remarkable discovery, Mr. Dedly has seen fit to grant you an A in your New York history class."

"What kind of discovery?" my mother asked as if nothing could surprise her any longer.

HOW TO GET READY FOR YOUR CLOSE-UP

At some point in your life, you will end up on television. Perhaps you'll be celebrated for your contributions to mankind. Or maybe you'll be captured slinking across the roof of a Monte Carlo hotel with a pocketful of stolen diamonds. Whatever the case, you'll want to be sure that you're ready for the cameras. These days, if you embarrass yourself on television, even your grandchildren may never live it down.

Be Careful What You Eat
To avoid a dry mouth that will leave you licking your lips like a thirsty cow, have a little something to drink before you go on camera. But make sure it's not carbonated, unless you intend to belch for your viewers. Also, you should try to eat beforehand, or your microphone may pick up the sound of your stomach rumbling. But be sure to avoid bean-based dishes.

Never, Ever Chew Gum
This probably doesn't need to be told to anyone whose name isn't Britney.

Don't Try to Dazzle the Cameras
If you want to shine for the cameras, do it with your personality, not your clothing or jewelry. Sparkling stones and noisy bangles will drive your camera crew nuts. Wear a brightly colored shirt and you'll look so washed-out that people will wonder if you have a life-threatening disease. And stripes and wild prints can confuse the camera and turn your outfit into an unflattering blur.

Don't Risk Wearing New Clothes
Whether you're accepting an award or pleading your innocence, you'll want to be comfortable. Wear clothes that you know fit well and flatter your figure. The last thing you want is to look bloated, lumpy, or in pain.

Prepare to Sweat
Television lights are hot enough to melt even the coolest characters. So take along some tissues and a powder puff if you want to avoid looking like you've been dipped in baby oil. And choose clothing that can help hide or prevent any dreaded pit stains.

Wear Your Makeup
This has nothing to do with vanity. Makeup on camera is a necessity if you don't want to resemble an ailing zombie. (This goes for males as well as

females.) But choose more subtle shades, and stay away from lip gloss and eye shadow that shine or sparkle—or no one will take you seriously.

Don't Get Flustered

Even if your heel breaks, your dress rips, or a bug flies straight into your mouth, never lose your cool. You'll just turn a mediocre TV blooper into a classic.

CHAPTER EIGHTEEN

Expect the Unexpected

The package arrived one week after the showdown at the Metropolitan Museum of Art. Tucked inside was a block of extra-sharp cheddar, a letter, and a picture of a mud-splattered Molly Donovan astride a fierce giant sow. One of her hands gripped a golden trophy. A banner in the background read *Borland Academy's Fifth Annual Pig Rodeo*.

Dear Ananka,

Don't get excited—it's just a second-place trophy. I've been at Borland for only a week, but I'm so happy Principal Wickham recommended it. There's a guy in my class who likes to set fires when no one's looking and a girl who thinks she's a vampire. (Really fascinating people once you get to know them.) They're the *special* ones here. Everybody's so busy with the fire alarms and bloodsucking that no one pays any attention to me at all.

Anyway, I never got a chance to thank you in person, so I've named my pig in your honor. If she's still around next year, we should take first prize at the rodeo. If not, I'll send you some pork chops!
Molly

As happy as I was for Molly, I was sorry to lose her. Atalanta had been far too quiet since she'd been expelled. I put her cheese in the refrigerator and checked my outfit in the hall mirror. Tweed skirt, tall brown boots, and a cute little coat. I'd spent hours searching for the right outfit. Principal Wickham had said there would be newspaper and television cameras, and I had no intention of being a fashion victim twice in one week.

"You look very nice, Ananka," my father said. He and my mother were waiting for me by the door, both dressed in their best clothes.

"Nice?" I winced.

"Your father meant to say that you've struck the perfect balance of stylish and nerdy." My mother laughed. "Now come on, or we're going to be late."

• • •

We passed our first giant squirrel at the corner of Bowery and Delancey. The charming creature with fluffy red fur and a tender expression was painted on the brick wall of a condemned building. The sign in his hands said I'LL BE BACK! The second squirrel drove past on the back of a delivery van. An adorable gray rodent, it held up a banner that read DON'T FORGET ME! By the time my parents and I reached the Lower East Side, we'd encountered more than a dozen rodents. For days, New Yorkers had been speculating about the meaning of the squirrels' messages. Many believed that the vigilante was leaving Manhattan now that his work was done. Lester Liu's imprisonment and the destruction of his Fu-Tsang smuggling ring had stopped the flow of endangered animals into the city, and thanks to Adam Gunderson's shocking exposé of the Tasty Treasures company, there'd be no more baby cobras on the city's menus. But only the Irregulars knew the true meaning of the squirrels' signs. Kaspar had been granted a scholarship to art school. Since getting the news, he'd spent every night decorating the city as a goodbye gift for Betty.

When we reached Bialystoker Synagogue, we found people streaming into the squat stone building. Principal Wickham was waiting for me outside on the sidewalk.

"Good morning," she greeted us. "I'm pleased to see that you brought your parents, Ananka, but where are your friends?"

"We've decided it's best if we aren't seen together in public for a little while," I told her. "We don't want any more attention."

"Ah," said the principal. "Well then, perhaps you can pass along some information when you next see them. I received a call from Mr. Hunt, the director of the museum, this morning. There's been a discovery regarding the Empress's mummy."

"We tried to be careful with her!" I blurted.

"The mummy isn't damaged. All things considered, she's in wonderful shape. No, what I meant to say is that the Empress may finally be exonerated."

"Exonerated?" my father asked.

"She's been called a traitor for the past two thousand years. But now it seems that might not be the case at all. When the museum's experts claimed the body, they found it wrapped in a piece of fabric covered with ancient writing. It was a message that had been smuggled into the coffin by one of the Empress's servants. Apparently the poor girl didn't take to life at court and tried to escape before she could be married to the Emperor's son. She didn't commit treason; she only wanted to go home. When she was captured, the Emperor had her poisoned and buried alive. Of course the experts want further evidence, but the museum has already performed some tests on the mummy and found the presence of a toxic substance in her body."

The principal paused and gave me a meaningful look.

"Unfortunately, the message also claimed that the servant slipped a small statue of herself on horseback into the tomb, but it doesn't appear to be among the Empress's possessions. It's a shame. It would add a great deal of credibility to the story."

I thought of the discovery that had kicked off the entire adventure. I'd almost forgotten about the clay statue of a woman on horseback that I'd hidden behind the clothes in my closet. The Empress's servant had served her well, and the time had come to reunite them. "I know where the statue is," I confessed. "Tell Mr. Hunt I'll have it to him tomorrow."

"I thought you might be able to shed some light on the mystery." The old woman chuckled. "And perhaps a few other mysteries as well?"

"Ananka!" Mr. Dedly called from the steps of the synagogue. "There you are. They're ready to start!"

. . .

Cameras began to flash as I entered the synagogue. At the front of the temple, Adam Gunderson from News Channel Three was testing his microphone.

"Here she is, the girl of the hour, Ananka Fishbein," Mr. Dedly announced. Since he'd read my essay, I'd become Mr. Dedly's favorite student. He'd even invited me to serve as his assistant on an archaeological dig downtown. An ancient cesspool had been uncovered near Wall Street, and there were bound to be some fascinating treasures hidden in its depths.

Gunderson regarded me suspiciously. "Have we met before?" he asked.

"I don't think so." I flashed an appropriately girlish smile. "Why don't we get started? I have another engagement this afternoon."

"Good afternoon, Janice. I'm here on the Lower East Side of Manhattan with a little good news for a change. This has already been a banner year for fourteen-year-old girls, and now comes word that another teenager has made a remarkable discovery.

"Ananka Fishbein, an honors student at the Atalanta School for Girls, has led archaeologists to a long-forgotten stop on the Underground Railroad beneath Bialystoker Synagogue. The subterranean

room is perfectly preserved, with ten beds and an escape tunnel that leads to the East River. It's an important piece of American history and a powerful example of the lengths to which people will go to secure their freedom.

"Tell me, Miss Fishbein, how did a girl your age manage to make a discovery that's been eluding the experts for years?"

"A girl my age?" I repeated, almost choking on the words. I saw my parents laughing, and if it hadn't been for the cameras, I would have taught him a lesson or two. *"Well, Mr. Gunderson, if you read the right things, you can find almost anything . . ."*

. . .

Closed for Renovations, announced the sign on the door of the Golden Lotus. But inside, Oona's nail salon was hopping with activity. The Irregulars, Verushka, Mrs. Fei, and Iris had gathered to bid a fond farewell to three of our new friends.

Luz and DeeDee saw me through the window and let me in. "Hey there, superstar," DeeDee said. "Saw you on Channel Three."

"I'm glad to hear that *some* young people are still watching the news these days," I joked.

"I'd rather *make* it than *watch* it," Luz boasted.

"How are you going to to make news if your mom won't let you out of her sight?" DeeDee teased. Oona had convinced Mr. Hunt to send letters to all of our parents explaining our disappearance and praising our contribution to the art world. Luz's mother had framed the note, but still couldn't bear to leave her daughter alone for more than five minutes. I was surprised to see that she hadn't invited herself to the party.

"She's getting better." Luz sighed. "She only followed me to the bathroom twice yesterday."

"Ananka!" Kaspar called from across the room. "I've got something for you."

He and Betty were huddled by the pedicure stations, enjoying their last few hours together. In the morning, Kaspar would be on a train to his new school. He had already assured Betty that he'd see her every weekend, but she was still looking a little forlorn. I said my hellos to the others and walked over to see them.

"What is it?" I asked as he held out a package wrapped in newspaper.

"A little thank-you present. For helping me find a home."

I tore off the paper. Inside was a painting of Bialystoker Synagogue. I tilted the frame to the left and a giant squirrel magically appeared on the building's roof.

"Thank you. It's beautiful," I told him. "And very unusual."

"I have one for Principal Wickham as well, if you wouldn't mind delivering it. Hopefully she'll find this one cheerful enough to hang on her wall."

"I think she'll be thrilled to display a painting by an artist of your stature."

Kaspar laughed. "If you want to see what real artists are capable of, have a look in Oona's office."

. . .

I wasn't even halfway down the hall when I heard the sound of Iris and Oona bickering.

"What's up?" I asked as I pushed through the door. "I thought you guys were all buddy-buddy these days."

"We are. Take a look." Oona pointed to the mural that Yu and Siu Fah were touching up. They had both stayed behind when their friends returned to Taiwan so they could finish their gift to Oona. Now that the mural was finally complete, they'd be leaving first thing in the morning. "I asked them to add Iris to the painting."

The lifelike image of the Irregulars battling the rats of the Shadow City took up most of the wall. The six older members wore dignified expressions and crisp, black uniforms with our *i* logo displayed on the front. Iris, however, was dressed in the same frilly purple frock she'd worn to the gala. I couldn't help but laugh.

"Yeah, yeah, very funny," sniffed Iris. "Why can't I have a uniform, too?"

"'Cause that's how I want to remember you," Oona explained. "You were wearing that dress when you saved my life."

"Don't make me regret it, Wong," the little girl huffed.

"What, now that you're all grown up you can't take a joke?" Oona asked. She spoke in Hakka and Yu grinned. Reaching up to the mural, he peeled off a strip of paper that had been fixed to the wall, revealing a slightly different painting beneath. Iris's purple dress disappeared. The image now showed all seven Irregulars in flashy black uniforms. "Better?" Oona asked with a wink.

"It's perfect!" Iris bounced up and down with excitement.

While Iris admired her portrait, Yu and Siu Fah stepped forward to shake my hand. As Yu spoke, Oona translated.

"He wants me to tell you that you did a wonderful thing. The hidden room should belong to everyone. It shows how hard people are willing to fight for their freedom." Siu Fah's head bobbed in agreement.

Oona said something in Hakka, and all three laughed.

"What was that?" I asked.

"I asked if they had time to draw a halo over your head," Oona replied. "And maybe make your mouth a little bigger, too."

• • •

Kiki covered one of the manicure tables with a tablecloth, and Verushka and Mrs. Fei set out three squirrel-shaped cakes.

"Hey! Everyone get over here," Oona ordered. "I have a few things to say before we start chowing down. First of all, I'd like to thank Kaspar, Yu, and Siu Fah for helping us put my father behind bars, where he belongs. We're really going to miss you all. And I've got to say, it was kind of nice having a couple of boys around for a change."

Betty sniffled behind me as Oona translated her sentiments for Yu and Siu Fah.

"Second, I'd like to announce the opening of two more Golden Lotus nail salons. And to introduce my new business partner—my esteemed grandmother, Mrs. Fei." The old woman beside her beamed. "Seems a lot of people are free now that Lester Liu's locked away, and they all need jobs. So I figure it's time to expand the empire."

"And will you be recording your clients' conversations at the new salons, too?" DeeDee asked.

"Absolutely! What's wrong with a little Robin Hood action?" Oona asked. "Speaking of which, I've got one more piece of business to take care of." She ran to her office and returned with a plain cardboard box, which she handed to Verushka. "I heard that rat Dr. Pritchard cost a fortune. Maybe this will help."

Verushka opened the box, and a tear slipped down her cheek. She reached inside and pulled out a fistful of diamond jewelry. I recognized several of the presents that Oona had received from her father.

Verushka planted a kiss on Oona's cheek. "Thank you," she said. "We will repay you very soon."

"Don't bother—it's all yours," Oona insisted. "Buy whatever you need now, and keep the rest for an emergency. You and Kiki seem to have them on a regular basis. But next time, maybe you'll *tell us*?"

"We will," Verushka agreed. She turned to Kiki and nodded solemnly. "It is time," she said.

Kiki stepped forward to address the group. "The money may come in handy sooner than you think. Verushka and I have made a decision. We can't keep hiding anymore. We have to deal with Livia once and for all."

"What do you have in mind?" Oona asked warily.

"It'll be in the newspapers tomorrow," Kiki announced. "I'm claiming the throne of Pokrovia."

Kirsten Miller lives in New York City, where she spends her time drinking coffee, exploring the city, and writing.

www.kikistrike.com

Rapunzel takes on the Wild West in
Shannon Hale's first graphic novel!

BLOOMSBURY